CARVED

THE CEORFAN GARGOYLES SERIES

MIKI WARD

GARRETT V WARD

Third edition - Ward, Miki & Ward, Garrett (Jan. 2019). Carved: The Ceorfan
Gargoyles Series (3rd ed). Cover Design provided by Christopher Coyle at A Dark &
Stormy Knight Graphic Designs.
Second edition - Ward, Miki & Ward, Garrett (Nov. 2018). Carved: The Ceorfan
Gargoyles Series (2nd ed). In. edits V. M. Duran and Michelle Hoffman
Cover Design by Francesca Vance at Reaper Designs/Editing by Sarah Williams
Formatted by Zoe Parker

ISBN-13: 978-1-949250-00-8

CONTENTS

CARVED

The Ceorfan Gargoyle Series

By

Miki Ward & Garrett V Ward

NOTE FROM THE AUTHORS

I dedicate this book to my husband, children, grandchildren, my brothers, and parents. There are no words for how much you mean to me. To Kit, who changed my world. To Kyle, whose memory will never leave my heart. Zoe, without you I would never have started.
-Miki

I would like to thank my sister Miki, who gave me the wonderful opportunity to co-author this book with her; my wife, Kathi, because without her love and support, so much of "my" accomplishments would have never been achieved; and my children and, grandchildren, who have inspired me to always push beyond any limitations.
-Garrett

TO OUR READERS

Thank you for purchasing this book and reading it! We hope you as the readers enjoy this book as much as we enjoyed writing it. We want to make sure you know that we feel this is a serious story about changing a world. It's an urban fantasy, a romantic adventure, dramatic, funny, and sometimes a heart-wrenching read. It's full of sex, drugs, and rock and roll. We didn't add a trigger warning in the blurb on the paperback. We added it here. Be warned: this book contains reverse harem relationships, graphic sex scenes, violence, and language.

Sincerely Yours,

Miki Ward and Garrett Ward

1

LOSS

Kendra

I'm numb and stare at the casket in front of me. Its wood glistens from the rain covering its dark polished surface.

My brothers, Jared and Dana, support me on each side, ensuring I don't collapse onto the soggy ground. Jared pulls me closer. Dana stands guarding my other side.

The drizzle is quiet. We listen as it softly soaks my love's casket. It sounds like a sad song calling me, playing on a loop.

I keep staring at the rich wood hoping he's warm enough. I hope against hope, he isn't getting wet. The cool wind blows my long dark hair away from my face.

Oh, my heart! David, I ache without you! My fists ball into my chest, to ease the pain. This is killing me!

A memory is being etched.

Startled and dragged back to reality, my body jerks when the Veteran's Honor Guard fire the first three shots of the rifle volleys.

I stiffen and steel myself for the remaining shots. I wouldn't change this ritual. My sweetheart served his country well in the U.S. Army Special Forces.

They remove the flag and fold it. A trumpet sounds taps in the background. It's breaking my heart. I want to withdraw into myself, to hide from this terrible pain.

I refuse to let tears fall. This is the closest I've come to losing it in public since David's death. I have to be strong.

The Honor Guard's commander crosses over, kneels, then he tucks a few spent shells into the flag, and presents it to me. I know he says something, but I'm lost in a haze.

The funeral passes in a blur. The chaplain's prayer, and the condolences of close friends are as unwelcome as the weather.

My brothers guide me away. They love me and take good care of me. I have their full support.

I shouldn't leave. I'm not supposed to leave. It's crushing me!

Jared whispers, "Come on, Kendra it's time to go. We need to get you out of this downpour, it's getting worse."

His normally blue-gray eyes are tight and wide. I gaze into them, they're gray today. They match the gloominess around us.

Dana says, "Come on, Sis."

I tilt my head. My baby brother's handsome face is before me. Tears blur my world. My head aches. I open my mouth to speak, but nothing comes out. I nod instead.

The boys use their bodies to protect me from the shower, and hurry me to Jared's limo.

My pulse thunders in my ears. I glance at David's coffin and gape as they lower the love of my life into the cold, wet ground.

Should I leave him? I left him at the hospital after they pronounced him dead.

Oh my God, I'll never forgive myself.

I'll come back, my love, my life, I promise. When my boys leave, I'll come back. I'll keep you company.

My shoulders relax. David always knew what I was thinking. Often, he would speak the words before they spilled from my mouth. I'm sure he hears my thoughts.

Jared puts his arm around me and I settle into him for the ride home. I rub my eyes and hold them open. Otherwise, I might sleep. I won't. The need to get back to the gravesite compels me and my body stiffens.

The limo bumps over the speed bump as we pull into the parking lot of my apartment at the La Caverna.

My brothers walk me through the front door. It's quiet in the elevator as we ride it up to the studio David and I had shared. They hover behind me, always overprotective.

I unlock my door and step into the foyer, then turn back toward them to say goodbye. An empty room at my back. The heater cycling on blows air across my shoulders. It's a relief.

Jared protests, "Please, let us stay."

I need them to leave, so I can get back to the cemetery.

I say, "No, I'll be okay."

Dana elbows his older brother out of the way and bends giving me his best bear hug and says, "I love you, Sissy."

My middle brother jokingly says, "I love you more though, Sis. You can tell by the size of my car."

That's an inside joke we thought was hilarious the first time he came up with it. Right now, it isn't funny.

I give him a fake smile.

"Shut up, dickhead!" Our baby brother retorts punching Jared's arm on his way to the elevators.

He never wastes time.

"Seriously, Sissy," Jared faces me, "you call if you need anything! Twenty-four/seven. I don't care what time, I mean it."

He waits for me to shut and lock the door before he jogs down the hall to our baby brother.

We live minutes apart in our little rural town of Cueva Hallow. After graduating from college, we moved here to spend more time outdoors away from big city pressures.

The window of my seventh floor apartment steams lightly from my breath as I stand near it. I watch as my brothers cross the parking lot.

Dana's dark curls blow in the breeze. Jared's short style is groomed perfectly and stays put.

The Macbard family looks are prevalent. We're all tall and dark-haired, with pale eyes. All different but light colored.

I need to pay the boys back for all of their help. I'll bake them something. They don't get homemade anything often.

I wouldn't want to go through this alone. It'd be torture. I can always count on them. It's a family trait, taking care of others.

I called them first when I got the news that someone had shot David in a burglary downtown. They were with me when the doctor told me my partner had died.

In a mental fog I continue to watch my brothers. It wouldn't surprise me if they wait in the parking lot.

They have a protective streak. Those two would charge an angry rhinoceros to protect me. The truth is, it's my job to protect them, not the other way around.

I marvel at what wonderful young men they've grown into. I'm proud of them. They're grown men, but they're my boys. The limo pulls away.

I take a deep breath, and sit on the sofa, then reach over to the coffee table, and pick up the pamphlets I'd left there.

I stare at the picture of the headstone I'd purchased for David's grave. My body shivers.

The one I chose is black granite with gray and gold inlay and two grotesques on each side. I insisted on one with two little gargoyles. I want him protected. Watched over.

Mama taught me that's what gargoyles do: protect... silly, I know.

Dana told me since I had picked an available sculpture, it'd be ready right after the funeral. I can't imagine him missing a deadline. Even one as impossible as this. It's his construction company. He's a stonemason of the highest caliber; I have no doubt, it'll be beautiful.

Time slows to a crawl.

The clock chimes bringing me out of my trance. I shake my head. What am I doing? I'd better get back to the cemetery.

I run to my room, and throw off my dress. I put on some jeans, a hoodie, and tennis shoes and grab the comforter off of my bed. I wad it up under my arm and snatch up my keys as I rush out the door.

I focus as I reach my truck, Jasper. He's a white F-150 and my white charger. I may not always be a knight in shining armor, but I try.

Although, right now, I can't save myself. Still, if I see someone in need, my fighting spirit will rise. After all, protecting the public is in my job title as a Federal Park Ranger.

Goosebumps rise. I shiver as a tingle goes down my spine. Out of the corner of my eye, I see something move.

On alert, I turn toward the motion, and see nothing... the whole parking lot is empty.

That's odd. I shake off the creepiness. I'm messed up today. I know that.

I jump into the driver's seat, press the button, start up my loyal steed, and lock the door out of habit. The plush seat envelopes me. I lean my head back, before closing my eyes and breath in deeply.

I'll wait just a little longer for a hard cry. It gives me a headache holding back the tears.

When I blow out my breath and sit up straight, I say, "Come on, Jasper, take Mama to the cemetery. We need to keep David company."

I won't let him down today. I shouldn't have left him this long. Can I get any more irrational?

It's not like I had my parents for long, but I had them. They loved my brothers and me. It's not by choice they're gone.

David was an orphan who grew up on the streets. I'm all the family he has, and we were inseparable for the last seven years.

***

Fifteen minutes later, I pull into the cemetery, everything's strange. It's like I put on a gray filter, but on a world-sized scale. I turn my head and everything is foggy. It's probably from the rain earlier. Because it's monsoon season here in the desert, the haze is inevitable.

Cueva Hallow is known for dry heat, not rain. Today, it's cooler, but still warm for February. The temperatures have been in the 70's for several weeks.

The parking lot is empty except for Jasper. I get out on unsteady feet, I lean on my truck for a second before pulling my comforter around me.

Finally, regaining my sense of balance, I start up the narrow asphalt path to the grave.

I've lost my way. A sweat breaks out on my forehead. My heart thunders in my ears. How does anyone ever find their loved ones here?

It's a limestone marble jungle. No, those two large pecan trees are familiar... I'm getting close. Oh, yes, I'm close. The fresh reddish-clay earth marks his grave more pointedly than any other marker and I stumble to it.

A headstone is before me. I stiffen as I read the big gray letters with a gold outline. It says, David Sean Ross.

I hold my breath. I lean forward and sway as I realize my baby brother has already delivered the monument. Though Dana promised me the gargoyle twins would watch over David from the first night. It's big and beautiful.

My vision is obscured by the falling tears.

That's enough, the dam breaks. I sink to my knees, and sob. The pain!

I mourn and pour my sorrow out into this empty, lonely place. Horrible noises escape my gulping throat. I don't care. Who's gonna complain?

Oh, God! How do people survive this?

"David, I'm so sorry I left you in the hospital. I didn't want to. I tried reasoning with the hospital staff. Anything to stay with you for just one more minute, one more hour, one more day.

"They wouldn't listen. Then they sent a stranger to get you.

Again, I tried to stay with you. They said leaving was the right thing to do. But right then, it was the all-time worst. Where are you, David? I miss you so much!"

I calm and put my face against the cold marble headstone. The stone feels good.

"I'm just going to lay here with you for a while, babe."

I mumble everything I'd ever wanted to tell him, but neglected to say. Time was usually the reason I didn't mention the things I thought didn't matter. Now those things seem to be of monumental importance.

Peace finds me and I drift off to sleep.

2

LIFE

Megahir

My team slowly edges up to the beautiful dark-haired mourner. It was hard for me to hold back and watch as she cried herself to sleep.

She is important to me.

I am not her father, and I have never spoken to her, but she is the closest I will ever come to having a daughter.

For my people, the Ceorfan, the Carved, she is the physical representation of a promise from long ago.

I struggled to keep my distance from her during this difficult time. However there are secrets we keep for her safety and for the safety of the Guild, or our race, as the humans say.

The monsters with me encircle her. We stay to protect her tonight.

I turn, face my squad, then watch them come to attention.

"We are ready, Commander Megahir, the Ducere" my warrior team" says in unison.

I stride down their ranks. They wait for my orders.

I unfurl massive wings, posturing, and flex my muscles.

This Elite team of gargoyles calls me Mega. I do not give that privilege to all.

I give an order to my third in command, "Kino, we need time to work."

The fierce red gargoyle begins to sings quietly, without question. He sits on the ground, lifting the girl into his lap.

Her still body, already relaxed and comfortable, sinks even closer to him.

He brushes the hair away from her face gently and rocks her body while he sings the sleeping spell over her.

His dulcet notes even relax me. They are beautiful.

"Flint, I need you to remove the boy's body from its internment," I say to my also red but short fat gargoyle Ducere member.

To everyone else I add, "The King said we only have one chance at Resurgere. I will not tolerate anyone taking a chance of being caught by humans. You each know the danger, keep yourselves on guard."

I turn to my second in command. He's a large obsidian gargoyle with thick horns curving up from above his temples.

I order, "Mica, help Flint with the digging."

I continue with my commands, "Amber, you and Mason, guard the gates and warn us of any who would approach."

Amber whips her birdlike head around then she asks, "Mega, my friend, are you positive you want to go through with the Resurgere?"

Resurgere means restore our family.

My little spy adds, "This is just a frail human. It's not too late to change your mind. As dangerous as this is I'm surprised King Findare is letting this happen at all. Are you creating a Cursed?"

The line between Commander and Ducere team warrior may have eroded in the many years we have served together. The insult stings.

I bring my shoulders up and point a clawed finger at her and say, "Amber, you know nothing of the Cursed! I would never do that.

"You weren't with us. It was torturous the way the evil mages controlled us by holding the smaller ones hostage. So many of us were destroyed! We had to comply. We did their dirty work. We became slaves to their wickedness.

"The only way we were able to end the nightmare was this female's human ancestors. Our king made a vow. The entire Ceorfan race made the same pledge. We protect the Macbard descendants for as long as we survive. Their sacrifice for us was great."

Amber's black little body folds in on itself as she says quietly, "I'm sorry, Commander. I sound selfish, but I'm thinking of your pain, and the cost to you personally."

"My little pebble, know this, the pain that I suffered in the past was so much more than this.

"The surgeon who carved out a piece of my flesh to perform the Resurgere is our old friend. He is a master of his craft. It will not diminish my magic or strength.

"It was painful, yes. I won't lie, but I do it gladly for Kendra. She is my charge, and I care for her. I owe her family a great debt. I gladly give myself, this time, as a gift to her."

Amber whispers, "One day, I hope you will tell me what happened. Right now, I'll go keep Mason company on watch, Commander."

"Commander, we have the human's body. We laid him on the grass, Mica says, motioning with a wave toward the pale and lifeless body.

"Come then, I will summon Jericho, then we will begin," I inform my second in command.

I hunch over and close my eyes to locate Jericho's mind with mine. It takes more concentration when the one I am speaking to is far away.

All gargoyles have a gift. My gift is telepathy; nous fārī, or mind speaker.

I can also tell what others are feeling. It grates sometimes. I keep myself closed and do not intrude on the thoughts of others frivolously.

When I open my eyes, my team is silent in front of me, waiting.

"Jericho is on his way," I say.

I add, "Ducere, I know some of you are uncomfortable around mages. Jericho is necessary for the spell to be completed properly. Treat him with the respect due to his station as the Royal Mage, and part of the High Guild which gives us our orders."

My team is the elite of the elite. They understand the need to work together, now that gargoyle lives depend on the wizard.

"Yes, sir," they respond. Long years have made us a smooth tight unit.

In minutes, a tall, slim, and robed man appears out of thin air. No theatrics, no smoke, no mirrors, only a slight breeze marks Jericho's entrance.

I have learned to notice the breeze when he travels; his stealth is remarkable.

He walks over to me with his purposeful stride. Thousands of years old, he still moves with power.

Shoulders squared, the gray haired mage dips his head toward me and says, "Commander."

I reply with a slight tip of my chin.

Jericho continues, "All is ready. I asked the spirit of this man, David, if he wishes to be restored and form a new family with you.

"I also verified that he will be raised as a gargoyle, to be exact. He fully understands what will happen. We spoke at length, not that he will remember, he likely will not.

"He agreed in total to the Resurgere, even acknowledging the fact he will become a warrior Elite serving on your team."

"Megahir, I ask one more time. Do you give your body, and magic to this man, making him your son for the rest of your lives?" the mage asks locking eyes with me.

My nostrils flare with the intake of air.

I say, "I do!"

"Beyond payment for the debt owed to Kendra's ancestors, I do this of my own free will. I have seen this man many times as we guarded the Macbard family. He was always honorable and trustworthy."

"Let's begin," Jericho says, with a bob of his head.

He spins me so that I am facing David's nude body.

The others had taken his clothes off after they laid him on the grass. A gargoyle does not always need clothes and he will be a gargoyle.

Kino is still holding Kendra in his arms.

He lifts his head to face me silently, mind-speaking, "*I will keep her sleeping.*"

I point a blue finger at Jericho.

He reaches into his robe and takes out a small metal box. It's shaped like something a jeweler might use. He opens it. Inside are two small round objects.

He had cut one from me earlier; the blue-gray stone, the color of my skin. It pulses in the night.

The other is a human bone. I know it is David's but wonder when my friend acquired it. A small knife appears in the sorcerer's wrinkled hand.

Chanting in his croaky sing-song voice, he picks up the blue-gray stone.

His eyes fastened on mine, he pins me in place understanding what I will endure.

Then he bends, with a quick flick of his wrist, he slices the skin of the boy, David's chest. He places the small blue-gray nugget into the exposed cavity. Continuing his mumbling, the mage holds his hand over the pulsing stone until the skin closes over it.

Turning to me with the same deft movements, he slices an opening in my chest and places the bone inside.

I grunt in pain and cover the wound with my huge clawed hand showing no other sign of how the procedure hurt.

I refuse to show weakness in the presence of my Ducere. They are the best and deserve the strongest commander.

My body shakes once before I tighten up and even out my

breaths to control the ache. This big body has been through worse in these long years. I am its ruler, not the other way around.

Jericho's voice moves into a gruff baritone growing louder. Still, no one can make out his words.

The wind blows.

My dark mane is whipping around my head. The pressure of the wind on my wings pulls at them. In response, I curl them closer to my huge body.

A storm rises and gains strength. Lightning strikes nearby. It was far enough away, but my warriors bolster their guard.

Kino protects Kendra with his huge red body, his wings fold over her.

The ominous chant of the mage's words fills the air of the cemetery.

Thunder rings through the night sky. Again, lightning strikes, closer this time.

There is an energy from the pulsing stone in David's chest that is spreading over his entire body. His back arches in pain. He is changing in the dark cemetery. His body is lengthening and growing larger. Transforming!

He is more lizard-like, yet still man-shaped at the same time. His skin turns a pale bluish-gray like mine. Claws form on his hands and feet which are a darker blue.

Wings grow from his back as he arches again. His wings furl around him then stop growing.

His hair is sticking straight out, a big mess around his handsome face. It was short, but now it is a mohawk the same as mine only golden blond.

My body tingles with electrical pulses. The wind calms, and the lightning ebbs as the Resurgere ends. Jericho stands quiet.

I glance at my chest as the bone is covered. Moving my hand, the slit Jericho had cut open with the scalpel's sharp blade has healed.

Only the blood that ran from the wound remains. The electrical tingle dances across my skin. My body is throbbing.

The storm has passed.

Jericho stands over David, waiting for something.

The new gargoyle opens his brilliant blue eyes!

Roaring like a beast, he stands, panting. He wobbles once then rights himself and shakes his head and body. Tilting again, his massive wings balance him with natural ease.

He swivels his head, his face a mass of pain. His body shivers with agony.

I speak to him telepathically to calm him. I groan as I feel his pain through the link.

Flint understands. He moves with purpose, putting his clawed hands on David to take the pain. The brawny gargoyle strains with effort to contain the torment and breaks out in a cold sweat.

Soon, the hurt they both share diminishes, and a shudder runs through my body as the pain is reduced.

The new gargoyle lets out the breath he was holding and drags in great gasps of air, moving away as he recovers.

I walk to David with open arms then enfold him in my embrace. It speaks volumes without any words.

He is my son. I cannot describe this kind of all-encompassing love.

Standing back, I slap a heavy clawed hand on Flint's shoulder and thank him silently for his help.

Only the strongest gargoyles can share pain. He might be short and fat, but he is mighty and powerful. He is fantastic, as are all my Elite Warriors.

Speaking to David, I say, "You are my son, and we are one flesh, one bone. Would you keep your human name, or will you accept a new one with your new life?"

I gaze at him with pride. I am happier than I can remember in an age.

"What would you call me?" he whispers in a gravelly voice.

Keeping the link open I can still hear his thoughts.

My new son contemplates, *I'm definitely not the same person. I'm not sure I'm a person. Everything is different. From what I can see of my body I can't be seen in public.*

I look like a blue monster... I like the wings and claws. Hell, I think I like it all. Big, I was always built, but now every muscle is defined. Only two of these other monsters are bigger than me.

I resemble the one who gave me this life. Mega is the name in my mind. I could feel his feelings. Mega, my dad. Why that feels so right is beyond explanation. It just is right. Someone told me it would be this way, I can't remember.

"Names have power," I say.

"They influence who we are and who we become. I want you to have a strong name, so you will be recognized by strength. And for you to have the ability to lift and guide others during their weakness and trials. I would give you a name that has promise. To build you up. I would call you, Spar, if you agree."

I hear my son's inner debate, *Okay, that's different, but again it feels right. Kendra and I have always been big on going with our gut.*

"Spar, it is, thank you. I've never had a father before. I know we're linked," He says.

Looking past my shoulder, Spar's eyes widen.

He walks slowly getting used to his new form. He bends to kiss Kendra on the head.

Quietly, he says, "I love you. I'll find a way for you to accept the new me as soon as I can, honey."

"She came here to keep you company. She didn't want to leave you by yourself," Kino shares.

Jericho steps toward me and hands me a jewel.

He says, "You must get the boy home. He will not be able to fly yet. He has much to learn, and cannot stay here. This aquamarine stone will open a portal home. I will see you when you have need of me, Megahir, old friend."

He is gone the same way he came.

I laugh at the stunned faces of my Ducere.

"We have less than two hours until sunrise. Mica, take over the cleanup. Make sure no one knows we were here. I am taking Spar home," I order.

Spar says, "Wait! I don't want to leave, Kendra. Please, don't make me leave her."

I answer, "You must. The humans do not know about our kind. Once we did live together in this world. That was before they tried to destroy and enslave us all. You would scare her if she saw you now, think of it. I promise we will come back. You will see her soon."

Spar dips his head, resigned.

Scrutinizing Kino, the new goyle says, "You take care of her. Don't let her get hurt. If she is, you'll answer to me."

Kino nods his assent. "It is my job. I will do the best I can."

His words put Spar at ease.

I open the portal and urge him toward it then follow him through.

***

Mica

Mica watches as the portal disappears.

He tells the remainder of the Ducere, "Wow! It's over already? I wanted a little more. Like fireworks, maybe, just kidding.

"It was amazing to watch the rebirth of the human into a gargoyle. There have been no children born or carved in a very long time. I feel privileged to witness it.

"Hell, that I was included in this company is cool. I only heard of it happening long ago. We'd better get this place cleaned up."

Flint and I return the grave site to its prior condition. He places the final piece of sod back onto the ground. Then he finds Kendra's keys on the ground and hands them to me.

I say, "Kino, lay Kendra on the headstone the same way she had fallen asleep crying."

The red gargoyle lays her down with her cheek on the headstone. Afterward, he tucks the thick blanket around her to keep her warm.

Surveying the cleanup, I deem it passable. Regardless, we're out of time.

After calling Amber and Mason back, I tell them what had happened. I say how Mega looked like a proud papa then I put Kendra's keys in the hand of the little gargoyle Amber.

"Hold these for the girl, gravel bits," I say.

Amber beams at the endearment, taking the keys. It's time to get back to our cave in the hills before the sun can change us to stone.

Amber and Mason fly up to sit on the headstone. I wave goodbye to them as we leave.

The little pair sit and talk together as the sun rises. Amber reaches out her hand, so Kendra will see her keys.

From experience, she knows the human will never even notice the change in her stance.

"Wings up, Mase," she says lovingly.

"Wings up, my love," says Mason grining at his mate.

He reaches for Kendra and pats her side to wake her as the goyles change starts.

The first touch of the sun's rays on their skin starts the process. They harden into stone. Although the pain is short, both grimace, making them look fearsome.

3

WORK

Kendra

While I sleep my back pushes up to the front of David. His hard, muscular body is warm as he pulls me close, wrapping his arms around me.

I love his rugged physical strength. He's an Army veteran, and working in the parks with me he stays fit. He's built like a brick house.

He shifts as I pull his hand to my chest. I'm filled with joy. There's a shift. I gasp, as a cold sweat breaks out on my forehead. I clutch his hand.

Wait, it's slowly melting—no, dissolving! Oh, my God! No! My heart speeds up. My leg muscles tighten. I struggle to breathe.

Little grains of his arm pour over me like sand. What the hell? I panic and turn toward him, and his whole-body melts into a pile of dirt!

Screaming, I roll over and push up with my arms jumping away from my imagined pile of nightmare. I shiver in the cool morning air, mostly from the terrifying dream.

I peer at my surroundings, turning in a circle.

Oh yeah, I'm still in the cemetery. I must have cried myself to sleep on Dave's resting place. How could I do that?

I say, "Kendra, twenty-eight is too old for teenage stunts."

Well, first time for everything. At least, David wasn't alone on his first night here. I smile. I'm glad I was with him.

The warm sun beams on me and heats my arms and face. I shift toward it. I'm going to have this moment with David.

No, not David anymore, my memory of him. I sigh, taking in the full realization he's gone. I have more peace now than I've had all week.

I accept I'm still here, and I'm going to live. I'll have to adjust to a life that's way different than what we'd planned for the last seven years.

I'll manage. I'm going to be okay, and it's going to be nice today.

As I search my pocket for my keys, I scan the area. The cemetery workers left some heavy footprints all around the fresh grave. The ground is a mess. How did I miss this yesterday?

Well, I wasn't looking—that's why.

I'll call to let them know later, so it can be fixed. I'm happy, however, that they put the nicest sod down. It just needs to be leveled up some. I roll up my dirty comforter to carry it back to Jasper.

There's my keys.

They're sitting in the hand of one of the little imps on top of David's headstone. I must have been out of it to have left them there!

Walking over the soft ground I reach over and pick them up. On impulse I rub my hand over the smooth black granite of the gargoyle then tap its beak-like nose with my finger saying, "Catch ya later, cute stuff. You keep guard on this man for me, will ya, huh?"

I better hurry. I need to be dressed and ready in an hour. My boss was so good to let me off this week.

David and I had never gotten around to officially tying the knot. Since there's no funeral leave for significant others in the National Park Service, it was a relief to get the extra time off. Now, though, I have to get back to work.

I love my job. I'm not prepared to lose it.

I have more than a little pride in my position as the only woman ranger for the famous Cueva Hallow Caverns. I don't want to give it up. It's a position where I believe I'm helping people.

I'm not even sure how I got to work so fast. The trip from the town of Cueva Hallow to the Caverns is about an hour drive. The trip shot by, and here I am at work–a little bit early even.

I need coffee.

"Okay, be brave," I say out loud.

I'm going in with a positive mental attitude, as Dave would tell me. I'm going to be nice, but I don't need pity.

God, help me control my temper if everyone pities me.

I make it all the way to the locker room, then to my desk without seeing anyone. That's not unusual.

We only have five employees who are in the office during working hours. The rest of us patrol, like me, or work up at the Caverns. The Caverns have hundreds of workers.

We're spread thin for park rangers.

After I'm on the road for a while, I hear my radio blare.

"Lima 26, we have a 10-15, in one of the campsites in Washburn Canyon." Great! 10-15, *a civil disturbance.*

I turn my patrol SUV around and start for the dirt road I've traveled many times to scout out the situation. I'm already halfway there when I push the mic button on my radio.

I respond, "Lima 26, 10-4, *acknowledge and in route.*"

It would be so nice to use the Bluetooth connection between my phone and the SUV to communicate.

But there isn't any cell signal this far out in the boonies. If I ever need backup I can't depend on having service out here. So, we must use the radios. I also know my radio has never let me down—the radio is my friend!

After a few miles of rugged dirt road, I pull up to the possible campsite. It looks as if a party was in full swing.

Several young people jerk their heads in my direction. They must be waiting for the law.

There is lots of trash lying around: empty cans, bottles, and food packages. Maybe it's a party that just gotten out of hand.

These young people are swaying on their feet—all but a few that is.

Especially, two young men, one who's wearing a ball cap have another man down on the ground. They're sitting on his back. The guy on the bottom of the dogpile is trying to fight the other two off and getting nowhere.

I decide to look at the auras around this group, just to be safe. It's a private thing—only my brothers know I do this.

It's my gift and I have to choose to use it. It's like turning on a switch, then I listen to my inner voice.

That voice tells me what the colors mean. The colors give me a vague idea about the character of the person I'm looking at.

A blonde lady in her mid-twenties runs up talking a mile a minute. She has a pink aura with some gray. She's safe.

This crowd is mostly pastel colors; some have a pale sick-gray, too. My guess is, they've had too much alcohol.

I keep a safe distance as I listen to her. Uh oh, I blinked, and my aura seeing switch turned off. No problem, I just pay more attention to her rambling.

She nervously blurts out,"My name is Julie, the goober on the ground and his girlfriend were bad drunk. They were cussing and being really, really hateful. Then that guy in the ball-cap . . . umm–"

Somebody interrupts her and yells, "His name is, Ray!"

Julie swipes her hair out of her eyes, chuffing, and continues, "–said something that made them mad. Then Goober started threatening us. He came over and took a swing at Ballcap Ray. He dodged, and that made Goober even madder.

"That's when he started digging that," she points to a large knife lying on the ground, "six-inch Buck knife out of his pants pocket.

Ballcap Ray and that other guy got him on the ground. That's when we called you guys."

I shake my head, that was as clear as mud. I tap the button on my shoulder mic, "This is Lima 26, I have a 10-10, *fight in progress*, and need a 10-78, *Officer needs assistance*, and please 10-26, *rush*, *detaining subject now*.

I raise my voice so the party of eleven can all hear me.

"Ma'am, I need you and all of you to stand right by this tent where I can see you," I say, motioning toward the tent.

Now, to get to business. Breathing deeply, I unlatch my pistol holster and approach the men.

I shout, "Calm down. My name is Officer Macbard. I want you to remain on the ground with your hands on your head. You two can get off your friend now."

They pause and don't move.

I say, "Right now!"

They move off Goober. I grab his hands and cuff him. He's only wearing a pair of worn dirty jeans.

I grimace, checking him for other weapons or drug paraphernalia. He's clean.

"You can get up now," I order.

I check the other two and find they are clean.

Goober gets up, stumbling. The smell of alcohol is strong. He reeks!

I walk him over to my SUV helping him into the back seat. Then I close the door. I hope he doesn't ralph in there.

His aura is fucking nasty with lots of black and muddy red. I bet he has blood on his hands!

Out of the corner of my eye, I see a blur of movement coming straight for me.

A screechy voice yells, "Leave my boyfriend alone, you fucking pig!"

I dodge and squat on my knees at the same time pulling my ASP, a collapsible baton. I strike out hard hitting her wrist—the one holding a crowbar and coming straight for my head. I'm quick; lots of drilling makes it possible. Thank goodness for leg training!

Crack. The crunch of bone is sickening as she screams and collapses cradling her wrist. I broke it.

She's whimpering and whining about how she's going to sue... go figure. I'm not happy with her.

I kick the crowbar, which I can now consider a lethal weapon, out of her reach. I cuff her then sit her up with her legs straight out in front of her.

I pull my service weapon, a 1911 Smith & Wesson. I aim at her, and wait for my backup to arrive. I'm furious but call the EMT's for her.

They're coming around the corner now. As usual, I can count on my backup when I need it. They are running up to us.

Good. I recognize Officer Gonzales.

He asks, "Officer Macbard, do you have everything under control?"

"I do. You ready to clean up and haul the perps to town?"

"Sure," he says.

We gather the crowbar and the Buck knife for evidence, administer breathalyzers to Goober and Harpy, then log the video evidence.

Officer Gonzales loads up both subjects in his patrol car.

He asks me, "Macbard, is this everything? Do you need anything else?"

"I think we got it all, including their statements, Jerry. Did the EMT's say if the girl's wrist is okay? Do you know?" I answer still excited by the fight.

"Yep, they said it is. She's happy now... they gave her pain meds."

"They're supposed to be hiring more officers, so we aren't spread so thin. This could have gotten dangerous," I say.

"I agree, you did a good job. Are you sure you're okay?" he responds.

"Yeah, I'm good."

He turns, nodding and leaves while I stay. I need to talk to the remaining campers. They've all calmed down and are opening up some.

I say, "I have to warn y'all that alcohol is prohibited in the federal park. Since I haven't seen any, I can't cite you, so consider yourselves warned. Have you had any other problems besides the two who just left with Officer Gonzales?"

They hang their heads, not making eye contact, then shake their heads no.

Ballcap Ray speaks up, saying, "You know, Officer, we did see some bones up the canyon to the north, just in case you need to know. We think it's a big deer or something."

"Would you mind taking me to the place you saw it?" I ask.

Before we left, his friends were teasing him by calling him Ballcap Ray. He's a good sport.

We came across the carcass about twenty minutes later. Hiking up the canyon is a good way for me to get my adrenaline under control. My job is such a rush!

"Thank you for showing me. You can go back to your friends. I can handle it from here," I say.

He smiles at me, pivots with a wave, and is gone.

I walk around the dead body of an animal I can't identify. I hate to say it, but I think it looks like a dinosaur. I take several pictures of it, and a few more of the surrounding landscape. I write down the coordinates and head back to my patrol. I'll notify Wildlife when I get back to the Ranger's Station to write out my shift report.

When I get back to my SUV, I notice the campers are quiet. They wave to me as I pull away.

I must have startled a few mule deer. Watching the deer take off running, I observe a little cave opening on the side of a rocky hill.

I spot a glimmer and wonder what could make that? I might come back with some caving gear to see what I can discover there on my next days off.

Right now, I've got to get back to the office and log my report.

I walk into the offices at the Ranger's Station and stop to talk to Chris, the dispatcher, who sent me to the campsite earlier.

She's older with a cheery disposition. Her shoulder-length auburn hair is pulled back into a ponytail. She says she's fifty-five years old but looks like she could be late thirties, tops.

Her gentle voice begins, "Kendra, firstly, I want to tell you how sorry I am about David."

I keep my face blank to be nice, but I'm ignoring that statement.

She adds, "If there's anything you need, just let me know. I want to help. Secondly, we're getting some new guys tomorrow. The boss said to set you up with a partner until his probationary period is over. Would you like to see the candidate files? I can let you have the first pick since no one'll know but us chickens."

"Well, Chris, let me look over these files. I'll see you before I leave."

I walk to my desk and sit down, then call Wildlife before I forget.

Darnell Johnson answers in his too-loud voice, "Wildlife! Whacha got, Kendra?"

I proceed to tell him what I've found, adding the report number, so he can access the photos I'm uploading to our network as we speak.

"Darnell, when you see this thing you'll probably know what it is instantly. I, however, am in the air! Will you please give me a call and tell me what the hell it is when you see it?"

"Why certainly, little lady. Give me a few days, and I'll get back with you. And... Kendra... I just want you to know how sorry I am about David. If there's anything I can do, just let me know," he says.

"Thanks, it means a lot, Darnell. I'll talk to you later."

I'm glad I don't have to be around lots of people. If I have to hear, 'sorry for your loss,' too many more times, I'll go fucking nuts!

Now, on to the new personnel files. Mica Jacobs is my choice. He's the biggest one of the bunch, and after tonight, I want all the muscle I can get. Which from his picture he's got muscles on his muscles. He has an excellent record and is moving to the area, so I might have a partner for a while.

Not too many people are staying here.

We're located in the dead middle of nowhere. Most families want more choices for schooling for their children, and a bigger city has more of, well, everything. I understand.

I've thought of moving before, but this is home. I like the sparse population. My family and friends are here.

It's the end of the day and I'm wiped out. I stop to see Chris on my way out.

"Chris, if it's possible, I'd like to be scheduled to work with, Mica Jacobs."

"Done deal, hun! Hey, did you hear yet? Those two you arrested in Washburn Canyon are wanted felons!"

"I've been busy, give me the cheese," I say.

"They're part of the Jessup cartel. Gun trafficking, drugs, money laundering, sex-slave trafficking. You name it. They're charged with the whole shootin' shebang. You may have inadvertently brought down part of the cartel!" she crows.

"That's great, Chris. Do you think it will help a lot of people?" I ask.

"You better believe it, honey."

I pat the counter in front of her and say, "Goodbye, I'll see you in the morning. Have a great night."

I stop at the Tastee Drive, so I can get fast food on the way home. No way am I cooking for just me. After today's excitement, I'm not that hungry anyway.

As I order, thoughts of the arrest and its implications start to overwhelm me. I'm thinking of David, and that I don't want to eat here alone. I get my food and head home.

I'm met by Brian, my doorman, as I open the apartment's front door.

He holds the door for me and asks, "May I carry anything for you, Miss Kendra?"

"I have it under control, but thank you. I'll see you in the morning."

As soon as I open the door to my apartment. I feel a coldness. It's empty in here. I want to shout, 'I'm home,' out of habit. Taking a breath, I put my food on the bar in the kitchen.

In the bedroom I get out of my uniform and head to the shower. I need to decompress and think about what happened today. The shower is wonderfully hot.

Dave used to tease me about how hot they were, "Your skin must be made of iron, you could peel pigs in there," he would tell me.

I want to stay in here for a long time. I feel much better and grab a towel, wrapping it around my body and wrap another around my hair.

I have a brilliant idea. I'm going to put on my pajamas then go to the roof to eat my burrito. I put on my favorite pj's first then brush my dark hair, so it can air dry. Before I head to the roof, I fill my thermal cup with ice water and grab my food.

I haven't been up here in a long while. It's a rooftop stone paradise, my own mini piece of Paris, or the Vatican, maybe.

A hot tub for eight sits in one corner under a beautiful stone awning. I understand it's made of fiberglass.

The hot tub is the only thing that looks like it came from this century. Yet it still fits, because of the artistic way the decorator added Victorian sculpture and greenery around it. The seating area is cement and has pale-green padding.

There's art all over the place.

We have a few donations from the local artists. Most of it is stunning statues original to the building.

There are gargoyles of every shape and color but mostly gray, blueish-gray, and green.

There is one that's a reddish color. It looks like red marble. He's a huge bat demon with pointed ears and teeth. If the artist had a man sit for the sculpture he had to be gorgeous!

I'm sitting by him, and I smile to myself.

Some of our friends didn't like to come up here, saying the statues are evil. They didn't want to be around them.

The reality is they're not demons, they're grotesques that we call gargoyles. I choose to think they protect us. They're magnificent. Their beauty isn't easy to describe.

I'm at ease and at home around them. I finish my dinner and wander around the garden.

I run my hands over many of the statues, talking about my day to them.

I go back to the red one and sit close, leaning on his legs, and let the tears fall.

"I thought I was finished with this last night," I say to my big red-stone friend, "I guess I'm just a big baby. Help me get over this, will you?"

After a bit I laugh at myself and get up to go inside. I'm ready to crash.

When I get to the door, I turn around and say to the garden, like it could hear me, "Thank you for listening and not judging. Good-night, all."

4

TROUBLE

KINO

I creep into Kendra's bedroom, singing a little spell under my breath, so she sleeps better.

Her sigh gives me tingles.

She has her uniform sitting on a chair with work boots under it, ready for her work day tomorrow.

I reach over to touch her on the shoulder, then run my hand across it gently, and say, "Sleep well, little one. We are guarding, so you can rest."

I leave. The way to the roof is nice, the carpet soft. I push through the heavy door, Amber and Mason sit together in the cool evening air.

"How are things going? Any trouble?" I ask.

"No, not trouble. We want to report, ya big boulder," Amber quips, knowing Kino's anything but a boulder. His good looks are part of his reputation.

"Can we put the permanent sculptures on the tombstone, so we can leave the cemetery?" asks Mason.

"I am not sure if it's okay. Commander Mica will know. We can go ask. There is a High Guild meeting we are supposed to attend tonight. You will get to meet Spar if you are lucky."

The other Elites, warriors, who perch on the apartment roof gather close for orders.

I say, "Mason, Amber, and I are going to Navan. Keep watch over Kendra. We will be back before dawn.

Navan is our cave city home.

Finally, the Imps and I fly into the cloudy night sky. Flying high, we shouldn't be noticed. Even if a human does see us, they will think we are bats from the Cueva Hallows Caverns.

My people have a contingency plan for discovery.

The Ceorfan High Guild negotiated a deal with a human group called The Alumbradai Sanctuary State, or TASS, as it is commonly known. A group with many members of all nations, they are the true power and authority of the human world.

TASS and the Ceorfan have worked together for as long as the gargoyle race has had their freedom from the mages of old.

We reach Navan in under an hour. I stay in the sky with Amber, circling.

Mason, known for his stealth and speed, verifies the sentinels are at their posts near the entrance. His little stealth body pulses an echo with the code frequency agreed upon for residents of the cave city.

Gargoyles have the ability to use sonar to pulse for communication, travel, and operate tools for day-to-day living.

This is one of the security measures used to protect the only city of gargoyles left on the Earth. Sending a pulse to me, Mason lets me know the way is safe and open.

Amber comes in first and meets up with her mate, the sentinels move to let them pass.

When I fly to the dark cave opening, my powerful wings are as wide as the opening, and the sentinels included. They bow.

I should be used to it and consider it an honor... but it is awkward. Being the King's only nephew means that some overdo the accolades.

I know, these two guards would have shown deference to me, anyway. I saved them once in the Mage wars. In my opinion, they owe me nothing.

I nod to Mason and Amber as they leave. The imps head up to their own room which they call home. I proceed to my own area above the armory and practice field where most of the warriors have their rooms.

The armory is big, with a sandy bottom; there are openings in the walls all the way around, rising into the cave sides. The openings are rooms, all different sizes. Each is big enough for the soldiers of the Elite Warriors to have a private room for themselves.

Some of the rooms are bigger. Those are used for soldiers with families, like mine; my mother and sister call this home, too.

Happy to be home, I send a gentle pulse to my sister, Sondra, and mother, Gem, so they know that I am on the way. Sondra shoots out of our rooms and hugs me.

"I am so glad you are home, Kino! Mother and I have missed you so much! Was the mission a success?" Her pretty face is all smiles.

Mother is at the jagged entrance. Her joyful face makes me happy.

"Let me get settled, and I will tell you everything as soon as we are all together," I answer.

Mother gives me a big hug. She is so warm and soft; the lavender scent of her is home.

"Come sit, son. Are you hungry? Have you eaten? I have venison ready from the kitchens, and fresh bread with prickly pear jam. We also have some of the best red wine left from your sister's trip up north last year, or maybe you would like water more?"

"Water, for now, I must report. Mega is expecting our weekly report in fifteen minutes, then there is a meeting in an hour. When it is over, I will return to eat, drink, and catch up." I finish drinking my water then hand the cup back to her as I'm leaving.

I fly down to the conference room. Some of my friends are on the path waving, but I do not have time for conversations.

I nod as I pass them; some give me bright smiles and say hello. I move by Eltira, a beauty who knows she is pretty. She crashes into me!

"Oh, my pardon," she scornfully cackles, raking me with her eyes.

"I am on my way to a meeting, Eltira. I don't have time to talk right now," I huff as I hurry away, avoiding her touch.

"Of course," she grumbles with a grimace.

Uh oh, not good. A tingle goes down my spine as I enter the conference room. Strange, everyone is already here, early.

Tilting my head, I acknowledge my Commander Mega.

Speaking telepathically to him I ask, *"What is wrong, sir? What do you need?"*

"Be seated, Kino. As my third in command, you need to know there is a new threat. The King will cover the problem in a few minutes. It is serious."

I sit facing Commander Mega. Spar, sitting close to his father, recognizes me with a smile and a wrinkled forehead. Best guess... he wants to know how the beautiful Kendra is.

High Guild member Reyder, the current chairman starts, "Since everyone is here we will start the meeting with information from King Findare."

Our king, Findare stands. He looks like a griffin. His head, wings, front legs and talons are that of an eagle. His body, tail and back legs are that of a lion. His head, chest, legs and the bottom of his wings are bright white. His countenance is serious and grave.

He says, "First, I would like to welcome to our midst Megahir's son, Spar. He is a newly-carved gargoyle with training and experience that makes him eligible for the Elite Warrior Guard.

"It was intended for him to start his warrior training and begin his tests for the Elites sometime next year. Given the circumstances, I must tell you his testing must begin in a few days. I am confident he is skilled enough to pass and integrate quickly.

"It is my wish that you give him as much support as possible, so he can survive and become one with the Ceorfan Guild.

"Now, for my other news. I have just gotten back from my trip to Europe where I had met secretly with TASS. I was given information that an old foe has resurfaced and is gathering forces. His purpose is to annihilate humans and enslave gargoyles once again.

"This foe is known to most of us from the Mage Wars. His name is Baratium."

The whole room breaks out talking at once.

The King holds up a hand to the members. "Hold on, let me continue, I understand your concern. It is also mine. We must remain calm and objective. We have decisions to make, and we will need all of our wits about us. Some of you were not born when Baratium walked freely among us. I'll catch you up quickly. You can ask others for more details later."

A murmur sweeps around the room.

The king continues, "Baratium is a mage of the highest order. In the twelfth century, he had a university of mages he was teaching the old ways of magic. He was teaching dangerous spells. Magic ruled off-limits, not to be used unless the then rulers of the world agreed and deemed it necessary. They were extremely controversial spells, producing as much bad as good.

"Under Baratuim's tutelage, the young mages became an army dedicated to putting him on a throne, a throne of the highest power. They started by using the gargoyles to try to kill every man, woman, and child of humanity."

I shift in my chair uneasily.

Findare glances with sympathy at me and resumes speaking, "We haven't been worried about him because he has been captive in what we had thought was a prison from which he could not escape.

"A few weeks ago, we learned that a faction of mages he had created by torturing our own, found him. They were able to perform the magic required to set him free. They are now in the process of creating a Crafted army to re-establish their power with the same goal as of old.

"TASS, however, isn't sure the army is Crafted or gargoyles.

They are in the process of verifying the facts. I gave them descriptions to tell the difference.

"They understand now that the Crafted are made of wood even though they look like gargoyles they are not Carved and have no souls. They are animated with evil magic and have no thoughts of their own. Their movements tend to be robotic as they are only tools.

"My people, we must put the genie back in the bottle. Commander Mega, you now have the floor," King Findare concludes by giving his military commander a sharp nod.

Mega stands, his appearance serious. He moves around the room with a military bearing and his wings around his shoulders as he speaks. His big body is graceful despite his size.

He says, "The enemy has been identified. The High Guild will be in planning for the next few days. Elite Warriors Guard, those of you who are listening on your tablets away from Navan, finish your assignments and return home to await further instructions. Everyone, check your B-board notices constantly. Prepare for the worst. You are dismissed."

Mega stops Mica and I telepathically, *"Mica I need you to continue Spar's training. Help him pass the tests. I have to be in meetings."*

"Yes, sir! I will do my best. Don't worry, Spar will survive the tests."

Mica looks at Spar who walks up beside Mega and says, "Meet me in the training field at sunset tomorrow."

I do not envy Mica. Spar is a big gargoyle. Training is not going to be easy.

I leave the conference room to Mica and Mega.

***

I wait outside the conference room following the meeting to get further orders concerning Kendra Macbard.

Mica and Jericho exit the room and walk directly to me.

Mica bends his head toward mine and says, "Tie up all loose threads on the mission code-named Carved. Set a warrior of your choice to watch over Kendra. You need to make your perch on her apartment building tomorrow then come back to Navan. Have sculptures of the little imps replace their watch over David's grave, their orders are to stay in Navan."

Butting in, Jericho hands a smooth dark jewel to me. He says, "This is a glamour stone. Mica doesn't need one, but you might. You need to look human working near the guarded one of the King; it may come in handy. You know the correct pulse to use it?"

I nod to the old mage.

"I must go, I have another meeting," he says and waves a hand at us, leaving.

I cannot help grinning at his back knowing the mage conserves his words.

Mica confides in me telling me not to worry about Kendra. He has been able to infiltrate the Park Rangers and is getting a job working in the same building where she works. If he needs back-up, I might need the glamour.

Mica repeats Mega's words, "Prepare for the worst. Get your affairs in order and good night."

***

Going straight home to Mother and Sondra, I can smell the inviting aroma of dinner.

"Hello, Mother, I am back," I say.

The cave room is big enough to accommodate my immense frame in the open area. The room is clear of the typical stalactites and stalagmites.

A floor of solid limestone shines from cleaning and use. Our furniture is not what you would see in a typical human home, it is made of stone. It is a different kind of beautiful. Each piece is a work of art and adapted from the stone of the cave. The seating is covered with thick padding of blues and greens found in the cave city.

I sing a spell to turn on a nearby light. The lighting is different also; it is made of clear jar-shaped glasses filled with a fluid that creates a soft glow. The glow doesn't express the harshness of human light bulbs.

"Let me get some food into my handsome boy before you waste away. Sit here, Kino, you look like someone just walked over your grave, son. What happened at the meeting?" she asks, her beautiful green eyes sparkling.

I sit on the bench in our kitchen to relate today's events.

The living and entertaining area is on one side, transitioning to the kitchen area. Niches in the walls are used for storage and shelving. Cooking is completed on various stones warmed with magic and activated by an echo pulse.

I tell her and Sondra everything: Mega, Spar, and the new threat of Baratium.

Afterward, I lay out a plan if worse comes to worst. I explain where they will be the safest as well as where to meet if we are separated.

This type of information is not kept from any Ceorfan the way it is from military families in the human realm. It is shared. No gargoyle would give out information to endanger others. They have all been tested and connected. The bond is strong, unbreakable.

"Son, they must be mistaken. Who made this report? Are they sure it isn't the Crafted that are with Baratium and not gargoyles?" Gem asks with disbelief.

"Mother, you are probably right," Kino answers. "The report was from TASS agents, and they might confuse the mage-animated Crafted with us. I will let my commanders know what we suspect to be the truth."

When I am full of my mother's delicious food and drink, I pat my stomach and say with a smile, "I never eat so well. Thank you, but I must get back to my charge and tie up some loose ends. I will be back tomorrow." I kiss her cheek to leave.

A slight frown marks the worry in her eyes.

Going by way of my favorite imps. I send a pulse to their room. They come out at the same time.

I say, "New orders... you must stay in Navan until further instruction. Baratium is a threat again. The High Guild, Commander Megahir, and the King are in meetings deciding recourse. I'll let you know when I know more. Did you put the sculptures on the headstone, or do I need to go to the human cemetery and place them there?"

"No, don't worry your pretty little head, boulder boy. We set them there before coming home. We had a feeling," Mason shares.

"Thank you, gravel bits. It will save me time. I'll see you both when I get back tomorrow," I quip waving goodbye to my friends.

5

ASSHAT

Kendra

Reaching my phone and shutting off the alarm is a challenge this morning. Finally! Note to self: leave phone on the night table... not the bed!

I hurry to the kitchen and start a fresh pot of coffee.

Getting it brewing I gather my uniform and underthings on my way to dress. Just maybe I'm learning to function. This is going to be my new normal.

I have a new partner to meet. Boy, I hope I picked well. I slather on some lotion and sunscreen on my face. I brush my hair into a low ponytail. Adding a little make-up, not much, just mascara and lip gloss. I'm ready.

I speed through the apartment. I'm off to get my coffee. It hits me now.

I pause mid-stride and bend my head. David always filled our cups... I fill my travel mug.

Just stop! Get tough, Macbard! It's a cold, hard world, and you have to live here for a while, so get your shit together!

I tighten the lid on my cup, grab my badge and purse, and head to the parking lot. I glance up at the gargoyles on the roof as I make it to my truck. My red boyfriend who let me cry on his leg last night is looking down at me as if he's alive. Something is different. Are his wings spread out more, higher maybe? I'm a nutcase.

"Come on, Jasper, let's get to work before I'm late."

Almost an hour later I reach the parking lot of the Caverns. I love working here. It's so beautiful. The rolling hills of this country, the sunrise just getting up in the clear blue sky, even the cacti are beautiful to me.

I grab my purse and my now empty travel mug, and step out onto the asphalt parking area reserved for Park Rangers.

It's my habit to check out my surroundings, but this morning I just want to look at nature. Everything looks normal, beautiful—but normal. I can't get a lock on why I keep having the idea people are watching me.

I better get control of my feelings, before they start dictating my life. I'm not a baby or a scaredy cat. I kinda like being the tough, smart girl no one messes with in my little world. Hell, my brothers call me Batgirl.

I start to enter my code to get into the front doors of the Rangers Station, but a big hand beats me to the scanner. I'm not surprised it's John Cooper, one of the other tough guys—he wishes—flashing his pearly whites at me as the doors auto-open for us.

"Gotta be fast, Kendra, if you're going to beat me through the door."

"Maybe I let you open the door for me, so you can practice being a gentleman, John."

"What are you talking about? I wrote the book on manners for gentlemen," he chuckles.

Maybe he did, he's never been anything else around me. His partner Paul has no complaints from everything I've ever seen.

Chris pipes up in her 'mom voice' from behind the front desk, "All right, you two, Captain Murphy is waiting with the new hires in Human Resources. You're supposed to meet them in thirty minutes. I suggest you get your stuff stowed in your lockers and clock in on your computers. Go now, or you'll be late. Murphy brought donuts, Kendra, will you bring me one back? I'll owe you."

I nod and smile at her as I salute and head toward the women's locker room.

John and I meet back up as we walk up the stairs to Human Resources.

I hear a raised voice coming from the building. My spider sense is tingling, something isn't right. Shushing John with a finger to my mouth, I reach for my side holster and unsnap it.

We both lean against the building close to the window, so we can hear better.

Someone is yelling, uh oh... I see the glint of a gun. Not used to having a lot of weapons drawn in our office we're surprised when we hear a shot.

Jumping while ducking is an art that can't be practiced. Yet it apparently works this time as another bullet is shot out of the window where we are standing/jumping/ducking. We're sure something serious is up.

"I see you out there, get your asses in here, and I won't have to shoot your boss. Now! I won't be waiting!" shouts an unfamiliar voice.

John and I both run for the door.

I surreptitiously press the emergency button located by the door facing sending an alarm to Chris. Hopefully, she'll figure out we're hostages to this madman before too long.

I'm fast, and John's beside me, so I know the crazy doesn't see me hit the alarm. He probably wouldn't have a clue anyway. There are cameras to catch everything almost everywhere here, let's see what happens now.

Time begins to slow. I feel myself calming.

We enter the office, and Captain Murphy's on the floor. He's breathing but not moving. Blood is coming from a gash on his head.

A gunman is pointing his weapon at one of the biggest sons-of-bitches I've ever had the privilege to see. Gorgeous, but really, really big.

Jackpot! If this is Mica Jacobs, I sure can pick 'em. He's not happy as I enter and rolls his eyes. Pretty sure we haven't met before, but he looks familiar.

The gunman is intently focused on the striking giant of a man I've just nicknamed Gigantor. How in the hell is time moving so slow? I swear I can count seconds between my heartbeats!

I've gone through too much to let some dickhead with a gun hurt any more of my friends.

For some reason, my mind plays "When the going gets tough, the tough get going." I almost laugh out loud.

Steady, Kendra, steady. John knows me. I'm sure he has an idea; no way in hell am I waiting to act.

After what seems like minutes, but is probably only a split second, I decide. I never stop from the moment I cross the threshold.

I run straight at the asshat holding the gun, jumping over Murphy in the process. I'm going to have to dodge John who is bending to check on our captain. He watches me as I jump, with a look of surprise.

Looking into the asshat's eyes, I can tell he has no compassion. His kind are killers.

In fact, I see his aura, and it's green and brown! That's really a sick-looking aura. He levels his weapon at me as I land.

He's not going to hold back, and neither am I. His mouth is open sneering through his crooked teeth. I bring my own pistol up and aim... a shot rings out.

Gigantor reaches out and backhands the asshat.

I hear his gun go off again as he flies through the air, hitting the wall near the window where he first fired at us. He hits the wall so hard he leaves a butt-sized hole in the wall.

My mind flashes to a time where I watched Jared take his 1st degree Tae Kwon Do test. He was sparring three black belts; they all kicked him so hard, he left a hole in the wall exactly like the idiot just left. Why do I seem to have lots of time available in my brain while life-and-death struggles are happening in front of me?

Gigantor is on the douche in a flash. After disarming him, the big guy has him cuffed in a snap.

I spin and ask John how's Murphy when... damn it... I think the asshat might have grazed me. I don't have time to check it out right now though, I've got to call for help.

I reach for my shoulder mic, keying it I say, "Lima 26, *officer needs assistance*, 10-26 *at my* 20 *in* HR. We have a 10-33, *emergency* and need 10-52, *ambulance needed* for a 10-78, *officer down*. I need a supervisor at my 10-20, the perpetrator is under control and cuffed."

I get over to John, who is making sure Murphy is still breathing and applying a bandage to his head wound.

Everything's under control. I amble over and ask Gigantor if he's okay. He studies me with the greenest eyes. I almost stumble.

Smiling he says, "Easy peasy, Princess."

"Easy frickin' peasy, huh?" I burst out laughing, "Thank you, I guess you might be..." Then before I finish, I lean forward, my knees going weak.

Mica, alias Gigantor, only has to hold his arms out, and I fall into them passing out cold.

***

Waking, I glance around to get my bearings. Great, just great! I'm in a hospital.

It's bright in this room, and the clock on the television screen tells me it's afternoon. I feel like a car ran over me and came back for a second pass just to be sure. My mouth is dry. I try to lift my arm, but it's velcroed to a plastic splint with an IV.

"Well, I definitely missed all the action," I say out loud. I can't even guess what happened.

Dana, my sweet brother, jumps out of a chair he'd evidently

pulled up to my bed. He's rumpled. Pretty sure he had been sleeping in said chair.

He says, "Way to go, Kendra. We leave you for just a few days, and you go and get yourself all shot up."

"What... happened?" I grate out of my sore throat and try to rise.

Dana proceeds to tell me yesterday during the ruckus in HR the asshat with the gun shot me.

Because I didn't take the time to notice and complain about my wound I passed out from blood loss. Apparently, most of the blood was on my back as I had been shot through the meaty part of my waist just above my pelvis.

The doctors were afraid it might have nicked a major artery. Against my black uniform pants, the bleeding went unnoticed until I passed out in Gigantor's arms.

Dana says my Irish luck is holding up.

"Arghhh, that's embarrassing. I bet you love the guy for catching me."

Dana says, "I'm happy you even have a partner, especially one who takes care of business."

I knew it. I knew they would love Gigantor for saving me.

He adds, "His name is Mica, Mica Jacobs.

I knew that, too.

"Mica picked you up and took you straight to the EMT's. He ordered them to help you and leave the idiot who shot you for later.

They airlifted you to the hospital in the Ranger copter where you had emergency surgery.

Jared was here but left to get some dinner. He was here all night, too. He's gonna be pissed that he isn't here now that you are up."

"Can you text him, Dana, pretty please, with sugar on top?"

"Sure thing, Sissy, and I'm going to text Mica, too. He gave me his number with an order to call him with any new information. I'd hate to get on his bad side. He's just too big an hombre to challenge. I thought me and Jare were extra-large. He makes us look all medium-sized and shit." Dana looks serious, his eyes big.

I can't help it. I laugh at him. Then I grab my stomach. "Oh, that hurts!" I say.

It's maybe thirty-minutes tops before Jared walks into my hospital room, worry written all over his face. After seeing me, he relaxes a little and kisses me on the forehead.

He says, "Don't do that again, Sis. My heart can't take it. In fact, how about you get a safer job?"

"Oh, no, don't start that again. I love my job. I'm good at it. End of discussion," I respond.

And here comes Mica to the rescue again. Taking up the whole doorway, he walks through. What's up with the look on his face? You'd think we'd been partners for years, not hours. He looks me over and evaluates my well-being. Satisfied he backs off a little.

"Nice to meet you, Kendra. My name is, Mica. We didn't get to talk any before you passed out in my arms."

Wow! Just look at those arms. My partner is so built. I'll have to work at it if I want to be able to work around him without staring.

"What do you think? Will you have me for a partner?" He asks.

He's asking? I'll have to fight the others off. I think I may have to adopt my 'don't-mess-with-my-shit' face until they get over him.

"Well, that depends," I start and smirk at their surprised faces, "it depends on whether you can handle having a shot-up, confined-to-bed, pain-in-the-ass, for yours."

"You better believe it, Hollywood. Just get better. We can discuss more later. I 'll be back tomorrow," he says, then adds, "Do you want a cheeseburger tomorrow for dinner?"

"Are you kidding? I want one now. I guess I can wait, though. See you tomorrow but be early, okay?"

He smiles and waves at me as he leaves.

6

FIGHT

SPAR

So much is happening right now that I hardly get to see Mega at all. We'd talked and yeah, I feel a son-to-dad type of love for him. This is something I've never had before.

It's all happening so fast. I just met him, but I feel like I've been part of the Ceorfan my entire life. It is kinda nice to have a real father. I laugh that I already have no problem calling him 'Father.'

I pause, adding to my thoughts, but in the field, I'll be calling him 'Sir' or 'Commander.' I'm pretty sure that's what his team calls him. Maybe Mica can explain how I've become part of this large family so fast.

I have a book I need to finish online. Mica assigned it to me. He's my father's second in command, and I'm sure he knows what I need to help me understand this new way of life.

One of the first things my father had given me was a tablet. He set up a sort of email for me on something called the B-board. He said it's shortened from bulletin board. He told me to check my notices often.

I'm checking right now, while I'm at it, and yep, nothing. I set my alerts to vibrate and to chime with a one-minute time gap between the two just to be sure.

Maybe, just maybe, I can read my book without letting my thoughts wander into an endless dream about Kendra. That's a problem for later.

For now, I'm walking around exploring my new home. I need to be able to find my own way. I'd love to be able to show Kendra around.

I slowly drift. We could hold hands as we walk just like we used to do. I can imagine the way her skin feels next to mine... so warm. Her hot breath on me everywhere. My arms long to pull her body against mine, to feel her heat, her passion. I'm completely lost in my thoughts of her as I walk.

"Spar, concentrate," I say.

I shake my head, hoping to fling the thoughts away. I don't want to run into anyone while I'm lost in my daydream.

I'm just feet from the lunchroom. Hmmm, I'm hungry; starving, in fact. I turn toward the cafeteria and absently wondering why they call it that. I'm going to eat before I go to our room, there isn't even a snack in there.

Stopping short before I run right smack into another gargoyle, I mumble, "Sorry." I guess I didn't focus fast enough.

The new gargoyle looks like the Sphinx. He's bent over another much smaller gargoyle. He raises his clenched fist to punch the other gargoyle. The smaller gargoyle is already bloody. Great wounds made by claws cover the bloody one's side and shoulders. He's about half the size of the Sphinxter-goyle assaulting him.

Sphinxter-goyle yells at me when he sees me staring, "On your way, fucker. This is my prey!"

"Wait a minute here, buster. You need to back off." Then I ask the bloody gargoyle, "Are you okay?"

"None of your business... unless you want a turn." Sphinxter-goyle smirks.

His victim slumps over and begs me, "Help, please?"

I'm on this, I think.

I launch myself at the bully without giving him a second to react. He drops his 'prey,' who slides down the wall. I'm breathing heavily, infusing my body with O^2. It's a trick I learned as a kid, okay yeah, I fought a lot. My heart rate speeds up sending the extra-oxygenated blood and adrenaline to my muscles.

I say, "Pick on someone your own size, Sphinxter-boy." My fist connects with his face.

Uh oh, it doesn't even faze him. His reaction is lightning fast. He throws a straight punch. I'm not nearly quick enough to dodge. I hit the wall and then the floor, hard. I get back up. Fuck, this isn't going to be easy.

In less than three seconds, I've learned Sphinxter-goyle is much stronger, faster, and certainly more skilled in combat than I am.

I go over my options and determine I must use my last-ditch, sure-fire, gets 'em every time, 'kick 'em in the balls' move.

Spinning backwards faster than I've ever moved I land a back-kick to Sphinxter's groin. It lands hard. Victory is within my reach. Completing the 360-degree spin I'm now face to face with Sphinxter-goyle. He's just standing there looking at me like I called his grandma a whore. Bloody hell, I'm fucked. My reward for failure is going to be very unpleasant.

Preparing for the beat-down of my short gargoyle life, an odd thought goes through my head considering the circumstances. Damn it all! I didn't even get lunch first!

The lights brighten. I didn't even notice they were low. Mica's voice booms around the area, "That's enough Apex, thank you for your participation on such short notice."

I tell the room, "What in the fucking-firetruck is going on here?"

Bloody gets up and hits Sphinxter-goyle in the arm. He says, "Good job," and both are smiling.

I'm seriously confused. Good thing Mica lumbers over to me with both gargoyles. He reaches to help me up. I brush off his help and get up by myself.

Now I'm pissed.

"Spar, meet Apex and Dolo," he motions to Sphinxter then he motions toward the bloody gargoyle.

"Dolo is just fine, and you have just passed your first test. It was designed to test your base reaction to defending others in the guild. Your actions have proven you will. Most gargoyles are tested to see if they'll defend humans. You can understand why that would be different for you. Your dad is going to be so proud of you." He grins at me as he explains his description of the test.

"I hate to tell you, though, that fight is going to make the best story ever. I can hardly wait to tell how you kicked Apex in the balls. I can still see the, 'Oh shit!' look on your face. Come on, let's go eat." Mica lets out a hearty laugh, and I join him.

"I'm so glad one test is over, but if they all go this way I'm going to be in sad shape by the end," I say as we walk.

"Not all of the tests are physical, Spar. I can't tell you everything, but this one's free," Mica says with a shrug. "Let's get some food and talk in the lunchroom. One good thing I can tell you is that while you sleep, you'll heal up and not even feel sore when you wake."

We sit, swapping stories and finishing our meals then Mica says, "I have a mission in a little while, so I have go get ready. I'll see you in training tonight." He pats me on the shoulder as he leaves.

Tonight? Oh, that's right. It's almost sunrise, and I'll be asleep all day.

When I get to my room, I'm tired and sore, ready to sleep, so I can heal. Dad's in our room getting ready to sleep, too. Meaning he's cleaning and putting up as much as he can before he sleeps.

He spots me as I enter the living area and says, "Mica already told me telepathically that you have passed your first test, son. I am proud of you.

Normally, gargoyles would have this test with humans to prove their willingness to save humans. In your previous life, you have already proven you will sacrifice to help them. That type of test was not necessary.

You will have other tests, five in all. Protecting is what we do as gargoyles. We protect others, even humans. Our whole lives are built on this premise. We must protect each other because of the dangers we face. There are those who think we are nothing but chattel to be owned, used, or thrown away like trash."

My shoulders rise, and I puff my chest a little. This man makes me happy with myself. I want to make him proud. I know I'm a large gargoyle inside and out, but I feel even bigger from his praise. Kendra's the only one in a long time who built me up the way he's doing now.

I smile at him and say, "Pretty much what Mica told me. Is there any way I can practice for each test Father?"

"Mica oversees preparing you. Listen to him, son. Disregard nothing, he says." His posture changes and he asks, "Can you feel the change about to come upon you? The sun is starting to rise."

I take a second to evaluate. "Yeah, I can feel a tingle all over my skin."

"Wings up, son. It is a good thing to pose until it becomes automatic. If you are in the human world when the sun rises they will come closer to believing you are a statue or art if you pose. It might keep you safe. See you tonight."

I raise my wings, "Goodnight. When am I going to get used to this? I mean, see you tonight, Father." The pain is fast but blinding. We harden to stone with a quiet crackling.

I sleep.

***

I wake, but I'm still in my hardened state. I'm rested! Even now I'm more relaxed than I can remember being. Waking while I'm still solid stone, I listen to the sounds of bats in the cave, of water dripping, and even the sounds from outside the cave which echo within our community.

The change is coming soon. My body feels energized and awake.

A tinkling, crackling, like glass breaking, and my stone body changes to flesh. I stretch and breathe deeply. I'm healed now, and not even a scratch remains. This sleep has its advantages.

I dreamed of Kendra! I want to see her, let her know I love her. I want to know if she can possibly still love me now that I'm a gargoyle. The sooner, the better.

I see my dad moving around. He's getting himself ready for his job this evening.

He says, "Keep yourself safe, son. Listen to Mica. He will help you. I have meetings most of the night. The High Guild still hasn't come up with a plan to implement, and we will have to work until we do.

"Spar, tonight I need to talk to you about your beloved Kendra. There are some things you need to know. She is safe. Do not worry. See you soon, son."

7

PISTOLS

SPAR

Mica moves like he's as refreshed as I am. That's a plus in the gargoyle column. He starts the training by motioning me to come over to him. When I get to where Mica directed me my mouth drops open. Row upon row of weapons line the wall and tables. Wow!

I feel like a kid in a candy store.

Everything I ever wanted to try or use is here, some of the oldest weapons and the newest. There is even a mini rail-gun. That reminds me... my favorite handgun is something I should probably get from the apartment. It's a sweet Smith & Wesson 1911 Spartan with an oil-rubbed bronze finish.

It's probably right where I left it, too, I'll bet—right where Kendra and I had made our lives together. Okay, I go from thinking about guns to Kendra. Yeah, that fits. She's a pistol all right, and I want all my pistols back!

Mica must see the look of want and lust on my face.

"I drool over them, too, but we're doing hand-to-hand today, Spar. I just want you to see that we do have and use weapons. However, we choose to use stealth and our hands as our first choice. If you're in a position where you need this type of backup, one of our Guild will be there to support and defend you."

He's in full training mode now. I listen intently to every word.

He continues, "You're stronger than any human you'll ever encounter. The Ceorfan have the best soldiers on the planet by a 100-to-1 margin. With that in mind, generally, you'll restrain and not kill humans.

But," he emphasizes the word and exaggerates the pause after the 'but' to drive it home, "if we're fighting for the safety of the Ceorfan, our freedom, or the people of the Earth—things along those lines, we fight to win. You will use EV-ER-Y," again exaggerating the word to give it more meaning, "resource to win. Win. Do you understand me?"

He's as serious as I've ever seen him. His expression is one of manic intensity. But, observing him closely, I see an almost hidden pain. "Yes, I understand."

"Spar, you know life is rarely black and white. I can't lay out every situation where lethal force is required. You would have to use your judgment. You already know this, but our decisions need to back up the needs of the Guild. Gargoyles have always been protectors. That's what we should be fighting for. Let the humans decide life and death for their own people.

"If you're fighting gargoyles it's different. I wish I could tell you there aren't any gargoyle enemies. Here in Navan, you're safe. Outside this group, you might have to fight enemy gargoyles. Use every weapon you have to destroy them. Most are evil twisted beings who live only to destroy. Long ago they were made for that very reason."

I follow as Mica moves to the center of the big room. The floor is sandy. I haven't fought on sand like this in a long time.

About a year ago while training on a floor like this, we were practicing throws and slap-out landings. I fell wrong and broke a rib. I hope I don't have that kind of luck here. Wait... ha! Who cares, I won't feel a thing tomorrow. I'll intensify my practice.

Mica says, "First, I need you to learn to use your wings for defense. You already know how to pull them around you like a cape.

Spar, you have large wings. When you need, you'll be able to protect others by folding them around those you wish to protect. Say, for example, something was thrown at you, or maybe during a short fall.

Today's training will teach you how not to hurt others or yourself. Now, let's see you try an offensive move on me."

Mica grabs me, using a throw stance. He physically moves my wings to a position encircling the area in front of me. "As you land I need you to 'slap-out.'"

I remember doing it this same way like I did when I was a human. "Got it."

This time, my other arm and/or wing will continue to hold and protect the individual I'm protecting.

Mica and I continue my training.

Hours must have gone by before he says, "It's time to stop for a break."

"I'm not ready to stop. I'm getting this, and enjoying every second of it."

Mica ends my protests with a wave.

"We're going flying in a few minutes. I'm going to talk to the imps, Amber and Mason, and have them come with us to watch our backs," he says.

Glancing around, I notice we have quite a few of the Ceorfan watching our drilling session. Several move closer to us. A tall blue-grey female rakes my body with her eyes.

She asks me, "So, you are Mega's son? I just want you to know that while he is busy, I can keep you busy. In case you get lonely, that is."

The others giggle.

I'm feeling a little self-conscious because, during practice, I'd removed all my clothes except a pair of heat gear exercise shorts.

Like most gargoyles in Navan, I don't need many clothes. We

aren't affected by temperature like when I was human. Even though the caves stay an even 62 degrees Fahrenheit this far underground, I'm still hot and sweaty from the exertion.

Another of the girls says, "No, Coral, I think he might need someone more like me to keep him company."

This gargoyle has a definite sneer to her speech, but she is cut off by yet another gargoyle.

"He might just like my team better girls."

"Get away, Jadite. We saw him first," Coral tells the large muscular male monster in front of me.

Okay, now what do I do? I don't want to piss them off. I only want Kendra. No one else will ever measure up to her in my heart. Besides, I know Mega wants me to focus on my training. I enjoy making him proud of me. My silence is stretching out.

Thankfully, Mica takes charge.

"Disperse, the training field is for training. If you don't have business here, you need to go," he says to my crowd of admirers.

Not one of them offers an argument. They turn and leave.

"Mason, Amber, will you come and meet Spar?" Mica asks.

Two small gargoyles about two feet tall come over to us. They are both solid black, shiny, and smooth. They're beautiful. The closest thing I could say they resemble is a lizard-kitten.

"Spar this is Mason and Amber. They're part of the Elites. Their specialty is speed and stealth. They were guarding the gates of the cemetery the night you joined the Ceorfan."

I bend and reach out to shake hands. They both react simultaneously, each extending a paw. I chuckle, shaking Amber's clawed paw first. I hope I can tell these two apart. They're a matched set as far as I can tell.

She asks Mica while looking at me, "We can fly. Are we going with stealth or will we be using glamors to be seen as human?"

"We need to remain unseen this trip, Pebble." He gives a knowing look to both of them, the kind longtime friends and associates share.

Mica, Mason, and Amber take me to the cave entrance. The

whole time they're explaining how to fly, things to avoid, and how to take direction from the stars.

"I know how to navigate, guys. The Army Rangers trained me well," I say.

The cave is a fantasy palace, beautiful and calm. A path leads to the mouth of this cave unseen from the outside. It's an easy upward rise. I'm not paying the training much attention and look up at the night sky as we exit.

I draw in a deep breath of the cool desert air. It is a little cloudy tonight. The stars that peek through are shining and bright. It's nice out here. I spot two guards near the cave entrance, and nod to them as we pass.

The small duo of our group drop to the ground and roll in the dirt, covering themselves. Mason says it's to dull the shine of their skin as we fly. It won't last, but it will be enough for this trip.

Mica pauses, glancing at the two small companions who scramble away.

He explains everything that happened at the Ranger Station when my girl got shot. He reassures me she's out of danger. Still, my heart is pounding. All I want to do is go see her! Now! They have given me an added incentive to learn to fly well tonight.

Mica turns me around and I'm facing a dark abyss.

"Okay, Spar, we're at the top of a 500-foot drop. This is the easiest way to learn, just run and jump off. Spread your wings, then if an uplift doesn't catch you start pumping your wings. I assure you they will provide all the lift you need with minimal effort," explains Mica.

I don't wait a second. I run to the edge and jump. What can happen? I've already died once, and I need to get to Kendra.

After a slight drop I begin to pump my wings, and up I go. I love it! I straighten my legs behind me to streamline my body, it helps.

The lights of Cueva Hallow are in the distance, and I angle in that direction. The others are by my side with pleased looks. Nothing needs to be said, we understand each other. I did it, and they approve.

I've lived in this area for years, so I want to lead the way to the hospital. Taking advantage of the darkness, we avoid the lights of Cueva Hallow and come in from the west. I first see the flume and then the hospital.

Mica's instructions for landing are pictured in my mind. I lower my legs, hold out my wings for stability, and slowly descend to the rooftop. I land roughly.

He pats my shoulder and in a low, quiet voice, says, "I'm proud of you. You did amazingly well. It'll get easier. She's over here. This is her window. I opened earlier before I left. We'll enter this way, silent approach."

The little ones are in first moving without a sound. Next is my turn. I catch my breath when I see her. I've seen worse on others, but this seems much worse because it's Kendra.

My anger is going to boil over. I should've been with her. She is mine to protect. I've always thought that, but now it seems amplified in my mind. I reach out to touch her face, and she snuggles into my hand. Drugged as she is, she stays asleep.

Mica passes me, whispering, "You can have fifteen minutes. The imps are checking the halls as well as her records. I'll be outside watching. Don't ignore the time limit."

I nod my acceptance as he leaves.

Bending, I get to my knees beside her bed and still tower over her. That's okay, I can better protect her with this body.

I can't wipe the smile from my face. I'm so happy to see her. She's so little, so frail-looking, and so beautiful. I touch her forehead with my lips and kiss her lightly.

She moans, I jerk back quickly, but not fast enough as she grabs my arm and brings it around her like normal. At the same time, she presses her face to my chest. I feel an erection begin, thankfully that still works. I continue to hold her for a little longer. I feel better, but I must find a way to be in her life. 'How,' is the problem.

"I have to go," I whisper to her, kissing her softly.

She says, "No, stay."

I smile... she always talks in her sleep.

As quietly as I can I step out of the window onto the roof and meet the others. How did the imps get out here? Maybe I was too busy to notice them passing me.

Mica gives them orders to take me back to the Navan. He needs to stay and go to work as a Park Ranger. What I wouldn't give to have his gift of glamor and the ability to stay flesh in human form until he chooses to sleep! What a perfect gift to have.

"Guard her well, my friend. Report to Mega and let me know of the slightest problem. Okay?" I ask.

"Of course, I'll let you know. Safe flying, Spar," he responds.

Eventually, the imps and I are off and flying again.

Gliding high over the city is amazing. I love this feeling. I'm looking around and following the little ones. The pure joy of flight fills my attention, and I'm not even sure where we are now. I'm sure they do, so I go with their lead.

They drop behind a hill, and I follow. Wait, what happened to them? They're gone, I can't find them anywhere. Those little jerks. I call for them and get no response.

Frustrated, I wait a few minutes. I look at my tablet for the time, it'll be light in about an hour. Great! Just great!

Okay, calm down! I look back to the sky and see the moon is in the west. Navan is south of Cueva Hallow. All I need is to travel south, and I'll start to see the hills near Navan soon. I fly in that direction. After a few miles, I notice Sandy River and know I'm headed in the correct direction.

I hear a rattling and the bleating of deer. Looking down, I see a large 10-point mule deer caught in the barbed wire fencing.

"Oh, bloody hell, could it get harder tonight?"

I check my tablet, and I only have forty minutes before sunrise. Fine, whatever. What can happen to me way out here anyway? I'll just hide in the mesquite bushes and wait for dark if I can't make it.

I land a little too close to the trapped deer which sets him off struggling. He's been here a while. I can tell because he's tiring and has several bloody scratches on his hide.

"It's okay, I'm here to help," I say, knowing he can't understand me, I try to make my voice soothing.

Having a little experience with trapped deer, I grab his horns, so he can't hurt me. Awesome! This isn't hard at all.

I'm stronger than he is, I discover. I hold him still with my left arm while I cut the barbed wire with the claws of my right hand. It parts, and the wire snaps back, and... yes, of course, it slices my bicep.

Damn it! That stings. It looks okay, ugly, but okay. At least my arm now matches my hands. My thoughts drift from holding the deer, and I relax my grip. My new friend notices and jerks his head up nailing me right in the forehead with one of his antler points!

Son of a bitch, that was dumb! Shaking my head, I clench tighter to hold him steady, not letting him move until I have the wire cut.

"There, you're almost free, big guy!"

I've got him free from the fencing. But, some of the wire is still wrapped in his antlers.

"In for a penny, boy you got this wound up," I say.

He calms. I outmatch him physically. He's also worn out when I finally cut the last strand free. Now the hardest part, setting him free. I've been lucky and never been kicked or charged when I've freed a deer in the past.

"Be careful," I say.

I set my stance, point his antlers away from me, and let go.

He jumps straight up kicking out with his back legs pegging me right in the gut. It propels me backward as he takes off.

"Yeah! Back at ya, buddy. See if I do you any more favors," I shout to the racing deer's butt.

Whatever, we'll both be fine.

Getting up, I scope my surroundings sure someone must have been recording the episode. It'd get lots of laughs on the internet.

"Like there could possibly be someone out here in the boondocks who saw my little show," I say to the bugs and rabbits in the area.

I look at my tablet. I have about two minutes to make a twenty minute trip. Let's see... what can I do? I'm going to have to stay out here for my change. How do I stay safe? How do I keep the Ceorfan a secret? There's a rock shelf about a hundred yards away which should help conceal me.

I fly over to the rocks. How many times have I said a rock, or a mountain, or a cloud looks like an angel or animal? Well, that's my plan.

I land and yes, nailed it! I'm getting better at them. This landing didn't jar me at all.

I take a deep breath of the dusty desert air. I see the orange rim of the hills surrounding me, and I pose. I hope this is right, I think as the first rays of morning touch my skin.

"Arrghh!" I roar! My skin is now stone, and I sleep.

Several hours later, I feel a little rabbit walk over my... feet? I think I might scare it when I wake in a few minutes. Naw. That would only be funny if it was those two imps from hell who left me on my own.

I'm kinda glad, though. It's nice to have some time, not training.

I detect the change coming. Waking up doesn't hurt like it does going to sleep. It tingles like a numb limb with no circulation.

I stretch, and there's the two imps from hades, right in front of me, waiting.

"Hey, you two, where have you been?" I shout, letting go of my anger as I lift my wings to fly.

Yeah, taking off is easier, too. Those little pests follow me up into the sky. The second test is almost complete. They tell me speaking together excitedly.

"What?"

Twenty-some minutes later we stop at the cave entrance as two Elites stop us for verification. Again, I get back to our cave room before Mega leaves.

My father has just enough time to tell me he wants to give me a briefing at lunch.

I bob my head once happy saying, "Okay, Dad, I'll meet you in the lunchroom at midnight. Ha, I'm getting it."

"Oh, and Spar, good job on passing your second test. I will give that information to the High Guild today. I am proud of you.

"The test was, amid finding your way, would you help the defenseless? This is part of who we are. How we change the world. The small things matter. You kept in mind the safety of the Ceorfan, which was also a big part of the test. You posed and changed in the rocks.

"Good idea, son. In doing so, you help keep our secrets from others. Mason and Amber were watching the entire time. They reported that you were able to navigate by the position of the stars and moon before you saw the deer.

" Knowing you might not make it in time to change, you freed a mule deer from where it had been trapped in wire. Not worrying about extra tools, you used your strength and claws to free the animal.

"You were never lost and made it home without help. Also, when you made it here, you showed no stress or anger to the sentries, or even to the small Elites. I am happy with the results."

Again, there's something about my relationship with Mega. His praise builds even more confidence in my belonging to this community.

I'm keenly aware I've left the human world, and the world of the Ceorfan is now my home. I feel like an adolescent speaking with their sports idol.

I respond, "Thanks, see you at lunch later. I've got to go find Mica."

8

HISTORY

Kendra

It's early when the nurses taking my blood and checking my vitals, wake me. I had the best dreams last night. I was certain David was with me, holding my hand. My body tingles with the memory.

Dr. Vargas enters my hospital room with a chart in his small hands. Scanning the paperwork, he asks to examine my sutures.

He says, "These are healing nicely. Kendra, I have never seen someone recover from a wound like this as fast as you have. How do you feel?"

"I'm sore, but ready to go home," I answer.

He grumbles, "Might be possible if you can meet a few goals. First, in the next twenty-four hours, you must have no fever. Your sutures must remain in place with no abnormal fluid discharge. Finally, you must be ambulatory. If you can do this, I might consider letting you go home tomorrow as long as you have someone who will stay with you. Again, you heal quickly. I'm impressed."

I get out of bed to practice walking and to go to the bathroom with the help of my nurse. The walk energizes me. However, not wanting to wear myself out, I lie back down after I finish.

Mica, good to his word, strolls into my hospital room at 6:30 a.m. sharp. The delicious aroma of the Tastee Drive burger he carries in a paper sack is a boon to my hungry stomach.

"Ahhh," I take a big whiff and lean back with a grin.

"You're my friend for life," I say stretching my stitches a bit.

I ignore the pain not wanting to let my new partner know I hurt myself.

"Good thing the diner is open twenty-four/seven, so I could get this. I wouldn't want to disappoint a lady. Well, what's the news from the doctors? It must be good, your brothers aren't here. I can't imagine them leaving otherwise."

"You would be correct, Mr. Brainiac. Visiting hours just started, and they aren't here yet. The doctor said they'll be letting me go in the morning. I'm not in any danger if I don't over exert myself. I need to be careful not to tear my stitches. Now give me my cheeseburger before I have to break the law."

"Well, we can't have that, your highness."

His gorgeous grin makes him look less tough, approachable even. No, I can't even imagine who'd brave walking up to him just to shoot the breeze, without knowing him first, anyway.

I don't have to wait for my burger. He brings it to me and even gets it out then puts it on the rolling tray where my water cup is sitting. I dig in.

Not minding my manners, I blurt out, "Mica, have they found any information on the dirtbag who infiltrated the station and shot me? Have they told you anything?"

"Yeah, I know a little." He pulls a chair close to my bed.

"I'm going to say one thing first, partner. I'll be open and honest with you at all times, but I need to know you'll do the same for me."

I nod my head up and down, keeping my mouth shut, so he can continue.

"Said dirtbag has a name. It's Jerry Drinker. He's a known hitman for the Jessup cartel. His rap sheet is filled with weapons violations, gang activity, domestic violence, theft, need I go on?" he asks rhetorically.

"He's been a suspect in several murders. He was acquitted every time, and Princess, he didn't make it to the hospital. The shot you fired was on target and did its job."

"Okay, I can deal with that. I don't want to sound uncaring, but it makes me feel better knowing he isn't out there loose to finish whatever he started."

"Actually, he was after you from the start," Mica says.

Air whooshes out of my lungs. I'm puzzled and shocked.

He continues, "Captain Murphy and I had just walked into his office, and Drinker was already there, waiting. He clocked Murphy before we even saw him, and he threatened to kill him if I tried anything.

"Drinker yelled at me to call for you, so he could take you out. I had a plan to storm him to control the situation right as you walked in, all pretty as you please.

"I've got more and it's highly classified. I don't know how to prepare you for it. It's strange and unbelievable. You might not want to have me for a partner, or you may want to have me committed to an insane asylum when you hear it.

"Can you eat your burger and think about it today? I don't have time to tell you right now. I've got to get to work. I'll see you tomorrow morning and even take you home if you want. Then, I'll tell you what I know."

He punches me lightly on the shoulder, turns his broad back on me, and walks out of my room.

"Wow," is all I can say to the closing door.

***

I considered what Mica wanted to share throughout the night. What on earth could he want to tell me? It's on my mind as I wake up this morning, too. Whatever it is I need to know what he knows, now. Why would he even think I might consider he's crazy?

"Hello, Kendra, how are you feeling today?" Doctor Vargas says as he walks in with his brow knit. I've known him most of my life. I can't remember seeing him smile. So, I do at him. One day, he might do it back, right?

"I'm fine, doc. I've been walking, and no problems have popped up that I know of. So, you think I might get to go home today?"

"Everything looks good, Kendra. I'm going to release you this evening. So, I know you will have a few more hours of supervision. The nurses will be here later to go over your release instructions. You can't return to work for several weeks. I'm sorry. Did you find someone to take you home?"

"Yes, I did, doctor."

Speak of the devil, in walks Mica. I introduce the two to each other. Then Dr. Vargas excuses himself to continue his rounds.

"I get to go home this evening. Will you take me?"

"I'll be here as soon as I get off work."

"Also, Mica—I need to know everything."

"Okay, Princess, as soon as I get you home. I'll tell you everything I know. I won't hold anything back. Have you told your brothers, or should I tell them I'm taking you home?"

"Please let them know you're giving me a ride. They'll worry less, and that way, they won't be there trying to compete with each other over helping me," I add.

I think it must have been a relief to me to tell him I want to know. Because as soon as I do, I drift off to sleep. The day goes by fast, and time to leave comes before I know it. Mica loads his truck with all of my stuff.

My brothers had left earlier. We had agreed Jared could spend the night tonight and Dana would the next night. But they also have to let me have my time alone and not come over until late or when I call. I think they felt better after hearing the doctor tell them about how well I'm healing.

I'm so glad to be out of the hospital, I can't get enough of the scenery during the trip home. It is quickly over however and we pull into the parking lot of my building.

Mica helps me out of the truck. Holding onto his arm, I make it to the apartment building doors. Slow and steady. I can tell Mica is a bit antsy with how slow I'm going. I laugh to myself. I'm almost to the elevators then before I know it he picks me up gently and carries me the rest of the way there.

I don't have the energy to argue, and it feels good to be held, so I let him without a complaint. I'm awake, though, and aware of every muscle in his chest and arms.

What? Really, Kendra? What's up with that? I am human. David has hardly been gone two weeks, and I'm perving on my partner. I take a few seconds, questioning myself.

The reality is I'll always love David. I've thought I may never find anyone who cares for me again, and here is this gorgeous man who has done nothing but care. My body is responding to needs I'm not ready for mentally.

I'm happy he's my partner. I don't want to ruin this new friend-ship. A girl can be proud of her partner, right?

Mica gets me into my apartment and sits me on the couch.

I ask, "Will you get me a glass of water?"

He answers, "Yes, are you hungry too? If you are I'll order something."

"Ummmm, let me think a minute."

He's back with my stuff in a flash."

"You want me to order a pizza or something else? I don't mind going to get dinner for us if you want. It's going to take a while to tell you everything."

"That sounds good to me."

"Do you want to talk or food first? Also, do you mind if I stay the night on your couch? I can call Jared and tell him I'm here, so he doesn't come and stay, too. If you're okay with that, that is."

"Can we order a pizza and talk until it gets here? You'll have to go down to get it, though. This building is protected from the evil pizza delivery people. You can stay, too."

"Good plan, if you get tired or it's too much just shut me up, okay?"

"Okay, I promise."

I settle into the back of the couch watching his face as he begins.

He's serious. I can't help but think his speech reminds me of what I have always thought a bard would sound like as he tells a story. His deep voice is soothing in the quiet of my apartment.

He starts, "Kendra, there's a race of people who I want you to understand first. If that's alright with you?"

I move my head up and down.

"These people were like us. They had families who they loved deeply. They lost family members and grieved each loss. They were travelers without restrictions. They weren't troublemakers. They lived in search of beauty.

"They made their homes in the cliffs of every nation. Mostly the cliff homes were carved in stone or had a stone edifice. Some were even built inside wonderful caves.

"These people were big, strong, full of confidence, and had a fierce determination to help each other. Their whole culture made it commonplace to be loyal and help others."

"Any questions so far?" he asks.

I shake my head no. I'm not sure where this is going, but it seems like a good story, and I don't care right now.

"You know as well as I do, there's always people who are filled with prejudice and hatred for anything or anyone who is different. We believe prejudice and hatred come from fear. It overrides any love or human kindness. That type strikes out and destroys what or who they feel is a threat. That happened to the dragons more than a thousand years ago."

Okay, so now I know this is just a story to help me rest or something.

I guess Mica thinks telling me this will put me to sleep, and I won't over do it. It's interesting, though, so tough luck, sucker. I'm staying awake to hear your story.

Mica continues, "The dragons weren't evil man-eating killers that made men sacrifice virgins. The real story is, dragons would save those sacrificed. Those saved were made a part of their people. They were all shapes and sizes. Some looked like creatures people think are just myth.

"We are called the Ceorfan Guild, all of us are different yet the same tribe. Sort of the way you have giants, little people, females, and males of different colors and shapes but you call them all humans.

"Anyway, people mated with the Ceorfan. Their children were different. They were celebrated for their differences. We noticed the difference wasn't just in looks. These young had abilities. Some could communicate telepathically, others teleport, or shapeshift, the list is endless.

"Sometimes family lines would exhibit the same abilities. One such family was the dragons. The females were beauties who were natural leaders. They had favor with the people because of their ability to make the ones around them stronger, heal them, and amplify the unexplainable. Humans called it magic.

"If you were near these ladies, the dragon-children, those without kids would be blessed with them. And the people had no deformities the way they are thought of today. If someone had a deformed limb, it could be magically reformed by a gift of dragon blood.

"These women were sought out by everyone for healing.

"During this time war broke out between men. The Scots and the Vikings fought over land and power. The Ceorfan stayed hidden and away from the fighting.

"However, the Vikings could see their cave city as they came ashore. Scottish royalty asked the Ceorfan queen to help them in their war with the Vikings. She declined. Our queen explained that we wouldn't hurt humans. Instead, she agreed to help heal the injured on both sides. Unhappy the Scots left and set about planning a way to force the dragons to help."

I startle as the intercom buzzer goes off and Brian, the doorman informs us the pizza delivery guy is downstairs. I guess the story was keeping me sitting instead of trying to do more than I should. Devious plan, Mica. But it's working!

"I'll go get it and be right back. You stay there," Mica says, taking his phone out of his pocket, I guess to call Jared while on his way to get the pizza.

I've got to move, though. I'm achy from sitting, and I just flat-out want to do something. I'll get the paper plates and drinks while he's gone.

Hurry, Kendra, you need to be finished before he comes back.

I glance at the door. Odd, Mica left it open. Oh, don't be silly. Go shut it. I walk over to the door to see if Mica is coming back. I peek toward the elevator to see what floor it's on and if the floor indicator is lit up. I can't see him, so I wheel around and shut the door.

A strong arm shoots out grabbing me around the waist while another holds my mouth. Ouch! Oh crap, his arm hurts my incision.

I can't fight because I'm concentrating on fighting the pain. Every time I move, lightning bolts of pain shoot through my torso. I can't see my captor, but I can tell he's dragging me to the roof.

Whoever has me is strong. He's so big my feet don't even drag the ground. He moves fast, it's like he's flying.

He carries me up the stairs to the roof. Mica's shouting in the background, but I'm confused and can't understand what he wants.

The arms holding me, throw me over the edge of the roof.

As I fall, I scream, knowing this must be the end. I'm not sure how, but I have time to say a short prayer, asking God to watch over my brothers and tell David I'm coming... then I hit.

Wait, what the hell! I'm not dead.

I stopped hard, but I didn't hit the ground. Someone, or more like something, has grabbed me out of thin air.

His arms pull me close to his muscular red chest. I see huge wings flying me back up to the roof.

Again, wait. Did I say 'red'? Great, I'm certifiable now!

My big crimson savior hands me to Mica who doesn't have a shirt on, and he also has giant wings. I study him with what I'm sure is what's left of my 'panic look,' combined with a 'what the hell' look.

He still looks amazing, so I hope my look isn't anything like, 'I just took a panic shit' look.

He shakes his head and carries me back to the sofa where he gently sets me down. Immediately he frantically examines me to see what my injuries are.

I bat his hands away and say, "What the fuck, Mica! What the fuck! What the fuck! What the fuck! Are you kidding me? What the fuck is going on?"

I stare him straight in the face and see his forehead wrinkled with worry and failure.

Kendra, get hold of yourself. I chuff and blow out a breath. I do it four times. One last intake of air, center yourself. Concentrate on calming down.

I need to take stock of my surroundings and regain control. Nope, not happening! Glancing around, I'm piling up questions. Several gargoyles now surround us, blinking, wide-eyed, and alive. On that note, I pass out.

***

I wonder how long I've been asleep as I wake. Now that was a freaky dream. I can't remember being so out of control in a dream since I was a kid.

"I've got to turn that shit around next time," I say out loud.

A voice breaks through my thoughts. I turn my head slowly, and see my outlandish dream come true. My red hero is staring at me and asks if I'm okay.

"No, I've lost my ever-loving mind," I say.

I'm pretty sure it's a him, and he's gorgeous, in a monster kind of way. I would love to reach out and touch him. Not gonna happen though. He might just suck me into those eyes. They are impossibly green, like diamonds in the dollar store lamplight of my bedroom.

"Well, maybe. Maybe not, little one. My name is Kokkino Petra. It means 'red stone' in Greek. Please call me Kino, and I am pleased to be of assistance. My commander Mica said to call him as soon as you woke. So, if you don't mind."

"No, I don't mind, I guess."

Kino takes out a tablet and talks into it.

I don't even care what he's saying. I just want to watch him. He must be real, including those wings. I know he saved me, plucking me out of the air like a baby bird. At least in my dream, he did.

I look closely to see if red is the color of his skin, or if maybe it's paint. Nope, it's a great airbrush paint job if it is fake because it looks as real as my own skin color.

"He said he is getting you a cheeseburger as a peace offering and replacement for the destroyed pizza. He will be here soon."

"That sounds good. What happened to the pizza?"

"Well, when the Crafted, that is what we call the creature who attempted to execute you by throwing you off the rooftop. Anyway, when that happened, Mica pitched your pizza to the ground endeavoring to save you. Even had it remained in the container, it would have been inedible. However, most of it landed on the floor of the hallway.

"Commander Mica is very fast, but I was already on the roof guarding. While I rescued you, the Commander destroyed the Crafted. They are nothing but tools and not real beings with souls like you and me. Their maker creates them like robots to do his bidding and to increase the size of his forces.

"I do wish, that you would have been able to learn of us differently. Commander Mica said he was teaching you the history of our people.

"I know this must be a frightening shock to you. Will you please give him a chance to finish? We have good intentions toward you and your family, but the world is a bit bigger than you have been taught."

Kino continues, "I require a promise from you. For you to stay aware of us and keep this memory, you must convince me that you will keep everything about us a secret. If you choose, we can make it so you do not remember any of this."

Really? I'm hurting, and I'm about to take out my anger on him. Instead, I should check whether my incision is bleeding.

"Kino, did you say your name is Kino?"

"Yes, Edling, that is my name."

"Do you mind leaving me alone for a little while? I want to check my stitches. I need to be sure my body is okay. I also need a sanity check."

"Of course. I'll be close if you need me."

After he shuts my bedroom door, I lift my shirt, so I can see if my wound has opened. I don't see any damage... nope, no blood. I feel better just knowing that, but my body is sore, and I'm exhausted.

What do I think? So many things make sense now. 'What do I want to do?' is the correct question.

I need more information. Okay, if that's the case, I'm moving on and keeping my memory. Yep, I want to know more.

I get up and go to the bathroom to comb my hair.

Looking in the mirror, I say, "Come on, Kendra, you can do this."

I walk over to the door, open it, and walk into my living room.

Mica's at the bar in the kitchen pulling my food out of a paper bag. I walk over to him and reach for the plate. I sit on a bar stool, and eat. They are silent until I finish.

I say, "Thank you, Kino, for saving me. I thought my number was up. Then suddenly you grabbed me. All I can say is, thank you. It doesn't feel like enough.

"Thank you too, Mica, for... just everything. Or is it Commander Mica? You've done nothing but help me. We have just met, yet you have saved me and fed me several times. I'll never be able to repay your kindness. I'd like to try, if you'll be my friend. Maybe someday, I can return the favor."

Speaking to both, I say, "I want more information. Right now, though, I'm very tired. Will one of you be able to tell me more about this fantastic world I've managed to miss? I'd like to know more about the beautiful things and people you spoke of. Later, when I wake."

I turn to Kino and say, "I'll keep your secret, you have my word."

He approves and bows slightly to me.

Mica says, "You're welcome."

He and Kino share a glance the way that close friends do.

Mica says, "Most certainly, we'll tell you everything we can as soon as you are rested."

9

KNOWING

Kendra

Seems like I've been asleep forever. I must have been asleep most of my life to have missed a whole race of people. Especially ones I've been attracted to forever. I thought they were myths.

Is that coffee I smell?

I glance out of my balcony doors and see it's still dark out. I didn't sleep as long as I thought. It's early in the morning 5:00 a.m. to be exact.

"Good morning, Mica. Thank you for staying last night."

He smiles at me. It's pathetic, I can't ignore his crazy good looks.

He says, "You're most welcome, Princess. How did you sleep?"

"I slept well, thank you very much!" I return with a bouncy quip.

He laughs. He's not fooled. I must have been caught looking.

I say, "Probably because I knew you and Kino were here to help protect me from the Crafted and the Jessup Cartel. I'll do better in a few days and not need so much help."

I fill my favorite coffee cup and sit on the sofa in my sweats putting my feet up on the coffee table.

I ask, "Well, when do I get to know more?"

"Now, if you'd like. Kino is about to sleep. Would you like to have breakfast on the roof, so you can watch him change? It's something we do as gargoyles. I won't have to tell you how the process works if you see it firsthand."

"Yes, I would love to," I answer.

We walk to the roof. They have a table spread with cut fruits, fresh bread, butter, and apricot jam, my favorites. We sit, and they eat with me.

I say, "Well, that answers the 'if you eat and what you eat' questions that I was going to ask."

Kino and Mica both chuckle.

Kino's brows furl.

He looks into my eyes as he says, "Edling, you are very important to me. It was my pleasure to save you from the Crafted last night. You need not ever thank me. It is to your credit you did so, but please promise me you will never thank me for me defending you again. It almost broke my heart."

I say, "Yes, it's a deal."

I'm a little choked up by his words.

"The change is painful for a split second then we sleep. There was a time before the Mage Wars where the Ceorfan did not turn to stone. They were full flesh and blood creatures. But, ahh, Edling, that is a story for another time."

He motions for me to come over to the edge of the roof telling me as we go, "This is where I stay during the light of day. At night, I wake and guard you as you sleep."

"Well, that's not at all creepy," I say half-jokingly.

The sun is just peeking over the horizon, and Kino lifts his wings to pose the way I usually see him. A pained look crosses his face as he hardens to the shiny red marble I'm used to seeing. I put my hands on him when I see the painful look. It hurts me.

Mica must know what I'm thinking because he says, "We have a word for this. We call it torpification. We heal in this state, as long as no one destroys us. We are at our most vulnerable in a torpefied state.

Many gargoyles have perished while sleeping by having their bodies broken."

"But you're made of stone," I start.

He interrupts, "It's not as hard as it seems when someone takes a sledgehammer to one of us.

Mica continues, "If you're wondering why I'm not stone it's because of my gift. All gargoyles have a gift. I was telling you before about the dragons and their powers. They were part of our race, the Ceorfan. Our gifts are all different. Mine is called glamour. I can stay in the sunlight and not be forced to sleep in the daytime and appear human. I do have to sleep at least a few hours every day. Otherwise, I'll get run down just like you would."

"That's wonderful. Kino looks like a gargoyle, and I can understand dragons could also be part of your people. But tell me, why do you look like a man? Do gargoyles look like men, too?"

Mica starts cleaning up our breakfast then with eyes wide he says, "I'll give you the short version. Again, my gift covers me with a glamor. Humans think this is what I look like, so I can operate in the open, in the sunlight. I can show you what I look like, if you want and if it won't scare you."

"Okay, Mica, I'm ready."

He says something I couldn't repeat if I tried.

The glamor melts off him. He stands still, almost as though if he moves, I'll scream in terror and run out of the room. Anybody that isn't ready would be terrified of him.

There's no telling what would happen, but I'd lay odds it wouldn't be good. I bet he thinks he might scare me, even though I told him I was ready to see his gargoyle self. I'm way past the fraidy-cat stage. I don't think anything can surprise me now.

Mica looks like a man-cougar as ebony as I've ever seen black. His amber eyes are a sharp contrast to his dark skin. He's still the huge muscle man I figured he would be. He has horns which curl back a little behind his temples.

I don't see any hair. His hands and feet—or claws—are as jet-black as his skin, but they have some white on them, too. He's absolutely beautiful! Not what I was expecting at all because of his usual blond, blue-eyed human guise. No wonder we all think they're just art or statues.

He hangs his head looking at the ground and says, "I'll put the glamor back as soon as I've rested. It takes a little out of me, and I'm tired, sorry."

"What?"

As soon as the question is out of my mouth, I figure it out. He must think I see him as an ugly horrific monster.

"W... why?" I stammer.

Who could have made him believe that lie?

"Mica, you're my friend and just so you know I think each of you look like the most beautiful people I've ever seen. You have nothing to be ashamed of, period!"

His eyes widen, a look says so much. His face says he's been shamed. Like possibly it would be too much to hope a human wouldn't think him hideous.

I don't like it one bit. I've seen that look many times, mostly on the homeless or crippled. I've seen it on others also. Anyone who is different from what 'polite society' deems acceptable.

Polite society, what a crock!

I hope to God, I build others up and not tear them down, and when I mess up, that someone tells me. Starting now, with my partner.

"I think I prefer you this way. Don't use the glamor around me, Mica, just the part to be in sunshine. Not unless you think you must for your safety or we're at work. I wish you never had to use it. I wish everyone could feel like it's okay to be themselves. What do you think... shall we try to influence our small corner of the world toward this kind of behavior, big guy?"

Beaming at me with a lift of the corners of his mouth he says, "I'd like that, Edling."

"Okay, what does 'edling' mean? I kinda like the sound. But if you and Kino have been calling me an idiot or dipshit in gargoyle-ese I need to be able to get you back," I tease.

Now he chuckles. I hold back, raising my eyebrows. Honestly, seeing him laugh would make most people wet their pants.

"Kendra, in all my years, I've never known anyone like you. To explain Edling, think of the warm feeling you get with children or small animals then add respect. It literally means 'noble family.' We don't use it lightly.

"I need to return to Navan, the gargoyle city, where I'll rest. You need to rest, too. There's still stuff I need to share with you. Do you think I could come back tonight?"

"You'd better come back! You're right, too. I feel much better. I think another day would be good. Then I'll be in a good enough state to move around outside of my apartment."

"Good, you go rest, and I'll lock up."

While taking myself back to bed, I almost felt as if I were flying. So many new people I've met. The world is so much bigger than I believed.

I can't wait for Mica or Kino to come back. The things I'm learning are so exhilarating.

I'm lost in a daydream. As I walk, I ram my left shoulder directly into the door jamb. Pain shoots through my torso as I impact. All right, dummy, watch where you're going before you hurt yourself. I make it to bed without any further accidents.

***

Mica

I fly to Navan. It's my day off from the Park Rangers. I have reports to file for Mega here. I'm going to my 'goyle-cave' room as I call it.

I've heard my human friends speak of their 'man-caves.' They don't have any idea what a real cave is.

As I sit writing out the reports to Mega and leave him a personal message asking if I can bring Kendra to Navan this evening. I believe she's healthy enough, and she's certainly ready for more revelations.

Sometimes, it's easier to show someone than tell them some things. That is if she doesn't take my head off when she finds out I hired an off-duty officer from the National Park Service as a guard during the daytime. One who is at her house right now.

We'll see.

Pulling out my tablet I leave a message for Spar. I know he misses his lady, maybe this will help. Message sent, now I'm going to rest until evening. I've been doing a lot and not sleeping much.

I stand and pose, concentrating on relaxing for the change. I roar. The pain is worse when I'm tired. Now to sleep.

***

Spar

"Dad, can you tell me, has the High Guild made any decisions yet?"

So strange, sometimes I'm comfortable calling him Dad. He's in my heart and part of me.

"Yes, I can tell you. We do not keep our plans secret from each other. The Guild has decided to send a contingent to the humans' Alumbradai to ask for their help. They need to know of the threat," he says concentrating on his tablet as he types into it. "Do you feel up to being part of the team?"

"Yes," I blurt out a bit fast and loud. Softer and under more control I add, "I want to help if I can."

Mega smiles. "I have news concerning Kendra."

I stop dead in my tracks, so I can hear every word.

"Mica has reported that she was attacked again last evening."

"I have to go. I'm going to go and kill someone," I say with gritted teeth.

Mega holds me back telling me the rest of the story. I feel grateful for Mica and Kino's protection over her. Yet, I still feel the need to go to her.

"Son, Mica has asked if he might bring her to Navan tonight, so she will have a better understanding of our people. The King and I have granted his request. There is a chance she will be ready to see you. You must trust my men to know if she can handle the stress or not. Is it possible you can wait if she is not ready?"

That's not what I want. I want to see her and be with her. For her to know I'm still me in this different shape. I want her to be okay, healed and whole, mind, body, and soul. I know Mega can communicate with my mind, but can he read minds, too?

I grudgingly say, "I'll be okay. I'll trust them."

He says, "I will need you to get some clothes made for the trip. The tailor is about a klick down from the lunchroom. Will you go?"

"Yes sir."

I've been wearing old jeans, no shirt, and no shoes. Heck, I'll bet I can't get into the lunchroom dressed like this. I wonder, what does a gargoyle wear to a summit meeting with humans?

Mega asks, "While you are there will you please pick up my clothes from the tailor as well? Earlier, he sent a message informing me they are ready."

"Yes, I will," I answer as he leaves for his business meetings.

I pick up my tablet and read a message from Mica. It says he's going to be busy and this is a day off for me. That's fine. I'm going to go get clothes, anyway.

I tuck my tablet into my pocket and take off in the direction of the lunchroom.

The air is nice in the caves. Nice doesn't describe how beautiful it is here. The formations are lit with lights from the mage jars. Some majestic formations that look like falls are up ahead. They are close to a circular area of stalagmites with a small pool that follows the wall of this room.

Some people are laughing close to the edge of the widest part of the pool. It isn't big, maybe only ten to twelve feet across at its widest, but it's much longer. So much so that I can't see the end.

The shrieking group is throwing something. Well, that can't be good. Working in the caverns, I learned how fragile cave formations can be. They take thousands of years to form, but only a few minutes to destroy. I marvel at how this cave has obviously been cared for since the cave habitat hasn't been destroyed. Well, it's been preserved until now, maybe.

I better go ask them to stop. I know the Guild wouldn't want our caves trashed; plus, I can't let go of that part of my former life.

When I reach the group, I verify my suspicion.

They are stumbling around, weaving on their feet, and shouting. They seem to be drunk, because they have beer cans and bottles thrown all over the place. Some of the glass ones are broken.

My mood is going from good to not so good after seeing the mess up close. A man-sized gargoyle sees me coming and throws his beer bottle at me.

I dodge. I should have tried to catch it or let it hit me. It would have made for a better entry. The bottle was full and breaks on the rocks.

I say, "Hey, no need for that. I just wanted to know what y'all are doing. Why are you tearing up our home?"

The bottle chucker says, "Uh, this is not your home, mister. It's ours, and we can do with it as we please. You can leave. We don't want your kind here. What are you anyway? Some kind of freak?"

Before I can respond, he turns and hits me with a hundred-pound tail, and it's sharp.

"Oomph."

It knocks me back, but I don't fall. I do have a cut across my chest, though.

"Will you just listen to me for a minute?" I ask.

The guy stops, his eyes wide.

"I'm Spar. What's your name?"

I stumped him because he's pausing. The rest of the group are lined up behind him. They're all listening to what I have to say. So, I start by telling them what I'd read.

"When we first came to Navan, we had nowhere to go. Our people had been used as slaves, as pack animals, and for sex long enough. We had just won our freedom.

Yeah, they're still listening.

"We made this place our home. Other races left us alone. They didn't see the beauty in what we had found. The dragons were all gone. Killed. Their heads mounted on human buildings. The big ones, along with some of the little ones. If we stayed here, we didn't have to see the sacrifice our loved ones had made for us by seeing their heads mounted. We recognized the caves are living, not just stone."

The gargoyle who had struck me says, "I remember."

He pats me on the back and says, "We shouldn't be doing this. Let's go."

Like ghosts, they disappear.

I have no idea why that worked, but I'm glad it did. I go to the lunchroom and ask for some garbage bags. They give me a whole roll. I return to the trashed area and start cleaning.

When I have the area cleaned up, I take the trash to a recycle enterprise beside the lunchroom. I give the trash bags back to a short gargoyle working there.

Completing my walk to the clothing store I ask, "Am I in the right place? I'm looking for the tailor."

A man walks out with a waddle. He must be the tailor. A younger, skinny, gargoyle follows close behind. I'm guessing this one is his assistant.

The tailor says, "Megahir has informed us that his son, Spar, would be coming in for clothes."

They introduce themselves and relate to me how excited they are to meet me. I stand while they measure, prod, and poke. Soon, they finish and don't need me anymore; they'll send me a message when my clothes are ready.

I shake hands with the tailor before I leave. Feeling my tablet buzz against my leg, I dig it out and check my messages.

There is one message: Good job passing your third test. Many people wouldn't have even tried to keep the cave from being destroyed. Your respect for the land is a testament to your ideals.

Mega

My spirits lift.

10

FLYING

Kendra

I've read the last chapter of my book three times, and I still don't remember a single word. It's time to put it away. I can't sleep. I can't read. I don't want to eat anything. I think I'll watch a....

What was that noise?

I'm sure I just heard something in the kitchen. As quietly as I can, I sneak my Glock out of the nightstand, tiptoe to the bedroom door, and crack it open.

Sure enough, through the opening I can see a man in my kitchen. Somebody's about to get shot!

Kendra, I tell myself, don't you dare make a mess in that fridge. Wait for him to close the refrigerator door first. That's a mess you don't want to clean unless you absolutely have to.

I open the door all the way and step into the living room and yell, "Federal law enforcement, dirtbag. Hands up!"

As the perpetrator turns with his hands in the air, I can't believe it.

"John! What in Sam-hill are you doing here?"

"Your partner, Mica, hired me. He said he had some business to take care of and he'd pay me to guard while he was gone. Kendra, please lower the gun. I promise, I'll put the sandwich back. Just put the gun down."

I lower my weapon, put the safety on, and then walk toward him.

"Sorry, John. I had no idea anyone would be here. You scared the shit out of me! Though, now that I'm awake and not likely to go back to sleep, you can go. I'm fine now."

John adds, "'After you finish your sandwich?' No, 'Come sit and have some tea with me?' No, 'How was your day, John?' Just, 'Get your shit and leave. I don't need you around.' Story of my life. See you at work. By the way, I'm glad to see you're doing so well," He says as he walks toward the door.

"Okay, okay, I get it. Sorry, I'm a little snarky. I just woke up. I don't need a babysitter. I'm better now. Come over here and finish your sandwich. Tell me what's up at work."

He's his usual silly self and has me giggling in no time.

"Ouch! No more jokes, John. Hurts, not as much as yesterday, though. Thank you, Lord, I'm getting better. I just wish it was quicker."

John and I have a good visit, then he leaves. There's no way Mica told him about the Ceorfan, gargoyles, or any other of the odd things I've recently come to know.

I think I'd like to go up to the roof. On second thought, I may be setting myself up to be an easy target. I'll wait for dark.

"See, I can behave, sometimes," I say to no one in particular.

I sit on the couch and turn on the television. I flip through the channels and find nothing entertaining.

When darkness starts to fall, I make a cup of coffee and tuck my book under my arm. If I go now, Kino will be coming to life in a few minutes, and I'll see how that happens.

I'll carry my gun in my sweats pocket. I'm pretty sure a 9 millimeter slug will break something off a Crafted, if not outright shatter one.

The air feels good after being cooped up all day. It's not too windy today, just a little breeze. It smells like jasmine up here. I love the smell.

I can hear a siren, but it sounds a long way off. I set my coffee and book on one of the cement tables.

When I walk over to Kino, I notice his eyes are still green. He looks scary with a grimace monsters make before they eat you. I'm ruined on that aspect. I already think he's a pussycat. Still not a pussycat to mess with, his claws look like they could take a head off.

I stop as I feel an electric sensation and smell, what is that smell? Not a bad smell, but different. Sort of like when you walk into a welding shop. The same, but at the same time, not.

Watching Kino, I can see a light surrounding him, and it looks like his body blows up in a shower of sparkles. He steps right out of the sparkles, putting large hands on my waist.

"How are you today, Edling?" Smiling doesn't soften his face. He looks sexy-scary now.

I snicker at my thoughts. "I'm better today. I'm starting to feel human again."

Is that a grimace? Who could tell?

"Good news then, Edling. Do you mind sitting over by the hot tub? I think it is a safer location if you insist on staying on the roof."

He gets this faraway look for a few seconds. Then he looks down at me and tells me he just heard from his commander. He said that Mica will be here in a few minutes.

I can hardly believe my life. How did I get so lucky? I've always thought my family and I are blessed. We tend to succeed at everything we decide to have or accomplish. I'm not saying bad things never happen to us, they do. Sometimes terrible things. We just tend to overcome. It's a character aspect, maybe something our parents instilled.

My parents did teach me the golden rule. I have known some who say do unto others before they do unto you. I have never been that way. I like to be an optimist, at least most of the time. Building others up is my goal. Judging is my pet peeve.

"Kendra," Mica's deep bass voice calls me out of my thoughts.

"Oh, hey, Mica," I say, rising for a hug and then sitting back down quickly. He smells like musky vanilla.

"Kendra, you're moving well. Does this mean you're feeling better?" he asks.

Then, without waiting for an answer, he turns and gives orders to the other gargoyles on the roof with us.

Kino is to fly above the building and recon the area.

The smaller gargoyles Mica tells to search the inside of the apartment and neutralize all threats.

One he calls Flint, who must be using a glamor because he looks human, he sends to get some dinner, Chinese. Sounds good.

"What do you want?"

"Oooh, I like cashew chicken and veggie egg rolls."

Mica adds my order and sends Flint on his way. "I have a lot to tell you Kendra. Please, let's sit."

We both take a seat on separate cement benches, allowing us to face each other. I can see others of Mica's team moving with a purpose. They obviously are not going to let anyone or anything near us.

"The nights were too short for me lately. So, Kendra, if you don't mind, I'd like to get to it."

"Sure," I answer.

"I have many discussion points I need to speak about to get you up to speed on the Ceorfan. Princess, we've watched over you for a long time. Sometimes, I feel like I've known you for years. Yet, you and I have only recently met. Because of this, I'm not sure how to approach certain topics.

"I need to tell you these things and many of them are going to be difficult for you to understand. I don't want to hurt you. So, if I tell you anything too far out of your comfort zone, let me know. I'll stop. After you're ready, I'll continue. I'll wait for you, even if it's days, months, or even years. Is that okay with you?"

"Please continue, Mica. I doubt I can be surprised any more than I have been in the past couple of days."

He rubs a hand over his face, doubt is prevalent, and a little hurt.

He says, "Remember me saying, the gargoyle's city is called Navan? The city is a sort of last refuge for the Ceorfan. It's near the Cueva Hallow Caverns. Yet it's far enough away that a tourist won't accidentally stumble onto it. It has its entrance disguised as well. Only a Ceorfan can see it."

He pauses and asks, "Are you ready for a break? This next part is going to be particularly difficult."

"It's okay, Mica. I can take it."

"Do you remember the night you stayed at David's grave?"

"Yes."

"Well, we were there, Kino, Mason, Amber, Flint, and," a breath of a pause, "Megahir, who we call Mega. And, after a discussion, Mega invited Jericho."

"Who are Megahir and Jericho?" I ask.

"Mega is our Commander. Jericho is a mage. My sweet Edling, Jericho spoke with David after you buried him. Mega gave him a carved part of himself which the mage used to bring him to life as a gargoyle. We call him Spar now."

I gasp! I can't breathe. I try to stammer something, anything, nothing comes out other than more gasps.

Mica continues, not giving my brain any time to process.

All right I was wrong. I'm not only surprised, I don't believe this! No way!

Trying not to look too mad, I rush away from him, and go to my bathroom, locking the door behind me. I can't contain myself. I cry like I did that night.

Why? I don't understand. Wait, don't answer! I've got to think. Is this all just a lie?

Are they fallen angels and not my saviors, like I've been thinking? That isn't consistent with their behavior. Mica and Kino have both saved my life. Then to lie to me? No. Why would they lie? I need to consider that Mica had told me the truth. David is alive, and he's a gargoyle.

If he is, I want to see him.

I feel like I've been sitting on the floor in here for ages when a knock brings me out of my mental retreat.

"Princess, I'm sorry. What can I do to help you through this?"

I'm not waiting. It's not my speed, anyway. I open the door.

Mica's very close, taking up the whole opening.

I gaze straight up into his amber eyes. He looks so sad. Imagine that, I mean something to this monster. I'm amused because of that thought, and he grins at me.

"Would you like to go to Navan with me and see him? I can take you flying."

Without a word, I grab his hand and start toward the roof.

When we get there, Mica looks over at Kino and says, "Come with us after you replace your stand with your 'ef.'"—short for effigy.

I give a little wave to Kino, winking at him, so he knows I'm okay.

My gigantic black gargoyle friend pulls me close to his body. My back is against his chest. He jumps into the sky.

I can't breathe. My initial feeling of fear is replaced with wonder. I love this! I know I'm stiff as a board, so I relax a little.

His strong arms hold me tight. The swoosh of his wings pumping surrounds me, then silence as he glides.

Can he hear me if I ask him something? I'll find out in a minute. I'm enjoying this. Nothing's like it.

I hope we can keep doing this. Oh, or maybe David. No, they said his name is Spar. Maybe Kino, if no one else will, this is amazing.

Next time I'll braid my hair back; it keeps blowing into my face.

"Mica, how long do we get to fly until we reach your city?"

"Princess, are you tired of this? Is it too scary for you? Your heart-beat slowed, so I thought you might be enjoying the ride. Right?"

"Oh, no, the truth is, I love it. How much longer have I got to enjoy this sensation before I have to give it up?"

"About thirty more minutes. If you get too uncomfortable let me know. We can always stop and rest. I'm happy you like it."

I can feel his breath on my neck as he speaks. It gives me chills. He doesn't have to talk loudly, because he's so close. I need to shout for him to hear me, there's no need to speak.

Soon, he starts gliding in a circle and tells me we're almost there. I feel a thump of air on my body and jerk a little surprised.

"Did you feel the pulse, Princess?"

"Yes, what was it?"

"It's an echo pulse I sent to the sentries, so they know it's me. All inhabitants of Navan pulse the code to the sentries to keep our city safe. It's a little like the codes your aircraft use, so your military knows which ones are on their side. They'll pulse me back when I can come in. Did you feel their pulse?"

"I didn't."

I look to see if I can see a cave entrance as we approach. It's not easy to see, but I finally pick it out of the surrounding landscape.

There are several people, or gargoyles, standing nearby as we land. Two are obviously sentries. Another is huge. His skin is bluish, and he has a long dark mohawk. Of course, he's beautiful. All the gargoyles are beautiful. I'm a gargoyle groupie, I guess.

I didn't feel the answering pulse, but I can see an aura around everyone. I have always been able to read auras. I don't talk about them, very often. Not many people will accept that without thinking I'm a weirdo. It helps me to know things about people. I can get information from the colors around them. The hues for certain emotions are the same.

Gargoyles' auras aren't faint. Unlike humans, their auras are easy to see. The big guy's is pink and yellow with orange. This tells me he has a lot of love. He's very intelligent and a warrior. I like him already.

I'm anxious and stay close to Mica. I look around for David. If he's here I can't tell who he is anymore.

There are two little gargoyles and a large one who reminds me of a sphinx.

We close in on the crowd. Mica nods at the blue gargoyle as if he'd said something to him.

With grace he introduces me to everyone. The small ones come forward and kiss my hand.

"Oh, can I take them back home?" I ask.

When I'm introduced to Megahir, he says, "You may call me Mega. Come with me into the city. You are welcome in Navan. Make Navan your home if you choose."

I giggle as I reply, "Okay, I will. As scared as I am, I probably couldn't even find the city by myself."

This cave is even better taken care of than the Cueva Hallow Caverns. It's a living cave, and the beauty is beyond description. The formations are lit, but I can't tell how.

I'm so caught up in the cave features, I don't ask where Mega is taking us. My giant escort touches my arm, bringing me back to myself.

"Princess, we need to go up a few levels. Will you let me carry you again?"

"Sure, I will. Why do you keep calling me 'Princess?' I understood the first time that was irony. You can stop any time."

"I know, but I like it. Now it's a habit. It fits you. Don't you think?"

I chuckle, "No, not really."

He takes me into his arms and we fly to where we're going. My senses are overloaded with the magnificence of this underground city.

When he sets me on the floor, I stumble. He brings one of his wings up to steady me. They are soft and warm like a living blanket. We are in a large room that must be at least fifty feet above the floor we started on.

The noise in the room quiets. I glance around, wondering why. There's a huge, muscular gargoyle standing just feet from us. He is... oh my... "David, is that you?" I ask the new member.

He gins, his handsome face is full of hope.

"I'm called Spar now, honey. But you can call me anything you want."

He stares at me, looks at the floor, then back up. He isn't sure I'll accept him.

I'll give him a reason to be sure he's loved. I run and jump into his arms, grabbing him around the waist and putting my head on his chest. He smells like home, all spicy, with a touch of a woodsy scent.

He catches me and wraps his wings around me, giving us a little privacy from the people around us.

I'm crying tears of joy.

"It's true, it's true," I keep repeating like an idiot. "I never thought this was possible, even when Mica told me you were alive. And your name is Spar? I'll have to get used to that."

I chatter on. But right now, I don't care what anyone thinks. I have my love back, and I'm not letting him go.

After what seems like a very short time. He whispers, "I love you with all my heart, Kendra. Are you okay?"

I search his eyes. Ha, I love it! They're still blue. His face looks the same, but now, gargoyleish, still my handsome boy.

I say, "I'm fine now. Better than fine, I'm happy. I love you so much. It was so hard to be without you! Let's never do that again, okay? Let me look at you."

I move back away from him a little, still touching. I ogle his new body from his clawed feet to the top of his head. His claws are bluish, but dark where the color of his skin is pale blue. He was always muscular, but now he's enormous.

I heat up. My mind goes straight to the gutter, speculating if his man stuff is the same or different. My mouth goes dry, imagining his penis in my hands.

The 'V' on his defined abdomen stands out and is shaking with laughter. He's smirking at me.

I give him a 'what' face?

He chuckles, then says, "I know you, Kendra. I'm so happy you still want me like that. I was afraid.... You're all I can think about. To be honest, it's messing up my training."

"Ahem." A loud throat-clearing sound behind us is telling us we can have more time together later. He opens his wings, letting them wrap around his shoulders.

I reluctantly step away. He takes my hand in his clawed one. Our fingers intertwine, just like when we first met. Well, maybe not 'just like,' his hands dwarf mine. He can only hold my hand with the top of his fingers because if he held mine normally, it would pull my fingers apart.

Damn, he has big hands, and you know what that means. Focus on the group, silly.

We turn to the others, who have stepped over to a table and are beginning to sit.

Spar nudges me forward. A griffin-like gargoyle sitting at the head of the table rises.

The Griffen amused says, "Kendra Macbard, I have been waiting to finally meet you. Let me introduce myself. I am the king of the Ceorfan, Findare Magas. I am happy about your reunion with Spar. We would like to talk to you. Would that be all right?"

We're seated at a long, beautiful stone table, one I imagine is used for meetings or other large gatherings.

Kino is sitting on one side of Mega and Mica on the other. Spar sits beside me, there's no way I'll let him out of my sight.

There are guards by the room's opening and no doors.

The king picks up a tablet. It looks like one you might see in any school or office setting.

"Kendra, I am ordering some drinks, fruit, and cheese. Would you like me to order anything special from the kitchens? They are fully stocked."

Without any clue what to ask for, I say, "Will you please ask them to bring me some cheddar cheese and some bread or crackers?"

He adds my request to the order. Standing, he takes my hands.

"Now, with that out of the way. On behalf of all the Ceorfan, I welcome you to our city. We are happy to have you here."

The others in the room stand and face me. The king bows deeply. Then each of them take a knee and bow their head. The room is dead quiet. As one, the Ceorfan return to their seats.

"My lady, before we move on, I have been told of your injury. Mega, is Jericho in Navan?"

"No, sir," He responds.

"Will you call him to us? I want our guest healed. She will need her strength in the coming days."

"Yes, my King. I will contact him immediately."

The blue gargoyle commander appears to concentrate. No, that's not right. He seems hypnotized. He snaps out of it, dips his head politely to his ruler.

The king explains, "Mega is gifted with the ability to communicate telepathically. He is friends with Mage Jericho, our surgeon and healer. He was contacting him on your behalf. Also, if you are interested, the commander will speak with you telepathically to show you what it is like?"

I'm a strong woman. I have an idea of what I want and don't want, yet all I can think to say is, "Yes, sir," which elicits smiles around the room.

"Commander, would you please demonstrate your gift?"

Immediately, I hear a deep bass voice clearly in my head.

"You do not know how happy we are to have you here, Kendra. You will soon, I promise."

"Thank you, Mega. I could not be happier myself," I think back to him, hoping he hears me as I heard him.

He did! He tilts his head in approval.

"That's great! Does every gargoyle communicate this way?" I ask.

"No, not many. Some have varying degrees of telepathy."

Just then, a man who looks like he just walked out of a King Arthur movie, beard included, comes into the room. Since the guards didn't try to stop him, I expect this is the healer.

He walks straight to me, kneeling in front of my chair. With tears in his eyes, he stares into mine.

Spar, noticing my discomfort, introduces him. "Kendra, this is the mage Jericho."

I don't know what possesses me to reach for his hands, taking them in mine, but I do. I'm happy.

"Mage Jericho, I thank you for your company. Will you gift me with your wisdom and healing?"

Where the hell did that come from?

Hearing Mega in my head, *"You speak respect to him in the 'old way.' In the old way, you would show respect to magi and gift them with your favor. Today, your favor was your kind welcome."*

The old man drew in a breath, surprise covering his face. "Edling, you are most welcome. My life for yours in every danger. Will you accept healing from me?"

"I have no doubt you can heal me. However, how is it possible? I'm as healed as I can be. My body needs to do the rest of the work. My doctor thinks I heal very fast. Always have, in fact."

"Let me show you." He takes out a deep green stone from his robes.

A mage's robe must have loads of pockets.

He starts singing.

Kino stands and crosses over to us. He joins Jericho's melody. Exquisite. Although, I can't understand a word.

The mage puts the stone against my forehead. His lyrics sound like a breeze in the forest. The pain in my body leaves. The desire of the stone questions my body and lines up with it. I'm sure the stone wants me healed; I agree with it. My head falls back, eyes roll up in my head, and I slump out of my chair.

Spar catches me, pulling me into his lap.

I watch as he does this. I'm wide awake and outside of my body. I glance around the room at each gargoyle. Each one is a varying shade and color of light.

The mage is different, though. He still has light, but I can see his face. He examines my expression while the others are looking at my body.

"Jericho, how did you do that? Will you put me back in my body?"

"My lady, I did not do this. You did. Just as you decided to absorb the healing stone. Your ancestors passed this ability along to you. You should know this is only the beginning. It is not your gift. You must still learn that. Lady Macbard, you and your family have been this way for many, many generations. You must will yourself back into your body and wake up. Do so now!"

I did. When I open my eyes, Spar's face is agonized. He's panicking and stiff, getting ready for action. I do the only thing I can think and lean over, kissing him lightly. His lips soften and turn accepting as he ceases to panic and returns my kiss.

I back away from him before this gets out of hand. It's not what I want to do, but necessary, all the same. I feel his grip relax. He's okay, so I stand.

The entire room is watching me.

I move around and regard them. "Well, that was interesting. Who's hungry? I think I could eat a horse right about now."

Kino is holding his mouth stiff, he looks upset, and says, "What? I feared we had lost you! Jericho, please attend to her."

Jericho simply pats his back.

"Oops! Sorry, my red-hot chili pepper. I'm just fine. In fact, I feel better than before I was shot," I chuckle.

Maybe I shouldn't have called him that. Well, it's too late now.

I need to change tactics a bit, because of the funny looks on every face around the room.

"Pretty sure y'all couldn't see everything that just happened. It was strange. I was standing outside of my body for a minute there. I could see you all and Jericho and I spoke to each other."

The gargoyles appear to be recovering, including the king.

I move toward him and say, "I know that must have looked bad, the stone sinking into my forehead and then my body collapsing. The reality is, the songs and the stone called to me. The jewel wanted me to let it in, to heal me. I agreed. When I agreed, I must have decided to spend some time watching the room, outside of my body. Jericho told me my ancestors could do this."

I need to spend some serious time thinking about what just happened as well as how it happened. I return to my seat, next to Spar. He puts his hand on my leg.

The whole room full of people erupts but not in a noisy way. It's like the echo thump I felt when Mica pulsed at the sentries. My body tremors from the feeling of the gentle throbs on my skin. The looks I'm getting are the type when your mama is about to take you to the ER. I understand they're concerned. Jericho sits and many of the looks subside with most of the pulsing waves.

Spar asks, "Do you really feel okay?"

"Better than ever, really."

He believes me and adopts his 'I'm watching you' face.

The food arrives. Spar grabs me some water and a plate of fruit, cheese, and fresh baked bread.

When we finish eating, the king asks me, "Will you stay in Navan for the day, Kendra? Please, make yourself at home. We will meet in this room again tonight. We could all use some rest, and it is time for most of us to torp."

Where has the night gone? I'm sleepy, too.

I'm given a room of my own. Mica tells me it's my room and I can stay in it whenever I want.

The kitchen staff has left food on my table.

I ask Spar if he'll stay in my room as he changes. He accepts, of course.

Mica agrees, then bows, and leaves us alone.

I promptly jump straight into Spar's arms. "I'm not letting you go. I'll give up everything and everyone I know if I have to."

He swoops me up and kisses me hard, holding nothing back. I wrap my legs around his waist and put my hands on his face, pulling it closer and kissing him back.

He moans into my mouth. "Kendra, the change is coming. I have to put you down, honey, or you'll be stuck here until I wake. I'll stand right here at the end of your bed, if that's alright with you."

"I understand, handsome. I'll be here when you wake."

He kisses me lightly. His warm lips smile at me in the kiss. He takes a step back, raises his wings, and, holding one arm in his 'look at this pose,' points to his bicep. Then he hardens into stone.

"You little pissant. Yeah, you got muscles. You must've ate a ton of spinach. I love you. Good, sleep, uh, torp? Yeah, that sounds good to me. Good night, hun."

11

CHANGES

Kendra

After I rest, I wander around the caves. There are interesting albino fish in a pool in one room. I find a formation which looks like a buffalo and another a mausoleum.

I text Jared and Dana a short message telling them I'm with Mica as I eat the food the kitchen staff left for me. If I spend much time in Navan, I'll have to bring books. The gargoyles have Internet, because their tablets work on a network of some sort.

"My Kindle should work just fine," I mumble.

Since the clock on my phone says it's getting close to dark, I head back to my room. I want to be right in front of Spar when he wakes.

Maybe, I'll tease him. Ding, brilliant idea! I take off my shirt and loosen my sweatpants until they are just hanging on my hips. I comb my fingers through my hair and stand in front of him. I hear a breaking-glass tinkling sound and he's loose from the stone.

Spar doesn't even look like he takes a breath before he's on me. Laughing, I bite his lip. We don't have a door. I couldn't care less. He's mine, and I want him. It's obvious he wants me back.

He pulls away and blathers, "Hun, I want you to know I'm still me. My memories of my life with you are all here. I have to ask, though, are you okay with how I look now? You love me, but do you want me as a gargoyle? Can we be a couple? I don't know what I'm saying. I'll understand if you can't. I mean, thinking about it, I can't be in public without causing a commotion. You probably don't want to live here in Navan."

He looks away as he asks the questions.

The speedy pace of his vocalized doubt, keeps me from interrupting him. I raise my hand and put my fingers to his lips.

"Spar, you're mine. I'm yours. I want you. How could I not? You're magnificent. You always have been. Now, you have a little, extra. Don't question whether I love you. You're perfect the way you are. Let me ask you the same question back. Can you be happy with a dinky human?"

"No, Kendra, you are the one for me. The..."

We both hear noise. Someone is coming, and it's not either of us.

Kino puts his hands on the doorway to my room and stops when he sees us in a 'getting it busy' position.

"Well, I believe I can deduce the reason for not answering your tablet messages." He smiles, then quickly recovers his usual serious demeanor. "Mica has sent orders that we are to meet in the conference room. Breakfast will be served there today. We are already late."

I pick up my shirt and pull it over my head. Kino never turns his head or acts embarrassed. Well, I guess it could have been worse. I slip my shoes on, and finger-combing my hair. I fix it into a messy bun. If I stay here often, I'm going to need to bring some personal items.

Off we go. When we get to the meeting, I smooth a hand over my wrinkled clothes and grimace. I add appropriate clothing to the list of things I need to bring. Especially if I'm going to end up in meetings with royalty.

Spar takes my hand, noticing my discomfort and says, "Don't worry honey, we both kinda look homeless."

I giggle in response.

The king followed close behind us as we entered the room. Find-are's grin is infectious. I smile back. As he greets me, the look on his face says he doesn't care what I'm wearing. Maybe it isn't such a consideration with gargoyles. With as little as I'm wearing, everyone in the room except the King and Jericho are wearing less. Thinking about it, it only makes sense.

The temperature in the cave stays a steady 62 degrees fahrenheit. Outside is much hotter in the summertime, often topping 100-degrees. Though, it gets colder in the winter. Does a gargoyle even feel the cold? There are many more things I want to know about the race.

"My dear child, please come to the buffet with me. You need to eat, and I want to begin the meeting. We face a desperate situation, which we must address urgently. I am hoping for your help."

"Of course, I'll help in any way I can."

Looking over the buffet, I take a plate and start filling it with food.

I say in an exaggerated southeastern New Mexico drawl. "Oh, yeah, one of my favs, jalapeno cheese bagels."

I sit between the king and Spar, and notice we took the same places as last night. There are a few more people here today, though.

As the room settles, a short, greenish-colored gargoyle with an obvious superiority complex blurts, "Your Highness, if you don't mind, I will begin. I have information."

The corner of the King's lip curls in annoyance. He controls his facial expression and waves toward the belligerent little goyle, motioning his consent.

Little green goyle apparently now becomes aware of me. He stops his prepared remarks, and stares at me.

He says, "I do wonder, Your Highness, why we have a human present in such a pressing meeting. I will have one of the Elite escort her from the room and take her to her own home. There she can be with her own kind." He points toward one of the guards to make his demand an order.

Feeling self-conscious, I start to get up to leave with the guard.

I'm not sure why I'm here and agree. Everyone is staring at me and I'm uncomfortable.

"No, Count," Findare growls.

Several goyles jump up, in an obvious attempt to defend me. Yet it's Jericho who speaks.

He sneers, "You do not know who you offend. Let me make the introduction. Count de Treon, I would like you to meet Kendra Macbard of the Tarragon family bloodline."

What on Earth is Jericho saying?

The little goyle, if it's possible, just turned even greener than he'd started out.

He kneels in front of me and says, "I humbly beg your pardon, Edling. I had no idea there were any surviving children of the dragon lords."

I hear Mica whisper, "Well, the dragon is out of the bag now."

I laugh at the movie reference, but I'm stunned at the Count's the statement.

Are they saying I'm a dragon child? That can't be possible.

Spar takes my hand and holds it tightly against his leg. We gape at each other, eyes wide, backs stiff. Neither of us understand what they're saying.

"King Findare," I start, but he interrupts.

"Edling, call me Findare or Fin, if you please. This meeting was meant to provide you information on many things, your ancestry included. I did intend a more diplomatic approach. Please be seated, Count. I'll continue the meeting."

The green goyle Count ducks his head and takes a chair behind the king.

"The subject of your ancestry is known to most gargoyles. The Macbard family have been watched and protected for more than a millennium. I'll have a historian show you the information and any proof later, if you would like."

I motion my assent without interrupting him.

"Now, as most of you know, Kendra is part of this community and is to be treated with the respect given royalty. Count, it is beneath you to belittle someone because they are human. Do not let that happen again. If you cannot properly eliminate your unfounded biases, I will exclude you from the coming negotiations with TASS.

"My Lady, with your permission, I must give you the history of the Ceorfan. I will be as succinct as possible. The humans have convened a secret multiumvirate in Scotland. This is similar to the idea of a triumvirate, yet the member number is larger. The group is called The Alumbradai Sanctuary State or, TASS. Its delegates represent the most powerful individuals in the world. I will provide you more information later. Suffice it to say, no world leader has any power which was not given them by TASS. Not even the American or Russian presidents.

"An old enemy of ours is gaining power. The last time this person held power, he tried to annihilate humankind."

The king paused, maybe for effect. I'd pause there if I wanted the words I'd spoken to sink in.

He continues, "Today while we slept, Baratium made another strike. On top of the devastation he heaped on the world last week, he has destroyed an entire African village. Thousands have been killed."

The room erupts in murmurs. Gargoyles fire question after question at the king. "Where is he? How will we defeat him? Do we have a plan?"

The king raises both hands, and pats the air in a downward motion. "I will answer your questions. Mega, will you finish reporting?"

A rumble of assent zips around the room.

Mega says, "Baratium commands several powerful mages and innumerable Crafted. The wooden Crafted who work for him are not like us. They have been warped by magic to go against their true nature. Our nature is to protect. Theirs is to destroy. We are sending a contingent of ambassadors to TASS. However, because of old prejudices, the humans still fear us. Kendra, we know we need to work together with the humans to win this fight. I humbly ask, will you be our ambassador at this meeting? Will you represent the Ceorfan?"

The king lets out a giant breath and flops down into his chair, all the steam let out of him.

I'm not a drama queen. I squeeze Spar's hand then stand.

In my most determined voice I say, "I'll do my part. I need to study a great deal to catch up on the politics and other important issues involved. I'll be your representative."

I almost said human representative, but I'm not even sure I am human anymore. Sweat breaks out on my forehead and I wring my hands. I've got to get a grip.

Everyone in the room is smiling. Pretty sure that's right. Some goyles look pissed off when smiling. However, their auras are showing me they're happy and not mad. The little green turd is even glowing a happy yellow brightness.

A clue to his real character is in his aura. I study him for a time. I see some crimson. I usually equate red with anger. It can also mean passion or a warrior's spirit. There's not much of the color, though. There are more purples. He might be angrier at himself than me or any of the others. There's a lot of purple that I have a feeling comes from being hurt at some time in the past. I'm choosing to give him a chance. I'll keep an eye on him, especially around humans. I might ask Fin if he needs the Count for the meeting or if he is included because of his status.

My degree is in political science. With all the reading I'm about to start, and with information from Fin, I'll brush up on my political skills. What have I gotten myself into? On second thought, I'm sure I have plenty of back up. With all of these goyles, I won't be going into a war zone alone.

"Kendra," the king says, "one of the subjects we have not touched upon yet is when you were shot. We have intelligence that the Jessup Cartel is targeting you. I understand you may have inadvertently arrested the son and heir of the head of the cartel. The very one who would take over if his father dies. If that was not enough, while defending yourself and others, you killed their chief strongman, Jerry Drinker."

The king motions to Mica to continue.

He stands and walks to the front of the room then says, "Drinker had been singularly responsible for the growth of the Jessups and was the linchpin to their organization. For example, your arrest stopped their sex-slave trafficking in North America. It won't last, but it is costing the cartel."

I continue to listen. My investigative and protective side is now taking control and the 'holy shit' side is retreating.

Mica adds, "They're losing men internally, due to the loss of Drinker's leadership. As an enforcer he was responsible to carry out Jessup's will. He was trusted by Don Manuel Jessup, the semi-competent but ruthless founder of the cartel."

I consider the angles of the situation. If Drinker was such an intricate part of the cartel, I'll have to be on guard. Not only against bounty hunters, but also assholes who want to score a name for themselves.

Mica, continues, "The contract that Jessup has placed on you is large. Everyone who can pull a trigger will be trying to collect the reward."

He fixes his gaze on Fin, who asks, "Kendra, I respectfully request you be our guest here in Navan. Will you remain until we have rectified this problem?"

"No, sir!" I state categorically. My response is too harsh.

I add, "Fin, I have a job. I have doctors' appointments. If Jessup is coming after me, he'll also go after my brothers. With a target on them, I'll do whatever I can to keep them safe. In fact, I need to call them. Then I need to get home."

I pause and look around the room for support.

Finding none, I say, "They need to understand the situation with the cartel. Also, I'd like any of the specifics on how you came by this information. How are you tracking the threats? Besides giving up everything I know, what can I do to keep my brothers and me safe?"

The king leans back in his giant chair, huffs and folds his arms across his chest. It's obvious he doesn't want me to leave. It won't stop me.

I stare back at him.

He focuses on me without blinking.

Adopting a new approach, he says, "Edling, I wish you would reconsider. If you must return to your apartment in Cueva Hallow, let me send a small force of my Elites with you. They can protect you and your brothers, and help you with security procedures."

"Thank you, that's fine," I answer.

Mica says, "You should avoid seeing the doctor for a while. Otherwise you'll have to explain the healing. Make people believe you're still on the mend. Besides, you'll get time off work too. I'm already on leave. I told Murphy this morning that I have a family emergency. I'm on leave for the next six weeks. That way, we'll be able to get you to Scotland."

King Findare says, "One more thing we need to share. We must restrict how many humans know about our race. As your brothers are also of the dragon line, they should be told about us. We will help you tell them, if you like. Seeing is sometimes easier, as you have learned. They need to be sworn to the same secrecy as you swore to Kino in your apartment. They need to understand the risk to our race. Is this agreeable, Edling?"

"Yes," I say.

The King turns and speaks to a skinny goyle. "Dolo, will you bring Kendra's tablet?"

Dolo walks toward me with a tablet in his hands. His shoulders are rolled forward, his arms are tucked in tight, and he's clutching a tablet near his chest.

"Hey, don't be afraid, Dolo," Mica says, trying to offer courage to the skinny imp. "She's not gonna hurt you. But she needs the information you put on the tablet. It'll make things clearer for her. You did a good job. Let her have it."

Backing Mica up, I smile my best smile at the timid gargoyle. He swallows hard and brings me the tablet. His voice is shaky as he explains how to use it and how to find the files I need to read. He says the tablet won't need to be charged the way I'm used to. It's something about the cave and magic doing it.

When I ask what happens when I'm away from the cave, he says I won't have to worry about it.

Once Dolo finally calms down and is enjoying teaching me about Ceorfan technology, I think to Mega, "I think Dolo would be an asset if we bring him to the Summit. What did they call the humans they were meeting in Scotland? I forgot."

Mega speaks in my thoughts, "The Alumbradai Sanctuary State. We use the acronym TASS a lot if that helps you remember the name."

I say, "I've seen others making calls on their tablets, Dolo. Will you please show me how to do that? I need to contact my brothers."

He lets me do the calling; he had already loaded their information into the tablet, making it easy for me. I call each of my brothers and tell them I need to see them for breakfast. I'll cook, if they'll come and eat. I add that it's very important. They both agree to be there before going to work.

I laugh. Maybe Dana has deadlines to meet, but Jared, he probably has a girl to get home. He makes his own hours, something I would never be able to do as a Federal Park Ranger. I make a decent paycheck. Enough to support me, but no extras. I'm okay with that. I don't need a whole lot to be happy. Spar is the thing I need the most.

Oh crap! I hope I never say 'thing' referring to him again. As self-conscious as he is, that would make him feel terrible.

After hearing the conversation with my brothers, my big blue boyfriend whispers in my ear, "It's not easy to let you go when all I want to do is love you. When you get back, I won't hold back."

His breath is warm on my ear and gives me shivers shooting straight to my core. Anyway, I have to leave, so I stand.

"Whatever, handsome, you'll be the one trying to hold me back." I hang onto him just for a minute.

He kisses me softly while Kino, who is taking me home waits. I walk away with my red protector before I can't.

Telling Spar goodbye wasn't easy. He'll be asleep until I get back.

***

KINO BRINGS me back to the top of the La Caverna before sunrise. I notice a statue that looks like him in place on the roof. Well, I guess he has to move around sometimes. Humans would spot the difference if he were missing.

He and Amber hide their effigies then stay on the roof to pose.

Mica said he'll be here soon. He'll stay on the roof until I take my brothers to meet him. I walk to my apartment with a lot on my mind. The first thing I do is make coffee when I get inside.

It isn't long until the doorman buzzes me that Dana and Jared are on their way. I hope I can explain this to them right. I've been practicing my speech all morning. If there's a way to soften the blow of this news, I can't figure it out.

Will the boys take me seriously regarding the danger they're in? Will they keep themselves safe? They both tend to 'pooh-pooh' me when I tell them how I need to protect them. They tease me when I say how important it is.

I'm positive the cartel can use them to get to me. Jared's a black belt in Tae Kwon Do. Dana is as strong as an ox. They're both powerful, and they're comfortable with multiple weapon types, too. Both are intelligent and always watchful of their surroundings. But damn it, they're my brothers. It's my job to protect them. I can't rely on their skills.

I'll be devastated if they get hurt. Devastated, to the point, I won't recover, until I burn the whole cartel down. Their safety and protection is my number one goal. After we all understand and agree how to keep everyone safe, I'll tell them about the Ceorfan.

It's funny that I worry about telling them about the dangers of the cartell. Yet, I'll just tell them about the Ceorfan. No biggie. Yep! The world is officially weird! Giggling, I'm ready to speak with them now.

I stand at my door, so I can hear the elevator when it gets to my floor. There's the ding and the doors opening. I crack open my door a little, making sure it's them. It is, so I open the door the rest of the way.

Their expression is as stiff as their bodies. They always know ahead of time when there's something wrong. Yeah, it's a gift. One that makes my eyes roll. It answers why I get irritated at people who don't know what I am thinking. And yes, I do know how that sounds, but honestly, some people are so clueless. Can't they just notice body language or something?

"Hey guys, the coffee's ready, and I have juice if you want some," I say, giving them big sister hugs.

They're so comfortable in my home they take over and fill their own cups while I pull the egg and sausage casserole out of the oven. Dana grabs the plates out of the cabinet and sets them at the bar. Jared is getting the butter and jam out of the fridge as the toast pops up; I plate it. We sit to eat. Scooping the hot cheesy casserole onto their plates, I give them extra, Jared more than Dana. He can eat more than anyone I've ever met.

"Okay, Sis, spill it. You look like you haven't slept in days," Jared says.

"Thanks for that. Yeah, I probably don't look my best. I'll nap in awhile. I need to tell y'all some serious stuff. Some of it sounds like I'm making it up. I promise I'm telling the truth. I'll show you the proof. I'll have to anyway.

"To start with, I'm afraid for your safety. The Jessup Cartel is involved. I've evidently stirred the pot where they're concerned. I arrested the son of the big cheeto. Then the guy who shot me, the one I killed, was their number one hit man. I have inside information that the cartel has put a contract out on my head, with a premium.

"You two, being my brothers, are also in danger. They'll try to harm you to get to me. We need to make a plan for your safety."

There isn't a way to live in Cueva Hallow and not understand the cruelty of the cartels in the area. I know I don't have to explain in detail, they know.

Dana raises an eyebrow at me.

I add quickly, "No, I don't think you're weak or helpless, and yes, I'm including me too. I'm taking safety measures that I need to explain. It's far-fetched. Keep an open mind, okay? I've been receiving help from a source outside of the police department or the Rangers. My friends are a little different. They're not from around here, so to speak. I'm also going to have to call in some old friends in politics, maybe DEA."

Jared takes his last bite and sits back in this seat, "Go ahead, Kendra. We're listening. It's evident you need to tell us something you're struggling with. We also sense you're doing very well after getting shot. How is that? That's what I want to know. Are you on pain meds to the point you aren't feeling pain anymore? You're getting around like nothing happened to you."

I say, "Well, that's part of the situation I need to tell you about. You're right, I'm fine. No, better than fine. Nothing's wrong with me, and I'm totally healed."

Dana says, "What the hell, Sis. What do you mean you're totally healed?

I answer, "That's part of what I need to tell you. I'll get to it in a bit."

"So, let's meet the friends you have hiding in the bedroom. We're ready," Dana responds.

"I do have friends here, but they're on the roof. I wanted to get you ready, but I don't know how to anymore."

"It's okay, Kendra. We'll believe you. Just tell us what's going on," Jared says.

"Y'all have been on the roof of this building. You know those statues that look like gargoyles? They are gargoyles. They're my friends, and they're helping me. In fact, they're helping us all. If you'd like to meet one of them, we can go right now. He's waiting for us, so you can see him. You guys can't tell a soul about them. The gargoyles live in a cave city a few miles away from the caverns. I've been there, but it's hard to find."

My brothers are quiet as we make our way to the roof. Mica meets us by the seating area. He reaches out to shake hands with each of my brothers as I introduce them.

"Okay, Sis, Mica, what's going on here? Who are we meeting?" Jared questions.

My new partner says, "Me, I don't look like this. I'm going to drop my glamour, so you can see the real me."

Just like he had shown me, his glamour melts off, and his gargoyle self is revealed.

Dana doesn't say a word, just smiles a crooked smile at me. It's his serious smile, though. Jared is nodding his head, not saying anything either.

"Well, do you guys have any questions?" I grimace.

12

UNSAFE

Kendra

I'm so worried about convincing my brothers about the dangers that I don't think about anything else. What I should've been worried about is what they would think about Mica being a gargoyle.

I feel a storm coming on. Static electricity builds and the wind begins to blow. Lightning flashes.

Jared has the shorter fuse of my two brothers.

There's more lightning bursts and the thunder rolls closer.

My boys are both unquestionably protective of me. With David passing, they're even more protective, if that's possible. Almost perfectly timed to the brightest lightning yet, Jared moves. He's quick, he moves around the furniture and punches Mica dead in the face. The thunder rolls on, louder still.

Mica is caught unprepared for Jared's attack. My angry brother is moving again, readying himself for a possible coup-de-grace. In a flash, my partner catches him as he's trying to land his usually devastating roundhouse kick to the gargoyle's torso. Mica pulls him close, hugging him as he pins his arms to his chest. This infuriates Jared even more. He's getting madder by the second.

Crash! That one was right above us.

Jared bashes the back of his head into Mica's nose, dropping them both to the rooftop. With my crazy-ass brother on the floor, the ebony goyle easily flips him over, sits on him, restraining his arms and legs. It's obvious my partner is acting to keep my brother from being hurt.

This happens fast. We haven't had a chance to react. Dana starts to move across the roof to help our brother. I know he'll try to tackle my partner.

I put my hand on my stomach as acid rises in my throat. I feel sick. This has to stop before Jared or Dana hurts themselves, or my friend. I can't take chances.

I point and yell, "Mica, get off him! Jared, Dana stop, just stop!"

Mica stands.

Jared loudly exclaims, from his spot on the floor, "Mica, you motherfucker. What the hell? You've been around our sister. What have you been doing? You're the reason she hasn't been home. You'd better not be using her."

The fight momentarily at a halt, I reach for my friend's big goyle mit and press it. I take my brother's hand, hold it, staring at him. Finally, he breaks eye contact with his nemesis and turns to me. The shit-storm is ebbing, and oddly enough, so is the one above us.

Jared stands and says, "Fine, but I need answers, and I need them now. You betrayed our trust. You let us believe you were someone else. If I find you've hurt my sister, nothing on this planet will stop me from ending you! Now, start talking," he lowers his volume of his voice.

Dana, my quiet brother, isn't fazed at what happened. He would have helped if he was needed. He's, for the moment, just standing there listening. I know him well enough to know he's calculating every detail. He must agree with Jared, or he would have spoken up.

It looks as if my partner has made enemies of my brothers. If so, I need a new plan. My brothers win, every time. I'm on their side, even if I can't be with the Ceorfan.

Mica steps closer. This better be good.

To my surprise, he kneels in front of them. With his head in his hands, he says in a voice full of emotion, "Please forgive me. What I did, I did to protect everyone. Kendra, my people the Ceorfan, and, yes, you two. I didn't understand you would consider my actions a betrayal."

I hear deep sighs from both boys, magic words. Jared is such a passionate man and he understands Mica perfectly and straightaway.

He says,"Forgiven. But, I still need an explanation. Can we all go into the apartment, before someone from space sees us talking to a moving art piece?"

Dana adds, "Yeah! Kendra might melt anyway in this rain. I'm getting the bottle of Johnnie Walker you have stashed in the cabinet above the microwave. Want some?"

After we get inside, Mica catches my brothers up on as much information as he can pack into a few hours, including that David is now Spar. He explains to them that they're welcome in Navan. He'd like to take them tonight, if they're up for the trip. Jericho had given him a portal stone, so we can all make the trip faster, without having to be carried by his gargoyle self.

With all the major information out, we order pizza, and stay out of sight. I doze off on the couch while we wait.

I wake hearing Dana's deep voice. "If I'm going to be takin' a vacation, I've gotta talk to my foremen. I trust 'em to do a good job, but I need ta tell him which jobs come first."

Noting I'm awake, he asks, "Sis, what do I need to bring with me?"

"You'll need clothes, nothing heavier than a light jacket. It's not cold down there. Also, some personal stuff like deodorant, tooth-brush, and a comb. I'd bring a handgun and a few magazines. You won't need the gun in Navan, but it's better to be prepared. I don't think more than that's needed. They have everything. The bathroom works differently from ours. I haven't figured out the specifics. It isn't three seashells, though like in the movie Demolition Man, where they won't tell Sylvester Stallone how to use them instead of toilet paper.

We all laugh except Mica. The three of us love to joke about the three seashells and what they might or might not do.

Dana quips, "Good, 'cause I'm not goin' if I have to use the seashells."

We laugh louder.

"I'll be back by seven, Sis. This'll be fun," my tall baby brother says.

"Okay, just keep your head down. If you aren't here by seven, I'll call the calvary," I answer.

He smiles, giving me a hug before he leaves.

Jared is right behind him with an embrace.

"Do you need me to get anything while I'm out? I should be back before Dana. The corporation can run okay from my phone for a few days. I do need to give some instructions to James, my personal assistant. He'll let everyone know I'll be traveling. I don't need them worrying and searching for me, or the advice they'll try to give because they're imagining me haring off with a blonde Hollywood type."

I answer, "I have everything I need. I'll be packed in a matter of minutes. Just, please, be safe. Watch for dangerous people. Trust your feelings. I'll see you in a little while. Mica is with me. I'll be fine."

After a few minutes I watch them walking across the parking lot. Old habits die hard.

I say, "I think you should follow them and make sure they're safe. Please, Mica?" I use the deadly 'please' word.

He huffs and squares his shoulders.

"I won't leave you here without a guard. Want me to call John, so he can stay with you while I follow your brothers? You'll have to explain to them why I'm slinking around in the shadows. A better idea might be to send John a text asking if he's close and would he want to follow your brothers?"

"Okay, fine! Do it, but it doesn't pay well. I hope John knows that. And tell him to bring a friend because I've got two brothers."

I stomp off to my bedroom to pack. Sheesh, I've got a bad attitude. I need another nap. My closet door is open, so I drag out my old purple Samsonite backpack from my college days. It looks good. It's just old. Packing is pretty easy, a few pairs of jeans, several tees, underwear, socks and I'm finished. I'll wear my hiking boots and a jacket when we leave.

On second thought, I take out a business suit I haven't worn recently and look it over. Better try it on to see if it'll work, for the meeting in Scotland. I'll need a better look. I'll have more influence as an ambassador, if I look the part.

The dress fits perfectly. It's still new, even if it's several years old. It isn't too out of date. Navy is a great color for negotiations, but I need a little power color. I pin an organza bag holding my ruby studs and matching necklace, to the shoulder of my dress. It's perfect, not too much, but gives me confidence. The jewelry was Mom's. By wearing it, she'll be right there with me. Now, a pair of nude heels will finish off the outfit.

Putting it all in a garment bag, I decide I'm going to trim my hair and get a shower. My sixth sense tingles, is someone watching me? I turn. There's Mica standing in the doorway with a faraway look in his amber eyes.

"You know, Princess, I saw your parents a few times. They were both wonderful people. Beautiful and brilliant in their fields. You're as beautiful as your mother, but you favor your father more. Thank you for helping my people. You're amazing for even considering what you are doing. Your brothers are on the way and fine. Their tails will drop when they get here. I'll wait in the living area while you shower. If you need anything, I'll hear you if you call me. I'll be here for you, always."

"Wait a minute. Would you do me a favor?"

His eyebrows raise a little as he nods slightly.

I share, "I feel like I'm stepping into unknown territory with a wolf at my back. I'm probably gonna mess up more than once. I'll keep going, though. I'm good at finishing. Will you guide me on protocols that I might not understand? For example, in my culture it's good manners to chew with your mouth closed. I noticed that's not such a consideration for Ceorfan. If I do something wrong, will you sort of give me the eye, boot me under the table, or interrupt before I make a fool of myself?"

He chuckles, "Of course, but I'm gonna remind you that you said that. Not really, I won't boot you, but a soft nudge if you're lucky."

"It'll help me a lot. I want to be respected and show respect. We're going into a political situation ya know? I don't want to start a fire. It would be wonderful if humans and Ceorfan could coexist. At least that's what I want. Do you think it's possible?"

He says, "It's a goal we can work on together. I for one, would like to live free and not have to hide anymore."

"Which reminds me, thank you for not putting the glamour back on. I'll be out soon. Should we cook before we leave, or eat dinner in Navan?" I ask.

He answers,"Navan, if it's okay with you. They're planning a feast tonight to welcome you and your brothers."

The doorman buzzes at 6:30 p.m. Jared's coming up with his bag in a hurry. When he gets inside my door, he's panting. He takes out his phone to call Dana. Okay, I'm watching his every move, waiting.

"Alright... Just making sure... Are you on the way?" His one-sided conversation with our baby brother is confusing and a bit unnerving.

"Make sure to keep to the shadows as much as you can. There's a crowd in the parking lot. I think they're just a bunch of kids partying... I'm not sure.... Something seems off." Finishing, he hangs up.

He warns, "Sis, stay away from the windows. Some of those people down there look kinda cagey."

"Okay, do you have a gun on you?" I ask.

I reach to touch my own concealed 9 mil at my waist. He nods, lifting his shirt showing me his gun, a Sig Sauer 1911 with wood grips. We are so related!

Right then, the doorman buzzes Dana up.

When he comes in, he sets his backpack on a kitchen chair, and says, "You're right. Something's off with this crowd. A little squirrely guy by the building's got my donum a singin'.'"

When our mom was a kid, people called it extra sensory perception, or ESP. Granny taught her it was a gift from God, and she called it 'donum.' Our mom continued the tradition with us. We know what it means, and we don't spend time with BS or unwanted input from people we barely know.

Mom and I both taught the boys to pay attention to their feelings. My speech went something like this: "If something feels wrong, it probably is. If you walk into a room, and it feels funny, don't wait, turn around, and leave. Don't ignore it. If you think a person or circumstance isn't right, just act like you know it's a fact, then leave it or them alone. I mean it. Call me, and I'll come get you, come hell or high water!"

Their response went something like this: "Leave us alone. You're not Mom. Stop. No, you're not fixin' my hair."

Well, strictly speaking, the bit about the comb was only said when they were getting ready for a date. I always tried to help.

Jared takes donum more seriously than Dana. He doesn't like to admit its existence outside the three of us. I know he recognizes it and reacts as needed to stay safe, and that's good enough for me. It's also why, with him calling it out this bluntly, it's more than just a feeling. Because he said it out loud, it means we need to take action.

We don't talk about it. We all pick up our bags and take off to the roof. Kino and Amber have woken from their torpefied sleep. Statues or 'efs' replace their likenesses where they had posed. Evidently, they keep them in a locked storage area up here. We won't be back for a while.

Mica holds out the portal stone.

"Is everyone ready? Here we go."

The portal opens. It looks like a large doorway. Light surrounds the rectangular opening, then the sound of shots being fired rings through the air. I glimpse chips fly off of one of the statues.

Mica motions for us to hurry into the portal, preceding him, then he comes last. The portal is closing when I see John on the roof with several others in his company. He takes aim, shooting his gun into the opening. The shot hits Mica in the back. My slow-motion time starts as I jump forward. I'm going to kill that asshole.

Jared knows me well. He jumps with me, catching me, holding me back. Mica leans forward, falling.

Dana, who is closest to him, pulls him up onto his shoulders in a fireman's carry instantly, asking, "Where's the medical facilities?"

The portal closes, and Jared puts me down.

I huff. Lips pinched, I follow as Kino leads us straight to the Ceorfan medical chamber.

The gargoyles respond and provide a floating stretcher out of nowhere. Dana puts a bloody Mica on the conveyance. A nurse shows us where to sit, so we're out of the way.

Kino is singing, low and calm.

A different nurse assures me our friend is in the best of care and Jericho is on the way.

While we wait I notice we're in a big cavern room. There are beds and what looks like a surgical table from a futuristic movie. There is a lounge area complete with coffee, and more chairs, or benches, made of stone. One area behind a ridge of stalagmites looks like a laboratory. It's closed off with glass much like you would see in the movies. In there, I see a brightly-lit pond, like a giant blue topaz.

I jerk my focus to Jericho as he bursts through the doorway, coming straight to me.

What? I know he can see our bleeding friend; we all can.

He takes my hand in his. "Edling, will you help? He needs your blood. He will not live without it, the bullet is in his heart."

"Of course, I'll help. He's mine to protect," I say.

We're standing at the floating bed. Mica is pale and unmoving.

I say, "I'm here for you." Then I spin around to Jericho and add, "Don't hurt him, mage."

Kino is beside me. His song speaks to me. I understand he's deadening my hand, so I feel no pain. I lift my head, letting him know I approve.

Jericho, quick as lightning, holds my hand over Mica. I don't have time to disapprove or make him stop. I guess it's okay, or I might try to fight him. He flicks his wrist, cutting Mica's chest, sticking a thin blade into the cut, and popping out the bullet. The next second, the old mage cuts my palm. My blood pours into the opening in the obsidian gargoyle's wounded chest. There's light connecting me and him by the blood. It's giving him life.

Weird. I'm full of energy.

Mica is okay now. My donum knows it. We're connected. I'm aware of everything about him and his body. He's healed. If there's anything wrong in his body, it'll be corrected. My blood stops, my hand heals before my eyes. My vision blurs the way it was when I was in my spirit form like yesterday.

I face Jericho. "Neat trick, Mage."

"Thank you. That was not me, but you, Edling. Thank you for the gift of life."

I turn and find my brothers, Amber, Kino, and now Mega with Findare, along with the medical personnel, watching me with wide eyes.

Mega speaks first, "Thank you, for saving my commander."

"Of course, I'm here for you, all of you. It's nothing," I say.

"No, Edling, not many others would heal a Ceorfan. The doctors tell me he's going to be fine, but he needs to rest," he responds.

"I have rooms for each of you. Will you follow me?" The king interrupts.

He shows me back to the room I had the night before. He also has rooms for my brothers and leaves me to show them their rooms.

Amber stays with me for a few minutes, letting me know this is my chamber as long as I want it.

She says, "Rest and clean up, I will be back in an hour to take you to dinner.

13

SANCTUARY

Kendra

I drag my way straight to the bathroom. I need Spar. Where is he? I take off my bloody clothes, then get into a pool in the floor. It's naturally lit with a clear-blue glow, and I sink into its warmth. I lean back, forcing myself to relax, making lists in my mind.

I'm calmer, but I'll take care of that Benedict Arnold, John. My anger is now a slow burn, not the raging inferno it was before. The question is, do I give him a chance to talk or just shoot him? Now I'm calm, well, maybe not calm, per se.

Betrayal is a big deal to me. I can't stand being lied to. There's no way to justify what he did as anything but slap out betrayal. His shot could've killed Mica, or one of my brothers, for that matter. No, I won't give him the benefit of the doubt. I've been to the shooting range with him. He's a crack shot, almost as good as me. No way was that an accident. He shot at us on purpose, he was aiming at me. Mica got in the way.

First step, tomorrow I'll call Chris at the office. I won't tell her what happened, but surely she'll tell me if John is working or not. Then I'll call Capitan Murphy. He needs to know I'm okay, but traveling. And I need to know how he's faring after the Drinker shooting.

Next, I need to get my tablet out and study Ceorfan history and their laws. I need to understand them better. They're more than protectors. Since I'm representing the Ceorfan, I need an idea of the people we're meeting for the Scotland trip. I'll need to meet with Fin to verify exactly what he's expecting from me. My most important job for today is to make sure Jared and Dana are protected there. Or are they coming?

A soft bell sounds from the rocky doorway and I feel one of those soft pulses.

It's Amber. "May I come in and help you with your hair?"

"I love for people to wash my hair. Maybe we can talk a little about what's going on. Do you know what's expected tonight? Oooooh, this feels so good!"

Her little hands massaging my head are going to put me to sleep.

"Nope," she taps me on the shoulder, "Rinse."

I sink into the water, obedient to her request. I pop up, and she starts rubbing my head with conditioner.

"Do you know how I can reach Spar? I'd like to talk to him."

"He's in the training room with Apex. I can show you how to write him a message on your tablet when you're dressed. And, I brought you some clothes for tonight. I unpacked your bag and noticed you didn't have anything appropriate for tonight's party. Oh, and are your brothers... umm... attached?"

Party! Great, just great! I don't want to party. I need to get started on the list in my head. I need some rest. She must feel my shoulders tighten.

"Party, really? Jared always has a lady on the line. Dana is quieter, but I think he just went through a breakup."

She says, "Relax, it is a dinner for you and your brothers to be introduced to the King and into the Ceorfan society at large. This is the way, Kendra. We are a people who have had to hide for long stretches at a time. So we are alone, confined to our cave city. During those times we are not able to go above ground. Or if we are stuck above ground, we can't return to Navan, because of the human threat. This forces us to spend lots of time together. We value every member of our Guild. It is a gift to be in each other's company. Does that make sense? You will honor us by accepting our presence in your life. It would be a terrible hurt not to be accepted by you and your brothers."

I relax. I understand rejection. Yes, it always hurts. I won't knowingly do that to this giving race of beings.

"Of course, we can party."

She smiles and holds a towel toward me and puts it on a bench, then leaves giving me privacy. Too bad I have to leave the bath. I do it anyway, and get out to dry off. I call out to her as I walk into my chamber.

She is in my room and fiddling with some material and looks over.

"Amber, are you any good with hair? Will you help me fix this mess?"

I have a good feeling, like I've made an instant, life-long friend. I made up my mind to trust her. Strange because I never need any help. I can do everything myself. Yeah, whatever, that's just me. I might have overstepped by asking for help.

She reaches out and hugs me. "I would love to help with your hair. Not all gargoyles have hair. I've always wanted to have some, but it would ruin my look. We're going to be the best of friends. I will even trust you when I'm torpefied. That's not something any of us do easily."

"Torpefied? I've heard of it, but I can't remember what that is. I'll do my best."

"It is the process of changing to stone when we sleep. It's the time we are the most vulnerable. It's precious to us when we find one who will guard our sleep."

"Oh, yes, I remember. I knew that. I'm tired, I guess and last I thought of it I was calling it torped in my head," I chuckle.

"Let's get you dressed."

She lifts the most beautiful pale material. It sparkles and glimmers like sandstone. When the light hits it, it shimmers.

I ask, "What color is this? This material is like chiffon-spandex."

"One of our number's gift is making material for clothing. The color is a changing color. Against your skin it's pinkish tan then against mine it's greener."

"That is amazing. How do I get this on?"

"Well, it's basically a wrap technique. You'll master it quickly. Let me help."

She wasn't kidding about a wrap technique. She wraps it up, around, and under my arms then voila, I'm dressed. It looks wonderful and sexy, yet was very comfortable.

We chat while she fixes my hair, leaving it mostly down. "I have some sandals to go with your dress. They don't have heels." She explains, heels are not for caves.

"These are beautiful. Thank you. Though, if I didn't know better, I'd say they're spun gold with inlaid diamonds."

"You are ready."

She stands back with her little hands on her hips. Afterwards she shows me how to access all the Ceorfan contacts in my tablet.

I write Spar a note.

I hope to see you at the party tonight, my love. -Yours, Kendra

---

We are so close, yet, I'm still so far away from him.

Amber says, "I'm going to go talk with Mason for a bit. I'll meet you at dinner, unless you need anything right now?"

"I'm fine. Thank you for your help, thank you for being you, and being here for me, most of all."

The small gargoyle lady says, "You are welcome, It is my pleasure. I'm sending one of the Elite Warriors to escort you to the celebration. He'll be here shortly."

14

TRUFFLES

Kendra

Where is Spar? I scan the crowd searching for him. I can't get over how many gargoyles are in this room. They're all different shapes, colors and sizes. No wonder we're welcomed into Navan, everyone is accepted.

The normally temperate cave is warm tonight with all the party-goers in one space. The area is as large as two football fields. I didn't know there was going to be a stage.

My eyes lock on King Findare, and calls me over to his side, where he's standing with my brothers. I didn't see them because of Fin's size. He has to be at least eight feet tall. He towers over my six foot four brothers.

When Kino brought me to the party, he said they would be here, and that Mica was asking for me. That gives me an excuse to eat and leave. Then I can go see how he's doing, hopefully. I might be here for a while. Someone is giving a speech. There's a lectern I spot. It's made of a clear stone shot through with blue veining.

Findare says, "You look beautiful, My Lady. Thank you for gifting us with your presence."

He motions for me to sit in a chair on the podium. Jared and Dana sit on either side of me.

"There's the Macbard blood sticking out. I love you for your protectiveness," I say, patting both of their knees at the same time.

Dana says, "Dadgum Sis, the king is right, you are a vision. You always are."

"You just love me," I return.

The king stands, raises his shoulders, and walks tall and straight. His face is blank as he grips the sides of the crystal podium to address his people.

"Ceorfan High Guild, Ceorfan Guild, and Macbard family," he starts.

This is amazing. No microphone is evident, but it sounds as if he's coming through speakers.

"I thank you all for being with us tonight. I have a few announcements, starting with our guests, Kendra Macbard and her brothers Jared and Dana, are joining us. They will help in our endeavor to overcome Baratium and his league of evil.

This plague has managed to murder another entire city, on an island this time. They left their calling card, as many of you have seen firsthand. Every man, woman, and child were guillotined. The heads were put on pikes and attached to the government buildings, much the way our ancestors were in the Viking wars. Even though our ancient grandmother's head can still be seen, these human heads were taken down, matched to their bodies on the ground, and given a respectful burial.

"We are collecting information, as I speak, to try to stop that vile army from committing another act of senseless evil. Commander Mega has many of the Elite Warriors collecting data across the globe incognito. If anyone can get any information, even if it is just from a dream, report it to the Elite Warrior Guard."

The king pauses to let the gravity of his announcement sink in with the crowd.

"Moving on, the Macbard family will be going to Scotland by the end of the week. It is our hope that TASS will work more freely with them than they have us. TASS has not always worked well with us. However, the Ceorfan are now considered a nation by the governments of Earth, and TASS is standing with us. We still have to stay undercover until they feel it's safe for the public."

At this statement a collective shout goes throughout the crowd.

I raise my eyebrows to my brothers. They already know how I feel. I can't fail at this. My job is to succeed.

"Another issue I need to address is that the Macbards have been targeted by the Jessup Cartel. They are the same people who we call the Edomant. They are doing what they can to take the families lives. This is why the Elite Warrior Guards' second in command was shot. Mica was bringing the Macbard family to Navan by way of a portal when a cartel member shot him in the back. We believe he was trying to get to any of the three Macbards. Does anyone have any information at all pertaining to the cartel or any of their attacks?"

A large Ceorfan steps up to the king.

"Ore, do you have something to say?" The king asks, motioning for him to come closer

He gestures in the affirmative and starts. "Sire, I have been on guard duty at the cave entrance for the last month. A few weeks ago, my partner Jerome and I were patrolling in a canyon a few miles away. He was shot while in his flesh form by the Edomant. I saw several of the Edomant around his body the next day. I'm sorry to remind you of his death. Jerome is now with the Creator. Flint, of the Elites, helped me take my friend's remains to an old burial ground which cannot be entered legally by humans."

Ore waits for murmurs and soft pulses of the crowd to subside and says, "Sire, a short time after we hid Jerome's remains he was discovered by Edling Kendra. She filed a report with the location, and pictures, at the Rangers' office."

Oh shit! I should've put this together. I need to call Darnell off the investigation, so no more questions are raised or searches begun. The way I figure it, what Ore said is; the Ceorfan have a lot of resources. If they know what's in my reports, their reach is beyond any I could imagine.

I speak up. "King Findare, I can help smooth this situation. I can minimize the humans' chances of finding Navan. We've had several dinosaur discoveries in New Mexico. The last thing we want is a team of scientists and media to show up to document a new dinosaur find. I'll call Wildlife and let them know I was looking over my film and I'm sure it's a deer. We get these reports often. They won't want to call out their investigators on a possible deer. Supervisors hate to have researchers grumbling and complaining about wasting their valuable time. Is this alright with you?"

The king answers, "Thank you, Edling. That would be welcome. Our goal is to do everything we can do to keep humans from finding Navan. Thank you, Ore. Jerome will be missed. We will not forget his name. It has been etched in the city many times.

"Now, Kendra, do you, Jared, or Dana have anything you would like to add?"

I stand, and indicate yes. "I'd like to say one thing. I'm honored that the Ceorfan people have welcomed my brothers and I into your company. Thank you for your protection and sanctuary. Keeping us safe is something I can't do without help. We also don't know your ways yet. So, if you will, please forgive us if we misstep. You're very important to us. We thank you again for your graciousness."

Jared stands beside me and signals his agreement. Dana stands on my other side with his eyebrow raised. They both wave their thanks to the crowd as well. As they do, a wave of echo pulses washes over us, followed by a few catcalls.

King Findare takes the podium, raising his hands, "You're welcome. Your names are also etched in the city. We expect they will be many times over. The three of you are now part of our number. We will protect you as our own! My life is dedicated to your life!

"Now," he continues with a twinkle in his eye and an excited undertone, "let's eat. The feast awaits."

I watch as the boys bounce off the stage, and laugh as they are surrounded by female gargoyles. I'm nearly crying with laughter when I spot Amber running in their direction.

Spar is coming toward me. I step off the stage into a pair of muscular arms that surround my waist. I sink into his chest, and smell his spicy scent with just a touch of a forest after the rain, ah, home. I hug him tight then swivel toward my brothers.

I say, "You guys remember Mica told you about the Resurgere of David? Well I would like you to both meet Spar."

They are all smiles, happy to meet him for the first time, again. They bump his clawed hand with chuckles.

"Come on, let's go get some food before you blow away!" Spar says.

We enjoy the laughter, and happiness, everywhere. I feel vibrations of the emotions on my skin and watch the excited auras around everyone. When I've eaten until I'm miserable, and bumped paws and claws for hours I get ready to leave. A girl can only take so much party.

Spar gives me the eye. "You want to get some air with me, honey?"

"Let's go, but first, do you mind if we go see Mica? Kino told me he had been asking for me. I want to make sure he's okay. What time is it anyway?"

"It's just after midnight, beautiful. You aren't turning into a pumpkin tonight, are you?"

"No, I want to see that he's all right my own self."

"The medical chamber is this way. Let's tell the others we're leaving, so they don't worry."

Soon, we are alone in a sort of hallway. Spar pulls me back, turning me, so my back is against the wall. His mouth slowly comes toward mine giving me plenty of time to back away if the answer was no.

The answer is yes, so I stay put. Of course, I want to kiss my gargoyle. I push into him at the same time he draws me closer, the evidence of his desire pressing into me. He has no problem lifting me, my legs close around him.

I can't think, much less stand up right now. His skin is smooth and tight from all the muscles. A tingle shoots down my back when he breathes on my neck, making it hard to wait. No, I don't want to wait. Do gargoyles fuck in the hallway?

Oh, hell no! Not again! I cannot believe my luck, or lack of it. I throw my head back in a defeated motion as a group of drunken party goers come around the corner into our part of the hall. Thank goodness they're so loud, otherwise, they might have caught us.

Spar pulls me behind a large cave formation that, in the heat of the moment, looks like a big dick. Well, excuse me! That's all I can think of right now.

He puts a large clawed finger to his lips while grinning at me. By the time the party goers pass, I can almost think in whole sentences again.

"Let's go see Mica. Then I have something I want to show you. Sound good?"

"You better believe it. I'll show you mine if you show me yours."

He laughs out loud. I love the sound.

I say, "I've really missed you."

He takes me to the big medical chamber, and I convey a look to the medical personnel. They understand and wave me on toward our friend's bed.

"He's doing better than expected and should be fine to torp out in his own chamber when the sun rises," the attending physician says.

I brush a lock of his sandy-blonde hair from my injured partner. He looks at me and takes my hand. Then he turns it over, palm up, and kisses it. He winks at me and falls back to sleep.

His kiss reaches all the way to my heart. Why do I feel this way? I must love my friend and partner too much. It feels like we've known each other for years, not days.

As we leave the chamber, I take Spar's hand and ask him if he thinks he can handle my new partner and I having a close relationship. We aren't fair-weather friends, but deep friends, the kind that are going to be there for each other.

Spar answers, "I'm okay with you having friends. Especially the kind who'd take a bullet for you. That ain't the first time Mica has saved your life. When you were in the hospital after that nut-job shot you in Murphy's office, I was happy you were alive. If I'd lost you before you even knew I was alive, I'd wish I wasn't. You're tough, making it through my funeral and all."

Spar talks as we leave the medical center and he takes me on a path I don't recognize.

He says, "Honey, the Ceorfan probably haven't told you this, there's so much that's more important. They're polyamorous. There're very few women gargoyles when compared to the number of males. They can't go out and have relationships with a human woman, either. That'd put the whole guild in jeopardy. When the mages in history took the gargoyles as slaves, they targeted the females to control the population. There are no children here. Even the few females who survived have been unable to have kids."

I say, "Seriously? That's terrible."

Spar continues, "And get this, Mica probably doesn't think about being jealous. The Ceorfan don't think like that. Honestly, neither do I. Ever since I was carved that night at the cemetery, I think different. I received part of Mega's thoughts and was rewired. I'm now gargoyle. Is that okay?"

"Of course it's okay, silly. It might change the way I think, but never how much I love you. You're mine."

He pulls me close to his body, stopping us. He bends his burly head, putting his forehead to mine and whispers, "Thank you."

I pull him closer and give him a quick peck and ask, "Where are you taking me?"

He smirks and pulls me along the path.

"Hey buddy, I have plans and wandering lost in a cave isn't part of it," I say as I jab a finger to his chest.

"I'll show you."

We're almost to the cave entrance before I figure out where we are. Ifeel Spar pulse to the sentries. This time I do feel the return pulse.

When we get outside we automatically look at the stars. The night sky is clear, and the stars are brilliant. Hmmm, I breathe in the clean country night air. A cool breeze blows my hair across my face.

"Will you fly with me, beautiful?"

I back up into his chest for an answer. He holds me tight. His chest moves against my back as he breathes. Can it get any better? Then he bends forward and bites me softly on the shoulder. I arch into him, moaning my pleasure. In seconds, he tightens his grip and takes a flying leap. We're in the air.

"This is amazing!"

Flying, plus the way he makes my blood boil.

"I'm praying for an eclipse," I shout.

His chest rumbles with laughter. He understands what I mean. I want this night to last forever.

I recognize where we are as Spar sets us down in a canyon: the one where I found Jerome's bones. They were right, I won't forget his name, either. I wonder if that's what they meant by his name being etched in the city? Maybe the 'city' is a generic term for all of us? I need to ask Fin.

Spar guides me to the cave opening where I'd seen something glittering. On the other side of the opening, a pool of clear spring water glimmers in the moonlight. Now I understand what I saw a few days ago.

The light reflects off of the water. Bats quietly click overhead. I raise my gaze and see that it's a round chamber with a hole in the top. Wild jasmine must grow in here, because the scent is heady. Rocks line the pool. A large rock sticks out of the middle of the pool and dominates the chamber.

I cut my eyes over at my big blue gargoyle hunk when I spot a blanket with a basket, near the water's edge.

He uses his sexy deep tone and wiggles his brow, "Where did you think I was before the party? I can only think of you. Do you like it?"

I may never get this dress wound back up right, but to show him how I feel, I start untying my dress, while I kick the sandals off.

"Is the water warm?" I ask.

He sucks in a loud breath as material puddles at my feet. I scoot it out of the way and stick my toes in the water. It's a hot spring. I love the water, and jump in. As I come up, I glimpse his beautiful aroused nude body dive in. He surfaces under me, kissing my inner thigh. Oh my, that's good.

I reach for him as he breaks through the water. He draws me in. Not wasting time, I rub my naked body against his, and wrap my arms around his neck. The pool's buoyancy lifts me to his beautiful sexy lips. I'm one lucky girl. I rake my fingers through his messy blond hair, pulling it away from his face.

He puts a big hand on my nipple tweaking and twisting then backs me onto the rock in the middle of the pond. I lean back while he lifts me onto the stone.

"I've had dreams of having you here," he growls.

I'm so turned on; the smart-ass comment section of my brain has officially disconnected.

I lift my hips saying, "I thought I'd never feel like this again. I love you."

Tears leak from my eyes. I hope he doesn't see them. He turns on the heat and I don't hold back the sound effects, as he kisses down my body. I squirm thinking about what he's doing. A groan escapes, and I'm panting as his mouth hits my clit.

All too soon the tickle is too much and my legs begin to shake. I try to force him up to me, as hard as I can.

There's no budging him, so I gasp, "I need you inside me before I cum. Please!"

He's inside me as quick as I ask. The stretch is good, and I arch into his body.

"Hard this time. We can be easy later," I beg.

He obliges and does as I ask.

I scream as my orgasm mounts and expends like waves breaking on the rocks.

My love comes soon after. He grabs my limp body hugging me close, and kisses me softly. Then lifts us, and flies us to the blanket.

Covered with his wings I snuggle into him... so soft. I feel like I can never get close enough to him. Right now, I'm okay with this.

"I'll always love you. You're mine," he says.

"I love you back! You make me feel amazing."

After enjoying the feel of him, I sit up. "What's in the basket, handsome?"

He chuckles, "Go ahead. Open it up, get us something to eat, and pick a wine if you want to. I'm a little thirsty."

He watches me as if he wants to remember every detail of this night, as if it were the first time we made love.

I open the basket and find two bottles of wine. The first one is one of my favorite sweet wines. It's a pomegranate wine bottled in Deming. The other is a Napa Valley Cabernet Sauvignon. He knows I love wine of all variations from everywhere, and I want to try all of them.

The rest of the basket consists of raspberries, strawberries, cheese, crackers, and cubes of ham and Angus beef. Yeah, he knows me. I set out the food and pour us each a glass of the Cabernet. The label says it's, 'a full-flavored wine with medium body and a rich concentration of fruit.' It'll be splendid with everything he brought. How does he do this?

As we finish eating, I dig through the basket. Something's missing, the one thing David would always bring on trips like this. Maybe in the transition to Spar he forgot. I'm a little on edge, because I don't want to hurt his feelings, but I've always said what's on my mind. Why should tonight be any different?

"Where's the chocolate?" I ask.

He laughs before handing me my favorite chocolate truffles. It's perfect with the pomegranate wine. I lean back on him, content. His heartbeat thrums in my ear, over the sounds of night all around us.

The boys are safe. Everything's right with the world. Let it spin on without us for a bit.

"Spar, how much time until daybreak?"

"We've got about an hour. Honey, I want to talk to you about the cartel." he says around a large mouthful of truffles.

I giggle at him for the way he is eating while talking. It's something David would never do.

"I want to make sure you're wearing your bulletproof vest when you get back to work. I know Mica will be there and I trust him to back you up, but just in case, okay? I won't ask you to quit working. And also for the next few weeks, you're getting workman's comp, so you're getting paid. I know you need the paycheck and you love being a Park Ranger. But did you get my insurance when I was killed?"

"Yeah, I got it. It paid for the funeral and a beautiful headstone. Dana made it. It's the best. Did you see it?"

"Yes, but you should've saved the money and used it for you. Heck, a couple of sticks tied together would have been fine to mark my grave." he guffaws.

I punch him in the side, hard.

"Ooopfh."

My heart melts when I hear genuine laughter from him, a belly-roll. I do love his enthusiastic myrth.

"Anything else," I ask?

I rub the spot where I punched him.

"Nope," he says.

"Handsome, there's not much left. I don't have to be rich. I might not have much, but I do just fine. My paycheck's enough. Thanks for asking, and I'll wear my vest. Just not right now, punk!"

My pet name for him is short for 'punkin,' which was short for my big pumpkin from the early part of our relationship.

I pack up the basket, pick up my dress, and tie it around me.

"Okay, yeah, I can't get it back on right, but all the good stuff is covered. You want to torp in my room today? I have to sleep while you're hard," I giggle.

He grins, "Yes, I do. Let's get going, just to be safe."

"Okay, I can feel the pulses when you go and come from Navan, so how do you do the pulse thing?"

"I'm not sure. I think it's just natural. When they taught me, Mega was in my head. He told me to think who I am and shove the noise at the guards. That's all I do. It just happens. When they send a pulse back, I feel what they're saying. It's like a motion on my body telling me words. When we get there, concentrate on the way the air pressure ripples across your skin."

We take off. When we see the guards, he warns me before beginning the pulse code for them. I do sense it on my body. It's like they're smiling, too. Okay, that's strange.

Spar takes me straight to my chamber. I get out of my dress and hang it in a stone wardrobe with glass doors. My pj's are a tee and sweats that are cut into shorts. His, on the other hand, is a pair of jeans. Yep, one lucky girl.

There's an area in the corner of the room which is raised like a mini stage.

He says, "It's time."

He goes to the stage, stands on it, and blows me a kiss as he hardens to stone, a beautiful blue marble. I catch the kiss and put it on my heart.

15

QUEEN

Kendra

Spar wakes me with a kiss. I slept all day. Well, that's weird. I guess I needed to catch up.

I stretch and ask, "Do you ever wake up with a song in your head? I woke up with Lady Gaga singing, 'That Boy is a Monster.' After yesternight, yeah, that is how it is. That boy, Spar is a monster, and I like it!"

He cackles and says, "Guilty. We're going to the lunchroom for breakfast. That's where almost everyone eats unless we have fancy visitors, like you, or the King orders a party."

Even though I've been to the lunchroom before, I've never stopped to appreciate it. Walking in, the entrance is like the portico of a large castle. Each end of the entrance can be sealed by heavy black stone doors which are two feet thick.

The kitchen has four buffet serving lines to the left. To the right is the seating area. It's massive, this room is capable of holding all the Ceorfan in Navan with room left over. Large pillars hold the roof in place each is lit with blueish lights shining upwards, providing a very nice sun-colored reflection.

I ask, "Spar, are you sure we should eat in here? It's really fancy. We could just take something–"

He answers, "I'm sure honey, it's okay everyone comes here to eat."

Yes, he knows me so well that he understands I'm not used to this kind of opulence.

Everyone must eat here because I notice that the stone seats and table edges are worn from use, but still beautiful. Some areas, near the buffet lines, might be new. These must be some of the areas Dana is helping restore.

There are several small kitchens, and they're all in use, with many gargoyles queuing near each of them. Wear patterns in the floor hint of many centuries of use. Spar and I head for the second buffet line. The sign above it reads –

ELK STEAKS
Eggs, your choice
Grilled Potatoes
Warm Bread and Prickly Pear Jelly
Your choice of beverage: Coffee, Tea, Almond milk
Cactus Juice or Cranberry Juice.

MY BREAKFAST IS DELICIOUS, elk steak, two scrambled eggs, grilled potatoes, onion and jalapeno pepper slices. The bread is still warm from the oven. The whole breakfast is a chorus of scents, reminding me of my childhood.

I giggle as I stare at Spar's tray. He has three steaks like mine, a dozen eggs, and a pile of potatoes, which are struggling to stay on his plate.

I hold back but chuckle as I ask, "You hungry, big boy?"

His eyes are on his food as he answers, "Yes, it smells delicious, you?"

He's so serious, I dissolve in laughter.

"Yes, I've already gained weight just from the smell. Hey, there's the boys."

I point to my brothers who are sitting on the inside of one of the larger circles of tables with two female gargoyles who I haven't met.

We slide into a rock bench beside them, then get and give good-mornings and introductions. The bench is silky smooth, probably because each tush has polished it over the centuries.

The room is alive with energy. A buzz is riding the deep tones of the conversations. It's strangely electric. People are pulled from all parts of Navan to this breakfast.

"I wonder what has people excited?" I mumble.

Spar, asks, "What was that, honey?"

"Oh, nothing."

Fin is making his way over. I detect him coming from more than ten yards away. Oddly, the closer he gets, the more the room buzzes.

"Good morning, all. I trust you rested well," he says.

Murmurs of assent and positiveness about their rest are returned in response. I ask him to join us and he does, sliding onto the rounded bench beside me.

The room quiets, as Fin leans toward me and asks, "Edling, after breakfast, will you please meet privately with me in my parlor?"

"Yes, of course."

Since he said, 'privately,' I continue eating and ask no questions.

Small talk resumes. Jared and Dana each provide me an update on their activities. Jared has been helping the Ceorfan with something to do with the energy source of Navan. He's working on improving the network as well.

Jared says, "The Ceorfan are teaching me more than I'm teaching them, though. I did help develop a plan to better utilize the vegetable fields, to use less water for irrigation and still increase the yield."

That was easy for him. He'd written a paper in college for Environmental Protection Strategies. Apparently, it fits the needs here.

I say, "I'm proud of you. I barely understand you, but proud. Dana what have you been up to? Following Jared around?"

He answers, "Noooo, Sis, I've been helping the Ceorfan shape some stone into stuff they can use without damaging the cave. I'm helping them repair the common areas, too. I figure, some broke from long use."

He explains that many chambers have weak ceilings or backs as they call them. My baby brother is demonstrating how to strengthen them, to make them safer. I have no doubt he'll teach them how to make them more beautiful at the same time. He has also taken on the task of reworking the gray water distribution. He's designing a new filter system so that the gray water can be used in the new irrigation plan that Jared is working on.

"I'm proud of you, too, little brother," I say.

I really am, they are amazing men. They love being busy and helping people.

Dana says, "It's all good. These people are taking care of us and hard workin' sons a guns."

I notice Kino and Amber and wave hello. She waves back, enthusiastically, adding a kiss, blown to both my boys.

Kino adds a regal tilt of his head.

As the small talk at our table dies away, Spar excuses himself to go to the training field. "Honey, if you don't mind. I need to get to training. They are teaching me all sorts of cool shit."

"No I don't mind. Wait, how did you eat all of that?"

He beams a toothy smile at me. It's striking. I kiss him, to a chorus of teasing, before he leaves.

All of us have work plans to get started on. The boys scoop up the last bites of their food. I was finished three-fourths of an elk steak ago. The boys and I are working on different projects in different areas of Navan, with different people. We make plans to meet for dinner. They head off to their task with the female gargoyles close on their heels.

I leave with Fin.

I was expecting the King's parlor to be larger than it is. It, like the many other rooms, it's brightly lit by wall sconces. A large, finely crafted, rectangular marble table dominates the room with detailed etchings in it. What the gargoyles etched doesn't seem to match anything I've seen in Navan. There are seats for maybe 14.

Fin and I sit near one end, facing each other. He's exploring my eyes intently. What is he searching for?

"Edling, the trip to Scotland has been moved up. We cannot wait. Baratium is murdering thousands. We surmise he will soon reveal the secrets of the Ceorfan," Fin says and lets his words hang in the air.

"The Ceorfan remain secret. Because of our differences, humans despise us. To integrate with others in the Earth, a change must take place in the opinions of men. TASS knows, but they want to keep our secret as much as we do. If the our race were no longer secret, the group believes their hold on power would evaporate. This makes us safe from them—for now.

"We will travel to Scotland before the end of the week, Edling. The High Guild, with your lead, will create the plan to destroy Baratium and the Crafted, once and for all time.

"TASS delivers influence on the powerful in the human world. If they don't want an individual in power, nothing will ever put that person in power. They do this for greed and control. The best interests of the global population count for very little. I must warn you, they can be very clever. They calculate every decision based on what advantage they believe will further their cause. Which they say is, 'To save succeeding generations from the scourge of war and to provide a vehicle for economic stability which shall be used to promote social progress and better standards of living and freedom.'

"However, I have watched them for hundreds of years. When the needs of individual members are pitted against the needs of the people, writ large, the needs of TASS inevitably win out. I do not want you to be fooled, so I am warning you. Some decisions seem correct, until you factor in what may happen to the greater population of the world, not just those involved."

"I understand, Fin. You've given me a great deal of information. I need a great deal more. I have a list of things I need to accomplish as soon as we finish, including checking on Mica. Before I leave, I do have some questions for you, if you don't mind?"

"Of course, Edling. We try not to keep secrets between the Ceorfan. I'll do my best to answer anything you need to know. What is it?"

"Last night, Jericho cut my hand, so I would bleed directly into Mica. I'd like to know why that made him better. It rapidly healed him. Does human blood do that for Ceorfan? Then I saw a light connecting us together through my blood. Can you tell me about that?"

"These are two of the most difficult to answer and most important questions. The answer to them both hangs directly on your ancestry. I know your ancestry because your lineage comes directly from the Dragon Rulers of the Ceorfan."

What have I started? Is this why Fin was searching my eyes so resolutely earlier?

He has to see my look of astonishment.

He says, "What you need to know is probably better told you by Jericho. I will send him a message. I am sure he will be here with all due haste. I will tell you as much as I can while we wait for him."

Little clicks echo in the otherwise quiet room as the king composes the message on his tablet. As he writes, I observe the floor for the first time. It's black marble. My eyes seem to focus intently on the black.

I try to focus back on Fin when he continues, with understanding pouring from his eyes, "Our precious dragons were healers. We judge that when your spirit detached from your body and your soul was dreamwalking, your dragon blood began transforming you, conveying your true nature to the forefront. It is possible that being with us in Navan is compelling your dragon core to develop faster than it otherwise would. Add in that you were shot by Drinker. Since then, your dragon-self—or that part of you—has forced its way to the surface, to keep your brothers, as well as others, safe. For years, we have watched as you have put yourself at risk to protect others. You have that protective attribute intrinsic in your soul."

The blackness, once confined to the now impossibly black floor, has begun to creep up the walls. The details, once so vivid, have blended to form still-recognizable shapes, shapes with little detail remaining. I sit back in my chair and cross my arms over my chest.

Fin, with a resolute voice, continues, "My Lady, dragon blood heals the most grievous wounds. It can alter body parts which do not conform to the body's needs. We, the Ceorfan, have been waiting and watching for generations to see a Dragon Queen rise."

My breath is speeding up. The room is drawing in on itself. The walls, once so brightly lit, have a foggy darkness creeping in toward each sconce. The blackness, looks like a void trying to drag us down. It takes my every anxiety and exposes them to every fear that drives them.

This is overwhelming. I'm stunned. Even though, on some level I knew this already. Why have I ignored it?

"I think I need a minute to process this. What do you have to drink in here?" I murmur.

"Here, Edling."

He pours me a glass of a spiced wine I hardly taste as I chug the whole glass. He pours me another. I take a drink, stopping there.

"I'm sure you are telling me the truth, Fin. I'm just not sure what it means to me. What do I do with it?"

On cue, Jericho enters the parlor.

Without fanfare, he states, "It means you are the Dragon Queen of the Ceorfan, Kendra Macbard, and we have great need of you. Your purpose is to unite us with the world of men, so we can share the Earth the way we were meant to, without fear. We are driven—to protect. Protect gargoyles, men, animals all equally, without preju-dice. The gargoyles need you to give that back to them."

I push back in my chair. The room completely overtakes me. The void where I was teetering a few moments earlier is enveloping me as I fall into it. My hands cover my face to hide from the void.

I respond, "I'm just a park ranger. How? How can I ever be a queen? What do I do? Queen, seriously?"

Each statement, each question is less clear than the last. My last words are a mere whisper.

"Never mind," I add.

I feel myself floating up from my chair. Without saying anything else, or looking at either Jericho or Fin, I flee to my chambers. I have no idea how I found them, but I'm glad I did. Breathe. My focus is on a single point on the wall in front of me. After a few minutes, I look away from the spot and to my clock. Thirty minutes have passed. I shake myself, grab my tablet, and call work.

"Hey there, Chris. This is Kendra. How's it going?"

"Hey back, lady. It's fine here, all quiet on the Southern front," She chuckles, "the question is, how're you?"

"That's why I called. So, I could let you know. I'm healing, but the doctors say it'll be a few weeks before I can come back to work. They're worried I might rip stuff open." All true, not a lie. "How's everybody there?" In other words, is that POS John still there?

"We're all fine. Concentrate on getting you better," she says.

"I'm going to call Murphy and check on him next."

That's code for, if that bastard hurt the Captain or anyone else, he will pay even more painfully than he already will!

Chris says, "I think Murphy's still at work. You should try his desk phone first. We're a little shorthanded with you and Mica out, so he's working late."

"I'm guessing no one will get vacation until we're back. Sorry about that. Apologize to the others for me, if they were wanting to take one."

"Nope, no vacations for anyone right now. No one's even tried to take a day off since you were shot. And don't you dare go apologizin'. We know the score. We'll all be just fine. You heal up and come back a hundred percent."

"Okay, I will. Thanks, Chris. I'll call you soon with another update."

"You do that. Goodnight, sweetheart. Goodbye."

Telling her goodbye, I call my boss next. We have basically the same conversation, only he thanks me for saving him. Apparently, he watched the camera footage. He only has seven stitches in the back of his head and is doing fine. After we say our goodbyes, I begin reading the Ceorfan history.

I've been reading for hours. Well, reading and thinking. I like who I am, dragon blood and all. I'm making decisions, big decisions. Decisions which will change my life, the boy's lives—hell, the Ceorfan's lives.

What was it that Jericho had said? His decree? Oh yes, he said: "Your purpose is to unite the Ceorfan with the world of men so that we can share the Earth the way we were meant to, without fear." Let's add a giant echo onto that statement! What the hell else?

I'm pretty good at calming myself down, most of the time. It needs to be instinctual in any life and death situation. Oddly enough, I've met my quota in the last several days.

While this is way out of my league, I've never been one to run away from doing the hard job. Deep down, I already know what I need to do. My fear is, I don't know 'how' to do what's needed. Before I do anything else, I need to talk with my brothers. They're good at helping me look at situations differently. They both come at them from directions I haven't considered. I also know I need to speak with Fin some more.

"I'm hungry," I say to myself, a bit more relaxed.

Standing lazily, I think I'll go to the lunchroom then I see if I can find the king or the boys.

Shit, shit, shit! Can you believe that? I jump up and put my tablet in a side pocket of my cargo pants. I forgot to check on Mica. I'm worthless as a partner.

I hurry out my door and turn right. Heading down the hallway I'm absorbed in focusing on my steps and with my thoughts, running through seeing my shot friend again. 'Hey, partner, I know you took a bullet for me—thanks for that. I've just been too busy to come see you!' Yeah, that's wha–

Thump! I run right into a hardened wall of man—monster—gargoyle. Mica wraps his huge hands around my waist, lifts me effortlessly, and sits me on a stone quarter-wall that makes up one side of the hallway leading to my secluded room. He stares at me, waiting to see how I'm going to react.

Spilling from me is a risky mix of, 'thank God you're okay', to 'holy hell, I want you, now!' I want him to kiss me.

Almost as if granting my wish, he kisses me—slowly, softly at first.

I kiss him back and yank him to me. I feel his heart, the one I helped heal, pounding hard in his chest as he wraps his massive arms around me. I like the feel of his monster-ness holding me against him. He crushes his lips to mine in a hard kiss. My body reacts, preparing for him. He forces his tongue into my mouth. I respond in kind. Need shoots to my core, and I moan into his mouth. Wow, this guy can kiss! He moves back a little and smiles at me. He's magnificent. His need is showing despite the thick jeans he's wearing.

"Now that's how to say hello to a fellow," he states proudly.

My brain is mush.

He pauses and waits.

My brain's still mush.

Before the silence gets awkward, he breaks it, "I want to tell you thank you for saving my life, Princess."

Before I say something stupid like, 'I carried a watermelon,' I try to calm my racing heart.

I say, "I think the saving was mutual. I saw John, and he was pointing the gun straight at me. I was his target. You took the bullet for me."

"Princess, I'll take whatever I need to for you. Are you hungry? Let's go get something."

So, my life is spinning out of control again. Am I collecting men?

I must tell Spar I kissed Mica. No way am I going to lie to him. Damn! I'm an idiot. What is Spar going to think?

"Yes, let's go see if they have pizza. You look fine now—is that true?" I ask, doing my best to focus on his face and not up and down his body.

He grins a knowing grin.

"I'm fine. Dragon blood will heal almost any injury. It's very powerful. It also connected us for life. If you don't want me, Kendra, I can respect that, but we will always be connected."

I need to talk to someone, and right now, that someone is him. I start spilling everything that King Findare and Jericho told me. Then I tell him that I'm attracted to him, and I do want him, but it's only right for me to tell Spar first. Spar has already told me that this was the way of the Ceorfan people. I have the feeling he expects this kind of relationship, but I still need him to know before I give Mica the go-ahead.

Mica says, "I understand. I'm here for you anytime you need to talk. I never thought I would love like this. I can wait until you're ready. Spar is important to me, too. I wouldn't want to hurt either of you."

"Thank you, will you show me to the King's chamber?"

He nods, takes me there, and pulses a greeting. Findare calls out as he pulses back. Funny, I think the prickle of the pulse is one of relief. Mica leaves me with the King, touching my back, giving me chills.

Seeing Fin when I enter, say, "I'm sorry, and I apologize, for leaving without an explanation earlier. Will you tell me what is expected of me?"

"Oh, Edling, I am sorry we shocked you so. Both Jericho and I should have been gentler in our delivery. The mistake is ours alone."

"Thank you," I reply.

"Kendra, we only want what you are able and willing to provide. No more, no less. The truth is, I am King in name only. I much prefer my previous title of Duke. We have not had a true monarch in more than eleven hundred years."

In a much gentler tone he adds, "You are the answer to our millennia-long search. You are the monarch that my people have loved for years, from afar. You are the queen we wish to lead us. It is you who will lead us to our freedom and prosperity. The core of my existence, over a millennia, has been searching for a Dragon Queen. You are that Dragon Queen. It is with the deepest hope and desire that I, your humble supplicant, ask you, Kendra Dawn Macbard, to accept the monarchy of the Ceorfan people."

"Fin, I do accept. However, I need to talk to my family before you announce this to the Ceorfan people."

A pulse booms through the whole room immediately after I finish my statement.

"I believe, my queen, it's too late. Your pulse proclaimed the commencement of your reign to the whole of the Ceorfan."

"Did that come from me? Oh, crap! Can I take it back for maybe 30 minutes?"

Several people come rushing into the chamber, including Megahir and Count de Treon. They all drop to one knee, with heads bowed. I look questioningly at the now Duke Findare.

"Yes, it is for you, my queen. You are the queen of the Ceorfan. No one has been able to code a pulse like that since the last queen. It has been over a thousand years since she sacrificed herself on the field of honor."

There are tears in Fin's eyes! I'm sure he's sincere.

"Uh oh, what have I done?" I mumble. "Get up! Oh, my gosh! Please, just get up. I don't have to have you bow to me. I'm just a person. I'm not even as physically strong as one of you. I make mistakes, lots of 'em. I know I'll need your help, and I most certainly will not have my friends kneeling in front of me. We're in this together. Okay?"

They all rise slowly, each with tears in his eyes.

One man, who I had not met, was still on the floor, prone, arms splayed in front of him, outright sobbing. I walk over to him and, squatting, I put my hand on his shoulder. I lift his face until it is level with mine.

"Don't cry. I need your strength now. I need it to help me transition into this role. You have not had a queen in over a thousand years. I will need your strength, your love, your help to learn this role. Will you help me?"

He grins, hiccupping as his tears stop.

"I will, my queen!" He answers, with so much affection, it can only come from his heart.

Okay, I knew this would be life-changing for me. The Ceorfan, however, think it's life-changing for them.

Megahir puts a giant clawed hand on my shoulder. Standing behind him is Count de Treon, Fin, and everyone else in the room.

Mega, speaks for the group. "I cannot thank you enough, chuisle mo chroi," pulse of my heart.' You will be known by that pulse. My queen, we need to get you to the underground amphitheater, so the people can see you. Your pulse had a great deal of emotion in it. Your people will want you to know they support you. We few just happened to be close to the King—no Duke's, chamber—so we came here. Your pulse indicated all Ceorfan are your family. I'll send messages to your brothers."

16

HOPE

Kendra

I pull away from the crowd of people surrounding me. Mega is sticking with me, though. Maybe he's my bodyguard. Well, I think he's always been, anyway. Leading, he begins, "My queen, the amphitheater is this way."

I follow closely behind. I'm in a bit of a daze. I keep my head up—regally, I hope, and watch the beautiful stalactites and stalagmites of my new kingdom. I admire the intricate frostwork as well as many other speleothems as we pass them.

One reason I work at the Cueva Hallow Caverns is my love of the cave features. I'm fascinated with them and want to be near them.

"Do I keep my job at the Caverns?" I wonder out loud.

We cross a wide, well-lit stone bridge. It's as well-lit from beneath as it is from above. In front of me, I see another substantial portico. It's intricately carved with what appear to be gargoyle muses, but small vertical openings are cut into the walls. I'm guessing these could be used to fire weapons though to defend the amphitheater. It's obvious now: the Ceorfan have built safe rooms in case they are attacked.

The amphitheater is not as long as the lunchroom, though it's still impressive. The difference is, as you walk in, you're looking down on a very large half-circle of a stage instead of finding the kitchen front and center. Lighting the stage are several of the same wall sconces I have seen throughout Navan. These, though, are much smaller than the ones I'd seen in the lunchroom.

In the seating area directly to the front-center of the stage sits a massive stalagmite. This stalagmite has been carved into a sort of reserved seating area. It looks as if it could seat maybe twenty large humans.

Ascending the steps leading to the stage, I have every conflicted emotion I've faced over the last few days come into my head at once. "Kendra," I say. I can't be heard over the din echoing throughout the amphitheater. "Focus only on the now. You can't fix everything at once. Right now, focus on your introduction only."

I step onto the stage and into my new life. I pause, scanning the crowd.

"Finally!" I yell and wave, "Spar, over here! Jared! Dana!"

They see me and hustle to me.

"Oh, big cluster-fuck, guys. I can't believe what I've done! I wanted to talk to all three of you and let us all think about it for a few days. But I guess as soon as I accepted, my body sort of just took over,"

I say. I begin to tell them about everything, as best as my addled brain could recall.

"Now, I've been accepted as the queen of the Ceorfan people. This has gone too far, too fast. While I didn't plan to do this, I don't feel stuck. I want you to know, this is what I want. I just never expected it would happen, much less happen without us talking first! But now everyone knows because that sonar thump thing. It evidently came from me." I run out breath at the last few words.

Dana squeezes my shoulder and says jokingly then serious, "Damnit. I love you, Sis. You can do this. Jared and I will support you every step of the way."

All three of them are touching me, each in his own way letting me know they have my back.

Jared says, "We all felt it. It was like we could hear it, but not really. Spar told me it was a code that the Ceorfan people will recognize. Your pulse said you're the queen of all Ceorfan, and your heart is for us."

"Well, if you are the queen," Dana says, "what the hell am I?"

I snicker at him. He knows how to ease the tension very well.

Findare takes the center of the stage, motioning the four of us to gather close to him. When the crowd sees us gather, they quiet and sit.

The rows closest to the stage are all packed.

"Is this everyone?" I ask my blue boyfriend.

"This is everyone here in Navan, but there are some on assignments, and some Ceorfan are nomads."

"Okay, I've been to high school football games with more people. This gives me an idea of the Ceorfan population."

I estimate two thousand, maybe a few hundred or so more.

"We're connected to each other. We aren't connected like shapeshifter wolves in the movies. We are connected more like a colony of bats. We feel things about each other. We don't keep secrets. We share and care for each other. If someone has a need, others help meet it, or figure out how," Spar explains.

"Queen Kendra, the pulse of the Ceorfan heart," Findare says. He's at the podium, and I didn't even notice. We snap toward him, listening.

He continues. "Today the Ceorfan people will etch your acceptance as Queen with reverence. For more than eleven hundred years, we have searched for a ruler with the dragon blood who could lead our people. Queen Kendra, through your pulse, you are known to the Ceorfan. None can ever masquerade as you. You have expressed your love for your people. You have told us we are one. This has long been our wish. Your Majesty, please come forward and, if you will, address your people."

As the Duke stands aside and bows to me. The room erupts. I feel pulses all over my body. The feeling is overwhelming. Their cheer buoys me as I slowly walk forward, to my place in the center of the dais.

I don't have the foggiest idea of what I should say. Thankfully, since it gives me time to think, the ovation of thumps continues unabated.

I stand, shoulders back, head up as I look around the room filled with my people–the Ceorfan. They are beautiful, so full of life. I find Mica, his face radiating his love. I notice Amber, tears are rolling down her face. I spot Kino, gazing at me in amazement, almost as if he's afraid this dream might shatter. I see many faces. In each, I recognize hope. Hope! I can't let these precious people down.

I begin, "With all my heart, I want to help and protect you all. You are my people, my family now. Mine. I'll do my best as your leader. I'm not perfect, though. I apologize now for my future mistakes. Please have patience with me as I learn how to meet your needs. No, not just needs, but your wants also. I know there are things you have wanted, things you want to do, maybe places you wish to see that you have not been able to. I'm going to do my best to rectify that. At the end of the week, I'll meet with TASS in Scotland. Instead of being your ambassador, I will be your queen."

The room erupts in pulses again. I hold both arms in the air and pat my hands downward, in what I'm hoping is a universal gesture of 'be quiet and sit, please.'

"I know Megahir. I'm pretty sure he and the Elites will act as my bodyguards. I obviously know and have an amazing amount of respect for Duke Findare. I have also met several others. Please don't be offended if I don't mention you by name. I'm a bit overwhelmed right now."

Breathe.

I continue, "I want to get to know each of you. It'll take time. Will you support me as your queen? Will you give me time to become the queen you deserve? If so, let's make that pact, right here, right now. All in favor stand, be seen, and say, 'Aye!'"

The entire crowd jumps and shouts, "Aye!" Now they are being loud and I feel pulses of support. A chant begins. I can't understand, but it unmistakably has great meaning to the Ceorfan. I wave Duke Fin to my side. Then Mega, Kino, Spar, Jared, and Dana move to stand with me. We put arms around each other as the crowd comes to offer individual congratulations.

17

ANCESTRY

Kendra

With the coronation complete, the Ceorfan crowd the stage to personally greet their new Dragon Queen as well as the Dragon Archdukes, Jared and Dana. It has been nearly eleven hundred years since the people had a queen; most of them want to meet, or at least, breathe the same air as their new queen.

Another bent knee, another introduction. "Queen Macbard, I am Ferre. This is my older sister, Barhaine. We are grateful you have accepted the monarchy. Our population has dwindled over the centuries. We hope you can bring new vigor... "

I steal a glance toward Dana. He's by my side, but facing me. I know he was bored two hours ago. Now—well, now I'm not sure what he is. He has the appearance of someone who's falling asleep. No, that's wrong. He is asleep.

Spar gently bumps into me, returning my focus to the sisters. "Ferre, Barhaine, I'm glad to now know you both. I'll do everything I can to help restore the eh... lost vigor you cited. Thank you both."

Ferre giggles, but Barhaine has a frustrated look about her. They curtsy to me and leave, chatting with each other.

The ladies were the last of the 'Thank you, my queen,' and 'Can you help us with this problem, my queen?' Thankfully, there are no more of the few surly comments we heard as well.

I stand, stretching my lower back by pushing it forward with my hands. My mind rambles through the many faces, stories, and even smells of the last few hours. My gaze treads upon the stalactite and stalagmite formations.

My eyes continue to drift. I find Dana again. Yep, still sound asleep, standing. Of course, Jared and Spar have already plotted some nefarious prank designed to embarrass or harass Dana. They'd better not hurt him. I raise an eyebrow at the two, curious of their intentions.

Spar moves, as if my eyebrow was the go signal in their execrable plot. He reaches his big, gray-blue hand around Dana and pats him on the bottom gently, then he starts massaging it.

Dana, immediately rejuvenated, springs into action like he was shot out of a canon. He high steps it across the stage, in his size thirteen boots, beating a hasty retreat from his assault. We're laughing, oh so inappropriately, at his embarrassment. I might call him cannonball soon.

"Damnit all to hell, Amber!" Dana roars.

Then, hearing Spar and Jared laughing uncontrollably, he realizes what's going on and spins toward them.

"You two buckets of turds! Just wait!" He's roaring with laughter and stumbling over his last words.

Jared yells, "Amber! You have every name in the Ceorfan book and you come up with Amber. Have you seen how little her hand is compared to Spar's?"

The chorus of glee morphs into a new one, "Amber and Dana sittin' in a tree, k-i-s-s-i-n-g."

More laughter follows, along with amused protests. Yes, my brothers and Spar are still children. I love them all the more.

Duke Findare, Mega, Mica, and Kino left about five minutes ago, before the last few introductions, because of previously scheduled appointments.

Spar, Jared, Dana, and I remain alone on the dais. Our smiles are fixed while we contemplate the recent events. The mental and physical exhaustion I feel must be mirrored on my face—and now, through my fading smile.

Jared jabs me lightly in my ribs, joking, "You look like you've been run over by a cave-sized gargoyle Mac truck!"

I gently chide him, "Well, little brother, you don't have room to talk!"

And I add a small giggle, so he knows I'm teasing. If I were talking to Dana, I wouldn't have given it a second thought. Jared had been treated a bit more harshly growing up and was more sensitive to this type of fun. He could certainly take more than his share, with our history, but I choose to take extra care with him. My brothers are mine to protect always. Don't worry, Jared, I got you.

"I could go for some coffee. A big Mega-sized cup! Haha." Laughing at my own token witticism, I punch Dana in the arm. Nobody thinks it's funny. "I'm your queen, and I made a joke, and it was pun-ny!" They all grin blithely.

Despite their brush-off, I ask again, "Anyone want to go to the lunchroom with me?"

It looks as though each one of these men has their 'adult' gene removed, and they've reverted to children who are spending the day at Disneyland. Being emotionally worn out is something these three have no experience with. They're all specimens who focus on the physical aspects of emotions. Each has known deep, emotional love; however, it isn't an area where they like to live.

Still, no one answers for several more heartbeats.

Spar breaks the silence and says, "I need to finish my training for today. I was in the middle of a session when we were called to your 'coro-NATION.'"

He accented the final word in his best impersonation of an

English Grandee for effect. He continues, in a totally non-sarcastic manner, telling me that once his training is complete, he will meet me in my chamber. Likely, it would take a few hours.

My brothers walk with me to the lunchroom. I lead us to the large circular seating area, since it will offer us the ability to see each other as we talk. And talking is what I want to do.

By and large, the room is empty, giving us privacy. The few remaining patrons seem to be hustling their way out. I sit so I can see the entrance of the lunchroom easier. It's then that I notice the reason the room is vacant. Two large Elite Warrior Guard members are at the door, ushering away any ravenous but apparently tardy visitors. I need to have a room where I can have meetings where they won't interfere with the rest of the community. I'll bring it up with Dana. I'm sure he'll know how to take care of this. The guards do let Kino in. I wave him over to sit with us.

"Okay, guys, we need to talk about this dragon ancestry. Have either of you had time to look into it?"

Jared and Dana both shake their heads. "No."

"No worries, I've got it covered. I found a short essay in all that stuff on my tablet. It tells the story pretty well. For the most part, the information comes from Fin and the reading material Dolo put on my tablet.

"Before the Trojan War, more than three thousand years ago, Helen of Sparta was born—an offspring of the god Zeus. When Helen hit puberty, she was kidnapped and raped by the King of Athens. This resulted in a pregnancy and a daughter. Helen's family had to hide the fact she'd been violated, or she wouldn't have been wed to any of the more powerful choices of husbands. That would have made her daughter Iphigeneia an outcast.

"Iphigeneia lived outside of the city, as an outcast. She chose to live in a cave on a mountain near Sparta, where her mother had married King Menelaus.

"Sparta used the strongest, most physically fit women to bear children. If a woman proved she could provide strong children, other men might request of her husband that she bear his children, too. This led to the strongest women bearing children from multiple fathers. Spartans grew into a polyandrous society, where the women held wealth and power.

"Sparta had a policy of leaving the malformed and weak to die on Iphigeneia's mountain. Sometimes, severely injured men would be left on her mountain to recover or die. Iphigeneia brought the outcasts to live with her, in her cave. She protected and strengthened them. In time, she learned her blood had magical qualities. It could heal the most severely injured, or even malformed limbs. At some point, her group outcasts grew to more than three hundred, large enough to become their own society. Their culture was different from others. Their guiding principal devised ways to help the living live to their fullest. They excelled at helping the disposed of—the injured and the sick. They even saved the same wealthy Spartans who tried at one time to have her burned out of her cave city when they had found out she was helping those they had left to die.

"Her people adored her and the Ceorfan made Iphigeneia their queen. Blessings followed the Ceorfan. After many years, Iphigeneia learned her blood made her immortal. This secret escaped the confines of her community into the larger world of the greedy. The magic within her blood made her a target for every would-be despot or upstart crackpot around. She was hunted. Without going into detail, she was eventually killed. She did have several children. One was a girl named Leta, who had long orange-red hair and skin like velvet. This girl was blessed with the same gifts as her mother.

"That's all, but guys, over the last few days in Navan, I'm starting to 'feel' more things. For example, I can feel the gargoyle pulses as they enter and leave Navan. I couldn't do that before. My seeing auras is more pronounced, too. Now, I'd like to see if we can find any other things the dragon blood does for the three of us."

Jared chimes in, "Do you have anything you'd like to add, Kino?"

"Some, the Ceorfan dragons have always been matriarchal. We

are also matriarchal as a guild. You two men, will have gifts like other Ceorfan. Even though your gifts are magnified by your dragon blood, your blood is not magic. Blood magic only follows the females. That means only your sister's blood can heal or transform.

"Only a Dragon Queen can pulse as strong as you, Kendra. Those who are privileged enough to stay in your company will enjoy better health. For a gargoyle, your blood gifts strength. Anyone around you will consistently have their gifts operate on a higher level, and they usually have children—something we have not had for nearly eleven hundred years, when our last queen, Leta died.

"Sickness, as a gargoyle, means weakness. It can also mean you lose your gift. Without a Dragon Queen, it is possible to lose all our gifts, talents, and even our ability to excel. In the last days, I have seen a remarkable improvement in my friends' strength. Their gifts are increasing in power also.

"The truth is, the male dragons always had gifts which exceeded most other Ceorfan. For all dragons, residing in the city amplifies their gifts. Navan has its own magic, too. You must pay attention to coincidences in your lives, projects you are drawn to, or even feats you excel at completing.

"While you are here, test yourselves. Find your gift. Dragons were known to have strong gifts. Not gifts like mine—I can sing magic, or my singing magnifies magic. Nothing to brag about. Sleeping a babe is the essence of my gift. Dragons could make the ocean roar. One of the old dragons was known to shoot fire from his mouth, an admittedly uncommon gift. I do not know if your bodies will develop stronger gifts. It seems likely. Also, all dragons can fly."

The three of us sit and stare at Kino as he finishes his speech. Spar has a big grin on his face as he looks at us.

He says, "You three look like a coin slot on the old-fashioned penny banks!"

The boys close their mouths as fast as I did, then chortle.

Jared says, "Thanks, Kino. That's a lot to absorb. At least we know what to look for to find our gifts. We'll pay better attention while we're here in Navan."

I'd better tell them when we leave.

"Oh, I forgot to tell you. Fin told me we'll be traveling to Scotland at the end of the week. How busy are you? Do you want to go with me?" I ask.

Before they worry about my safety I add that I'm sure I'll be okay surrounded by gargoyles.

"I would like to go with you, Sis," Jared says.

Dana follows with, "If it's okay with you, Sissy, I want to stay here. They have some bad back ready to cave in. I have a design to fix it and make the cave chambers more useful and nicer. If you want me to go, though, I will."

"Not a problem. Stay and help. It's what we do. Right? What's a bad back? Do we need to worry?"

"No, don't worry. We have restricted access in those areas. Back is what we call the ceiling underground. There are some needing strengthened."

"Okay, gotcha. Maybe you'll figure out your gift while we're gone. Could you please try to find a room I can use as an audience room/meeting room? I'd like it near my room, and I want a big round table that can seat fifteen to twenty people. It doesn't have to be fancy. I just don't want to keep using the lunchroom and having people get locked out."

"No problem, Sis... I mean, your queenliness!"

I give a quick elbow into his ribs as I stand and say, "I'm going to head to my room and get ready. If you guys need me, you know where I'll be."

Kino told me he'd walk with me to Mega, who was waiting to speak to me in my room. When I get there, I realize I'm going to be a poor host.

I say, "Mega, I don't have anything to drink in here, or I'd offer you something. I'm not exactly sure where everything is yet, either. How can I help you?"

"You have already helped in many ways, my queen. In the days to come, I am sure you will be able to see the difference your presence is making with the guild. I need to keep you informed regarding what your military is doing. You need to know your soldiers, our number, and what our capabilities are. When we arrive in Scotland, to meet with the humans, we need a strategy. You need information to devise this strategy."

While he pauses, I interject. "Please call me Kendra, Megahir. You are so right, I do need this information. Can we agree to meet every evening after breakfast for a short informal meeting, just to exchange information? Another thing—you spoke to me in my head the first time we met. You haven't done it again. Can I ask why?"

"Of course, you may. I will call you Kendra in private, if you also call me Mega. I gather that to do so in public or with the humans would be disrespectful. It would take away respect for your position. Politically speaking, the power and prestige of your position is not just a token sentiment. If you are treated with dignity, others will follow the example automatically. We want your word to hold power from the start.

"To address the telepathy, I do not wish to intrude on your privacy. My gift is one that gives me access to emotions as well as thoughts. I am beginning to understand that with you and your brothers, I can access you when you are farther away than what I am able with others."

I have a little seating area in my chamber where we were relaxing when Amber walks in with a tray of tea and sandwiches.

"Wow, thank you, Amber! How did you—oh yeah, Mega. Thank you both. Mega, we should stay as connected as you deem. It'll be a safety issue and will save us time. I have nothing to hide from you. I trust you. I'm sure you'll consider my privacy. We'll figure it out as we go. The question is, if I reach out to you telepathically, will you hear me? Telepathy is too long I think I'll call it tele-speak or some such."

"That will be fine. With most, that only works if I am in their minds when they respond. With you, I thought I could hear you earlier. Making a joke about something–coffee, maybe?"

"Ha, that's right, shall we practice?"

I think without speaking, "*I need to practice steeling my facial reactions. So, in a conference meeting, we can tell secrets, and no one will be the wiser.*"

Mega thinks back, "*That would be a good practice. Let us also try to strengthen the bond, so I may hear you farther and farther away. For emergencies, in case you are ever lost, or in case I am taken by the enemy, or vice versa, we can find each other.*"

Then audibly he says, "You have some very talented warriors at your disposal, Kendra. Did you know Amber is one of your best?"

"Well, that stands to reason! Nope, I didn't know it. What can I expect from you, little lady, do you also communicate telepathically?"

"No, my queen."

"Kendra while we're in private. Please?" I ask her, whispering.

"Kendra, I'm extraordinarily good at infiltration. I can sit as an ornament to the unknowing, with few ever detecting me, then slip into a building under the radar. I gather data, files, or evidence and get back out undetected. Mason and I both are gifted similarly. He likes to say he has a better sense of humor. I like to let him believe it," she says.

The time gets away from us as we strategize and talk.

Soon, Spar returns from his training and backs away saying, "I didn't know you would be in a meeting. I'll come back later."

Mega stands and tells him no; he has monopolized me most of the night. He tells Spar to clean up and take me to eat something. We had only eaten some small sandwiches for our lunch.

Amber had left much earlier when our conversation had become too boring.

Mega says, in tele-speak, "*I will talk to you again in the evening, tomorrow after breakfast.*"

My Commanding officer leaves me with my love.

I'm hungry, but with my big boy all sweaty, I think food can wait for a little while. We have hours until sunrise. That's amazing—I can tell what time the sun is going to come up just by feeling! I love it.

One more look at my big hunk of monster and I forget I even had a stray thought. I invite him into my bathing pond. We're into water sports—well, something like that. I forget my name in the next few minutes.

18

SCOTLAND

Kendra

This is the night Duke Findare had told me we are going to leave for Scotland. I didn't pack because Amber made me leave that to her. However, I did check the bathroom to see if she at least packed my comb and brush. Of course, she did, but one never knows what a soldier might think is or isn't important. The soldiers I know like to shave their heads and pack light—nothing that can't be left behind and all that. I seem to be surrounded with soldiers. Thank the Creator! At least they understand me.

When I was younger, I was a square peg in a round hole. A woman in a man's world needs to find a way to make it work, if that's what she wants. It's what I want. I love what I do. I just need to figure out how to make my new position fit into my old life as a Federal Park Ranger.

A Park Ranger might be right for me now, but I'm reminded of my first love... politics. I had achieved my Bachelor of Arts in Political Science, emphasizing in both public law and political policy. I'd given it all up when a randy Senator accosted me sexually. I was too young to handle that kind of pressure. I decided to quit. At the time, I thought it was a good decision.

Yeah, running is sometimes a good decision, but not from your own fears. Better to confront them head on. I'm tougher now. I handle myself better.

I've had enough of it happen that I teach others to map out a system. Here is mine; Option one, punch them in the chest and yell at them loudly enough that others can hear details of my disgust. If that doesn't work, go to option two, kick them in the balls if the perpetrator is a man, or punch them in the face if a woman, before screaming, "The children are hungry, they haven't eaten in days! You should be ashamed." Finally, option three, pull my weapon.

No, I rarely go through the first two options. I skip straight to option three. I'm too old to put up with that shit.

I'm curious if any of my old contacts in the political realm are involved in TASS. Arden Kelly is an old friend I met during negotiations the US had in Ireland, when I was still a lowly intern for the dirtball Senator from Michigan. Arden would look at my role with the Ceorfan and take me seriously.

Coming back from my thoughts, I hear a conversation I don't like in my front chamber. It seems the Count has come to visit.

The lovely Count de Treon has just informed Spar he'll have to stay behind to finish his testing.

"No," I say firmly, "Spar is going with me. I need his expertise with me in Scotland. Please make him welcome on the trip."

If the Count wasn't so temperamental, he'd be okay. As it is, he irritates me so badly that I don't want to hear what he has to say. It's such a shame; he's a stunning gargoyle. He has a perfectly demonish look, including the big pointed ears and pale-green skin. He's rather short compared to the Elite Warrior Guard, but he'd look perfect torpefied on an old French castle. Whatever. He's one of my people now, so I'm going to have to do my best to build him up—maybe help change his superior attitude. I'll protect him the same as any of the others.

Without a word or sideways glance, the good Count executes my request.

Yeah, it's a gift. I've always been able to get my way in those kinds of situations. Wait a minute. Hold the phone. Could it be possible I might be gifted in that area? I'm going to test my theory soon, and a lot.

I test my link with Mega to see if he can hear me. *"I'm so bored waiting."*

He responds immediately, *"Yes, Kendra?"*

"Where is everyone? I'm ready to leave. I'm also bored. Did I say I'm bored?"

"Do you remember where we had the party last week? The entire team picked for Scotland is meeting there in a few minutes. Can you remember the way? If you do not, I can send someone to get you."

"I can get there. See you in a minute."

All three of us, Spar, the count, and I make our way through the cave chambers, finding our small crowd of travelers sitting around talking. As soon as they see me, they stop gabbing and stand.

"At ease, at ease, you don't have to stand for me. We can be more formal in Scotland when everyone in our company isn't family, okay?"

"Mega, there are some people here I don't know, who shall I ask to introduce us?"

Without a blink, he says, "All of you know the Pulse of the Ceorfan Heart. In public, you may call her Queen Kendra or Your Majesty."

He continues speaking and begins the introductions, "My lady, beside the Count de Treon is High Guild member Reyder, Marquis de Roat."

"Please, my lady, call me Tobert," says the Marquis.

I blush, and nod as my commander moves on, "Flint is part of the Elite Warriors. You already know Mica, Kino, Amber, Mason, and Spar."

Then he moves toward the last gargoyle to be introduced. She is exceedingly beautiful as well.

"This is Eltira, the Count's daughter. She is fluent in languages and will assist us in that capacity."

In my mind, I hear him say, *"She is also a spoiled brat. Her father could not say no to her when she demanded to accompany him on this trip."*

"Shall I make her stay here?" I ask.

"Let us indulge them this time. I think we want to start easing the High Guild into taking orders from you. Let us not make enemies in the beginning."

"I agree, but I'll give a warning, so they know I'm the one in control."

"Agreed."

Jericho makes his way to us, stopping when he is standing beside me. I sense he is content. I view his aura. Here in Navan I hardly need to concentrate—I can perceive them clearly. His is very yellow, with orange. That tells me he's not only intelligent, he's happy; the orange is the fact that he commands authority.

I'm satisfied, and turn to look at Eltira. She flares red, but the color around her is mostly blue. Is she a musician? The red flares are not a good sign in her. She has a temper, I bet. I should keep an eye on her. That's enough; I blink to quit seeing the lights, and they all disappear.

I search Jericho's face. I hope he can read body language. I want him to know I'm about to speak. He motions to me, a tiny fraction of a nod.

Standing straighter and using my formal voice, I say, "Thank you all for being part of this team. You are brave to stand for our guild in a human council, one which rules the world of men. I have a few instructions.

"Our primary goal is to make allies to help us defeat Baratium. If not allies, then friends. I need your best. If someone offends you, I'll correct the situation. Please don't take matters into your own hands. Do your best not to give offense in return. There will be some men who will undoubtedly look to cause trouble. Do not let them do it."

I look at each of the gargoyles, emphasizing my point.

I continue, "If you receive information pertinent to the business of disposing of our enemy and his horde, give it to Mega or one of the Elites as quickly as possible. Please, do not sit on it, no matter how insignificant. Mega is point on any issue regarding Baratium."

Mega nods his concurrence.

"Our secondary goal is to reintroduce our people into regular everyday society. The Earth is as much ours as it is theirs. I intend to have us live with humans in harmony. We will no longer live in secret and shame. Kino will take point on this. Direct any questions to him."

As with Mega, Kino nods approvingly.

"During the talks, I speak for the Ceorfan. In meetings where I'm present, only speak when I give you the floor. Most of you are coming on this trip to make friends. Let's help the humans learn to be comfortable with us, as they once were. Thank you for your assistance in reaching our goals."

I watch Jared strolls up to our group of travelers. He stops beside me. I think that is everyone.

I ask, "Jericho, are we ready to travel to our destination?"

"Yes, my queen we are." He removes a smooth rock resembling a big blue sapphire from the sleeve of his cloak and mumbles something. A portal opens in front of us.

Mega orders Mica through first. Before I follow, I see not only Jared guarding me, as he always does, even though the Elites are here. I recognize Eltira has also noticed. The scowl screwing up her lovely face says she isn't happy about the fact.

Mica enters the portal, turns, and extends a hand to me. I take it, and he draws me to him through the portal. Here we go. I'm kinda scared. It's not bad though it's a good excited feeling of adventure.

Mica stops once we are through the passageway. He holds my hand still on his arm.

I gape and the countryside. I'd bet there are tons of books describing this magnificent land we just entered. It is beautiful! In the darkness, I can still see rolling hills surrounding us. Up against a huge cliff is a sensational old castle. In the moonlight, it looks ominous.

From this distance, I can't see a single gargoyle. Maybe there aren't any—maybe out of respect for our troop? We'd been told that if any of the Ceorfan torpefy outside or on the castle, no one will make anything of it. Most humans will think my Guild are part of the castle's art and history.

"This is where we're meeting?" I ask Mega.

"Yes, it is, Edling."

I'm so happy he used the old endearment instead of calling me queen again. I don't want to be above the Ceorfan. I want to be a part of them. I'll find out if that's possible soon.

"Let's see how they welcome us, shall we?"

We pass through the open portcullis and into the courtyard, or bailey. The doors of the keep are lit with ancient ironwork lamps. The doors themselves are an imposing thirteen or so feet high and made of iron and wood. I'd like to stand here a while and enjoy the beauty of the architecture around me, but the doors open.

A tall man I would estimate to be in his fifties stands before us.

"You are welcome to Fiatril Hall. My name is Thurston. I'm the steward of the castle. Please come in. Let me show you to your quarters. Have you eaten yet?"

"Thank you, Thurston. I'm Queen Kendra of the Ceorfan Guild. We will be happy to go with you to find our rooms. We haven't eaten. Do you have a meal prepared, or are we ordering out?"

Thurston smiles at me and returns, "You Magesty, Queen Kendra, I believe we are going to get along swimmingly. Follow me, please. I intend to take care of you personally."

Thurston takes us to our rooms, putting me in an opulent and surprisingly up-to-date suit of five rooms with a large patio. He explains, one room—the largest and most girlie—is for me. Then there is one for my personal assistant, one for my bodyguard, a lounge area and a small kitchenette.

"Thank you, Thurston. When can I expect to see the council?"

"I'll return in a half hour to collect you for your breakfast. After that, I'm told you will be taken to the great hall to begin your meetings. You will receive your itinerary then. If not, tell me, I'll have one made for you. I'll see you in just a few minutes."

Then he leaves to show the others to their rooms.

Mega tele-speaks to me.

He says, *I am assigning Kino as your personal assistant, Mica as your bodyguard, and Spar as your escort.*

I hear a commotion in the hallway. On my way to check it out, my retinue fall in directly behind me.

I open the door to see Eltira pushing her father away from her screaming, "I will not stay in that closet! I shall find Kino and sojourn with him!"

They notice us watching. Immediately, they cease their commotion and face us chagrined. There must be steam coming from the top of my head. Their looks change to dread. How dare she make a scene. I don't want her around Kino.

What am I thinking? Kino can do as he pleases. I have no rights where he's concerned. Why would I even go there?

As I stand there arguing with myself, Kino comes forward and states, "Eltira, you have your room. I am staying with the queen in her suite."

The look on her face is priceless. I can't help it. I feel happy. Even if he forgot the part about having his own room.

I save him right back and step forward.

I grate, "I'll ask Jericho to provide a way home for you if you give me any trivial reason. Additionally, if you find the room is inadequate to your needs, I'll happily call him this instant, so you may return to Navan without delay."

She chuffs before turning on one foot and returns to her own room. Her father apologizes before following her.

I face the floor to hide my uncontrolled smile. I move back into our suite, so the others can't read my face. I enjoyed this whole situation more than I should've.

I need to appear queenly, so I go change for breakfast. Amber had my business suit copied in multiple forms. Now, I have enough clothes to last several weeks. God help me, I think I like this. I pick out a red suit with a cream-colored silk blouse. My nude pumps will do fine with this. I want to make a powerful first impression. I decide to improve my telepathy skill with Mega, asking if he knows where the little Elite is. I need help with my hair.

Oh yes! The tele-channel with Mega works fine.

He answers me, *"She is on her way now."*

The men are lounging in the living area outside my room. They're dressed in formal business suits. Oh my, they're a handsome bunch. But maybe I'm partial. I try to think as a stranger would... and, no. They're still handsome. I can't imagine anyone thinking anything else.

Knock, knock.

Spar opens the door to Jericho and Amber. After they come in I ask, "Amber, would you mind helping me with my hair?"

"No, it will be my privilege."

It might have taken her ten whole minutes to make my hair look amazingly queenly. I put on my shoes, and another knock, knock.

Spar again opens the door. This time it's Thurston coming to get us for breakfast. His blueness returns to me and offers me his great gargoyle arm. I take it, feeling special. I simper, intent on following Thurston.

Jericho holds up a hand and says, "My queen, one moment, if you please. I have glamor stones for the gargoyles. Do you wish for them to use them? They have always been glamoured to fit in here. We have been told in the past that it was more palatable for the humans if they didn't have to bear our differing forms."

"Well, my dear Mage Jericho, thank you for the information. I believe it isn't necessary to carry a glamor here. TASS knows our true identities. Let them truly know us."

Thurston hides a grin, then takes us across the castle to a large dining hall. It's decorated in Tudor meets goth, but nice. Very nice.

This room has exposed beams, open fire places, chandeliers, and rugs. The rugs on the floor are Persian. I don't know about the tapestries on the walls. Some of them are more than twenty feet high and tens of feet wide. They hang, somewhat precariously, on large bolts sticking out of the wall every foot or so. These rugs show scenes of the castle in various historic battles.

Large tables are in several places through the hall. There's still a large area which I can only suppose is used for dancing. I could stay here all day, soaking up this history. Everything has been updated and modernized. Yet, the castle still maintains its ancient beauty.

A man in a blue wool suit that fits him like a glove has his eyes on me and he's slowly, almost suggestively, walking my way. He's one who makes the suit, not the other way around. Tall, dark, and young is not what I was expecting. I'm glad Amber saw to my wardrobe. Even a real queen could feel frumpy in his company.

The stranger reaches for my hand, bends, and kisses it. I feel the Ceorfan stiffen. Funny, that's new—I can sense each of them. I can discern their emotions. I can only communicate with Mega, but I like knowing I can feel my... my what? 'My people' falls short of what is in my heart for these men.

Jared comes forward and says. "Glen Hughes? As I live and breathe... get your lecherous hand off my sister!"

He's chuckling, reaching to pat the man on the back. Before Jared can touch his shoulder, the man grabs him up in a fierce hug. I feel the Guild prepare... for what?

"My queen, this is my old friend from college, Glen Hughes. Glen this is my sister, Kendra, the queen of the Ceorfan Guild. You possibly already know, but it is correct to call her, Your Majesty. Usually, you must ask to touch her. You'll be forgiven the breach in protocol if you'll show us to our places and instruct us on how to get some of the delicacies this castle has to offer."

"Don't listen to him. He's teasing you—well, mostly," I say, taking his hand, so he can lead me to a seat around the table.

He seats me and sits next to me. A waiter promptly provides us a rundown of the breakfast offerings. Glen tells us they knew our schedule was reversed to their own, and they changed the menus to accommodate us. The waiter surreptitiously takes each order and disappears.

Seconds later, the hounds—I mean bitches—descend. A willowy blonde sits close to Mica and places a hand on his shoulder, turning her upper body to face him. A redhead slides so close to Jared, she may be partially on his lap. A brunette, with the greenest eyes I've ever seen, pushes her boobs right onto Spar. I mean, each of these women look to have known these three for months. This is not going to work for me. Well, except for Jared. He's always had a thing for redheads. Even so, for Spar and Mica, I feel rage starting its burn.

Mega tele-comms me, *"Edling, do not let the anger show on your face. They are testing you. They know we often have many mates. They think you, as a queen, have all of us as consorts. If they can cause you to make a scene, they believe they will have just cause to excuse us from these talks."*

I take a deep cleansing breath and say out loud, "Oh, my, will you look at that? I didn't know it was that kind of party."

I laugh and resume my conversation.

I can feel Mega's approval.

He tells me silently, *"Mica and Spar have successfully backed the women off."*

I wonder how?

The breakfast is superb. Different, but fine. I love tomatoes, so that was great, black pudding was on my plate, too. It was good, but I didn't ask what was in it. We Macbards have a rule about food: just taste it. If you don't like it, at least you tried it. I found over the years if I don't know how something is made, I can usually eat it a lot easier.

We finish eating and gather for the meeting.

19

MEETING

Kendra

Glen Hughes is an interesting fellow. I already knew he was a good friend of Jared's, and make a mental note to ask Jared about what 'good friend' means. As a Park Ranger, observation has become second nature. In this meeting, I know I'll need to employ as many of those skills as possible.

When Glen guided me to my seat, I could tell he was six feet tall, maybe, an inch more. His eyes, wow. They're reminiscent of the ice-blue water flowing off a glacier, and are eyes I would love to get lost in. His chiseled jaw could cut your lips, if you happened to be kissing his neck. Not that I wanted to. Well, maybe a little. He also seemed to be fun and flirtatious, almost to the point of being a Casanova. However, when the 'distraction ladies' plopped their boobs down next to Mica, Spar, and Jared, the look he gave the maître d' was not one I would have wanted to be on the other side of.

While eating our breakfast, I had the opportunity to learn about his professional background. He explained he was one of three people in the U.K. involved in TASS. He is prior SAS. Apparently, he was part of the 21st Regiment, called the Artists Rifles. I guess it's exactly what it sounds like. In 1859 it was originally made up of artists, poets, musicians, actors, and other imaginative people.

It's at this point that Mega tele-speaks, "Ask him about the Increment, or Group 13."

I ask, as I lay my hand on his rock-hard forearm and pushing as much sincerity into my words as I can, "I know you are a member of TASS."

"Yes."

"Well, I'd like to know more about you and the deeper aspects of what you do."

I pause for a heartbeat and got lost for a blink in those eyes. "Will you tell me about the Increment, or Group 13?"

I could have said, "Tell me about the color of grass," for all the impact it had on his expression. Not a single twitch of a muscle on his face. This guy must be a master in the poker room.

Our eyes lock. We gauge each other, in a rather bold manner for having only just met. His eyes search my soul. Me, I get lost in his them again. But the pregnant pause has now turned into an elephant pause and is verging on the uncomfortable.

I know I must keep my poise. Don't lose eye contact. Don't give any hint of a problem. If I misjudge this, even a little bit, this conversation will turn cold and professional, and after the meeting, we will never speak again. I will then lose a potentially powerful resource for the Ceorfan.

"Well, Kendra, both of those organizations are considered confidential."

"But," I say, drawing the word into a couple of syllables

"TASS is, too, isn't it," he finishes, with the wryest of smiles.

Then he adds, "I'm sure you have what it takes to persuade me to open up a little more. Let's get through what we need to, then there may be enough time to talk more, at length."

He escorts us to the large meeting hall. It feels like most government rooms—pretentious. There are few decorations, and those are red and black. The front of the room is dominated by a raised dais.

It's striking and seems to be reminiscent of a judge's bench, but more pontifical. The church-like feel, while not overwhelming, can't be denied. The base of the dais is decorated with scenes from Macbeth. The two pillars anchoring each side of it appear to be decorated with scenes from the struggle for Scottish independence. One pillar is dedicated to Robert the Bruce's victory at the Battle of Bannockburn, where the Scots routed the forces of Edward II of England near Stirling Castle.

The dais, walls, and ceiling, as well as the roof supports, are made of rich woods. I'm not sure what kinds of wood are used. If it was mesquite, I'd know. The wood has the feel of old, but not out of date. Even the seating is made of wood. It may be torture if we're to sit here for the next several hours. Not looking forward to that, thank you very much.

"Pardon, Kendra?" Mr. Hughes asks, as he pauses briefly.

"Oh, nothing."

He continues to lead us to our seating area, then left to do, no sure what but other Glen stuff, I suppose.

The seats are pleasantly comfortable. They are padded with lush red fabric, perfectly matching the rest of the red in the room. I sink into my seat and lean back in a most un-queenly manner to take in the wonder of the rest of this great hall.

Dracula has nothing on these people in the decor area. The blood red of the decorations is toned down by the ancient, black iron work throughout. The iron lighting is modern, but still manages to add to the old-castle charm of the room.

After the last of our group file in and sit, I check-in telepathically with Mega, seated to my left.

"Are we all here, Mega?"

"Yes, Edling, we are all here except for Eltira. As you may know after her tirade at our arrival, she and Kino are no longer together. She is looking for a suitor in the human contingent. This means Kino is alone for the first time in a long time.

I surreptitiously search to Mega's left for Kino.

I find him sitting next to his commanding officer, as stoic as always.

"*Mega, what is your title, and what do you want me to call you?*"

"*I am the Commander of the Elite Warriors Guard, as you correctly called me earlier. In formal settings, you should call me Commander. If you prefer the less formal, Mega. I will answer either way you decide. You also may, if you will, change our titles as you see fit. My small team of specialists are called the Ducere. I trust my life with them. They have demonstrated both loyalty and bravery, many times over. You may consider us the gargoyle special forces.*"

Mega is continually ensuring I know I'm in charge and have the power to do as I wish.

I respond to him, "*Oh, new titles... that might be interesting. For now, 'Commander' it is. Although you are Ceorfan family, I'll call you my in-law, too because Spar is my gargoyle. Is there a title for the queen's lover?*"

"*Consort, just like in the human world. We are more like the English version of titles than any other country or group. A simplified version, though. I guess the titles were shared the same way we once shared the Earth. When the consorts are recognized publicly, they are acknowledged as a Prince.*"

I wonder what is taking so long for the meeting to start. I look to my right and Spar is looking back at me.

I let my eyes wander and notice a pale-blue banner directly behind us. Large block type spells out, 'The Ceorfan Guild' in big black letters across it. No other country seems to have a banner with their name on it. They do have electronic numbers on the table in front of them. I wonder why that is.

I touch Findare, seated in front of me, on the shoulder and lean forward secretively.

"Fin, what is the flag of the Ceorfan? Evidently, they know our people have been to these meetings before, correct?"

"Yes, my queen, I have been here a few times. We once had a flag, or banderuola, as we call it. When our last queen fell, we decided that in her honor we would not have another flag until our new queen took her throne."

"Do you know someone who can design one for us?"

"I believe Kino and his family have been involved in the process before. In Navan, we have others talented in design and still others gifted in crafting material. These Ceorfan will make it to your exact specifications. I will ask Jericho to take Kino back to Navan to oversee the process when we leave here, if you agree."

"Yes, that's perfect. I'll speak with Kino before he leaves. Fin, I've also noticed we've been placed several rows away from any of the other participants in this meeting. We're seated in the proverbial corner. Can you tell me, if you know, why that might be? Should I take offense?"

"My queen, many humans still have many fears concerning our kind. They do not want us here. We are little more than animals to them. However, they know we can be a great asset as well. They know that in you, we have a great advantage, and they are willing to do as they see fit. Know this, they will go to any length to secure that advantage. Some, you will see, are so averse to our kind, they will not touch us and will go to great lengths to avoid us. They also believe our kind has caused the problem, so we should be the ones who clean it up." He just finishes whispering to me as a much older gentleman walks to the lectern.

I feel sorry for the older man. He is bent from age, and slow to climb the few stairs to the dais. As he takes the mic, he surveys the room's inhabitants. I think, Well as I live and breathe, it's Scrooge in the flesh. Kendra! Stop that. That's not how we think of people! Grow up.

He begins the meeting by introducing himself as the Chairman of The Alumbradai Sanctuary State. He looks in my direction. Is that a sneer on his face?

His voice is weak and shaking from age, he asks, "Will each member please introduce yourself to the new, eehhmm, queen of the

Ceorfan and contingent. I'll begin. My name is Jose Brinker, Chair of TASS.

As if bored by the process from its outset, each member stands and turns to me, introducing themselves. Some look at me with a genuine smile, many don't bother to even look in my direction. After the room has completed their introductions, the Chairman asks me to introduce myself.

I stand, taking my time to look graceful. Squaring my shoulders and using my most commanding voice, I say, "I am Kendra Macbard, Queen of the Ceorfan Guild."

I make eye contact with each of the 50 members while I'm speaking.

"I am here to represent my people in this meeting. I come with my Elite Warriors Guard, as well as a few of my most senior council members. If you would like to meet us personally, I'm sure lunch will be a wonderful time for introductions. I along with my staff, fully intend to assist with the development and implementation of a plan which will lead to our victory and the total annihilation of our common enemies. I have also noted the Ceorfan Guild does not have a permanent representative in TASS. I would like you to include my brother, Jared Macbard, as my representative in this membership."

As I say this, in the most genteel manner I can muster, I slowly raise my right arm and, using my whole hand, direct it toward Jared.

I risk a quick glance at Jared to see if he is upset with me for giving him a job he may not have wanted. One which I haven't asked him about. He flashes me the slightest of grins, one that only the two of us can share because we know each other so well. I relax. I know we'll have to talk later about me volunteering him. But in this setting, he's going to go with the flow. Yep, if I need to fly by the seat of my pants, then so do the rest of the Guild.

The collective intake of breath is an indicator of the shock I just delivered. They don't have the nerve to turn me down... do they? They've gone to great lengths to get us here. They've even set the meetings around our schedule. Without another word, I return to my seat.

Glen Hughes pipes up, "I'd like to make a motion."

"The Chair recognizes member number three-zero-three."

"I move that we increase the number of members in TASS from fifty to fifty-one, and I hereby nominate Jared Macbard as the TASS representative from the Ceorfan Guild."

"Member one-zero-five seconds."

"We have a motion and a second. Discussion?"

The Chair looks around the room. Someone screams, "Hell no, throw her out!"

Others mumble support.

"Hearing no discussion, all in favor respond with 'aye'."

A cheery chorus of "Aye's" follows.

The Chair says, "All opposed respond with 'nay'."

A volley of "Nay's" echoes, some screamed and repeated—but certainly far fewer than those in the affirmative.

The Chair interrupts, "All those who abstain, please stand."

The Chair, Mr. Brinker, looks around the room and, after seeing no one standing, he gavels.

"The motions carries. Clerk, please ensure Mr. Jared Macbard has the proper credentials by the close of this meeting."

I can't tell if he's happy or upset. His face is simply a permanent grimace. He continues with some small subject that I completely miss as I revel in my small victory.

Mr. Brinker's voice gains some gravitas as he begins a new portion of the agenda. "Do we continue to allow larger countries to sanction smaller countries in an effort to stop behavior we deem not for the greater good?"

The Chair states, "Discussion? Seeing none, all in favor respond with 'aye'."

Most of the members respond with, "Aye."

The Chair comments, "All of those opposed, respond with 'nay'."

I hear a few of members get out the "N's" as the Chair dropped his gavel with, "The ayes have it."

Clearly, not following the standard rules of order, I note.

The Chair adds, "Moving on to the matter at hand.

"Queen Kendra, a few hours ago, a small village in Mexico was attacked and destroyed by the Horde of Baratium. Will you please give us an assessment of the capabilities you and the Ceorfan have to help us win this war? Also, we have not had the pleasure of addressing the Ceorfan Queen before. Will you let us know what you, personally, are willing to do to help us?"

I answer, "Chairman, I have only a few thousand people in total. I do, however, have some of the most talented warriors on the face of the Earth. I can support—"

I hear Mega giving me the details and repeat what he is telling me, "—this council with three teams of specialized soldiers, including black ops intelligence officers. I don't have access to the type of intelligence apparatus which you have. I need detailed intelligence concerning the enemy. We will need as much information as you are willing to share. I ask that you work with my General, Megahir, to plan a strategy. If you do, we can be well on our way to securing victory. We will brief your commanders and start implementing plans as I've laid out."

A middle-aged, olive-skinned man shoots to his feet, shouting, "You do not give orders here. You and your pack of freak-show animals are here to listen, and we decide how to use you and your soldiers. So, shut up and sit down you wretched woman! I will give the orders to your pathetic group of shit!"

The volume in the room is turned up a few notches as the other members begin discussing the outburst, maybe even choosing sides. Almost as a reflex I think, If they are choosing sides, I need to give them a reason to choose mine.

I turn on him before the Chairman can say anything.

As I speak, I push my will throughout the room, forcing it into every crevice, "You, sir, are out of line," I said, trying to maintain the formal tone I had set earlier. I can't let them get under my skin.

I continue, "We don't need you. You need my warriors and me. The Ceorfan have fought and defeated this mage before. You, with your high-minded superiority and high school behavior have only watched as Baratium has destroyed whole villages and towns. We wish to assist you in ending this scourge, once and for all. We will do so in the name of helping all humanity, even those like you who have an irrational hatred for us. No matter the names you call us we will fight and, if needed, die to protect the population of the earth. In return, we only require that we no longer live in the shadows. We must become full members of society."

The volume in the room is much higher now, and still growing.

I need to quickly reach the conclusion of my little speech. "Sir, before you offend the wrong party, I suggest you sit and possibly have one of these other fine people teach you a little about diplomacy. Nonetheless, no matter what names you call us, we'll protect the population of Earth."

The volume is at full now; sides are solidifying. I can't tell if my remarks have opened more doors than they have closed or not.

The Chairman continues hammering his gavel and shouting for order. The belligerent man is being held back by his delegation as the Chairman releases the council to reconvene after lunch.

***

THE CEORFAN GATHER to my suite to discuss what occurred in the council meeting. I notice Eltira isn't with her father.

"Maybe you should let me take over, my lady," the good Count relates, "some of the members do not want to hear from a woman."

"No, they get me. Thank you for the thought, but they get me. We have already made headway with them accepting Jared as my representative. Jared, I'm sorry, I just volunteered you without an overture to you."

My tone is still formal from the meeting.

"Edling,you handled that situation quite well," Mega interjected.

"Thank you," I repy.

"I would also like to add, if I may steal one of your phrases, that 'gentleman,'" over-stressing the last word, "is a real dip shidiot!"

everyone laughs.

"Thanks, Mega, I needed that."

"Sis, at first I was going to ask if you would choose someone else. For now, I think I'm the best option. I accept your appointment. I think I'm going to like this appointment. Hell, it also gives me a chance to take some upfront and personal care of a few of my European companies."

He finishes with a bow.

I decided on a course of action regarding our seating, while in the meeting earlier, and now is the time to let everyone else in on it.

"When we go back into the meeting, I want you all to follow my lead. We aren't going to sit in the corner anymore. Kino, I need a flag. I understand you might be able to help with that—what do you think? How fast can we get one made?"

"Edling, I have been planning a design for you for as long as I have known you. I have several sketches completed already. When we finish here, I will show you the sketches I have. Then you can tell me what your ideas are. You have a royal designer. It will only take him a few minutes to transform raw goods into materials. Any design you choose is possible. Quickly. I will ask Jericho if he will supply a portal stone or take me to Navan to see the designer. I could fly home, but that would take days."

"Awesome! That makes me happy. I need it hung in the meeting room ASAP. Spar, please find someone to help you hang it and remove the current banner by tomorrow night's meeting. If we aren't going to be equal with the other members in number of citizens, at least we'll have flair. I'll also do my best to make some friends at lunch.

"Mega, what is your take on the TASS members?"

"You have most of them eating out of your hand, Edling. Most were impressed. Others hated you before you spoke. I now believe you are correct. Persuasion is a gift you control. Even the chairman was taken with you. There are a few who resent us being here. They will never want the Ceorfan here and may cause trouble. I want you to have a guard with you at all times. The feelings of hatred in the room began to show depth after your speech. Both jealousy and fear were very present with the hate. Edling, remember, all three of these, regarding us, have an irrational basis. They fear us from a place they never saw. We were there. We know how the humans learned to hate us."

Mica speaks, and it startles me a bit. He has been in the background, focusing on my safety so I'm not prepared when his deep voice booms out, "If you do have the gift of persuasion, my queen, and it's anything like I have seen of old, gazing into the eyes of the one you want to persuade will help. You should know, though, there are those who can resist it. I'm not sure how it'll work. Let's test it and see. Will you?"

"Sure."

I turn to Flint, gaze into his eyes, and plead, "Will you please get me some hot chai tea?"

Without a word, Flint jumps right off to the kitchen. My eyes widen, I'm surprised.

"Now try on Jericho. He might be more resistant," Mica says.

"Okay,"

I start, but Jericho isn't looking at me. With one finger I push up gently on his chin raising his face to mine.

"Jericho, will you make me a portal stone?"

Immediately, he responds, "Here it is, my queen. I have this one in my pocket, just for you."

He snaps out of his trancelike state when he sees the beautiful blue portal stone in the palm of my open hand.

I hold it out to him. He folds my fingers over it.

He says, "My queen, it is a gift I should have given you much sooner."

Right on cue, Flint returns with my tea.

I take it from him with a smile and say, "Thank you. Mmmm, it's very good. Flint, can I make you the royal tea getter from now on?"

Everyone laughs; Flint blushes.

"I'll get your tea, any time you wish, my queen," making the others laugh louder. On which he grumbles at them, "Shut it! While I was getting tea, my queen–"

"Kendra," I interrupt.

"Kendra," he repeats, "while I was getting tea, the chef told me to let you know lunch is being served."

"Sounds good to me. Does anyone have anything to add before we go eat? "No? Okay, let's all go make some friends. Mega, I can hear you wherever you are. Is it alright to keep Mica close to me?"

"That is most acceptable, Edling."

***

IT IS the most amazing thing to watch the Ceorfan in action. They're working this room like a used car salesman with a chance to win a trip to Hawaii. It makes me happy to see them this way. I make my way around the room with Mica. I talk to a few people and meet a few others before we sit for our lunch.

The waiter says, "The chef has prepared your lunch, Queen Kendra. Would you like it served now?"

"Oh, yes, please. I'm hungry."

The waiter returns with a dish of salmon and something called neeps and tatties. I eat it all, surprising myself.

"That was good. I've got to tell the chef how much I enjoyed it. Do you mind?" I ask the waiter.

"Let me bring him to you, Queen Kendra."

The room quiets some as the chef makes his way to me.

Not knowing how to properly thank him as the Ceorfan Queen, I say, "I've not eaten so well in such a long time. I thoroughly enjoyed my food, I wanted to make sure to tell you, face to face. I almost licked my plate."

I add a gentle giggle. I push a bit of my persuasion gift to set the compliment firmly in his mind.

He beams. Then he takes my hand, after verifying with a questioning look to Mica.

"I am Chef Ron. It's my honor and privilege to cook for you, Queen Kendra. May I say, the stories of your gratitude are only outdone by those of your beauty. I'll happily pass along that both are true. Whatever you wish to be served, please only ask. It will be my pleasure. I'll provide you an epicurean adventure during your stay."

I grin and thank him.

I'm about to devour a just delivered chocolate dessert, when I notice Eltira talking to the olive-skinned man who had yelled at me earlier. Good. Maybe he'll like her better than he likes me or the others. I nod my head in her direction, then glance at Mica. He takes the hint, looking where I nodded. We agree she has captured the man's attention. We both eat the most decadent chocolate dessert I have ever had the pleasure of tasting.

My stomach is full, I'm ready to take on a bear. Time to wash up and head back to the meeting. I have about 30 minutes left when I enter our suite of rooms. Just inside the entry, on the floor, I find a note. Someone must have slipped it under the door. The note is written in cursive and has this warning,

"BE CAREFUL WHEN YOU SLEEP.

Hammers are cheap."

. . .

ANGER FLARES, as I read the note.

"Just try me, asshole!"

We've taken measures for our safety. Mica and I will stay awake in shifts to guard the others. In fact, now that Jared is staying on in a more permanent basis, he can also be part of the watch rotation. I hadn't considered that others might think I torpify the same as the gargoyles. I hand the note to Mega.

Amber comes forward and sniffs the note.

"It smells like cinnamon. I will see if I can find who wrote it, but it's a long shot."

"That's a good idea. Let me know if you find anything," I reply.

I take a minute to get control of my thoughts. This is going to take me a while, and I only have minutes before I have to be back in a meeting. I'll consider more options for recourse later with my advisors. What I can do is pick one of Kino's flag designs. At least, if TASS is treating us differently we'll have class.

"Kino, let's look at your sketches before the meeting reconvenes. Shall we?"

His room is just like most rooms in a luxury hotel. What's somewhat unique to Kino is that nothing is out of place. He's very neat. Sitting on his nightstand is a beautiful wooden box. It's made from burl wood, and darkly stained. There is a sizable lock on it as well. He takes a key from his pocket and opens the box. He pulls out a book filled with sketches. We sit on the bed and review the relevant ones. His work is amazing! I stop on one I like—a red dragon with wings extended, stalagmites in the foreground. Gold shoots through the picture like sun rays on a solid black background. There are four stones above the dragon's head: blue, green, red, and purple.

"Tell me about this one, will you, Kino?"

"It is black, because we are creatures of the night. The red is for you, Kendra, you are a red dragon. The gold is your gifts to the Ceorfan Guild. The stones above you are representations of power.

Power, I have faith, you will control. They represent Water, Earth, Fire, and Magic."

"I love it. Do you mind going now to get the designer to make it before the meeting tomorrow? You might have to torp in Navan. If you can get back tonight, make sure I know, will you? With the threat to our people, I want to make sure I know you're safe."

I keep turning pages in his sketchbook as I'm talking and come to a picture of a beautiful, nearly nude woman relaxing by a pool of blue water. The pool is constructed of white marble with marble columns. The view to the water is protected by vines and bushes. The lady has a towel arranged across her lap, protecting that part of her womanhood. Looking closer...

Kino takes the book gently from me and closes it. Too late, I've already figured out the sketch is of me. He lifts me to my feet, he holds onto me.

"When this is over, and you have time to have a life, will you consider my suit?" he asks, glancing at the floor.

What is it with these gargoyles? They're terrific examples of male magnificence that any woman should want, and he's acting like I might turn him down.

I wait until he raises his eyes, my heart thumping uncontrollably.

"That would make me happy, Kino. Give me time to tell Spar and Mica. You understand they're also my consorts?"

"I do," he says, the excitement evident on his face.

I lean into him and stretch up on my tippy toes, as tall as I can. Even though I'm a tall girl, he still needs to bend, so I can kiss him lightly on his perfect mouth. He doesn't pressure me, letting me set the tone. I back away from him. I can tell he's happy.

I say, "You had better get going, so you can get back to me."

He nods and backs up running into the dresser. Taking out a portal stone of his own he disappears into the opening.

I wonder what the limit is on consorts? I better have a conversation with the others, just to be sure I'm not going to mess this up.

How can I want them all? The way I feel about each one of them is so different.

"Time to go, Kendra," I hear from the doorway.

Mica is waiting for me there. I can tell he knows. I take his arm as he leads me into the hallway toward Spar.

"I need to speak to you both before sunrise. If that's okay with you?"

"It is okay with us, Kendra. Don't worry, we love you. It's our way. You'll get more comfortable as time goes by, and you're able to learn more about our people. I'll always love you. We'll all be happy together. If we have problems, we'll work them out."

I should have known he'd have everything figured out. He already knows me so well.

20

NUMBERS

Kendra

Entering the meeting hall, I remembered an area in front which had previously been unoccupied. I make my way there and motion for the others to sit with me.

Mega tele-speaks to me, "I have placed Mason and Amber in the back of the room to guard our backs."

I say, "Thank you."

This time when the chairman takes the stand his sour old face turns to surprise as he notices I've moved the Ceorfan to the front. He says nothing. I say nothing. Now, it's just the way the world will turn. The room knows we'd been slighted. They wondered how I would react. Now they know. I won't put up with it. I might as well set the tone from here on out. I'm not the roll over and play dead type.

Staring at the chairman and not diverting my eyes from him, I ask Mega, "Do you know where Eltira has gotten to?"

"I believe she is with the dark man who challenged you earlier. Do you want me to find her?"

I say, "I don't like the idea of her taking liberties with a member of TASS. I think it'll cause problems, but let's not rock the boat right now. As soon as she's back to her father, send her home. She will have to prove herself to ever be included on a trip with me again."

"I understand. I will see if I can mind-speak to her."

I notice Mega is concentrating. It lasts several minutes when he stops.

"Eltira has a gift that can prevent me from speaking to her. Not only can she protect her mind from communication, she can even prevent anyone from reading her feelings. We had not thought it a useful gift until now. I believe she can stay hidden from me until she decides otherwise."

By the end of the meeting we had set a tentative schedule for each of the planning stages involved to catch what TASS is calling the Horde of Barat. The first meeting would involve only the intelligence parties. It would be held after dinner and until the Ceorfan depart to sleep.

This meeting is long and boring, but necessary. The council assigns tasks to various members. Each task is voted on electronically then it has to be accepted by the member or members who will perform the task.

The Chair stands to release the members. He clears his throat before speaking. "I want to thank Elite Warriors Guard for being a part of these meetings. We try, in most cases, to eliminate the need to call each member group by their country name. Our goal is to stand as a unified world body. In your case, we have not stuck to our charter very well, and I would like to apologize for that and ask for your patience and understanding. We are assigned numbers. If you will push the button on the screen in front of you, you will produce a random number. Or, if you would like, you can choose your own, if it is not already in use."

Reaching out I push the button on the screen. It stops on 505.

The members clap, then the Chair says, "The dinner bell will be ringing in about twenty minutes. Your butlers will collect you from your rooms at that time. The groups numbering 1, 40, 72, and 505 will meet in the library at 4:00 a.m. Meeting adjourned."

Crack, his gavel hits the wood on the desk where he is sitting.

On the way out of the hall, I manage to look down and see Mason. He's so still, he looked like a statue. So cute! So beautiful! I could feel he's concentrating on what is going on. No wonder he and Amber can infiltrate so easily; I almost didn't even notice him.

Getting to my room to change for dinner is a chore. I have only a few minutes to get ready. Good thing Amber followed me here to help again. She has my clothes laid out. I guess this is a little more formal, just by observing the dress. She helps me slip into the form-fitting black evening gown, turns me, and zips up the back. Well, what there is of the back. It's low-cut, with pleated draping in the front. The neckline is scoop-shaped, showing off my mother's necklace beautifully. She sits me down and starts on my hair. She combs it lifting one side then clipping it with a graceful red dragon clip. It must have cost a fortune.

"Where did this come from, Amber?"

"I hope you don't mind. I gathered it and a few other things from your vault."

"I have a vault?"

"Uh huh, dragon..," as if that were the only explanation I would need.

I titter at her. "I love it, thank you. Thank you for helping me dress and making sure I look like a queen. I've never been able to spoil myself. I kinda like it. I wouldn't know what to do if you weren't here to help me, though."

"We are family. It makes me happy when you are happy, Kendra."

When she sees my eyes glisten from unshed tears, she adds, "Get up and put on your heels."

She hands me some slim, glittery black heels. Thank goodness, they aren't that tall.

"You look amazing, and all in five minutes flat. Let's go see your consorts."

"What? Who told?"

"You! You can't fool a gargoyle, Edling."

We walk into the living area and Kino is already back. Oooh, he gives me shivers. He, Mica, and Spar are standing together talking. I secretly hope it's about me. They look so nice in formal wear. I know it's not fun for men to dress up sometimes, but damn, they look sexy!

They turn as one. My face heats up when I see they're feeling the same about me. Thurston is at the door, waiting for us. Spar holds his arm for me. I take it, making sure to rub it across as much of me as I can.

Okay, cocktails first in the waiting area. It looks like a ballroom. My preparation guide told me this is where the real politics are orchestrated. We make our way to as many of the members as possible, trying to appear friendly.

I feel like I'm on repeat.

"The Ceorfan are not violent and protection is in our DNA."

Each restatement is pushed with as much of my belief as I have. Later, I'm hoping, when enough of them believe me, we can vote the Ceorfan reintegration into regular society into law. Some of them have already gone to bed, but we were still able to influence quite a few.

Dinner is as wonderful as lunch. This time the waiter doesn't even pretend to ask me what I'd like from a list of choices. He just brings my plate. If I continue to eat like this, I'm going to need dieting advice.

I tell my waiter, "You're wonderful, and can I keep you?"

He's taking pains to care for my people and me. I also ask him if he will hug Chef Ron for me, as he has, once again, outdone himself. I'm pleased.

21

DECISIONS

Kendra

WHEN WE GET BACK in the common area of our suite I say, "I need to speak with Mega. I'll be out after I change."

I put on comfortable clothes for when I need to stand guard over the torpified Ceorfan, ones that will be loose enough to take a short nap in when Jared takes over his shift.

For now, I need to meet with Mega. I find him waiting for me on the patio.

I say, "Mega, have you found our absent miscreant?"

"We have found Eltira. She has been with the olive-skinned man the entire time. She told me she wishes to leave with him and start a life with him. I must admit, I am at a loss of what to do."

I pause for a moment, reflecting on the bigger picture, and say, "Well, we do want to live in the open. If Eltira begins a new life with him, that's part of what we want. Tell me about Eltira's background. I know it's different from most of the Ceorfan. I'd like to understand her."

Mega, looking solemn and as if this past was part of the troubled times the Ceorfan have faced, says, "The Countess could not have children when she was alive and young. She begged the Count for a child. When they found the young woman, who would become Eltira, she was nearing her last breath. Conveniently, they found a wandering mage nearby to inquire if she would consent to be their daughter and to explain the Resurgere to her. She agreed. However, the Queen, fearing something of which she never spoke, denied the Resurgere request from Count. Edling, it is important to understand that all mages are not like Jericho.

" Many mages during that time were not affiliated with any magical order. They were usually not trustworthy, and many fought against us. I believe the Queen feared something in the Resurgere process would endanger the Ceorfan. Nevertheless, and despite the Queen's edict, the Count requested the mage complete the Resurgere. Accordingly, the old wizard carved out a piece of the Count to make Eltira his daughter, and a carved gargoyle. We know Eltira has always been hard to handle. She is willful, and cares more for herself than others. Even when the Countess died, Eltira hardly noticed she was gone.

"It is rare for a gargoyle to behave this way. I believe the mage may have intentionally made her hard-hearted and obstinate, thinking she would help him by betraying the Ceorfan."

"Where is she now?"

"I still cannot feel her. She is blocking me from her mind."

"Okay, give me some time to think about it. I'll come up with something. In the meantime, don't push her away. Let her believe she'll get her way. Let's not shame or embarrass the Count, either. Right now, I need some rest. I need to stay awake for guard duty while our team is torpified. Mega, when you enter the strategy meeting, be careful. Don't give away much about our capabilities, just give them enough to finish the job of destroying the Horde. Volunteer for the jobs we need to complete and tell them you'll report any results."

"Yes, my queen, I will do that. I will see you soon."

He leaves, and I motion for Spar to join me on the patio. The rest of my Guard, recognizing I want some privacy, slip away, leaving my sweetheart and I alone.

"Spar, tell me the truth, can you handle me having Mica and Kino as consorts and as part of our relationship? I know it's the Ceorfan way, but I won't do it if you say no."

"Kendra, my love, my life. Please, let me explain my feelings. I love you no matter what you choose. I've been reading about our people for a while. Never has a Carved had children. I know you want them someday. Don't make me live knowing it's my fault you'll never have them. This isn't the only reason you should choose the others as consorts. It's a very good one, though."

"I understand your reasoning. But—" I try to interrupt, unsuccessfully.

"Kendra, please honey, let me finish. The Ceorfan haven't had children since the last queen. You're queen, and it's important for you to continue your line. You've seen our suffering etched before your arrival, and the joy that followed your ascension to the throne.

"Our history is clear: Dragon Queens heal those in need and bring prosperity to the Ceorfan. So much so, that not only does the queen have children, but our people and even non-Ceorfan who are around her do, too. When the ruler has children, our people have a better chance at survival. I like the idea of knowing someone will be with you when I can't. I won't have to try to be everything you need. We three can share the load of your needs to make you the happiest woman ever. Would that be so bad?"

"I just want to be sure you won't stop loving me. I don't want you to be jealous, either. You do know that if I choose you, Mica, and Kino, you will be princes to our people?"

"Yes, honey, it'll be okay. We'll be okay."

I snuggle into his broad chest and ask him if he'll hold me until I fall asleep. The release of pent-up worry about talking to Spar about Mica and Kino has drained what little energy I had left. I fall into a deep sleep.

What feels like seconds later, My blue warrior wakes me as he moves to get off the bed.

"Kendra, you need to wake up now. The others are waiting in the living area."

"How long was I asleep?"

"Almost two hours."

"Wow. I feel better, though. Let's go to the meeting," I say, rubbing the sleep from my face. I'm glad everyone's back together.

he says, "Good you needed the rest."

We make our way into the other room where the others are waiting.

I ask, "Do you want to stay inside or be on the patio?"

Almost like a football team chant, they roar, "Patio!"

I'm just waiting for the, "Ready, break!"

"Mega, how's the security situation if everyone's on the patio?" I ask.

"We are on the first floor with a patio and long sight-lines. Torpi-fying on the patio or in this room is irrelevant to our safety. A committed team in a determined assault will take either location in the same amount of time. At least if we are on the patio, our protec-tion—You, Jared, and Mica—will be able to see all of us. If we are inside, one of you three must stay inside to guard the door, leaving two outside. All in all, I do not like the situation and will ask that we adjust tomorrow. However, we have been given no cause to worry. Consequently, I do not have any major concerns about our location."

"Outside it is then," I add.

Eltira comes in at the last minute before dawn. She does have to torp. Her smug expression doesn't faze me.

A few minutes later, my commander moves to the middle of our delegation, holding our guns and extra magazines. We take the weapons and holster them.

The sun begins to rise, Mica takes my hand, and we watch as our people torpify into their hardened state.

I recline in a chair near a wall of the castle, while my blond partner stands watch further out in the garden area. I hear voices approaching from an area that's supposed to be off-limits. When the strangers approach, Mica disappears into the brush around the garden. Quiet as a mouse, I lay down on my stomach and inch back into the hedge behind me, my gun drawn, phone in front of me.

Why would I have my phone out, you may ask? For one, I learned the value of video in my time as a park ranger. I had several cases dismissed for lack of video evidence. For two, well, I don't know. I just did, okay?

Adrenaline is coursing through my body. Time and activity around me begins to slow. My body prepares for the fight. I'll protect my people, I vow.

I start the video. I'll have something to show my team, as well as the other members of TASS, after this is over. My adrenaline-soaked senses tell me where my companion is as he moves through the garden. The strangers cut through the bushes. No wonder they chose to come through there. That's the perfect spot if they're avoiding our sight-lines.

"Oh, what do we have here?" slobbers the greasy-looking one. Looking at him, it's apparent he hasn't focused much on his personal hygiene. He stumbles slightly as he wipes at the slimy shine on his oil-covered forehead with the back of a hand that holds a beer bottle.

"I knew they were here," says the tall one contemptuously. He wiggles his ass as he digs for his pecker. Finding it, he tugs it out and urinates on several of the Ceorfan.

He says, "I hate them. Let's destroy them and go back to Jafer and tell him we couldn't help ourselves." Completing his desecration of my friends he mostly avoids urinating on his pants and fingers.

"I thought you wanted to fuck that one Jafer had in his bed last night," says Greasy-guy.

"It'd make me puke, but it'd be fun to rape or torture a few of them," says Little-pecker.

He adds, "Did you bring anything to destroy them with?"

"No, you don't, do nothing! We're to report if it's true that they turn into stone in the daylight and where they're staying. Once Jafer gets enough information from the two that're helping him, he'll send a missile to wipe out their hiding cave. Then these ones'll be easy to get," Greasy-guy says.

Well, it looks like Greasy-guy is the 'brains' of this operation. I'll snap his neck first.

Little-pecker asks, "What else does the boss need? The fat gargoyle told him how to destroy these things. And the girlgoyle told him where the gargoyle city is. We can destroy them all now, and get rid of this filth forever."

"No! He needs to know how to control the mage, so we can use his magic to run the world, remake it the way we want, with our laws and our culture."

Just for pissing on my friends, I'm going to kill these two. Maybe, just maybe, we should capture them for now, then take them to Chairman Brinker.

Bam! As soon as I think it, Mica swings a shovel and cold-cocks Greasy-guy. He turns, hitting Little-pecker in the face so hard I hear the bones in his jaw break. Both dirt-bags drop like shit from a horse splashed onto the curb.

I check to see if they're breathing, while not touching them. Yeah, they are. Too bad.

Mica says, "Hey, beautiful, there's a shed a little way down on the right. It has rope in it. Do you want to stay and guard them or go get the rope?"

"I'll get the rope, Sis," interjects Jared.

"Damn it, Jared, you scared the daylights out of me! Don't sneak up behind me. Damn it, I forgot you were out there."

Laughing, Jared continues, "Well, I was hanging further out from Mica. I saw the two coming. I couldn't get close without them seeing me. Besides, with our warrior friend near, they didn't stand a chance."

"Jared, you tow stay and watch our friends and these two bag-o-dicks. I just might shoot 'em if I'm left pointing a gun at 'em."

I find the shed. Inside, I find the rope as well as two large animal nets. I bring it all back to the scene.

"Well, Princess, I'm not sure what we need the nets for. Do you want to let me in on the plan?" asks Mica

"I don't know how to restrain these two. They're too gross to touch, and I don't want to catch anything. I think the net'll work just fine. We only need to close it around them and tie it up in a tree. When everyone is awake, we'll figure out what to do with them and find out who's trying to kill our whole Guild."

After we have the two ass-wipes trussed up a tree, I replay the video for my cohorts.

"Guys, I'm sure the traitor who was in bed with Jafer is Eltira, and there's only one fat gargoyle with us: Flint. Will you help me drag them over and put them in the second net then hang it beside the two bag-o-asses over there hanging in the tree."

The two possible traitors were too far apart on the patio to make it easy, so it takes us a while.

About one-o'clock, some of the humans are starting to get around. Mica takes our prisoners to Chairman Brinker, along with my phone to show the video, while my brother and I continue guarding our friends as well as our two traitors.

After seeing the video, Chairman Brinker and a quorum of the Council send Glen, along with some of the castle guards, with the guys to relieve me while I returned to speak with the Chairman.

After sitting in his office talking about the situation he let's me in on a secret.

"Queen Kendra, there's an underground prison here in the castle. We can lock these two in the cells until tonight's meeting. You should rest," said Mr. Brinker, as I've been instructed to call him.

"Mr. Brinker, I need a plan to keep the Ceorfan safe while also keeping humans safe," I say.

"Your Majesty," Mr. Brinker says with more authority than I've heard from him before, "you will return to your quarters and retire until breakfast tonight. I will ensure my personal guard, headed by your brother's friend Mr. Hughes, will protect you and the gargoyles until each of you can join us for breakfast. We've apprehended Jafer and the rest of his men. I swear to you that your friends will be safe."

Feeling I'd entered a battle of words and that I wouldn't win, yet feeling no duplicity in Mr. Brinker, I agree. I return to my suite, and tell Mica what's going on and that he should also sleep. He's as exhausted as I am, so I don't have to talk him into it. He feels the guards that the Chairman supplied are competent and trustworthy.

I go to my room and set my alarm for 4:30 p.m., so I can get several hours of good sleep, and wake when my team is waking, then I lie down in my clothes and fall fast asleep.

I wake before my alarm, my donum singing. I hurry to the patio to see if everyone's safe. They are. I'm hungry and want a snack so I call Thurston and ask if he'll bring me some chai tea and maybe some shortbread if the kitchen has any.

Sitting on the patio in view of several of the castle guards, I ask one of them if he knows if the council is meeting. He says he's just left the meeting room and no one's in there.

That's strange. I thank the house steward for bringing the tea and the most melt-in-your-mouth shortbread cookies I've ever had.

"Queen Kendra, if you want more biscuits, I would be happy to bring as much as you would like."

"Thank you," I respond.

He offers a slight bow as he backs away and leaves.

I have my notebook out. I need a proposal to suggest to the council for what to do with Jafer and his crew, as well as a location where my people can sleep that's more defendable and safer than our current suite.

Finally, the sun is gone. I'm more comfortable when it's dark. My friends are now fully awake and looking at the net containing Eltira and Flint. Eltira's screaming her head off. Flint's quiet.

Mica lowers them and secures them in place. Eltira is still screaming, now with her father, Count de Treon, at her side.

Flint is still quiet, but now sitting on the paving stones near the patio.

I tele-comm Mega a run-down of what happened while they slept. He says he was aware for part of the night and knows some of the story, but not all of it. He asks Spar, "Will you move the television to the patio where we can all see it?"

I play my video on the TV, where everyone can see it, including the irate Count. By the time the video is over, the Count is crying into his hands. His daughter is quiet, Flint's ashamed, and everyone else is waiting for orders.

22

BETRAYED

Kendra

We leave Spar to guard the two prisoners and go inside, so they won't have any more information to give away to the highest bidder.

"First, Mega, we need to be sure our people in Navan are safe," I say.

"That is not a problem. I have contacted Jericho. While this has never happened before, we do have an emergency plan in place for this type of betrayal. If needed, Navan can be moved. However, for speed and immediate security, he will hide the old cave opening and make it impassable. He will then open another, hidden entrance, and make sure it can only be opened via a portal-stone. Jericho is already in our cave city. He has assured me the previous entrance is now gone, and he will soon have the new entrance completed."

"Thank you. On to the traitors." I'm so mad, I can't even bring myself to say their names.

"You are welcome, Edling. What shall we do with the traitors? The worst thing a Ceorfan can do is to betray the people."

"It is terrible. I believe we should lock them up in cells here in the castle. Mr. Brinker has provided me with several in an area we can control."

"I agree. We have all of the evidence we need to move forward," Mega responds.

We leave the room, and I instruct the guards to take Eltira and Flint to the cells under the castle. Mica and Spar will keep them restrained. They will verify the cells are strong enough to keep gargoyles locked up.

After breakfast, we return to our rooms, shower, and prepare for a night full of business. Amber dresses me in blue today, again with the nude pumps. She brushes and weaves my hair in a serious-looking librarian bun.

Before the meetings, my commander and I go to the cells to speak with the traitors.

"Flint, why did you betray us?"

He doesn't answer. In fact, I notice that he has not spoken since waking from his torpification.

"Please tell me what's going on. At least, tell me why you're silent now, after this betrayal."

Flint says nothing in return.

Finally, I ask Mega, *"Please tele-speak to Flint. I know we have an agenda, but I have a funny feeling he's being manipulated in some way."*

My commander nods.

After we leave the dungeon, I say, "Eltira is a serious problem. She isn't sorry. She could have killed everyone."

"Yes, my queen. Jafer is being paid by the Jessup cartel to kill you. Flint is convinced the cartel has his older brother prisoner. He left the threatening note you found. He hoped the cinnamon would be a clue since earlier, he had made you chai tea. We can use this situation to our advantage. Someone will have to infiltrate the enemy. I will tell you more after I gather more information. If you agree, Edling."

I nod slightly to Mega, not letting on that he'd spoken in my mind, "I think I have enough of the facts. I need Jericho to return here for tonight's sentencing. I'll proclaim the sentences for the traitors. For now, I need to find Mr. Brinker. I need to borrow the meeting hall."

My soldiers all have parts in the various strategy meetings. We come up with plans for collecting intelligence, so we can devise the correct plans to catch the Horde of Barat. I'm satisfied, and we have full schedules for the next few weeks. I add in a few fake doctors' appointments for my boss, to make it seem like I'm still healing. Then I check in with Chris back at the ranger station. I'm also able to put off work for a few more weeks.

With Jericho's return, I ask to speak with him privately. After doing so extensively, we enter the meeting hall, where we find the Guild members who arrived with us on this mission in attendance. The old wizard told me the laws concerning the criminals. It's not good.

Spar and Mica bring the prisoners in. Both stand shackled in the front of the hall, facing the Guild. I let them stand there, pausing.

At last I motion to Spar. He brings Flint to stand in front of me, facing me.

"Flint, do you have anything to say in your defense?" I ask.

"My queen, I will, without complaint, take whatever punishment you deem fit. But, please, I beg of you, find and free my brother. He does not deserve to die alone at the hands of the cartel."

I nod to Jericho. He opens a portal. Through the portal comes Flint's brother. It's easy to see the relief on Flint's face when he understands his brother is safe.

I say, "Your brother was never taken by Jafer. He's been on assignment, collecting information for the Guild regarding the cartel. After this meeting he'll return to his assignment. You see, your treason was for nothing."

I finish, playing up the situation.

"Flint, face me and look at me. I've wondered how a gargoyle would mete out justice. But, I'm not a gargoyle I'm Dragon Queen of the Ceorfan. I will mete out justice as I see fit. You have endangered my people by telling an enemy how to kill a gargoyle. It was your job as a Warrior Elite to protect all. Your creed is, 'Protect Ceorfan, human, and animal.' Your actions have deliberately put others in danger to protect only you and your brother. This is a betrayal of the highest order.

"You are stripped of your Warrior Elite status, your rank, and any etchings of achievement. You are stripped of all titles and property. Your word is worthless to this Guild. Your name will be etched as a traitor in Navan. Until a short time ago, your life hung by the thinnest of threads.

"Megahir pleaded your case. Prior to tonight, you've served with great valor and distinction. Because of this, you may reside in Navan until the end of your days. I hope you find a way to be of use to the very people you have betrayed. You are ordered to remain in Scotland so that we may keep an eye on you. What say you regarding my words?"

"I am sorry, my queen. I'll do whatever I can to make it up to you and our people."

"Gargoyle, I have heard your words. Now get out of my sight."

Mica takes him in hand, guiding him out of the room. He ducks his chin, tears running down his face, shocked at his sentence. He knows a betrayer has no place as a goyle of any consequence in Navan. The few criminals we have live out their days in back alleys and gutters with the drunks and malcontents.

"Eltira, face me and look at me to receive your sentence."

She is confined by magic and must be held by a spell, one that she is fighting. Only her lips can move. Apparently, Jericho doesn't want to take any chances on her drama or possible escape.

I say, "You have lived many lifetimes because of your father the Count. Yet you worked with an enemy who wants to murder him, a man who gave of himself to give you life. You have told the cartel, and ultimately the world, of our secret city, Navan. This secret is death to reveal. What you have done could have killed the entirety of the Ceorfan Guild. Do you have anything to say?"

"I hate you all. I wish I'd never become a part of this cursed race. It's too bad that Jafer didn't kill all of you all before you caught us."

"Then you'll truly be at peace with your sentence. I'm afraid yours is different from Flint's. When your father gave a part of himself to you, he did so to let you live. For you to become carved, he needed permission of the Queen. She denied his request. I now undo what should never have been done. Jericho, if you please."

The old mage steps forward.

He says, "My friend, Count de Treon, please remove your shirt."

The count, heartbroken, responds, "No, please my queen. No."

His pleading continues as Spar and Mica restrain him.

Jericho closes his eyes and begins a hushed chant as he cuts through the braiding on the Counts shirt, revealing his chest.

The Guild watches, transfixed with the events unfolding before them.

I feel an outpouring of love and support for the count. It grows to a point where I not only feel it, I hear it.

With a weirdly imperceptible glance toward me, Jericho flicks his wrist and cuts deeply into the Count's chest. He had told me earlier that this cut had to reach the pneuma, or 'that which is breathed.'

That is where his soul is, he said.

He continues his chant even more loudly. The distressed green gargoyle continues pleading, no not pleading, groveling for me to save his daughter. A divot of bone pops out of his chest.

Jericho catches it. While staying near the distraught gargoyle, the focused mage continues chanting until the wound closes.

Mixed with love and support for the Count, I begin to sense goodbyes to the unrepentant female before me. The first goodbye to reach my ears is mine.

"Eltira, goodbye. I don't love what you did. I do love your soul. My hope is that you shall find the peace and happiness in death that you could not find in life."

Then more of the Ceorfan add expressions of compassion and love for her, containing no condemnation of me as I fear. None are accusatory. None condemn me, their queen for only a few days. A queen who, in her first acts of discipline, demands the execution of Eltira, a member of the Ceorfan for centuries. There is no hate today. None for the betrayer. None for me. Only love and support for the Count, his only child... and for me.

My mage moves to the defiant traitor lifting her magical restraints. Still, nothing emanates from her but hatred. With her arms outstretched Jericho cuts her shirt loose. She is as exposed as the evil within her. Still defiant, she solicits anyone within hearing to carry out her one last desire—to kill the Guild.

Our room fills with somber pleading. Not for the Queen to intervene, but for death to treat Eltira with kindness. The compassion being pressed toward her is crushing me. I no longer feel the way a human woman does. I feel like a Ceorfan Queen. I add my force to the entreating, impressing my own hope for her to be treated well in death.

The lights in the hall begin a dance, dimming and brightening with no detectable sequence. With remarkable speed, Jericho cuts open her bare chest, painlessly. Out pops a stone, which he hands to the Count, who places it near his cheek, covering it with tears. The mage replaces the piece of bone, earlier removed from her father, back into his daughter's chest. Her wound closes as the chanting diminishes, then ends.

The room is silent. The lights have dimmed to a low level. A chill fills the room, almost as if death were personally coming to claim Eltira. It's astonishing to see a woman dissolve into a pile of dust. Even more so, to see the dust fade into eternity in a matter of seconds.

The Guild waits. The count, in shock, stands.

I take a few steps toward him. As I do, the room begins to clear. I walk toward him, searching his eyes.

"You did the best you could with her. I'm sure the wild magic of the rogue mage is what caused the evil to fester. I'm sorry for your loss."

Tears continue to stream down his face.

I continue, "You're a good man, and I'm certain you'll do mighty things for the Guild. Our people need you, Count. Will you step back into your rightful place of leadership, or would you prefer I replace you as a member of the High Guild?"

He sobs on the intake of a breath.

Controlling himself just enough to speak, he answers, "My queen, you have my loyalty and my love. I hope the Guild will be improved by my understanding of this pain. My daughter did evil, I know that, but I love her. My wife has gone on long ago, and she will not feel this grief. Of that I am glad. I will have to learn to live without my daughter. I will miss her for the rest of my days."

I hug him and say, "Go home. Rest, heal, and help Jericho keep the Guild safe. The Ducere and I will be there soon. Be sure to tell Eltira's story, so her name will be etched forever in the city."

All Ceorfan birth and death records are kept. It's a small conciliation but a tradition to remember the dead with this phrase.

Jericho gives me a hug then reaching out for the arm of the count, taking him by the elbow, he guides him into a portal and leaves.

I feel sick. Dinner time is approaching, but I'm not hungry. I go to my room to speak with the others.

"Jared, what do you want to do? Do you think you need to go home or stay here? I'm second-guessing my decisions."

"No, Kendra, you're right. The Ceorfan need representation with TASS. Our culture must be understood. If we can't convince this small group, we'll have no hope of convincing the world we deserve a place in it. I'll do fine. You, of all people, know the way I've set up my companies. I can handle them remotely, easily."

I hug him and say, "Thank you. I guess the real question is, do you want to stay in this decrepit old castle or get one of your own?"

Jared laughs, a small subdued laugh.

"I'm sure I'll be okay here until I can find my own place. I need to figure out my options. I have a real estate company in London. I'll have them take care of my accommodations in the long term."

There's a knock at the door. Thurston is there. He's brought a waiter, who has a cart with trays of food.

He says, "The chef has sent your dinner to you. Would you like to eat it here at this table," pointing at the coffee table in the living area, "or out on the patio?"

"The coffee table is fine."

The waiter sets a tray on the coffee table and takes the rest to the dining table. There's enough food for an army! It smells so good that everyone excuses themselves from their discussions to go eat in the dining area of our suite. All except Spar. I ask him if he'd like to eat with me in the living area.

"I'm your Huckleberry," he responds, which gets a smile out of me.

We sit and talk over all the 'what ifs'.

"You did the right thing," He says, peering at me with his big blue eyes. I can just fall into them.

"I believe in you, Kendra. I'll try to always be here to back you up. I'll make you a deal, honey. If I ever think what you're doing is wrong I'll tell you before you go overboard, okay?"

He puts his big hand on mine making me feel so much calmer.

I answer, "Thank you, it's a deal. I guess it's just a wake-up call to the hard decisions in life. She really had relief in her eyes. I'm going to remember that instead of questioning myself anymore. Thank you for believing in me, I needed this talk."

The realization of how much he cares pulls at my heartstrings.

Just then, a waiter comes and removes the empty trays, bringing us a bottle of rich burgundy wine. Spar opens it and pours us both a glass. I enjoy it with a sigh.

He hands his glass to me, and I take it with a question in my eyes. He picks me up carrying me to my room.

He says, "Come here, I want some alone time with you."

I sigh and say, "That would be really nice."

"Be careful—don't spill. Well, if you spill, I'll have to lick it off you."

"Okay, now I need to spill it on purpose. Maybe pour it." I tease.

He sits me softly on the edge of the bed. Then he takes our glasses and places them gently on the nightstand.

Standing in front of me, he pulls my head toward his abdomen. I open the snap, using my teeth, and lick his skin softly, using as much of my tongue as I can.

My blue goyle pulls back slowly, then pushes me softly toward the bed. He caresses my neck, working his way toward my stomach. As he moves down, I check to see if he's biting off the buttons or unbuttoning them. I grin to myself—he's very talented with that tongue.

It takes a few more seconds for him to get my shirt undone. Using one hand, he pulls it the rest of the way off. He kneels in front of me, holding my back and kissing my neck.

"Oh, that feels so good," I moan.

He continues kissing my lips before he moves lower down my body. His hands on my breasts, rubbing them gently through my bra, is driving me crazy. His hair is tickling my stomach as he unbuttons my pants with his mouth.

Next, he undoes my bra with one hand taking time to kiss me deeply. I pull it off and throw it across the room.

He moves a little to suck one of my nipples into his mouth, taking it slowly. I moan into the silence.

A soft push and he climbs over me and begins rocking back and forth. My brain is fried. I push him back, so I can unbutton his shirt.

To hell with that.

I pull as hard as I can, and the buttons spray across the room. He bends to take his jeans off, pulling them over his clawed feet. I watch as the muscles of his ass bunch. He reaches for me and helps me the rest of the way out of my own pants.

Now that we have the clothes out of the way, he climbs onto the bed with me. He lifts me by the waist to put me on top of him. Leaning into him, I bite his ear, and I tell him he's mine. I'm never letting him go. I lift and slowly guide him into my body. The stretch hurts just enough to feel good. He's making deep gargoyle satisfaction noises—sort of like a moan and a growl together. I'm not going to last long. He puts a thumb on my clit, making a circular motion. That's all I need, and I'm gone.

I stop for a second when he flips us over and keeps up the rhythm. Slow and steady, he doesn't rush. It's like one long orgasm that keeps going. Then, my big Spar finally gets to come, too.

Exhausted, he says, "Kendra, I love you. I'm so proud of you. Don't question your decisions. I'll tell you if I ever think you might want to reconsider. I love you with everything I am."

We talk until I fall into an uneasy sleep. I wake a few hours later and reach for him. He isn't there. Instead, my hand touches Mica on the chest. He rolls over to me and presses his body to mine. I can feel his big claws, smooth and gentle, on the small of my back. That's a very sensitive part of my body, one that I love being touched, especially by this big hunk. I'm not ready for this yet, with him. But kissing is good.

All right I have no idea what's going on. He's too wonderful. I can't even think of anything but him now. I need to take a breath. When I do, I want to stop and talk to him for a bit.

"Mica, I need to stop for now. As much as I don't want to. I'm not ready yet. I want our first time to be different. Special. Okay?"

"Okay, I understand, my beautiful lady. It's still a few hours until sunrise. Mega left word that he wants to talk to you as soon as you wake."

I fidget with his chest and say, "I talked to Spar already, so he knows. I guess you know because you're here with me and not him. I need to tell you about Kino, though. I want to make sure you're on board with all of us being in a relationship. What do you think?"

"My beauty, you've chosen well. We'll be the best family. I can't wait to start our new life together, Princess."

"Well, let's go take care of some business." I begin to get up, not thinking about being naked. Oh, well, he's mine. I know I'm his, just as much. I don't mind teasing him a little. It'll make the wait that much sweeter.

I get up and let the covers drop. Slowly walking to my bathroom, I turn, and, oh, yeah, he's staring wide-eyed.

"Mica, I'm going to get a quick shower. I'll be out as quick as I can. Will you meet me in the living room?"

I have a fleeting thought to run over, kiss him, and run. I'm afraid that it would be too much for either of us, and I wouldn't be able to stop. I really want to plan something special for him.

23

FRIENDS

Kendra

I dress in some tougher clothes today. I'm not out to impress anyone. My mission: protect my friends while they torp. After yesterday, I need to be on my toes at all times.

Walking into the living area, I say, "Hello all, I trust y'all are okay?"

They answer in the affirmative, though I can tell their spirits are down. The thought 'like mine had been before Spar and Mica came to visit' jumps straight into my mind. I stifle the blush before it reaches my face.

"As soon as we get back to Navan, I think we should have a holiday. How does that sound?"

The room perks up, smiles on everyone's face. There's even a small murmur of conversation now.

"Mega, will you come walk with me?" I say out loud. Then I start our conversation in tele-speak as I walk out onto the patio with him behind me.

"Mega, does Flint understand what his job is now? Does he understand the sentence was a farce?"

"Flint and I spoke at length about what his role would be in this mission. I believe he understands it. I also believe Flint was hurt a great deal by his public humiliation."

When we reach the patio, I end the tele-speak.

"We need more information, and I need him to know we are on the same side at all times. At one of his next dead drops, make sure you have my coded thank you, with my love for him and my promise that I'll bring his work to light as soon as we can. Mega, he must play double agent for a little longer. We need more information from Jafer. How would you feel about telling the others in our party that the sentence in the meeting hall was for the cameras only?"

"I believe there are others working with Jafer and against our best interests. I caution against that and advise patience."

"I know you're right. I feel awful for Flint right now. We do need to find out who our enemies are. Baratium is obvious. He must have friends to help him travel the globe the way he is. I can't help but think we were brought here as part of some elaborate trap," I add.

"TASS does not look out for the Ceorfan. In its hundreds of years of existence, it has never had one of us as a director, so I do not think they ever will look out for us. With that said, Edling, I do not see any further evidence of a direct plot. Kino, Amber, and Mason have all worked in constant patrols, searching for such evidence."

"You may be correct, General. Maybe it's best if y'all pose on the top of the castle to sleep today. As high as you can, so no one can get to you. I'll still be able to watch, but it'll be safer. I'll have the castle guards with me. That'll allow Mica to sleep today, too. I need him frosty for tonight's strategy breakout, because this'll be the last of the planning. Then we'll start on mission 'Horde Be Gone.'"

"Yes. Let us return and tell the Ducere, so the castle surveillance will think everything is okay."

When we return, I let everyone know Mica will sleep today. When I do, they immediately balk at the idea. Mega explains our reasoning, and they grudgingly give their approval.

The Ducere fly to the uppermost parts of the castle turrets and pinnacles. The sun is close to rising.

Watching them pose, I say to myself, "Wings up, Ceorfan."

They may even have heard me; as one, they immediately raise their wings. When the first rays of sunshine fall upon them, they harden into their torpified state. Amazing. They're breathtaking.

"Sleep well, my family. I have work to do."

My first stop is the kitchen and Chef Ron. I want to tell him, 'thank you,' for taking such good care of me. On my way, I run into Thurston and walk to the kitchen with him.

I ask, "How is your family, my friend?"

"Queen Kendra, my wife is down with a cold, but other than that, everyone is fine. Did you know I have a daughter attending university in Glasgow? She's studying medicine," he says, with a lift to his chest.

"That's wonderful. I bet she takes after you," I reply.

He continues, "I have a son named John. He's at home with his mom, sick. John has always been a little sickly."

His shoulders drop noticeably.

The despair he has for his son's sickness is overwhelming me. I've always been able to perceive others feelings. Thurston's are no different, except it's much more intense. I'm not sure why, but when I accept the feelings, it seems to ease the intensity a bit.

"Thurston, may I visit your family after I'm finished in the kitchen?"

"I would very much like that my lady queen. I'll be back to collect you in a little while. Chef Ron is right through those doors."

He gives me a little bow before turning and hurrying away.

At his bow, I wince a little and quickly turn away, so he has no reason to assume I don't appreciate his manners. The fact is, I'm still slightly bothered by the royal treatment. Thurston is a kind gentleman who has done his best to make the entire Ceorfan delegation feel welcomed here. I consider him a friend.

It's loud in the castle kitchen—not so much from voices, but from grinders, blenders, beeping from alarms and microwaves, the clicking of utensils. All the chefs are bustling over their work.

Over the din, a familiar voice rings, "Hey, my queen. What has happened that you would visit my humble kitchen?"

"Humble? Well, my friend, I think our definitions of humble differ," I playfully say as I move in and collect a hug.

"That is very nice. I can't remember the last time I received a hug, thank you," he says smoothing his jacket and apron.

"You're welcome. I came to tell you thank you for taking such good care of me. I was feeling down last night and wouldn't have attempted to eat if you hadn't sent dinner."

"It was my honor, Queen Kendra. You're a worthy queen. You show me kindness. You show kindness to the least of all of us. That is how we have measured you. The thanks go to you."

I blush deeply at the kind comments.

"Chef Ron, you and your staff are wonderful. Everything you've cooked is delicious. In fact, I'll need to start exercising if I continue to eat so well. I'm going to get bigger than a house."

"You're most welcome. A chef does what a chef can. You're the first to complement my meager offerings in a long while. Your kind words are further proof of your magnanimity. My staff and I appreciate that. Sit here, let me get you a treat." He waves to a tall bar stool next to a granite counter.

I perch on the chair and lean on the table's cool surface.

He brings me a plate and a cup of tea.

"This is an old family recipe for apricot scones. Tell me what you think."

I take a bite for him.

Closing my eyes to enjoy my treat, I lean back and say, "Yum-mmm. Oh, that's good. Do you think I can have some of these sent to my room? Oh, and maybe, if you don't mind... I'm going to visit Thurston's family. Will you share some so I can take his wife and son some?"

He beams.

"It is my pleasure to make the world happy with food. Simone, please prepare a basket of goodies for Queen Kendra to take with her."

A short pretty lady with a dark pixie haircut and a bandana tied around her head answers, "Yes, Chef."

She is off to take care of my treats.

I say, "Chef Ron, thank you again. Is there anything I can do for you?"

He grins and says, "It's enough that you asked, and you love my cooking."

When I finish my scone, I leave the kitchen with my basket and spot Thurston coming for me.

"Are you ready to take me to meet your family, Thurston?"

"Yes, but you do not have to do this, my lady queen."

"Oh, hush, I want to, you nut."

We talk and walk for maybe twenty minutes before arriving at his little cottage. It's old, like the castle. I ask him if it's one of the older buildings.

He answers, "Yes. It was part of the original stewards' residences that belonged to the castle when it was built in the 1600's."

The tall steward leads me through the front door. It's a very nice cottage. He and his family are not lacking for nice furniture. The decor is more modern than what I'd expect, all dressed in a blue and gray color scheme.

He calls out to his wife and takes me by the hand, leading me to a bedroom where his wife is sitting in a comfortable-looking lounge chair in the same hues as the rest of the house. She's bundled up in a thick quilt. The quilt looks old and worn, soft with age. She has thick fuzzy socks on her feet. Her hair is long, a thick steel gray braid hangs over a small shoulder. She's a tiny lady, maybe five feet at the most, and I doubt she's a hundred pounds. She lowers the Kindle in her hands and smiles at her husband.

"Who have you brought to visit, husband?"

Her voice is beautiful and matches her perfectly. A high soprano voice if she were to sing, I'm sure. Thurston introduces us, and I bring out the basket of goodies Chef Ron sent and give them to her. She's very happy, even though I can tell she isn't feeling well. With all that's been happening to me over the last weeks, I'm questioning many aspects of my life. Such as, I can't remember being sick. Do I have a protection inside me? How can I pass that on without using my blood?

I give her a big hug, so I can have a reason to breathe dragon breath in her face. I hope it will help her to get over her cold faster.

"I can't stay for more than a minute or two, but I did want to meet you and John. Meg, please, get some rest, I hope to see you again."

I call her by the name Thurston had called her earlier when he introduced us.

Next, Thurston takes me to John's room, where his son is sleeping. John is obviously frail-looking, but a very handsome boy. His dark hair is messy from sleep, and his fair skin is red in places where he laid on his pillow. His hands and arms are on top of the covers. There are blisters on his hands.

"What is it?" I whisper.

"They fail to know, my lady queen. I hope they find out soon. He weakens daily. I'm afraid we will not have him too much longer if we can't find help."

John hears his dad and opens his eyes and smiles. Thurston goes over and fusses with the covers, straightening them and combing his son's hair off his face. I'd notice a small pocket knife on the bureau beside a wallet and comb. I pick it up and used it to prick my finger. As I do, I hide it from sight and squeeze it a bit to get the blood to pool on my finger.

Thurston introduces me to John. When he does, I butt in between them, so Thurston won't see what I'm doing. I reach for John's blistered hand with my bloody fingertip, rubbing the blood into the blister.

I pick his hand up and put it under the covers while saying, "John, I'm happy to meet you."

He relaxes and drifts off to sleep again.

"Well, I should be going, Thurston. I'm sure I can find my way back to the castle. It's a straight shot on an easy path. You stay and help your family for the time being."

Thurston tells me he'll see me at the castle later, after dark. I reach for him and give him a hug before I leave.

I say a little prayer for John as I start back to the castle. I haven't had any exercise in a while, so I decide to run back to the castle. I need the exercise, or I might lose my edge. I was so weak when I was healing in the hospital after being wounded by Jerry Drinker. I thought it would take me weeks, or longer, to feel good enough to run again. The run feels good. I slow to pace myself. It's only a few minutes to the castle. but still I'm starting to sweat as I arrive.

I plan best when I'm running or walking. My plan is to go see if the Chairman will let me speak to Jafer and his men. Afterwards, I'll go shower, sleep, and get ready for the gargoyle day to start. I want to finalize our mission plans and get back to Navan.

Also, I need to do some work to control the cartel, so I don't have to keep dealing with that problem. Perhaps I can persuade the prisoners to help. Lastly, I don't want to forget to ask Jericho to use a spell on them to make sure they forget the location of the gargoyle city.

Entering the castle through the front doors the guards recognize me, without a problem. I go straight to the Chairman's office, and his administrative assistant rings him announcing my presence. She introduces herself.

"My name is Cecile and if you need anything just let me know."

Then she goes to the door and motions to enter.

His permanent grimace is still in place, and his happy expression has my mind wondering if that's for me or not. That's creepier than seeing a gargoyle smiling by a long shot.

The Chairman seats me in a leather chair opposite his with his large wooden desk between us. He buzzes his assistant and asks her to have the kitchen send us some lunch. He doesn't specify what he wants.

He glances at me and says, "Don't think I didn't notice you not asking for specific meals. The best meals are never specified. I've been trying that, and my meals are much better than before."

We sit and visit over our lunch, talking of our families and what we want to see for our people. How we think we might best achieve peace across the world. I comment that in my opinion we can't enjoy peace until we get the despots under control. He agrees. The fight is never-ending.

I ask, "Would it be possible to question the prisoners."

He answers, "Yes, but I would like to go with you. I would, with all due respect, like to take my guards for your protection. We do have cameras in the cells and the audio is very good. Let me give you the codes to access those files while you stay here."

He punches information into his computer and provides me with the access information.

"Also tonight, Queen Kendra, there's a gala being held in the ballroom. Would you and your Ceorfan warriors please attend as our guests? If you need something to wear I have a designer within my reach—if you like."

"Mr. Chairman--"

"José, please, while we are not in session. May I call you Kendra in return?"

"It would make me very happy if you would. I'll also take you up on your offer of using your designer, if you don't think it'll be a problem."

He reassures me it's no bother and picks up the phone.

"Yes, Jamie. I need your help. Queen Kendra of the Ceorfan delegation needs a gown and other essentials for a gala tonight."

I'm only able to hear one side of the conversation. It sounds like a flurry of talking, followed by a pause in the conversation.

He continues, "Yes, yes. She's a dear friend, and I do know this is last minute. I'll owe you dearly, my friend... I understand, and you're too kind. Please make sure you bill me for the expenses...Thank you,

Jamie, I'll give her the tele, and she'll provide you with the important details."

I receive the phone from José and speak to the unidentified person on the other end, "Yes, this is Kendra Macbard. To whom do I have the pleasure of speaking?"

"Oh, darling, you do not need that pretense with me. I'm Jamie Serge. Please, call me Jamie." His beautiful sing-song lilt captures my attention.

I say, "Okay, Jamie. You can call me Kendra."

"I will be at your suite in two hours. We will begin your transformation and have the best day ever. Is that okay with you?"

"Yes, that would be wonderful," I answer.

"Of course, dear, and thank you for letting me dress you, darling."

I return the phone to José.

As he takes it, he says, "Let's go see the prisoners now. The guards are waiting outside."

24

FUN

Kendra

Well, I'm not let down on my vision of a medieval dungeon. This one is as dark and dank as I expected. Although, there aren't any torture devices that I can see. I do see the guy who pissed on my men in the first cell. Instantly, I become serious. I still think he's scum, but I'm not in the killing mood I'd been in.

I walk with José to Jafer's cell. The Chairman tells him he has some questions for him.

Jafer says, "You can ask all you want. I will not give you any information." His accent is thick with innuendo.

I stare into his eyes to see if I can call the magic persuasion up and ask him, "Are you sure you wouldn't tell us just a little? It's very important that we get some information."

When I finish speaking, he asks, "Exactly what do you think is important?"

"I think that knowing where Don Manuel Jessup and his top lieutenants are located is important."

"They are in Morocco right now, on vacation. They are planning to go to the south Caribbean next."

This persuasion thing is making this much easier than I thought it'd be. The more Jafer speaks, the more the other men yell at him to shut up.

One by one I examine them and say, "Your behavior isn't nice. I need the information, and you're the ones who should shut up."

Now I have the opposite problem. Each of them is frantically trying to provide the information I want. They speak over each other so much, I have to have different people listen to different suspects. Unfortunately, that leads to crying among the ones not speaking to me. I choose to ask each of them a question in turn. They are spilling the beans so fast, I need Merry Maids to clean it up.

We learn the names of the yachts the cartel uses. Various other names, places, some telephone, and bank account numbers are filled in. We've been at it for more than two hours when Jafer speaks up.

He relates, "Queen Kendra, if I do not report in by our 7:30 deadline, the cartel will send someone to check on us."

I thank him for the extra tidbit. José then asks me if I have enough information.

"I have more than I thought I'd ever get."

He replies, "I'm surprised it was so easy. If men spill their secrets that easily to you, I may ask you to be available to interrogate any other prisoners we have to incarcerate."

Then he adds, a bit forlornly, "I hope we never have any more though, Kendra."

"It's a deal. I know you're a man of honor. I'll stand with you. Now, we need to verify all the information they've given us," I chuckle.

***

I'D JUST FINISHED my shower when a knock sounds on my door. Calling out, I ask, "Who's there."

The designer I'd talked to on the phone answers, "Open the door, hun. This stuff is heavy."

I let him in with a few others carrying boxes and dress bags.

"I am Jamie," he says as he puts a hand out to me.

I'm not sure if he wants me to kiss it or shake it. Before I have a chance to do either, he pulls it back, puts it to his chin and walks around me making 'uh uh' noises. Stopping, he looks and waits until just before it becomes uncomfortable.

Then he speaks, "What on earth, hun? Have you been cutting your own hair? We have so much to do. Oh Lord, this is not good."

I bite the corner of my lip, then say, "I know I'm not all that--"

But Jamie interrupts me. "Noo, nooo, noooo, you, my dear, are very fine. It just looks like you have been trying to copy a bag lady for beauty tips."

Jamie has a delightful tilt to his voice. Each syllable at the end of his sentences always trails up, almost musically.

I giggle as I watch his hands waving with each word. If I hold his hands, he won't be able to speak.

The pure joy of him being himself effuses the room. Jamie loves who he is, and because he does it with such verve, I find myself feeling incredibly confident in his forthcoming choices. He calls Thurston, who brings an equally vivacious girl with a suitcase full of make-up and another full of pedicure/manicure stuff. I forfeit all my choices. Jamie makes them all. I will say it makes my day so much easier.

The three of us talk about every subject imaginable. Well, except for everything that doesn't involve make-up, jewelry, clothes, boys, and things that fit in one of those groups. Sunset comes and goes before I know it.

My gargoyles wake and come into the room while Jamie is still ordering how he wants my hair fixed. We have already taken care of which dress and underthings to wear. We finish a bottle of Joyce Eloise Malbec from Argentina and are starting on a 2006 Annabella

Cabernet from California when Spar comes into the room. We're all laughing, then quiet.

Without warning, Jamie says, "I see what you are talking about, Kendra. Can I have this one?"

"No! I like that one a lot—in fact, I think all the best ones are mine. But I'm sure we can find you one when we get home. Will you come with me when I go home?" I plead.

"I don't think I can make a living that way, hun. But I will visit. How's that?"

"I'll go for that," I answer excitedly.

"Spar, will you come and meet my friend, Jamie?"

"I, um, actually have something to do. I'll be back later, I promise, honey."

"Okay handsome. Just make sure you dress formally—we have a gala tonight."

He kisses me on the cheek and leaves. He must have warned everyone away, because no one else comes in while I'm getting ready.

Jamie stands me up in front of the mirror.

Wow, who's that? That can't be me. That woman, even I think, is beautiful. My wine buzz is gone, or I wouldn't believe I could look like this. I'm wearing a floor-length gown which shimmers every time I breathe. It's red, one of my favorite colors. I'm wearing stilts, not heels, but they aren't bad. In fact, they're as sparkly as my dress. I turn and hug Jamie, with my heart beating out of my chest.

"Thank you, Jamie. You're amazing. You've turned an ugly duckling into a queen."

"No, hun, you are beautiful. I just help with the trim."

I ask him, "Will you always be my fairy godmother!"

He says, "Yes, of course, my dearest Kendra."

Jamie gives me his number. I call him, so he has my number as he packs up and leaves. He says he'll walk out with me; he wants to see what my guygoyles think.

He wings an arm to me, and I take it, walking out of my bedroom door. All of the talking we'd heard in the living area stops. They turn toward me, except Jared, who is still telling a story to them—oblivious to their sudden inattention. Their mouths drop open at the exact same time. Their eyes go wide, shoulders going back like strutting peacocks preparing for their mating dance.

Mica actually drops a cookie, totally forgetting he was holding it.

Jamie walks me toward my trio, stops, and lifts my arm. I take the hint and do a little spin for them. I chuckle at the looks on their faces, feeling very happy that those looks are for me. I air-kiss Jamie's cheek before he leaves with a wink. He's as happy at their reactions as I am.

Mega says behind me. "Edling, you are more beautiful than any woman I have ever seen. I am proud you are my queen. I have always known you were smart, talented, and honorable. I have also known you were beautiful, but tonight you bring us all to our knees."

"It's the dragon blood, General," I say flippantly.

Jared pipes up and says, "That's what I always say when people call me beautiful."

We all laugh. "So, is everyone ready for a gala?"

It sure looks like we are. Kino is closest to me, and not about to be outdone by the others, offers me his arm impishly. I set mine on top of his, and we start for the party. Spar and Mica follow then the rest of the Ducere. We stop, so the Herald can announce our entry into the ballroom.

It's Thurston who's acting as the Herald. He grins slyly at me, and in his best Scottish Crier impersonation says, "Her Highness, Queen Kendra Macbard of the Ceorfan, and Her consorts, the Marquis Kino Magus, Commander Mica Jacobs of the Elite Warriors Guard, and Spar Megason, Cadet of the Elite Warriors."

He bows to us and lets us enter the ballroom. We all glow at hearing our names and titles sung out in this setting. It makes it even more real to us.

Spar says, "Well after that, I think I need a drink. Kendra, would you like a drink?"

"Please, just a white wine."

"Mica, come with me to get her wine."

Mica asks Kino, "Hey, do you want me to get you something?"

He answers in his stately voice, "I would like . . ."

While he pauses I say, "Milk in a dirty glass?" Now we're all laughing.

Kino says, "Any whiskey they have is fine."

After the others leave, I say, "I'm sorry for the joke."

He bends close and whispers, "Don't be. That's part of what makes you, you. I love you just the way you are."

I shiver, his breath hot on my ear is a turn on. I straighten and get a hold of myself.

I move closer to his face and growl under my breath, "Keep that up and I'll forget what we're here for. And thank you, let's start making our way to 'work the room.'"

When Mica and Spar come over with our drinks, I'm so ready for it. We sit on a bench close to a large balcony. We're in such a wonderful mood. This is what memories are made of.

Jared's with a beautiful redhead on his arm. I'm not up on these things, but, I'm pretty certain she's an actress. Leave it to Jared to find the stunningly beautiful and the talented all in one.

José Brinker is standing by the orchestra, readying an announcement. The crowd quiets to hear him. "I would like to welcome Queen Kendra and the Ceorfan Guild. These talks have produced great plans with input from both her and the Ceorfan. We are sure these will help to bring peace and prosperity to the world. I propose a toast to Her Majesty."

Everyone raises their glasses.

He continues, "Here is to health, peace, and prosperity—may the flower of peace and love never be nipped by the frost of war and hate, nor may the shadow of grief never fall among a member of her Guild. May the Ceorfan one day be accepted by all."

The whole room cheers. I have happy tears as I clink my glass to everyone's around me.

The music starts, and Kino asks me if I'll dance with him. I nod a small, tilt of my head to accept. He leads me to the dance floor. He puts his strong arm around my waist, I sigh and trimble when his big hands warm my back. Holding me close, he leads me across the dance floor.

I love dancing. Even with clawed feet, Kino is a splendid and graceful dancer. We just make it to the others when Mica collects me, and we start the next dance.

"A girl could get used to this," I say.

"Then let's have lots of dances and reasons to dress up." He sweeps me into a turn, and I lean into him for balance. Yes, I can get used to this. We talk as we dance, then Spar cuts in just as the next song begins.

This song is a slow one. Not a waltz but a two-step.

"I'm so glad you didn't forget how to dance. Don't you ladies always tell each other, 'the best lovers are the best dancers.'"

"The old wives tales are true," I flirt with him.

"Of course, they are, Kendra, my love. Are you ready for a rest?"

"Yes, and some water if you don't mind."

He sets me on the bench we'd claimed and heads off to get my water.

I look around the room for the others. My donum begins to speak loudly. Worrying, I stand as a loud boom next to the balcony shoots through the ballroom, knocking me onto my face. I feel hands on me. I start to fight them off when something is sprayed in my face.

Then blackness.

25

CAPTURED

JARED

It's been this way since we were kids. One of us is in trouble, and one or both of the others is there helping. No one tells us anything's wrong. We just know. We have a name for it—donum—we just never speak about it to others, because we're certain people will think we're nuts. Well, my friends from school would say I'm nuts, regardless of the reason.

Kendra says it is God who allows it. I say it's my ESP. Dana, well, he pretends it doesn't exist; but come time to help, there he is, right in the middle.

Tonight, I have one of the most vivid impressions I've ever experienced. Kendra needs help. It makes no sense. She's with Spar, Mica, and Kino. All three of these goyles are built to be the last survivor in any fight. If they're alive, nobody can touch my sister. But, there is something wrong—or it's coming.

I run as fast as I can toward the ballroom in the castle. I only left for a minute to relieve myself. I look around the room for Kendra. I see her, she is sitting on a bench, I run toward—

I'm blown back by the blast and slam into the wall behind me.

The force of the blast is like a hammer blow to my chest. My wind is gone, and my consciousness is fading.

I can stand, so I push away the dizziness the way Master Ghasanie taught me during my Tae Kwon Do training. I'm slow to move sometimes, so I used to get hit a lot. That means I was able to practice fighting through dizziness often. Right now, I need to find my sister and my date! Dizziness be damned, I'm moving.

My first impression is the bomb produced very little damage. Other than the hole in the wall and lots of broken dishes and over-turned furniture, there's little physical damage. Several people are lying on the floor near the hole. It's obvious that many of those in the room are suffering from some sort of shock. Many are just wandering.

I head to where the hole is blown out of the castle walls. The last I saw, Kendra was sitting on a bench near the balcony right by the hole. On my way, I find Jolie Woods, my date. Jolie and I had been dating for about a week now. For me, that's almost an eternity. I prefer not to have a steady girlfriend. Jolie is different. It isn't the beautiful red hair, or her knock-your-socks off-looks, or even her skill as an actress. This girl has everything.

Jolie's sitting on a bench opposite where I'd last seen Kendra. She has a cut on her forehead and several scratches on her arms. I pull out my silk handkerchief and use it to stop the bleeding on her fore-head. Then, despite my racing desire to find my sister, I hold her for a bit. She stops me, telling me she's fine. I look for any hint of a concussion.

"Jolie," I say, "I need to find Kendra. Have you seen her since the explosion?"

"No." She takes my hand and squeezes it.

"Do you mind if I go find some help for you and look for my sister?"

"Jared, don't be silly! I'm fine, look for Kendra. I can get my own help!"

I gently kiss her on her pouty lips, holding her face in my hands. She returns the kiss adoringly.

At the end of the kiss, she holds my hands in place and says, "I love you, Jared Macbard, and I'm going to marry you."

I look at her and smile. I don't need to say anything.

As I move through the crowd, I keep stopping to help people. Some need serious medical attention.

I yell to the room, "Does the castle have a doctor? Are there any nurses?"

"I'm a doctor. I just got here. Do you know who's the worst off yet?"

"This lady is bleeding badly—I think you should start with her. I'll find you some help. I've got to find my sister. If you meet someone named Kendra, tell her that her brother is looking for her."

"Wait, Kendra Macbard? She's a friend of mine. I came tonight to see her. My name is Arden. I'll keep a look-out."

Arden grabs a guy who seems to need a purpose at that moment. Together, they start to triage the patients.

I walk away, toward the bench where I last saw Kendra. I trip over a body. Even from behind, I can tell it's Kino. I turn him over gently to see if he's all right. I don't see any sign of trauma, so I risk moving him out of the traffic lane, so no one else will trip over him. Dang, he's heavy! I rely on my first aid training: turn him on his side, bend his top leg, so his hip and knee are at right angles, gently tilt his head back to keep his airway open, keep him warm.

After I've arranged Kino, I take my jacket and lay it across him. I hope he's only knocked out from the blast. There's nothing left for me to do but tell Arden. "Hey, Arden, check on this guy when you can!"

He yells back, "I'll be right over."

I get to where I last saw my sister. The bench is overturned, and debris is spread all over the place. I see a guy sitting on the floor, so I walk to him and ask, "Do you need help?"

"No, I'm okay."

"Have you seen, Kendra?"

"The Queen. These guys in all black sprayed something in her face when she got up. It knocked her right out. They took her out that way... where the balcony used to be."

"Thank you. Did you recognize the men?"

"No, they weren't from the party. They had on masks."

"Thank you again. If you feel okay, do you mind helping with the injured? I need someone to help take the doctor to the people who are the worst off. He's the one right over there."

"No problem. I'll start right now. Good luck finding the Queen. You know, I think this was all just to get to her," he yells to me as I leave.

I lean out of the hole in the castle wall, where I find two ropes dangling into the garden below. The ballroom is only on the second floor, so the drop is only about ten feet or so.

Mica finds me, and I tell him what the guy I just spoke with had said.

"Jared, do you want me to take you to the garden?"

"Yes, as fast as we can."

He grabs me and flies out of the window to the garden at the base of the ropes. "You go that way, I'll go this way."

I take his lead, and we both take off in different directions. I head to the parking lot, Mica heads toward the road. He's the only one who finds anything, and all he finds are footprints leading to the street. I gather some of the guards and start organizing them into a search party.

Eventually, we all meet up with him. He gets the rest of the ground search under control. He's flying—maybe he can locate things from the air. Amber, Mason, and Spar join him in the air, searching for any clues. Out of my depth and knowing the search is well in-hand, I head back into the castle to help with the wounded.

Arden seems to have the triage well under control, too. I let him know the ambulances are within sight.

"Jared, when they get here, help the EMTs as much as possible."

"No sweat!" I see Jolie helping, and I stop to check on her.

"Hello, beautiful. How are you feeling?" My sister's missing. The most prominent female I've ever had in my life, next to my mother, and the only thing I want to know is... will Jolie help me calm my panic? I need her to keep me strong, and she is willing.

"Hey there, handsome. Any luck on finding Kendra?"

"Not yet. We're pretty sure she's been kidnapped. Mica has the goyles up and flying, looking for any clues. There's also a ground search party. Right now, I'm waiting for more information. Hey, come check on Kino with me."

I find him in the same place I'd left him. He's still groggy, but sitting up now and wondering what the hell happened. I sit beside him to break the news.

"Kino, Kendra's been taken. We have search parties already hunting for her, but she's gone. We're pretty sure she was alive when she was taken."

Mica finds us and sits with us.

He says, "We didn't find anything regarding Kendra. Also, the prisoners are gone from the cells."

Arden joins us and fills us in on the wounded.

He says, "The injured have been transported to local hospitals. Kino, you appear to be the most seriously injured gargoyle."

"I will be fine after I rest this coming day. Jared, you said you are pretty sure she is alive. Why?"

"Well, for one, I haven't felt anything else, bad or odd. Also, I found a man who told me he saw men in black ski-masks grab her, spray something in her face, then carry her off."

Mica takes over again. "I found the container that they used to spray Kendra. It's in an evidence bag. Jared, will you get with TASS? I need the can examined for prints, and see if they can figure out what was inside it. I need any video that will show the grounds around this room and the interior of this room for thirty minutes before the bombing and for five-minutes after."

"Arden, are you leaving or planning to stay?"

"I'm staying. I came here to see Kendra. I'm not leaving until I do," Arden answers.

"That's good. I need you to go to the hospital and find out what kind of injuries there were. Next, see if any of the injured are from the people who took Kendra. Finally, while you're there, examine the stuff in the can of spray, too. Maybe you can find out what it is faster than TASS."

"I can do that. Hey, Jared, let's trade numbers, too, just in case."

Mica continues, unabated, "Kino, I need you to spell the grounds. Keep any clues from being destroyed while we search. Then, go get Jericho. I'm going to keep the others searching and report to Mega. We'll meet back in Kendra's suite in two hours. See you in a while."

I speak before anyone can leave, "Mica, I think you should get to bed. You're the only gargoyle who can be out during the day. You need to let Mega or another investigator work at night, and you handle the day shift."

"No, Jared, I--"

"Mica, don't make me pull rank on you." I add a laugh to make it less of a demand. "I need—better yet, Kendra needs you to run the day shift. We can wake you if we need to at night."

"Thank you, Jared. I know you're right. Wake me if anything important happens. Promise me!"

"I promise, big guy," I say, disregarding the fact that I'll need some sleep sooner or later, too.

Two hours later, we gather in the living area of Kendra's suite. We only have a few hours until sunrise.

Mega begins, "At approximately 12:57 a.m., a bomb was detonated. We have a witness who saw the Queen lifted from the ground and something sprayed into her face. Arden, have you or TASS identified it yet?"

"Yes, it's nitrous sulfide. To a normal person, it can kill, depending on how long it's sprayed in her face. How directly it was sprayed would also have an effect," Arden says.

Mega answers Arden in his powerful 'I'm in charge' voice, "Well, given that she is a Dragon Queen, I believe she will only be disabled by nitrous sulfide. Jericho is on his way to perform his investigation.

Similarly, given that the prisoners were taken, I believe it is a strong possibility the Jessup Cartel did this."

I add, "TASS is currently conducting an extensive search of the property around the castle and in the village, looking for more clues. We have not had any communication from the kidnappers yet."

Just then José Brinker walks in.

He says, "Jared, you need to correct your last statement. We have received a note from the cartel."

"I'll go wake, Mica."

I return with Mica and find Jericho stepping into the room from an open portal.

"Tell me, Mega, what's happened to our queen?" he asks.

Mega gives a rundown of everything we know while everyone listens again.

He says, "Jared, you knew of a problem before it happened and witnessed the explosion. Will you show Jericho the crime scene?"

Mica, Spar, and Kino join us while I show Jericho where I last saw Kendra. Jericho lifts the largest remnant of the bench with ease and begins mumbling a spell. I see light take form, rising out of the debris of the bench.

He asks, "Was Kendra wearing red?"

As one, we answer, "Yes."

"Mica, may I trouble you to carry me and follow the red light of the sprite?" he asks.

Spar looks questioningly at me, as if to say, 'Do you want me to follow along?'

Without waiting on him to speak, I say, "Damn straight I do."

The light leads us down a worn path about two miles in length. At its end we find an abandoned grass airstrip.

He tells us, "They flew away from this location. The sprite can lead us no further."

Unable to continue, Jericho and the gargoyles returned to tell Mega what we'd found. I decide to take time to finally call Dana. He is going to blow a gasket.

I have to leave a message for him to call me back. In the meantime, I sit outside the castle, waiting. I don't have to wait long before my phone rings.

He says, "What in the hell's going on?"

"Man, I don't want to have to tell you on the phone," I say, then I proceed to tell him the whole story.

I'm sure Dana just threw something when I hear a crash on the other end.

"There is nothing we can do until we get some leads. I'll call you as soon as I know anything."

I can tell he's as angry and as frustrated as I am when we hang up.

I've just lost my sister to some nutcase, and now Dana is pissed at me. He'll come around when he thinks it through. But for now...

"Damn it all to hell. I need to take a walk."

I take a literal hike, over to the top of a bluff where there are several boulders and rock piles. I stand there reviewing what happened. Sis gone, brother pissed, and Jolie hurt.

"And where the fuck were the guards?" I yell as I tear off my shirt and slam it against the rocks.

As I pick up a large rock to smash, I scream, "Don Manuel Jessup, I will find you and I will end you!" grunting the last words out as I smashed the rock to smithereens on one of the big stones.

Grabbing an even larger rock, I pound it repeatedly on a flat rock. I'm hammering it with all my might when I smash my hand between the immovable object and the thirty-pound boulder I'm beating against it.

Roaring with the pain in my hand, I feel a sharp pain in my left—no, both shoulders. It's growing worse. Great, throw a tantrum and now I've torn something in my shoulders! Nice.

It gets worse. Now my whole body is on fire. I roar. My growl becomes louder and deeper, more feral.

Suddenly, Jericho is beside me. What the hell? I didn't even see a portal.

The pain is astonishing. It feels as if my whole body's on fire!

Jericho speaks to me—do I hear him, or is he in my thoughts?

"Jared, the pain is your dragon-self. It's okay. Let it overtake you. Let it become who you are. Become the dragon. The pain will end."

I'm doing my best to listen and do what he says. I feel his hand on my chest and visualize myself as a dragon. I don't know why, but I push. Don't ask me what I push, I just do. I push, and the pain eases. I push more and keep pushing. When I gazed at Jericho's hand on my chest, I see that my skin is bluish now, more muscled.

Jericho is saying, "That's correct, Jared. Now, unfurl your wings. You must use them. If you do not, they will stunt, and you will not fly."

I do as he says and relax those muscles. Wow, I have wings! I feel like I knew this was going to happen one day. I don't know why, but I'm not surprised.

Jericho says, "Jared, you have chosen very well."

"Look at my wings—they're massive! And strong."

"You must try to move them... fly."

I begin moving them and feel the mass of air move around me. I struggle to stay on my feet as they try to lift me.

Jericho points to a small cliff and yells, "Jump! I will ensure your safety."

I run straight at the edge of the cliff and leap into the black. My wings catch the wind, and I fly. Easily, I fly.

Raising myself into the air, I roar at Kendra's abductors, "I'm coming for her, and I will utterly destroy you!"

Wait, problem. I need to land, so I can call Dana. Now!

I make a not very graceful landing. I'll do better next time. Now that I have it figured out.

"Jericho, I have to call Dana. I think I can carry you if you want to fly with me."

Without a pause, he raises his arms to me. Grabbing him, I take off toward the castle.

This time I set down easily on the patio outside of Kendra's suit and I put the mage in a chair. I pick up my phone off of the table where I'd left it and call Dana.

"Arghhh!!! What's going on, Jared?"

"Okay... Dana be calm and don't fight it. Go with it. You have dragon blood, remember? It's who you are. Hurry and get outside. You need to relax and push it out. It quits hurting so much when you push it out."

"I am outside! I was looking for rocks to smash!"

"Okay, can you feel wings?"

"Yes, and they hurt!"

"Relax, Dana, help them uncurl."

"Whew, that's better."

"Dana, you have to fly now!"

"What?"

"I'm not kidding. It just happened to me."

"Okay, I'll call you back in a minute."

I wait, excitement bubbling around me like a baby in a bathtub. In a few minutes, Dana calls me back.

"Did you fly?" I ask him.

"Yes, it's great. My skin is a little aqua colored. Not full on like a crayon, just a shade."

"Well, mine's blue. But, like you, just a shade. I think me being so mad at whoever took Kendra and not being able to do anything forced it out."

"Okay, Jared, I have to go. Love you."

"Love you, too, little brother."

I've never felt better, I feel great. Give me five minutes, and I'm sure I'll feel the crash. I'll be exhausted and need a nap. Probably not a bad idea, anyway. I need to be awake when TASS is ready to give us the information we're waiting on.

26

BATTLE

Kendra

When I wake, the only light I can see is that which comes with each heartbeat pounding into my headache. The fear resulting from not knowing where I am, is compounded by my nerves.There is pain thundering through each joint in my body.

I put my fingers to my eyes, checking to see if I'm blindfolded, or maybe worse. I touch knots of swollen flesh around my face and head as well as many areas where my hair is matted to my scalp and face. I assume it's blood that's dried. My eyelids are moving, blinking. With my eyes open and not feeling a blindfold, have I been blinded? I have a vague recollection of having something sprayed into my face before the blackness.

Claustrophobia is setting deep into my gut. I can't see. Risking, I'm not sure what, I try a soft, "Hello?"

What comes out is a cross between the sound of a saw cutting wood and the moan of a ghost. The sickness in my gut grows more intense; I imagine the latter may be close to a reality.

I risk exploring the rest of my body and gingerly rise to a seated position. Chains clink and a heavy weight pulls at my waist. My fingertips are my eyes. Using them, I find a thick, wide, hard rubber piece of something which feels like the steel-belted tread of a tire. The chain on my stomach has four bolts coming through, from my stomach, outward. These hold the tire together, along with a thick metal shackle. A heavy chain is attached to the shackle. The entire device is so tight around my waist, it's staving off my attempts at breathing deeply. This doesn't bother me, because the pain in my ribs keeps me from breathing deeply anyway.

I follow the chain until I reach another shackle, secured to a type of stone or concrete wall. Checking my arms and legs, I find that one arm and both legs are cuffed to chains attached through different holes in the wall.

Astonished at the turn of events in my life, I slide to the floor. It feels like only minutes ago, I was being escorted by my three handsome consorts, wearing a dress that was given to me specifically for my pleasure. Now, I sit on the dirt floor of a building, being held by any number of foes who want me dead—not for anything I've intentionally done, but more because of who I am, who I represent.

My eyes burn as the tears fall. Angrily, I wipe them away. I have no shame for these tears. I don't see them as a sign of weakness. They represent my growing anger, anger that's squeezing out the claustrophobic fear that had taken hold. Tears mean I'm mad. Someone targeted me, hurting my friends and my lovers in the process. I'll get my revenge. And when I do, it'll be a worse day for them than they ever thought possible.

Okay, Kendra, calm your ass down. Anger won't help right now. Making a resolution to find an opportunity to escape, I call out in a slightly stronger voice than before.

"Hey, is anybody out there? Hello? Hey," I try to get someone's attention a few more times. A shaft of light bursts through an opening in my cell. The light punishes my optic nerves and fortifies the pounding headache I've been fighting, dropping me to my knees.

Holding my hands to shade my eyes, I say through gritted teeth, "I can at least think now."

There's a bell, a church bell maybe, ringing in the distance. My senses are beginning to stir, and I notice things that I'd been missing. There's a definite heat radiating through the daylight. The room smells of dirt and rot.

I hear a man say, "Conseguir el jefe."

Then the light, my shaft of hope, slams shut. Somewhere in the back of my mind, I know I'm not in Scotland. A jungle? Central America, maybe?

A short time later, the door opens. More light, more air—closer to freedom. A short stout Hispanic man enters. I stand, shaking, and face him. At once, I know the face: Don Manuel Jessup.

My brain's still foggy. It isn't so bad that I can't keep looking for my one opportunity. He walks around me, sniffs. "So, you are the maldita puta that made so much trouble for me. You don't look like much. My men said you are someone special. A queen maybe? You cost me a lot of money. I want it back and interest. Then, maybe, I'll let you go. Yes?"

I answer with the weakest voice I can, hoping for mercy, "I have no money. I'm a no one. No one'll pay."

"Oh, come now, Kendra Macbard, sister to the famous playboy Jared Macbard. Your brother Dana has a nice fat wallet, too. Queen of the Ceorfan tribe.

Who are the Ceorfan anyway, bitch? Where are they from? A poor native tribe? It doesn't matter. I sent your ransom note to TASS. Someone will pay, even if it's for your dead body. Which was my intention when my men took you. They sprayed enough nitrous sulfide in your face that you should be dead. We were so convinced you were dead, we took pictures of you laying on the ground. I sent them with the ransom note. Then something interesting happened. You lived. You slept for more than a day, but here you are. How? The stories must be true you are superhuman."

Through all the questions and other comments, I remain quiet. Better to seem completely ignorant of what he was speaking about than to give him something to hurt me with.

Don Manuel Jessup comes closer to me. He studies my face and scrutinizes my eyes.

I ready myself to use my gift to convince him to let me go. "Mr. Jees—"

His slap is fast and hard. Blackness highlights a single tunnel of light, the extent of my vision. I'm not sure if his slap is as hard as he can hit, but it's hard, as if he had a metal plate inside his hand.

Reeling from the slap, I fight to stay upright, to regain my bearing. He kicks my feet out from under me. I hit the ground like a bag of concrete falling from a truck. When I land, he kicks me in the ribs. Bones grind, and my breath involuntarily departs my body.

I roll onto my knees and elbows, trying to catch my breath, and there's a sickening crunch. A heartbeat later, a towering wave of pain from my left forearm destroys any sense of hope I have left.

After a wave of pain attempts to drown me, I try to roll onto my side and curl protectively around my broken arm, cradling it gently with my other arm. I'm trapped by my left arm. It's pinned in place by Jessup's heel. I watch as he does his utmost to pulverize my arm with his boot heel.

Don Manuel Jessup kicks me until I pass out. It takes forever, but one more good kick to my head and lights out.

Again, I wake. I try to move, but the pain stops me. I lie still for a minute. Well, I need to find a way to keep from getting the shit kicked out of me by this asswipe. I'm not sure how much more I can take. I bump something metal with my foot. Oh, a present. I hope it's a tank!

Nope. It's not a tank. But it's almost as good! The water tastes terrible, yeah, and I still drink it, a little bit at a time. The pain in my arm is unbearable, but not so bad that I can't hold the bowl.

I need a plan. No more Ms. Nice Bitch. I finish the water and use the side of the metal bowl for leverage on the bolt in the wall. Before I can get to work on it, the door begins to rattle as someone opens it and walks in. I'd already stopped working on the bolt and began pretending to drink from the bowl.

"Well, that's a good queen. Again, you are alive when you should not be." If it wasn't Mr. Asswipe Jessup himself... again. He's wearing different clothes than earlier.

"I have beaten many people to death. How is it you still live and are moving around after less than 24 hours? Have you been given something to make you heal, maybe? Answer me, bitch, or I'll use a bullet to your head to see if you can survive it."

"Will you promise to stop beating me if I tell you?"

"I'll promise you this: tell me and I'll not try to beat you to death again."

"Okay, okay," I answer. "TASS is part of a top secret multi-government program to help keep soldiers alive longer and heal faster. I was given the serum. It's what has kept me alive. How'd you know about it? Was it Jafer? Did he tell you? It doesn't matter—he's probably dead anyway. I'm part of the experiment. I volunteered last year and have been in the project since then."

"No, Jafer did not tell me. In your words, Jafer is already e-lim-in-at-ed," he stretches out the word for effect. "I'll send a doctor to collect some of your blood. You may have just saved your own life, for a time. I'll make more selling the secrets in your system to America's enemies than as a ransom. So, you will be my new queen of the lab rats. Enjoy living while you can. No telling how much of your blood they will need. In the long run, you will likely hope for death. By then, my buyers won't even care if they kill you when they take your organs to find your secrets." He sneers.

As he leaves, he tells the guards, "She's yours. Enjoy as you want. But do not kill her."

I quickly count the guards. Okay, there's five. Hit the weak points: nose, throat, eyes. I don't care how weak I am from the beat-ings, I'm not giving up. The first guard reaches for me, and I punch him in the throat with both fists. Pain stabs through my broken arm. Another grabs me around my waist from behind. More pain flashes through my body as he squeezes my broken ribs. I use the pain as a source of energy and back this guard into the wall as hard as I can. A low "Umph!" escapes his mouth as I break his nose with the back of my head.

The other three use the chains running through the walls to end the fight. With my legs yanked from under me, I'm quickly subdued by three large men.

The leader, Broken-nose, spits the blood pouring from his nose, and reminds them that they can't kill me.

He bellows, "I'm going to fuck that puta first!"

I can't fight them off. They're too strong, too many. Somewhere along the way, I give up struggling. I'm not sure when I black out. It's a blessing, though.

After I wake, I tie the ragged edges of what is left of my dress together to cover me. I find the water bowl and gulp it down.

I'm so tired, but there's no time for rest. I've got to get out of here. Using my bowl again, I shove the edge under the bolt. Leaning my weight on it I bounce on it. Thank God, it shifts. It takes me several more hours to get it out of the wall. It's very long and has a pointed end. Clearly the wood it was in has partially rotted. I gain a small part of my freedom. It comes, though, at a cost. I'm panting like I've just run a marathon. Trying to not pass out again, I push the chain into the hole the bolt came from to make it look like it's still attached to the wall.

I'm not done. I won't give up.

"Never give up! Never surrender!" I say through gritted teeth. My brothers thought that movie was so funny.

I stumble to the door and slide down it. I'll sit behind it and rest until I hear someone open it. Then, I'll do my best to kill them with my bowl and chains, or even the bolt I just put back in the wall. I lean back and drift off to sleep.

I wake with a jerk, not meaning to fall asleep. Sleeping on the job will ruin my plan. I'd better go back to the wall and play like I'm still chained. That's a better plan anyway. They'll walk over to me, and I'll attack.

I sleep again. I reach for my bowl and it is full of water again. I must be out of it for someone to bring me water ,and I don't even know it. Good thing for me, I appear as if I'm still chained to the wall. I'm glad I thought of that. I sip my nasty water like it is brandy. It feels good on my throat, even though it tastes like elephant ass.

It's the water! The shock of my sudden revelation bursts through me, jarring me awake. It's drugged! That's why I can't stay awake.

I've sat here for what feels like hours. Have they forgotten me? Maybe they're busy with something more important for now. If so, maybe I can heal some before they start experimenting on me. As soon as I form this thought, the door lock begins its familiar rattling. I ready myself.

The light from the doorway is so bright. I can't see. Are there only two of them this time? I'll take the one in front first. Burning tears run from my eyes as I grab him and stab the bolt into his neck, using it to rip through it. He goes down hard, and I go with him.

The other guy is yelling at me. I turn, ready to attack him. I set my hips, preparing to lunge, but his hands are up in the universal, 'I surrender,' position.

Confused, I pause for a heartbeat.

He's yelling, "Kendra! Kendra, it's me. Kendra, remember Arden? Your friend Arden. Remember the fountain at University?"

"Oh, my God, it's Arden. The doctor is Arden. You're the doctor! Yeah, I remember the fountain."

I collapse into him as he pulls me to his chest. I cry. He continues to hold me.

"Kendra, I don't know how much time we have. I was sent to collect your blood samples. Your Ducere are in the jungle, waiting for my signal. They're coming. Well, that's the plan, anyway. I'm not sure any of this crew will wait. They're not very patient where you're concerned.

"Amber and Mason snagged the keys for me. Let's see if they work on your chains, shall we?"

I nod at him and say, "Thank you, Arden, I'm so glad to see you. I can't believe you're here."

He lifts my arms to get at the locks. He takes sharp breath when he sees my wrists and arm are mangled. Bone shows through in several places. Blood covers most of my body. Arden does his best not to hurt me when he removes the cuffs.

That's when we hear the first blast. We look at each other with big eyes. He moves even more quickly to unlock my leg chains. Finally, finding the right keys, my chains fall one by one onto the ground beside the dead guard. Arden pulls the AK-47 from under the guard.

I watch, surprised, as he goes through the AK like he was born with one in his hands. He checks to see if it's loaded, checks the magazine load status. He racks it and thumbs the safety off.

"Grab his extra mag," I say pointing to where it is on the dead guard.

He opens the door, motioning for me to lead. He whispers, "I can keep an eye on you better this way."

I crouch low, walking out. Directly in front of me is a large window with bright lights shining in. Damn, it's dark out. Those are giant flood lights! That's why my Ducere are here!

Continuing down the hall, we stop to check every door we pass.

"Doors and corners will get you killed." I remember an old detective telling me that. After a few turns, the hall opens to a large court-yard that easily encompasses a couple of acres. It appears to be lit with floodlights. There's a high fence, maybe ten feet tall, surrounding the parts I can see, and a large house anchors one side of the compound wall. My intuitions were spot-on. I find myself in a compound butted right up against a jungle.

Much of the compound is beautifully landscaped. There are two swimming pools. One, near the house, has what should be a waterfall, with a large grotto at one end of the pool and a large hot tub at the other end. The pool is empty; it's still under construction. The other pool is for children. That little fact jars me, as I realize there may be children in the area.

Jessup's men are fighting a fierce battle to control the area.

They've employed machine guns from the towers, small rocket-propelled grenades (RPGs), and at least sixty-five soldiers. I even see a tank and a helicopter preparing to take off. Luckily, I don't see the tank moving. The helicopter is our most pressing problem.

Searching for a path forward, I find myself perpendicular to a line of soldiers in cover, with more coming towa--h, hell—Mica! He's right in the middle of the line. No armor, no helmet, just his bad-ass bravado going full blast. Using his... is that a 50 cal.? Whatever it is, he's chewing holes in walls, buildings, any place that Jessup's men might be. Any time a soldier gets within range of him, he pauses, grabs them and kills them on the spot. He is covered in shithead blood.

Out of the blue, I catch a glimpse of three men running at him with a tomahawk in each hand. They appear to be out for blood.

I yell, "Run, Mica!"

He deliberately stops and waits for these three. He sets his stance, his balance low. When the first one reaches him, without hesitation, he grabs him and uses his body to beat the other two. Repeatedly, he pounds the two on the ground with the one he caught. The pounding continues until the man is dismembered. His legs and hips are beat from the rest of his body. Guts, blood, and bile spill from the bifurcated parts.

Mica, left holding only the man's legs, grabs the two men on the ground and, without so much as a trifling effort, removes both of their heads. He returns to his machine gun again. This time, he targets Jessup's men deliberately, not just the buildings. The 50 cal., tears holes through them, spilling even more gore. The smell of the blood and ruined bodies permeates the air. He turns and spots me. The smile on his face settles me. No way in hell will he let them hurt me again.

Mega runs to help him and now, together, they form the middle of the phalanx pushing Jessup's men. The gargoyles try to change tactics. Even though they stay back, Mica chews them up with the machine gun. If they rush him, they're torn apart.

"Nobody attacks my family without facing death," I say out loud to anyone around. The love I feel for these men because of the risk they are taking for me is indescribable.

There are others in this fight. Two of them are flying; they have no weapons in their hands that I can see. These men have wings. They aren't men—per se, more like dragon-men. They both have clawed feet, scales, long tails, larger armor scales throughout their bellies and chest. Their arms--

"Shit! Holy fuck-fire... Jared, Dana! What the hell am I seeing?"

They're so handsome, and... in so much trouble! The clouds behind Jared are rapidly building, and the lightning is shooting through the sky behind them. The helicopter lifts off and is angling toward them. Lightning flashes, and thunder rips through the compound. Boom! The helicopter explodes in a flash of fire and electricity. Damn, that was good luck.

The rain is pounding now. Any fires nearby are doused.

Just then, Jadite, my beautiful warrior, lands in front of Arden and I and begins yelling for us to move out.

He shouts, "My queen, now is the time to leave. Our mission is to save you, not destroy this cartel. There'll be time for that later."

I'm in awe of the fighting force decimating the cartel. Arden is holding me, almost carrying me in the direction of the pool that's under repair. We round the grotto and arms grab Arden. Well, if it isn't the top asswipe himself, Don Manuel Jessup, and he has a gun pointed at Arden's head.

He barks, "Make them stop, or your friend dies. You," now talking to Arden, "drop the weapon."

Arden drops the gun. "Don't do anything. I'm dropping it," he says.

Jadite was ahead of us and spins to end Asswipe. He begins to reach out, but suddenly stops and slowly backs up several steps.

Out of the corner of my eye, I see Dana moving to help, waving Jadite off. Dana starts to make his move. Asswipe sees him and point-blank fires two shots into his face. Dana drops to the ground near the edge of the pool; the momentum from the fall carries him into the pool.

Panic, dread, terror, resignation course through my hopelessly hysterical brain. My Dana, my precious little brother, is gone.

Jadite roughly seizes Jessup and plants him in his place in front of me, daring him to move.

"It's your choice, asswipe. Move, and I'll make sure today is the day you pay the ferryman."

Jessup arrogantly points his chin at me, talking. He's talking. What's he saying... something about 'making it worth my while' if I let him go?

At this point, Mica steps from behind me. He takes my hand and gently pulls me to him. I feel his heart beating and smell him for the first time in what feels like forever. I start to lean in, then pull away.

"I'm not done!" I say, as I place my hand on his chest.

My tears are falling like the rain. My anger is growing.

Jessup is screaming. Threatening or pleading, I don't know. I don't care. I can't understand a word he's saying. Right now, the entire world sounds like it is speaking to me through a giant can on a string—all mumbles, no detail.

"Dana!" I cry. This mama bear bites!

Anger floods my feelings, overwhelming every rational thought. It turns to rage, rage to hatred, hatred to a deep, visceral scream.

The "NO!" that I exhale is filled with all the anger, rage, and hatred I have for this man and his men.

Brilliant light fires from my mouth concurrent with my scream. Like a laser, it hits Jessup in the dead center of his forehead. I keep screaming until I have no more breath left. I collapse onto the ground, sobbing. Don Manuel Jessup, his entire upper body completely burned away, has fallen to the ground in front of me.

Jadite lifts me to my feet and says, "Kendra, we need to move you, now!"

"Wait. Dana."

I hurry to the edge of the pool where my baby brother had fallen. Horrified, I stare down into the pool.

Sometimes in my life, I see things others can't. Often, those 'visions' have led me to decisions that I struggle with; some change the plane of my life. But this is no vision! This is real! My heart skips a beat. Staring into the pool, I see Dana standing there looking back at me with the biggest shit-eating grin on his face.

"Hi, Sis," he tells me, his dimples in full force.

"What? He shot you in the face... I know he shot you. He shot you twice."

"It's okay, Sis, I'm fine."

"Thank you, Lord!" I launch myself at him and grab him in a fierce big-sister hug. "I thought he'd killed you."

"My skin isn't stone, Sis. I think it's harder than stone," he tells me as he points to his aqua-colored skin. Weird, it looks good on him. He tells me he was hit several times today and thinks all he got is a chip in his front tooth.

"We need to remember to keep our mouths shut in a gunfight," he chuckles. "Jared's the same way, I'm just prettier."

I would have laughed, too if I wasn't burning so badly. The storm, which was raging, is ebbing now. Now that the fighting is ending.

The burning is getting bad, and the cool rain isn't helping.

I crumple, looking to Arden for help. The battle's over; Jared and Mica are with me now, too.

"Ouch! It hurts everywhere! Help!"

Jared answers me, "Look at me, Sissy. I can help you, but it isn't easy. You need listen to me. Remember, you're part dragon."

"I do, but this is burning! It hurts so bad!"

"Sissy, let the dragon come. Relax into it."

"What?"

"You can push your dragon blood to the top if you try. Visualize what you would look like if you were a dragon. It doesn't have to be right. Just see it. Concentrate and think of it. Push your dragon blood to the top."

I do, and the burning subsides. It feels better. A little, anyway.

Jared continues, "That's it, Sis—concentrate and push it to the top."

I hold my breath and push all over, and I feel better. I relax, and wings shoot out. They're much longer than my arms.

"Alrighty then, I'm not sure why, but Jericho said it's important to fly right now. So, can you flap your wings?"said Jared.

I can and do tentatively.

"Okay, so do that and hold our hands." Jared and Mica both take a hand as I flap, and up we go.

I yell, "Holy crap! We're flying. Okay, I got it now, but catch me if I fall."

Mica answers in his deep loving voice, "Always, my love."

I take a short flight around the compound. It looks like most of the cartel is dead or has retreated. The TASS soldiers are cleaning up, checking for wounded. Jadite is attending to those at Arden's direction.

Time to land. I watch Mica, he gently guides me through the landing process. We touch down, light as a feather.

Arden says, "That's amazing, I'm never going to forget that, Kendra. You probably need some water, though. Even though your skin is naturally red now, you have some dry spots. Stay here, I'll see what I can find."

He's right; I'm very thirsty.

One of the TASS soldiers says, "Representative Jared Macbard. We've cleared the entire compound. We're now collecting any prisoners and are trying to find any useful information. Do you and the Ceorfan Queen mind the wait? We can make it back to the plane in a few hours. It won't be much longer. Is this Don Manuel Jessup?"

We tell him it is. He takes a kit from his pack, collects blood and tissue samples. Then he snaps a picture of his burnt body before he walks off.

Arden brings me a bottle of water. "I'll get you something better when we get to the plane, but for now, this should help."

He's right; I need the water.

"Dana, can you deal with these remains."

"Sure, Sis."

We move away from the body. As we do, the grotto near where Jessup lies, crumbles. Thousands of tons of rock, iron, concrete, and dirt bury Jessup in an unattributed tomb.

Dana says, "Well, that saves some time. The piece of shit's buried. That's more than he deserves."

"Jared, am I going to stay like this or can we look human?"

He chuckles and tells me, "You're beautiful either way. I really like the red."

Dana takes over and says, "The same way you pushed your dragon blood, push your human blood."

I do, and in seconds, I look human again. At least what I can see. I lean back into Mica's hard chest and take a deep breath.

"The first thing I want to know is, where is everyone else and how did you find me?"

Mica answers, "Everyone is safe at the castle. They all sleep as high on the parapets as they can. They're safe anyway—TASS has added to the guards around them. Anyone who works there signs a non-disclosure statement. Since you got your way with the members, they're treating us like gold. It's hard for Kino and Spar. They're not happy about having to stay there."

Arden said, "Your brothers told them they would bring you back to them or call if it was worse than we expected, so they could come, even if they had to sleep in the jungle. TASS had the intel that Don Manuel was needing a doctor to do testing on a new queen of the lab rats. We knew it had to be you. We figured that would get me into the compound. They had all the information we could possibly need to get to you. They must have had someone on the inside. I'm not surprised by them anymore. They did put me on staff and made me sign loads of paperwork, including a non-disclosure. They basically get everything I own if I ever tell a thing."

I lean closer to Mica, breathing in his smoky vanilla smell. He tightens his hold on me.

It turns out I wasn't the only prisoner in the camp. The cartel had half a dozen young women and girls handcuffed to beds in a common room. The TASS soldiers let them loose. The girls told the soldiers they were from tribes that live close to the compound. They can make it home without help. The TASS soldiers divided all the money and valuables they had found between the girls before they left to go home. We'll take the cartel's vehicles back to an airstrip where we'll board the plane to go back to Scotland. Since we're in Mexico it'll take us about 11 hours to get to the castle. It's almost 1:00 p.m., so when we get there everyone will be awake.

I fall asleep in my seat while Arden tends to my wounds.

Waking up after a few hours' sleep, I feel wonderful. It must have something to do with the dragon blood. Mica tells me all my cuts and bruises are healed, too. If the others saw what he did when Arden first found me, they'd go crazy. The way I did when I thought Don Manuel shot Dana.

"Mica, did you by any chance think to bring me some clothes?"

"Yes, they're in my bag. Are you ready to change now?"

"Yes. Is there a reason we're flying home with TASS instead of using a portal stone?"

"Yes, Princess, I want to give you a little time. When we get back, there'll be a lot of people who want a moment of your time. TASS will want information. I just wanted you to have a minute to yourself."

"Oh, thank you, Mica, that's what I need. Will you guard the door for me while I change?" I shouldn't think I need any extra protection. What's wrong with me?

"Anytime anywhere, Princess. I mean, my queen."

"No, you have called me 'Princess' since we met don't change that, okay?"

He hands me some jeans and a white Henley tee-shirt, underwear, and socks. "I'll get you a pair of new boots when we get home. I forgot to bring you some shoes."

"This is just fine. I'll be glad to get this torn-up, filthy dress off. I liked this dress, too."

"So did I," he says. "We can get you as many as you want, in any style."

I nod my head and go into the bathroom. I remove my destroyed gown and throw it into the trash. Then splash water on my face to clean it as well as possible. I do the best I can on the rest of my body. I need a good soak.

My hair is impossible. I reach into the trash bin and tear off a piece of my gown, finger-combing my hair, I begin braiding it into a French braid. I tie the end with the torn scrap of dress. I put on the clothes as fast as I can. I hate being alone in here. I don't want to be alone at all! In fact, I open the door, reach through, grab the front of Mica's shirt, and pull him into the bathroom with me. Pulling the door closed, I push him against it and wrap my arms around him. He holds me tight to his chest.

My body is shaking uncontrollably.

I whimper, "Mica, don't leave me alone. Please? I don't want to be alone."

I start to cry.

He holds me and rocks me, telling me he's not leaving me alone.

"I'm sorry, I wasn't there for you."

He thinks he let me down when the cartel took me.

"No, don't blame yourself. Just don't leave me alone. Please, I can't take it at all." I clean my face up again.

"Mica, please don't tell anyone I cried. Okay?"

"There is no shame in crying, Kendra. After what you have been through, crying is normal. No one is going to blame you for crying."

"No, they won't blame me, but they'll feel guilty. I don't want that. I want to be strong, if that makes any sense. When we get home, I want to talk to you, Spar, and Kino alone to tell you what happened while I was a prisoner of Don Manuel. That way I only have to say it once, then never again."

"You're strong. Whatever you want is what we'll do, Princess." He bends toward me and kisses me lightly on my lips.

I kiss him back. Breathing in his smoky vanilla scent, my blood heats up.

The pilot makes an announcement: we are descending and need to return to our seats. I smile at Mica, opening the door.

In minutes, we land and are disembarking. I can see Spar and Kino in front of a crowd of people. I must know some of the others, but Spar and Kino are who I'm looking for. I feel like I can't get over to them quickly enough. I quicken my pace. No, I'm running to them. Just like a commercial or a romance movie when the heroine runs to her love. I understand the feeling now. Only I'm running to two loves.

As soon as I reach out for them, they both gather me up together. I laugh. We must look weird to the others. I don't care. I want them both. Mica is behind, me adding to the hugs. Perfect! They pass me to Spar, and I sink into his spicy, rainy forest smell. I'm such a drama queen—I'm tearing up. I spill a few tears on his neck. Then he passes me to Kino, who gathers me close, putting his face into the crook of my neck, his hands in my hair. He's humming softly to me. I calm, feeling at peace. Happiness overtakes me. Taking a deep breath of his bergamot citrusy scent, I kiss him lightly on his soft, full lips.

"Thank you."

Kino smiles and says, "You have a friend who would like to say hi, Edling." He motions to a young boy, around twelve years old, standing beside his parents. Oh, it's John! Yay for dragon blood.

Standing directly in front of him, I reach out and shake his hand, putting my other hand on his shoulder.

I smile, "John, I'm so happy to see you feeling so much better! Thank you for coming to see me on my return. It's a gift to my spirit."

He leans close to me, and whispers quietly, "I know what you did. I don't know why, but it worked. Thank you, my lady."

"Let it be our little secret, please, John?"

He nods an almost imperceptible nod to me in conspiratorial assent.

I take his mother Meg's hand and give her a little hug. "Meg, you look wonderful. I take it you're feeling better, too?"

"I've never felt better, my lady. John is a living miracle. We've decided your presence in our lives has saved us. We had to be here to welcome you home. Well, our home. It's your home if you would like it to be. We are so glad to see you back and safe!"

Stepping closer to me and taking my hand, Thurston says, "It is so good to see you safe, my lady queen. We are in your debt."

"Never—you're my friends. Let's go to the castle and celebrate. I'm starving. Wonder what Chef Ron has for me?"

"I'm sure it will be something wonderful. This way to the limo, my lady queen."

I never thought, even as many times as Jared has used his limos for me, that it would feel so normal. It did, though.

27

PLANS

Kendra

Mica is holding my left hand and Spar my right, while Kino leads our little procession from the TASS private airstrip. I'm not sure how we chose this arrangement. It just happened rather organically, as if it was meant to be. If it was planned Jared and Dana are in on it, too. Which, now that I think about it, is exactly what they've done. Anyway, if they did, Jared and Dana are in on it, too. Jared also has his personal security force ringing the entire operation. Dana is walking behind me with his NODA look on his face.

Dana always has that look when he's in protection mode. He developed it when we were children. We were playing in a park in Pampa, TX. Jared was at the bottom of this bowl-shaped park, and Dana was near the top. I saw Dana run down the hill into a group of boys who had decided it would be a good idea to gang up on Jared. Dana was only nine, but when he hit the group, all of them went down like bowling pins. None of them ever bothered us again. We call that look on Dana NODA, for 'NOt a DAmn thing.' We were kids, it sounds edgy when you're eleven.

There's a total of three limos waiting. I'm escorted into the second with my consorts, while Jared and Dana ride in the first and third one, separately. The security force takes four black SUVs, two in the front, two in the rear. I am pretty sure I saw at least four machine pistols while they were getting organized in their vehicles. With all my goyles and friends in the limo train, we head to the TASS castle. Spar is on one side of me and Kino on the other; both are holding my hands. I could stay right here for a long while.

I thought about using the time during our ride back to the castle to talk to my guys. But it just doesn't have the privacy or the familiarity that I want before I open up to them about what happened. I need a different setting, so if they feel the need to leave, they can, without it being so obvious and uncomfortable for them. I guess that is my real fear... I'm damaged goods, now.

I do however, tele-speak to Mega who is in one of the other limos. I lean back with my guygoyles all touching me in some way and listen to Mega give me the details of my rescue mission from his perspective.

We arrive at the castle and head for the dining hall. Counter to what it seems many people believe, I'm not bothered by returning here. For me, returning is validation of my victory over those who tried to ruin me. I will not be undone by men of evil intent. Mica opens the doors for me. I will not be undone.

"Surprise!" Everyone yells, "Welcome back, Queen Kendra!"

I immediately feel shock. I can't understand what's happening, or why. I'm just standing here, with my mouth agape, trying to process what's going on.

Spar squeezes my hand and tells me, "Kendra, it's okay. They want to say they love you."

Recognition dawning, I realize how touched I am by this event. Wow. That some of the most powerful and prestigious people in the world would do this for me is incredible. Whether the world knows of them or knows that they make many of the most influential decisions every day doesn't matter. Outside this small group, few will ever even know what happened here—doesn't matter.

Chairman Brinker takes my hand.

He says, "Your Majesty, we're here to celebrate your return to us. If I, or any in this company," spreading his arms toward the others in the room, "can do anything for you, you have but to ask. This celebration is in your honor. Please enjoy. Today is not a day for details or questions. Today is a day of celebration." He motions me to my chair and seats me.

Chairman Brinker sits to my right and Spar to my left. Mica and Kino sit at my table, beside Spar. Near the front, I see Jared with his red-headed date again. Beside him is Dana, with a beautiful brunette I've never seen before. These two sure have a taste for the beautiful women. Or maybe the women have a taste for wonderful, handsome men—and they'd better not hurt them.

After I'm seated by Chairman Brinker, a bevy of waiters magically appear. To my right, I hear a baritone voice informing me.

"My lady queen, my name is Tito. I'm your personal steward for the remainder of your stay with us. Chef Ron has prepared your meal. I will be out with it soon. What would you like to drink?"

I respond, "I would like a glass of water and a glass of wine appropriate for my dinner, selected by the glorious Chef Ron."

I really accentuated the word 'glorious' for the crowd, playing up the event.

As I order my drinks, the rest of the guests are seated. I'm amazed at the coordination that is going on with the waitstaff. They are assigned, two to a table. The drink orders are taken, and drinks are returned almost contemporaneously with mine. I watch the waiters with rapt attention.

Chairman Brinker, sensing my fascination with the functioning of the waitstaff, leans in and says, "They use microphones and ear plugs. Notice how they lean in to each guest? It lets the microphone pick up the conversation. The bar makes the drink. The waitstaff only need remember who orders which drink."

Tonight, Chef Ron made me salmon crepes. They are my all-time favorite crepe, and he paired it with a Pinot d'Alsace. Its honey-ginger undertone mates perfectly with the meaty flavor of the fish. I have always been a 'burrito and a beer' type of girl, but Chef Ron has certainly added to my delight of food. I'll still love burritos and beer, but I'll also be happy to reach beyond that from now on.

The conversation at the table is unimaginative and stays within the confines of polite dinner banter, with the only stray being how I feel about my security situation, as well as the security of TASS. The conversation never wanders into what happened to me while I was in captivity. The discussion, while it doesn't seem forced, does feel planned. Ask her how she feels. Check. Ask her if she needs anything. Check. Ask her if she feels her security is strong enough... While I don't feel any irritation at the ad nauseam list of questions, I do feel a sense of awkwardness.

As if on cue, as my level of awkwardness is increasing, my personal waiter returns with my dessert wine. How does Chef Ron do this? He found my favorite wine again. This time it is a Grenache, Mas Amiel 10 Ans d'Age. I have always enjoyed Grenache wines. Previously, I have maybe enjoyed this version more than I should.

Tito leans in and politely informs me that Jared had told him this was my favorite dessert wine.

"Thank you, Tito, for going above and beyond. But I wish I had a piece of chocolate cake to go with it!"

Once again, perfectly timed.

"Would you look at that?" I say to Spar, who is leaning toward me with his hand on my knee. Chef Ron is rolling a huge layered cake into the room, stopping it directly in front of me.

I lean in a little more to Spar, in an almost conspiratorial manner I say, "If a man pops out and ruins my cake, he'd better be very good-looking!"

Spar laughs at me, then needles right back, "Kendra, my love, the cake is only two feet tall. I can get Mason to pop out of it, if you'd like."

Giggling, I sink back into my seat. Loudly, I proclaim, "Chef Ron, that's enough chocolate to keep me happy for weeks."

With him standing beside the cake, using his best inspirational voice, he says, "Kendra, I hope this cake meets with your approval. It is sweet, sexy, and magical like you. I made it with you in mind. Made with love, my friend."

He cuts into the cake and gives it to me. Everyone is watching so I make sure and ham it up a bit. I stick a healthy forkful into my mouth and moan, arching my back a little and titling my head back. The room bursts into laughter at my antics.

I say, "You have made me feel very special. Thank you, Chef Ron."

The cake is served throughout the room. And no, there are no good-looking men, even the small variety, who pop out of the cake. Now I see a few of the waitstaff begin to fade from view. Tito leans in one more time.

"Your Majesty, a call button has been installed in your chamber. If you require anything, my job is to ensure it's taken care of. It's my honor to provide assistance to such a lovely individual. I know what you have done for my nephew. You are our family now. Thank you."

Well, I think we're going to have to figure out what to do about that bit of information. But for now, cake!

I notice Spar doesn't have any, and I ask him if he wants a bite. He says, "Yes."

I guess he's thinking I'll hand him my fork. Instead, I pick up a bit with my fingers, holding it in front of his lips. He leans forward and eats it from my hand, licking the rich chocolate from my fingers.

My heart speeds up, and I'm all but panting. Who was I teasing? Well, that backfired. Everyone is staring, feeling the heat—maybe a bit uncomfortably. Kino smiles a crooked smile at me. Holding Spar's hand, I lean toward Kino, "I think we need to go to our room. I need to talk to you three privately before the evening gets away from us."

I stand to address the room. Everyone quiets as I start, "I would like to thank TASS and the representatives from every member nation. Your welcome, on my return, has made what could have been a difficult reunion with this room into a pleasurable evening.

However, with my apologies, I must retire to my suite for the evening. I promise I'll make myself available and thank each one of you at my earliest opportunity. Thank you and good evening."

While it's subdued for a standing ovation, the passion—bordering on adoration—is more than suitable for the occasion. I blush as I embrace the waves of emotion that crash through me with the ovation.

I turn to Chairman Brinker and say, "I'll be in your office at noon tomorrow, if it's acceptable."

He nods a polite agreement.

28

SHARING

Kendra

The Ducere are waiting in my suite. I explain all that had happened, except some details that only Mica, Spar, and Kino will know. Mega is very direct when talking about how TASS had gotten the information needed to find me so quickly.

"It is unequivocal: one of the Ceorfan provided the critical information. It was also done at great personal risk to that gargoyle."

I take over and continue, "Ceorfan, I need to make you aware of this, because we take care of our undercover agents. We knew the Cartel was trying to recruit within the Ceorfan. As you know, they succeeded with Eltira and Flint. What you do not know is the depth to which Flint had to operate."

At this, the room starts to gain a bit of buzz. I even see Amber raise her hands to cover her mouth, covering her look of surprise.

"Eltira," I say, continuing, "began colluding with the cartel before we arrived in Scotland. We needed an insider who Eltira believed she could manipulate. Flint was that insider. He accepted being the bad guy, being humiliated in front of the entire Guild, so the cartel would let him in. It was all to help bring it down and save those being destroyed by the cartel's actions. What we didn't know, what we never expected, was he would be the one to save me. He was able to gain the needed information from our home in Navan that allowed TASS to find the Jessup Cartel compound so quickly."

The room erupts in high-fives, or high-fours in some cases, cheers, and lots of 'I knew it.' I observe Amber, with tears streaking down her face, laughing and joyously hugging Mason.

Sensing this may be a time where I can rule and have the ruled vote for my wish, I ask, "I would like a vote. Who is with me in giving Flint his job back with the Elite?"

The immediate roar of "Yes," is unanimous.

Amber says, "I knew something was wrong with that picture. I never believed Flint would let anyone hurt us."

I say, "I'm going to declare a day of celebration when we get home to Navan." Listen to me calling Navan home.

"During this celebration, I'll properly award Flint for his courageous sacrifice in saving my life."

I ask Mega, "What's the reward for saving your queen and being selfless enough to lose your reputation in the process?"

Mega answers without a pause, "Having your story etched into the halls of history."

"Okay, when we get back to home, Mega, will you help me with that? I don't know enough yet to understand even the word etched as y'all use it. I'm sure it is a great thing because you say it so reverently."

"That is true, Edling. It may take a while and some education to fill you in on the subject. I shall be honored to help teach you."

"Thank you, Commander. Now, I have another issue. Since we can't easily go undercover in the human world—except for Mica, Jared, Dana, and myself— the ability to befriend trustworthy people is important. Arden Kelly was already a friend to me from college. He's proved very valuable in the past few days. What do you think we should do with Arden? I'm thinking of making him a representative for TASS, if it's what he wants. I'd like him protected by the Ceorfan. He's a doctor, but has been in politics for a good many years."

Mega agrees, and as I look around, everyone else does, too.

"Finally, before I take Mica, Spar, and Kino to speak privately, I need to tell you something. I didn't think when I did it. I just acted. John Collins, Thurston's son, was very sick. He'd been sick for a while. I was visiting Thurston's family before the gala, and I noticed John had a blister on his hand that had opened. I punctured my finger and rubbed my blood into the wound, hoping it would help him."

I can feel their approval. Their feelings told me they would have expected me to do this for John. There are no alarms in their feelings.

"However, at the airport, John told me quietly, he knows what I did. I'm not sure what to do, if I should do anything, or if I've inadvertently given us away."

Mega says, "In the past, we have found friends who are extremely loyal. Humans are not fooled. They have a way of putting information together to understand what happens around them. I think you should be honest with Thurston. Make him part of your inner circle. I believe his family is honorable. If he proves to be other than honorable, Jericho can take the memory of us from him. It will be as if they never knew us."

"Mega, that's the most wonderful news. I believe I'll do just that. Now, I'm going to my room. I have more to tell my consorts. Goodnight and good torp, everyone."

***

ALONE, in my private room with only my consorts, I start to question my rationale for telling them everything that happened to me. I steel myself for one, or maybe all of them, to decide I'm not for them anymore. Yet it's my obligation to be honest with them. Even if they choose to not stay with me, they should know what happened at the Jessup compound.

Nothing, not a word's spoken, as my loves patiently wait for me to speak. They simply wait for me to start. Needlessly, but to buy myself a few more seconds to think, I ask them to sit on my sofa. But they're so big, I have to pull up a chair beside the sofa for Kino to sit in. I pull a smaller chair in front of them for me.

"This is going to be difficult to get out," I start.

Trying to catch my breath, I pause. Unfortunately, the pause only allows more negative thoughts.

Damnit, how do I start? My hands are shaking, and my mouth is dry as I try to think of a way to tell them my story. I stare at my hands, trying to summon my flagging courage. All three of them watch and remain silent for me. Their pained expressions show the level of the pain they feel for me. I'm going to take that away. I can take away their pain.

"The first thing I want to say is, I love you each more than I can ever express. What I'm about to tell you will be difficult to hear. You should know, I want to share this with you. I trust you with this knowledge, and I don't want it between us. I'll answer all your questions. Afterwards, I want this conversation to be the end of it. I want it to be like so much smoke blown into the wind.

"I've no idea how I got to the compound. I woke up chained. I'm pretty sure they'd beaten me, though, because I was bruised and cut up. They'd shackled me. At first, I was terrified. And, after the second beating, I wanted to give up. I hoped for death.

"After a day or so, someone brought me a metal bowl of dirty, nasty water. I felt the water was like me—it was dirty and nasty, and still good for something. I'd still be good for something, more maybe. The water was dirty and nasty, but in that darkness, it helped me stay alive.

"Using the metaphor of the water, I began planning ways to get back to you three. You know, I'd heard that when soldiers say they have their girl on their mind, it makes them stronger and gives them a reason to fight on, even when they want to quit. That girl waiting for them is what gets them through the awfulness of war and home again. I learned that's how it really works. Don Manuel Jessup tried to kill me several times. They spit on me, peed on me, stomped on me, beat me, and ultimately raped me. The whole time, I kept your faces in front of me for hope."

Tears leak out of my eyes, and my voice shakes a little, so I clear my throat.

"I decided I would not be poured out. I would remain useful. I'd get back to you and love you with all my heart. I'd take this world and make my mark by loving everyone equally, by building others up and not tearing them down. I want to help and protect others even more than I did before. If what's happened to me is too much for you to handle, and any of you want out of this relationship, I understand. I won't hate you. I want you to know you have a choice in this, too. That's all I have to say."

Kino scoots onto the floor at my feet and puts his large hands around mine, laying his head in my lap. Mica also sits on the floor beside my chair. He puts his arms around me, his head against my arm. Spar, standing opposite of Mica, squats with his arms around my shoulders and his head on my neck. I can feel their love for me.

We stay that way for a little while. I know they love me; I just needed to feel it again. Taking a deep breath and letting it out, I start to giggle. Oh, my God, I'm such a girl! Now I'm laughing hard.

Kino picks me up and spins in a circle, holding me close. Spar starts his party playlist on his tablet. We just jump around and play with each other. Somewhere along the line, we start dancing.

If you can see two men who love you with this intensity dancing, you'll understand my heart when I say, "It is magnificent."

After a bit, we change partners and keep dancing. It's getting close to sunrise, so my gargoyles put me in bed for some sleep. They don't leave me, though. They stay, and I drift off quickly in Mica's arms, Spar and Kino next to the bed. I wake several hours later and lie there looking at Spar and Kino. It takes me a minute to recognize what they had done. But when I see it, it's obvious. Those two have put their hands together in a heart shape.

"You crazy boys. I love you back."

I wake up Mica, but he's so tired. I tell him to torp; I'm going to take a long shower then a bath. I cry in the shower, so no one hears me. When I finish, I soak in a hot bath.

Reflecting, I make a plan for my life. I'm not doing this anymore. I'm moving on and forgetting what happened in the compound. I might talk to Jericho or Arden in private. Maybe, but I'm not sure I can tell anyone else. Until then—fake it 'till I make—it is my new motto. I'm tough. I do not want pity! I especially don't want to make everyone around me feel my pain. I want to make them happy, myself included. So, I'm not bringing what happened up, even to myself. I'll deal!

After I bathe and dress, I go to Chairman Brinker's office for our meeting. His assistant tells me, "Queen Kendra, the Chairman has left instructions that you are to be his priority today. He'll see you as soon as I alert him. In the meantime, Chef Ron sent this." She delivers to me some chai tea and biscuits.

"Queen Kendra, is there anything more you would like?"

"No, Cecile, and it's Kendra unless we're somewhere we have to be formal, okay?"

She smiles her normal warm, congenial smile and answers, "We're in your corner. You have many supporters here." Then she departs to Chairman Brinker's office.

José Brinker leaves his office with another person. My eyebrows rise slightly as I figure out who that prominent person is. My all-time favorite superhero. José brings him over to me and introduces us. I officially like this job now. Meeting a sexy movie star makes my day. Too bad TASS has rules about telling who we see and what we do when we are together.

There is absolutely no media, anywhere. Meetings are conducted in different locations each time. No one would believe us even if we did tell what happens here and who we see. TASS is a propaganda machine. They'd be able to prove the opposite of any information they don't like at the drop of a hat. Most of the members are above such antics, though, so it's a non-issue.

José asks, "Will you have lunch with me."

"I will, but the biscuits and tea filled me up." I ask Tito for water when we're seated. He tilts his head in acknowledgment and offers a sly smile.

"José, I'm not sure what information you need, but I can tell you what I know. The cartel is preying on the indigenous tribes in the area. Most are slaves to the cartel. Some are used as security for moving into a new area. These men are forced to intimidate the new people into also working for the cartel. Additionally, these 'security' men have little choice. If they don't intimidate the others, their families will be denied food and water, or even killed.

"Others are forced to grow the drug crops, refine and prepare it for shipment north. We also have evidence they are enslaving the young girls and selling them as sex slaves. Some of them are even very young children. My people saw this while at the Jessup compound, and I want to fight it with extreme prejudice."

"Kendra, do you have any names of people in the area who are involved? If so, how badly can we hurt them? Will it provide us a window where we can focus on the Horde?"

"José, if TASS were to make this a priority, I can, through my job as a Park Ranger provide some information—names, pictures, and such. I have friends at the FBI and even the CIA that I can trust. We do have more information regarding cartel activities. However, there's at least one Ranger who's working with the cartel. I must find more facts and if anyone else is working with them, so we know our evidence is secure and correct.

"Also, although we decimated the Jessup Cartel in this last skirmish, his son will be taking control. I know this kid. I arrested him last month. He is a punk kid and doesn't have the brains to run it. That will only lead to someone else killing him and taking over.

"My point is, our Ranger station can't keep up. There's always someone to step in and take control. But we know who's in line, basi-cally. While the Park Rangers don't have the resources or mandate to go after the cartel directly, we can curtail some of the abuse of the indigenous peoples. I'm prepared to have my Ducere take this if TASS can't at this time."

"Kendra, this is hitting close to home, especially with your recent kidnapping. I would like to put it before the board and see what direct intel we have on this cartel. Then we can see what resources we can allocate to help. If we get it on the list, at least it will not be forgotten. We might have other priorities, however. One of which is, we must take care of the Horde of Barat. We had all but fixed our strategies before your abduction. Do we need to readdress those strategies concerning the Ceorfan Guild?"

Our lunch is being served. Thank goodness for small favors; my favorite chef only sent me a plate of fruit and cheese. I love him. I ask Tito if he'll bring me some coffee. I believe I'm beginning to feel like my old self.

"Is there more information concerning the Horde, José or are we still trying to find their base of operation?"

"Nothing as of this morning. We believe we will need to act with haste when we get the needed information. Kendra, what is the best way to contact you?"

"My tablet is always the fastest. Sometimes I forget my phone, or I just don't have a good signal when I'm home. I'll send you the link. If I'm not fast enough, try Mega's, then my phone. Enough business now—I want to know how you are."

We talk like old friends for the next half-hour. Afterwards, I call Jamie and ask him if he has some time for pampering, or if he will send someone. He asks if it is possible to meet him in town. I really want to go out into the town. I've only seen it through the limo window. And I won't have to be concerned with my security. Jared has his security force following... leading... whatever, they're with me wherever I go.

So, I spend my afternoon getting pampered. Jamie comes to the spa and takes me to his shop. I buy lots of clothes, including some sexy lingerie. I also get some booties to wear with my jeans.

I head back to the castle to have a nap before the guys wake. I'm glad to smell and look better for them, even though they'd said nothing about it last night.

29

PREPARING

Kendra

Jamie Serge has been working with me to make me clothes that will stay on a dragon queen. I've been able to keep it a secret because the others are torping when I go to Jamie's shop during the day. I'll have the most wonderful fighting clothes, even some new dresses and gowns. He makes me several versions of fighting outfits before we hit on one that works for me. The top looks like a vest. It's a halter that ties around my waist and neck. It velcros together behind my neck, and also in back under my wings. He made me some low-cut, hip-hugging pants that zip in the front. They have a keyhole opening in the back; the two pieces overlap to Velcro together over my tail. They're made of black bulletproof material. He put red trim on the pockets.

Always the designer he ordered me boots to go with my skin-tight fighting clothes. I wanted witch boots, so he found me some that are more combat style, but with a pointed toe. Yay, and they lace up the front, so he put red laces in them for me. He says they're fireproof. I love the whole outfit. What will the guys think when they see me wearing this? Jamie told me he's finished them, and they'll be delivered today.

I can usually sleep 3 or 4 hours at a time. Then I wake up, checking to be sure I'm not alone. I can sleep a couple times a day just fine with the castle's schedule. Today, I'm excited about getting my new clothes, so no sleep.

We've been here in the Scotland location for several weeks. We spend most of our time in combat training. I've been learning how to fight as a dragon, what to avoid in flight and maneuvering in air.

The Ducere are training Jared and Dana this same way. The more they know, the safer they'll be. I'm not too keen on them being in battle. I'll get over it.

A knock at my door has me running to see if it's a delivery. It's Thurston, and he has three large boxes for me. A full on guffaw escapes from me. I can't help rubbing my hands together. I ask him, with a big smile I can't wipe off my face, to put them in the living area.

He does and leaves, telling me young John has football practice, so he can't stay. That's wonderful. John's never been able to play sports; they won't want to miss this occasion.

After he's gone, I throw open the boxes and put my clothes away, all except one set that I take to the bathroom with me. I shower, then dress in my finery. I braid my hair, flipping it behind my back. It's a few minutes until the sun sets. Posing, I wait in front of my guygoyles. Opening my tablet, I make sure I'm up to date on my messages. I get a tickle the minute they start to change and watch them. They stop mid-stretch to stare at me.

Mica says, "Sexy lady. Will you look at that hot stuff?"

He makes me feel very happy.

"Pulse of my heart, you look exquisite," Kino tells me.

Spar just whistles.

Okay, I got what I want; all the attention from these super sexy monster boys. Yeah, they love me.

We've been making it a habit to fly fast and hard for at least 10 miles, then go wash up and break our fast. Mega says we do this to increase our endurance for battle. Kino's been my partner for training, while Mica's been working with Spar. Today Mega wants us to learn to throw an opponent with wings. He thinks Barat will be using Crafted to kill hand to hand. They are quick but not agile.

While we're practicing, Kino manages to come up behind me, putting his enormous arms around me, pinning my wings in his strong hold. I lift with them as much as I can while bending at the waist, then pull him over by his own wings. Ha, I knock the breath out of him. He's face up on the ground, struggling to catch his breath. Looking into his face to make sure he's all right I breath on him to help.

He instantly catches his breath and says, "I love to feel your hot breath on my body."

We glance over in time to see Spar rush at Mica, who bends his knees and plants his feet. As Spar gets to him, he shoves into Spar's abs hard, pushing straight up. Spar sails through the air toward the castle wall. I wince—that's gonna hurt. To my surprise, though, he just sails right through the wall like a ghost. I can't believe my eyes.

Mica turns, "Did you see that?"

"We saw! Spar went straight through the castle wall. So, do you think?" I start when he walks right back out the same way he went in.

"Well, I guess I found my gift. Did you see that, Mega?" he asks his dad proudly.

We laugh, and Mega pats him on his back, telling him that was his fourth test. Now, for the fifth and final test—which is combat in the arena. He's got to clean up, then go to Navan and meet with the High Guild to prepare for the next test. I'm excited and anxious at the same time. I'm left out of the loop on Spar's testing. They said a queen usually knows the details, but because he's my consort, it's too touchy. The High Guild won't let him integrate with the Guild or become an Elite Warrior if they're not sure he did it all on his own.

Knowing Spar's gift and practicing it daily makes us thoughtful of everyone's gifts. We should be figuring them out—at least, where Jared and Dana are concerned. Everyone else is perfecting their own.

It doesn't take us long to discover Dana's gift. Dana's a workaholic and goes back to our cave city several times a week. He's helping restore the city. While he's been working there, he's found that working with stone is part of his gift. He places his hands on whatever he's molding then concentrates on the shape he wants. The stone forms in the pattern he dictates. He's testing different types of stone to see if one is easier or harder to manipulate. He dropped a wrench and discovered, on accident, he can shape metal too, because he squeezed the wrench. Now it has his finger divots.

Not long after that, we figure out Jared's gift... also by accident. We're in the middle of a hot, sweaty practice. It's a cloudy, muggy day, one of those days you want to be in the pool, not near the pool! A short redhead I can't place, who looks familiar walks toward the pool in a very small string bikini. When Jared sees her, the temperature shoots up about 10 degrees, and the low-hanging clouds shoot straight up in the sky. It doesn't take us more than a few seconds to piece it together. Jared can control the weather with how he's feeling. Today, he has extra training to control that, to make sure it isn't always storming in our battles—unless we need it to storm. Nice thing is, if we get too hot he cools the air down around us.

I've been practicing the gifts I've discovered. I don't have to do much about health. Everyone at the castle is healthy while I'm here. I only help heal one soldier who'd been injured in combat training. He had a compound fracture on his right leg below the knee. The laser I can shoot from my mouth is dead on target every time. I control it with my mind: think of using it, and I'm ready.

Persuasion is the gift I work on most. I've found being nice sometimes is too much. One day, half a dozen young men followed me to Jamie's shop when I stopped at a bakery and was joking with them while the baker packaged my order. Jamie told me anytime he needs a sexy date he'll call me; if I'm going to bring men into his shop, he isn't going to say no. He makes me laugh. I'm so glad we met.

There's a meeting with the Ducere soon. I'll tell them all about the gifts. They'll have a fresh perspective on how we can use the gifts. Maybe they know someone who has them and can give us more ideas about training on their uses. I'm sure Jericho and Duke Findare will be able to help in this area. The more we know, the better we can use them to help others. Jared's already made it rain in an area that has been in a drought for months. Findare is talking to the villagers in the area, so they'll welcome TASS workers to learn planting. Afterwards, Jared's scheduling to make it rain enough to grow food without changing the ecology too much.

Today, Mega tells us our training will include weapons. He wants us proficient with as many as possible. We'll try everything, to find something special to us, individually.

We're going to home to train today. Jericho's escorting us through the portal to the training grounds. I remember being here not long ago, but I don't remember weapons. Spar tells me I'll be impressed. I guess we'll see.

Mega leads. The cave is different to me. I sense something strange, like fright but not. I'm happy to be here and am greeted by the entire Elite Warrior Guard. I touch each and every one of them in some way.

Amber and Flint get big hugs. "I have not forgotten you, Flint. We're planning a celebration in your honor. I intend for the Ceorfan Guild to know that you're a hero. One who saved his Queen."

He shakes his head at me with a smirk. "No, don't downgrade what you did. It's very important to me.

"Now come and help me pick a weapon, will you?"

Oh, my! I love this room full of arsenal! There are knives, but not many, I notice.

Flint says, "Let me see your claws, Pulse of the Ceorfan."

I do. He looks them over scraping one with his own then scraping it against the cave wall.

"How is it we haven't taught you to sharpen your claws yet, my queen?"

Now that's a thought. Why didn't I sharpen them myself? Amber's been on assignment collecting intelligence until today.

Kino's with me at my shoulder and asks, "Flint, where are the files and polish?"

Flint answers, "I've got some in my quarters, I'll go get them and be right back." Then Flint flies off to retrieve his kit.

Kino apologizes. "Beloved," he speaks quietly, "I am so new at taking care of my lady, I have forgotten this. Please forgive me."

"What are you saying, Kino? It's meaningless, a little thing, don't worry about it, okay?"

"It's very personal to a gargoyle, beloved. In days gone, it was a warrior's duty to sharpen his love's claws and ready him or her for battle. I had given up all hope of having a mate, much less one as impressive and beautiful as you."

Flint hands his kit straight to Kino instead of me. I'm sure it's the custom, and gargoyles follow the process accordingly.

I smile at Kino and hand him my hand.

Mega tele-speaks to me, "I have fallen down on that score also, my queen. I apologize also. It might take a little while for your first trim. When he finishes, it is customary for you to run your sharpened claws down his arm without cutting him. Don't worry if he gets a small cut, though it is considered loving."

"Thanks for the tip," I answer.

"Take all the time you need, later we can do some target shooting and see if claws interfere with your aim."

Mega starts to show Jared and Dana how to sharpen their claws. He sends Mason to acquire kits for all of us.

"Good idea, General, that's something I need to know, if I can shoot with them or not. If I can't, I wonder if I can morph my trigger hand in flight. If it's possible, let's have Flint's award ceremony quickly. I don't want it to be forgotten or late."

"We can do that. I will get back with you on the specifics. That is something we do need to practice. It will be good knowledge to have," he says.

Kino continues working on my claws. I thought they were sharp before, they're deadly sharp now. They look nice. He's putting something on them and polishing them up.

"Beloved, this is a mixture of oils to penetrate your claws. It will keep them from getting too dry and flaking or weakening," he says as he wipes off all the excess oils.

"I will make some for you. This one smells like patchouli—what do you like?"

Wow! My claws look wonderful; the deep red shows up against the black quick. "I like the smell of oranges and citrus, but I like the musky spicy scents, too."

"In that case, I know just what I want," he says with an impish grin.

I smile and scrape both of my claws down both of his bare arms while I keep his gaze. His pupils expand, darkening them. I add a little pressure from my right hand and cut him on the bicep. He draws a quick breath. I lean into him, putting my lips on his, keeping my claws on his arms. Just a soft touch of our lips.

I breathe on his lips, saying, "We need alone time together soon."

"I want to be alone with you now." He growls a little, his hot breath on my lips sending a tingle straight to my core.

"That turns me on, my hot goyle."

Mega marches closer to us and says, "Nice job, Kino. Are you ready for your lesson, Edling? I have the targets ready."

Nothing like a commander who can sense your passion! Thank goodness he didn't say, 'break it up, lovebirds.' We get the hint.

I grin at my red goyle and say, "More later."

He says, "The longer the wait, the sweeter the fruit."

Fuck that, I'm hungry now. Guess I'm on a fast of sorts.

Mega teaches me how to shoot like I'm a beginner. That's what it feels like, anyway. I cut myself twice before I figure out not to dig my left pinky claw into my right hand. I figure out my claws don't make a difference in the way I shoot, for the most part. I was a fraction of a second slower at first, because I was thinking about getting my claw through the trigger guard. I still pull the trigger with the pad of my finger. No difference. Still, I need practice, so I keep pulling until it becomes second nature.

I tele-speak to Mega. "Thanks for the claw-arm scrape tip. I need to show my consorts more attention, and the little things seem to count."

"I understand, Kendra. You are like my own daughter. I will guide you as much as possible. In the gargoyle tradition, all children belong to all of us. There have never been many. None, for hundreds of years, except for the humans we protect. I had been assigned to watch over you when your parents died. I am proud of you. You can always come to me when you need anything."

"Thank you. I knew I always had a guardian angel—I just didn't know it was you. I feel you in my heart. In fact, I feel all of you in my heart. Even the Ceorfan I don't know. At dinner, sit with me and explain if you've ever heard of dragons sensing stuff. Anything will help."

"It would be my privilege, pulse of our hearts. It would be my privilege."

30

HONORED

Kendra

We are all sitting in the castle dining room. White table cloths, napkins, and all. Mega sits on one side of me and José Brinker on the other. The tables are round and fit ten humans easily. Five of us sit at our table comfortably.

Mega says, "We should have Flint's award ceremony tomorrow night."

"Perfect, if we don't find the Horde and have to change our plans. Tell me what to wear for this ceremony my friend," I ask.

My General answers, "This is a time you must be Dragon Queen of our people. There is not a set uniform more an overall formal look.

"José what are the chances you'll accept an invitation to this affair from me?"

José looks surprised that I'd ask.

"I would be most honored, Your Majesty, but I will need a ride."

"I'll send a car around about 10 of the clock tomorrow. Reception to follow," I joke, and we all laugh.

I ask José, "I wanted to ask if you were ready to let out our rooms yet? We have good communication. Our plan is sound and prepared.

It's time we returned home. I'll need to get back to my job soon. The doctors have said I'm doing good."

Thanks to Arden being in on the secret. He'll release me when I tell him I'm ready. Battling the Horde and winning before I return would be wonderful. Otherwise, I have an alter ego to conceal. Jared is covered, he'll be here and in touch with me. Most of the others are free. Dana needs to go back to work also. As soon as you pinpoint the Horde or we do, then we can proceed with our plans."

José responds, "Of course, Your Majesty. I'll miss you. Please consider the room you are in yours any time you wish to return. I will not 'let' it out to anyone, in hopes that we will see you often."

"It's a deal, my dear Chairman. I'll visit and consider this my home away from home. Mica, will you bring José to Navan tomorrow?"

"Yes. I'll see you tomorrow," he answers.

***

JERICHO BRINGS me to part of Navan I've not seen before. Everyone is asleep, and we are going over the ceremony. The mage calls the room we're in the Halls of History. It's magical. The whole cave is magical.

Dana has been in this room to repair some broken formations. He'd created a table of solid crystal in the middle of the room. This table isn't just art—it's useful, too. I set the stylus, Jericho hands me, on the table on a velvet cloth. While I smooth the cloth with a hand, I have many thoughts in my head at once. Jericho's gravelly voice breaks the silence of the room.

"I'll be here to guide you, Kendra. I don't want to worry you, but I do need to explain a few things. One is why this room is so important to us all."

I can sense the importance. There's an echo of reverence in here.

I relax as Jericho puts his hand on mine then says, "Observe and be amazed."

He gives me a video in the air. Like a hologram but with feelings and smells.

In the pictures I can see my ancestor grandmother. Odd, I know who she was/is. She is bestowing a reward on one of her soldiers in this very room. There's light when she picks up the stylus and touches it to the soldier's head, then to the wall. It smells like apple pie baking when a light glittery writing appears on the wall of the cave. I know it says his name is Jerome. My Jerome! The same one we'd found. It says he had saved the dragon queen's oldest child by taking a wound intended for him by an evil mage. Baratium.

Then the hologram is over. I'm bereft of my grandmother's strong presence. I caress the place on the wall where she'd touched the stylus, writing Jerome's story on the wall. Beautiful, the same as the day it was written, the story is there—etched in the city. I get it now.

"Yes, you understand a little now, my queen, but there is so much more. Etching is more than this small bit. It's part of a bigger process. We need to spend some time together, Kendra. I can teach you more. What you are doing for Flint is a forever gift. It will tie him to you as your friend past this life.

"Flint has no family but the Guild. We are all the family he has. It has been this way for most of his life. When you touch the stylus to his head, they tell me it asks questions and gives one answer. Just warning you.

You are the queen. You have lived in a democracy all your life. This is your wants, your rules—you are the monarchy. There are those who wanted the throne before you were made known to the Ceorfan. I fear they have not given up. Be on guard for those who would try to manipulate you or your consorts.

"Concerning them, you have done so well with your choices. I am proud of you being able to accept the way of life of the Ceorfan people without judgment. If you had chosen only one or made that a law for them, it would have been a change that would have caused problems. Worse, something like that could tear them apart. Civil war. eventually.

You do know Kino is the nephew of Duke Findare? He would have been next in line for the throne. Now that you and your brothers are found and have been proven dragons, your brother Jared is next in line if anything should happen to you. Your brother Dana is next, then Findare and Kino."

"I understand, Jericho. I didn't know about Kino. If I did, I'd forgotten. I'm starting to care for him very much. I'm sorry to usurp his position."

"No, never be that way. You are the queen. We are blessed because of you. With the others, we can just survive until—or if—we ever find another queen born to the dragons. Very unlikely."

"Okay, I'm going to do my best to believe that, Jericho."

"Go get ready then, my queen, Pulse of our Heart. The ceremony will be in a few hours."

That's just what I intend to do but first, a relaxing soak. I love the pool in my bathroom. I could stay in the water for hours. But I need to look queenly, and Amber has checked twice on me to see if I'm out, so I get out and wrap a towel around myself.

Spar comes up behind me as I pick up my hairbrush to untangle my wet hair. He puts his hand on my hand, taking the brush. Without a word, he starts stroking through my long locks. I close my eyes and lean my head back, arching my neck. Awhh, a little moan escapes. I feel him press his chest up to my back, reaching around me, setting the brush on the vanity top. I stare into the mirror at him. Holy cow, he's fine!

"I just want to see you for a second before the ceremony. I'm not staying, so you can get ready. Amber would skin my hide if I try."

I catch hold of his hand, turning into him. "Would you like to go flying with us after the reception? I'd like to spend a little time with you all. To get away for a few minutes. Stress-free."

"Sounds like a plan, beautiful. Get ready. I'll see you in the Halls of History."

Amber makes my hair look amazing in a complicated queenly updo. She's unpacked the dress Jamie sent and is figuring out how to get it on me. It's more beautiful than the one from the gala. It's a deep blood-red covered with tiny crystals; most are a matching red on top fading to black. The hem is solid black, as are the wrists of the long sleeves of the jacket. I guess I can call it a jacket—it's sleeves going across my upper back. The dress is cut low to ride under my wings. Stiff with boning to keep it up in the front. The back has keyholes, each closing with a ruby button, the last one for my tail—then the rest is solid.

Jamie sent me the most beautiful stilettos, matching my dress perfectly. The red crystals are a little bigger on the shoes. Amber brings out a stone tray full of the most gorgeous jewelry; black onyx and diamond teardrop earrings, a matching necklace and ring. Then she places a crown on my head that any beauty queen would adore. It has a dragon shaped of onyx and ruby, lifting its wings amid a white gold crown full of diamonds and rubies. The very last thing she hands me is a pair of black silk gloves that fit like a second skin.

"Now, Kendra, if you'll drop your wings and hold hands with your little hands—the ones on top of your wings—we call these chir, short for chiroptera. Oh, you are beautiful. See what your designer has done? Your wings look like a cape—they fade from red to black like your dress. I see your beautiful ruby buttons are showing. Finished! You can look at yourself in the mirror. 'Pulse of our heart' seems like not enough, Your Majesty."

Jericho pulses me. He's outside my door, ready to walk me to the ceremony. Going out to meet him, I smile as he offers me his arm.

"We will meet the Consorts in the Hall along with the Ducere. Are you ready, Your Majesty?"

"As ready as I've ever been."

Navan is silent as I make my way to the Halls of History on my mage's arm. He stops as we come to the opening to the Halls of History, motioning me to proceed. Nodding my head slightly in his direction, I move into the room slowly. I see my handsome consorts, I walk forward to them, stopping in front of them I turn to the crowd. My brothers stand on each side of me, as heirs to the throne.

"General Megahir, it's my honor to reward the Ducere's Elite Warrior Flint tonight. Will you come forward with your warrior?"

Mega motions to Flint, as they move down an aisle of gargoyles on each side of them.

"Ducere Warrior Flint, you have honored your queen. I honor you in return. You and your deeds will not be forgotten as your name is etched in this city. Please come forward."

Flint stands in front of me. I take the stylus from the stone table. It vibrates with power.

"I hereby etch you into the Halls of History."

I touch the stylus to Flint's forehead as I had seen my grand-mother do in the vision Jericho had shown me.

What I couldn't see in the vision, I now know. The power of the vibrations become a hologram in front of me. So real I'm there. I see Flint being born, his childhood, how he became a man, how he became a warrior. Everything he felt, I feel. The care he has for me, the loyalty of the man is amazing. Lastly, I see how he saved me. It's a magnificent story. He's my hero.

I pivot on my heels. The stylus guides me to the spot it wants to etch his name in this city. I touch it to the wall. It's electric. The words shimmer and sparkle as they're written. It takes just a few seconds and very little space, but is a whole biography. It smells like cake in here now. Wonderful!

I peer at Flint, his eyes are glassy with tears. I may not be the most decorous queen when I go to him, gathering him up in a hug.

"Thank you, Flint, my warrior. You are my hero."

Applause breaks out, and the Ducere roar! The room pulses like a heartbeat. Next thing you know, we're all roaring and laughing. Duke Findare comes forward to make an announcement; there's a reception in the throne room. He tells me it's the room with the crystal podium. I see my brothers walk ahead with others. Jared needs to get back to Scotland and is taking José with him. Jericho had given him his own portal stone earlier. Dana says he'd see me later. He has to be up early; his crews are starting a new project.

Kino is beside me, offering me an arm. He says, "You are gorgeous, beloved. The crown suits you."

Mica and Spar are behind us as we casually walk to the reception. Mica informs me, "We'll see you in at the reception. We forgot to get something."

It sounds like they made a deal, so Kino and I can have a stolen moment together.

As soon as they're gone, Kino guides me to a little pool in an enclave on the trail. He bends down and shines a light on the pool; it's full of little white fish. Wonderful, oh so beautiful. Does the light bother them? No, they've adapted to the dark. They're albino and blind. It doesn't seem to hurt them—they get around fine without sight.

He stands. I know his heartbeat speeds up. Mine does, too. He curls a finger at me to follow him into the dark. I hold his hand tight. He stops after only a few yards. We come to a bench in the wall; he sits and invites me to sit with him. There's not much room. I crawl into his lap, hoping to surprise him. One corner of his mouth lifts.

"Kendra, may I kiss you?"

"If you don't, I'll have to kiss you."

He presses a soft kiss to my lips. He smells wonderful. His wings go around us. I keep mine down. He traces my face with a finger then pushes up on my chin.

He says, "Kendra, you are more than I could ever hope to dream. You make me very happy. If you ever, at any time, have enough of me, tell me, and I will leave you alone. I will pine my life away far from here, as I could never give up wanting you. You make me feel desire in every cell of my body. When you teased me with your claws, I wanted to make you mine right then and there. Show you pleasure until your body screamed for release.

"You are mine. I'm not letting you go. I don't want to lose a minute with you."

He crushes me to him in a hard kiss, his tongue moving deep into my mouth. I crawl up him. We make out until my lips chap. I pull my dress up to press my overheated body against his hard manliness. My body has a mind of its own, and I'm getting carried away. His hands on my breasts are driving me wild. He holds me close with his wings.

He puts a clawed hand into my panties. With a deft slice he cuts them off. With the back of a claw, he presses into my clit. kneading it. I'm so ready. I don't even care if he accidentally cuts me. He knows what he's doing and maneuvers me without a scratch. He slides a finger inside me, still rubbing my clit, and in seconds I come on his big hand. Leaning on his chest, I catch my breath, wondering how to return the favor in this dress. He must read my mind.

He says, "We have all the time in the world. I will wait. We can enjoy the chase. They are probably missing us at the reception. Let us go, so we might leave all the sooner. Shall we?"

Holding his hand in mine, I look to see how he managed to get a finger inside me. I hold his hand up. One finger has a perfectly rounded-off, smooth nub of a claw.

I say, "Thank you, for me?"

"After I sharpened yours, I did mine."

My singer gives me a wicked grin.

When we get to the throne room with my slightly rumpled dress, we talk to the entire Guild, it feels like. I give eye signals to my guygoyles. They get the hint, and off we go. I'm glad they know the way to the entrance, given it's changed places.

31

CAUGHT

Kendra

"Where do you want to fly tonight?" I ask.

"You're the queen—you decide. We'll follow," Spar says.

"Let's check out the Ranger post. It isn't that far away. I want to do a trial run in my dress, so let's go a short way then rest a bit, talk, then head home."

After we start, I call out to them, "So, I guess I'm flying high enough no one can see anything, right?"

I'm not telling the others I'm flying commando. That's for me and Kino alone; we share a conspiratorial grin.

Mica immediately flies under me and says he can't, no matter how hard he tries. Chuckling, he tips my tail up and causes me to plummet. I giggle as I fall. I know one of them will catch me, I hope. Spar catches me, steadying me while I get my wings again. Turnabout is fair play, Mica. You just wait.

We're at the Ranger post now. Without making a sound, I set down on the roof. I sit to look over the installation. Mica sits behind me, with his big legs on either side of mine. Kino sits on my right, and

Spar lies on my left, with his head on my leg. Could life be any better? I don't think so.

The wind is calm, the air is clear, and the day is perfect. We perk up when a couple of guards walk around the corner of the building we're facing. I watch, and I stifle a giggle. It's like when my brothers and I would pretend to stalk our parents. We were so sneaky most of the time that they never knew we were there. It gave us a rush because it was fun. That's what this feels like, kids sneaking up on an adult. I need to ask Amber and Mason how they sneak so well without laughing.

Is that John? No, I can tell now it isn't John, the shithead who shot Mica. What's he doing since we decimated the Jessup Cartel? Speak of the devil... he walks out a door and is talking to one of the guards. They have a short discussion about a shipment of cocaine coming through, then he leaves.

"Did you guys hear that?"

I ask the most handsome guys I've ever known. They acknowledge they heard him, whispering in case someone hears us.

I motion for the guys to follow me. We lift off and stay low and out of sight, following the terrain of the small canyon we used to get to the station earlier. On the way back to Navan, we make plans.

The most important step is to gather as much evidence against Shithead John and his cohorts as possible. Mica and I will bring them to justice in the 'real' world with real-world consequences. My partner will begin by calling work tomorrow to get reinstated from his leave of absence.

Next, I'll visit Arden and skip Dr. Vargas, so he can release me for work. No questions asked. Nope, on second thought—Dr. Vargas is the norm, but I can give him Arden's results. This will keep us busy until we find the Horde, unless TASS finds them first.

When we make it back to Navan, Spar stays with me in my room.

Mica and Kino go to their own cave rooms, giving us some privacy.

It's only minutes, it feels like, when Spar gets up and says, "Wings up, beautiful," as he hardens to stone.

I need to get with Mega to find out about his final test. I also want to know what they mean by integrating him into the Guild. Neither my brothers or I have had to do that. Why? What's the difference? Is it a warrior thing? I should ask Jericho while everyone sleeps.

***

I'VE SLEPT as much as I can, so I call Dr. Vargas's office. The receptionist tells me the office schedule is full. They can't see me until next week.

"The flu has covered this town, Kendra," the nurse relates. "Is 10:00 next Thursday alright with you?"

I tell her it is, making a notation with an alarm on my tablet. Then I write Mica a note, telling him I won't be going back to work for at least another week.

I call Murphy and check in. His relief is evident in his voice when I give him the information that I'll be back next week. Happy I accomplished something, I head off to see if I can find Jericho.

The old mage has a laboratory and an apartment in a cave room in the lower part of the city. I walk the whole way, making sure to stop and window shop on the way. It's quiet and calm in the city, like Cueva Hallow in the middle of night. When I get to Jericho's lab, he's focusing on his work.

I clear my throat.

"I hope you don't mind me coming to see you now. It seems like a good time, with everyone else asleep."

He replies, "It is always a good time to visit me. I'm happy to have your distraction. You have brought so much joy back to the Ceorfan. I often do not know what to say, but today is especially good for you to come by. I'm working on an invention. This is something to help the bats in our caves, though, not the Ceorfan. Did you want company, Kendra, or is there another reason for your visit?"

"I came because I want more information about Spar's testing. Can you tell me what 'integrating' means? I heard Mega say it. He said, 'Spar will integrate into the Ceorfan Guild when he finishes his test.' I haven't remembered to ask what it means. Will I need to do anything as queen for this event, or whatever it is?"

"Yes, easy question. It is not like etching. It is important, though. When we select a warrior for the Elite Guard, he must prove his character. We must know his intentions toward gargoyles, humans, animals, and the Earth. In the old times, there were more gargoyles. They didn't have only one city.

In fact, gargoyles didn't have a city. They were safe in the world. They worked with men but tended to be loners. They lived in parks and buildings. Many stayed in the hills when they were sleeping as stone. It was normal to see them asleep as stone. People respected them, watched their beauty, but did not try to destroy or mark them. They were like everyone else: neighbors. Gargoyles had no reason to mistrust. They were loyal to each other. Crime was not something they were ever part of. They are tight-knit, and they flourish when they are able to care for and protect others.

What Eltira did is such a shame to the Count. I'm sure he is wondering how to make it up to you. In fact, that he is in Navan is a testament to his character. Most would become nomads, hide in shame, or even find a way to destroy themselves. I'm getting side-tracked—I am sorry.

Kendra, during the Viking wars in the 10th century, there was such treachery. Several warriors betrayed their fellow gargoyles to evil mages. Those mages used them for terrible and shameful purposes. They put evil crooks on the thrones of men for their own gain. Many of these mages gained world renown, working for enthusiastic nobility. Some of the horrors the gargoyles faced were so bad, they never say what happened.

The High Guild petitioned the Dragon Queen for help deciding who the Guild would trust. She instituted the tests for warriors. This made it so gargoyles could trust who was protecting them. Spar is caught between a rock and a hard place. Oooh, pardon the pun," he chortled. "Instead of the High Guild taking his case, to discover his character they want to stick to the ancient way. Their poor choices hurt them before, and they no longer trust themselves. They put the strictest restrictions on the Carved. Those strictures remain, even though we are not in the same situation.

"Spar has passed all his tests except the last. The last test is for strength. The High Guild will select several opponents for him to fight in the arena or a similar challenge. We have not had a queen in a long time, or it would have been you to set the date for this test. Additionally, you have been away. We have had much to do and not enough time to do everything. Given your relationship with Spar, the High Guild thought it would be best if they conducted them.

"If you would like, we can convene with them tonight, learn their timetable, and settle your authority. You are the queen. Some of them need to remember that fact. You need to assert your position and show them the leader you are, my dear. I urge you to get to know them, make friends with them, know their needs. You need to do this to lead well."

"You're right, Jericho. Is it possible for the queen to have a personal assistant? I haven't a clue most of the time how to be a queen. Especially of a people I only recently discovered existed."

"I will help you as much as you need, Your Majesty. Which brings me to another subject. When we are all settled, I need to figure out how to get your ancestry into your memory. I know that blank look by now, Edling. It will take awhile for you to figure out this new life. It will get easier, but the ancient dragons had a private ceremony for new rulers. It didn't happen often, as a dragon lives as long as any of the Ceorfan. When there was a new queen, the old queen would take the young one on a short trek. When they came home, the young knew everything she needed to rule without question. You could find a reference in the Halls of History."

"I'll do that, Jericho. How do I read the etched word without the stylus?"

"I'm giving you too much information at a time and am not remembering everything. Thank you for the questions. Never be afraid to ask me, please. To access the Histories, you do use the stylus you used before. It is yours. You touch it to the cave and ask what you need. It will lead you to the information.

"You know, we have been at this discussion for a while, and I have been remiss in my duties as a host. Would you like anything to break your fast or something to drink? Walk with me, Kendra. Let's go to the lunch room. I want to make you lunch, if you will let me."

"Of course. I'll be glad to, thank you."

We spend several hours together before I start to tire. I excuse myself from him. "It was a wonderful day, Jericho. I have the strangest sleep schedule now and need my naps."

"That is the way it is with dragons. Get some rest. I will see you tonight when I convene the High Guild."

***

I DREAMED.

I should be getting to know the Ceorfan better. I should lead them to ease their lives. This is my priority, and John and the drugs he is selling are a part of helping my Guild. I should have the Ceorfan assist. It'll give them purpose.

Waking up and remembering my dream, I know I made a great plan in my sleep. I often use dreams to solve problems. When I face a difficulty, my subconscious tackles it, and many times, I wake with an answer. I pick up my tablet and write myself a note, so I don't forget.

My blood is resonating, building excitement. It's time for gargoyles to wake. Do gargoyles dream? I need to ask one of my consorts. I know how important training is, but I want my consorts with me in the High Guild meeting. My support system. My tablet notifications beep.

I READ A NOTE FROM JARED;

TASS has some leads, nothing much yet. Soon, with hope. I'll let you know. P.S. I love Scotland.

I'LL BET it has something to do with that little redheaded actress?

It's time. Spar wakes and stretches with a low roar.

"I had the best dream about you." And that answers that.

"Me, too." He kisses me good morning.

"I need coffee. Want to go get some with me?"

"Yes, I do. We can do that on the way to find the others for our wake-up flight." It has become our habit when they wake.

I relate to the guys the talk I had with Jericho. I focus on the part about the meeting.

"I want you all to be with me, so let's fly fast and hard now to make up for me cutting into your training exercise."

That's exactly what we do. Even in flight, we have different talents. My goyles think I'm graceful and look beautiful in flight. We found that I'm quiet, too. None of us make much noise. But—yes there is noise.

We try something. They want to see if I scare cows. We're close to the Smith Ranch, so as stealthily as I can, I fly up to a small herd. The cows act like I'm part of the scenery, until I growl, a low one. They take off like a herd of buffalo.

"Well, that's new. Can't say I have ever seen cows run like that," Spar laughs.

"Well, I haven't, either. I don't like that I scared them. I'm not doing that again. Feels like I kicked a puppy."

I receive a message from Mega on my tablet; the High Guild is meeting at ten. I need to get a shower. We fly hard and fast back to Navan.

We sit in the conference room, clean and refreshed. I'm excited and want to get this show on the road. My consorts sit around the table, letting Jericho and Findare sit on either side of me. I've met the members of this council and remember all their names. Thank goodness, I won't be stupid on that point. I don't know what they do here and don't know what they expect from me.

One of the members, called Traver, calls the meeting to order and starts. Findare shuts him down.

"We have a queen, Traver. It is her prerogative to start the meeting or order one of us to the position. You border on extreme disrespect to her. This is the second time I've had to remind the members of this group of the respect owed. I will not abide a third. We are blessed to have such a wonderful queen. Your insults are not appreciated."

The skinny gargoyle sneers an apology, setting a tone for my own attitude. I decide to change things right off the bat.

"Count de Treon, would you please chair this meeting?"

His surprised face immediately changes to a take-charge one, as he brings the meeting to order. Very well, I might add. Then he gives me the floor.

I begin by asking, "Who is the secretary?"

"There isn't one," Member Alexandritana responds.

"Okay, then who takes the minutes, writes the calendars, and sends reminders for actions?" Silence. I use my business voice, "Volunteers?" Silence again. "It seems you might consider the job beneath you, so for today, I'll do the job."

"I motion that the Queen choose a personal assistant. We will add this assistant to the High Guild to assist her in these duties," Alexandritana pipes up.

Out of the twenty Ceorfan present, all second the motion at the same time.

"I will assume, with all Members seconding the motion, that the motion carries."

Great, they want to impress me now.

"Spar, will you please use your tablet for now to help me record the minutes?"

Immediate sighs and groans from several of the members has me raising my eyebrows. One of the older gargoyles with a turned-up nose and huge ears petitions for the floor. When he has it, he uses the time to dress me down. Telling me, he knows I'm new to the queenship, but this is not done. Spar should not even be in this meeting, much less collecting information from it.

"Do you know what lesser gargoyles could do with the details gathered here?" his tirade ends with a sneer.

I eyeball the Count and take back the floor. I'm fuming mad.

Emphasizing his name I command, "High Guild member Traver, as the queen I revoke your power and position in this Guild. We don't have lesser or more important Ceorfan. I don't know if that's a tradition common to you alone, or Navan in general. It changes this instant. It's the job of every one of us to protect and serve each other. Everyone is equal. This includes me and my family. We do have different jobs. Mine is as the ruler. I make the decisions. I listen to my advisers. Each member of the High Guild have a say. I will not allow this type of behavior, especially in my advisers. You may go, Traver."

I ask Mega to escort him from the room. A fight breaks out, between Traver, his several supporters, and the other High Guild members.

Jericho immediately spells the agitators into submission. After which, the Elite remove the troublemakers.

After they're gone, I speak to the remaining fourteen members.

"This government has changed. You're here right now not because you're a trusted adviser, but because you inherited the position. If you do not support this matriarchy, you may leave the city with no repercussions. If you intend to support this matriarchy, then feel free to stay and prove your worth. I'll be as fair as possible until I get to know you and your character. First order of business, how are we to deal with the dissenters that I ejected from this group?"

Count de Treon put forth the following motion, "Mega will send an officer of the queen to each of those removed. The officer will give them two options. Either support the queen or leave the city. If they decide to stay, they will pronounce fealty in the presence of Jericho. He will spell their fealty oath into their memory, making it impossible to break. Otherwise, the mage must spell them into forgetting our location, including its inhabitants. Afterward, they must leave the city."

"I second the motion," Kino says. No one in their right mind would cross him.

"On a voice vote, who votes in the affirmative?" I ask.

I hear lots of ayes' around the room.

"Who votes in the negative?"

Silence.

"Abstentions?"

Silence.

"The next order of business, does anyone know the schedule for Spar's last test?"

"We do, Your Majesty, but the candidate cannot be in the room." Member Slateri, a pinched little goblin-looking gargoyle, informs me.

I listen as Mega tele-speaks, "We will be outside. Call me to come back when you are ready."

As they leave, their display of military bearing is better than I'd thought doable, given Spar's sporadic training.

I motion for member Slateri to continue.

"The High Guild has scheduled the final test for the next full moon. It will be in two days. The test will be conducted outdoors with five combatants. Spar must retrieve a stone from an area he has known. We chose the middle of the Ranger post building where he worked in his past life. Once he has the stone, he must bring it to you. When it is in your hands, the test is over. We do understand you can change this at any time, Your Majesty."

"Thank you for the information, Member Slateri. No, your test is fair." In secret, I realize he can do this with ease.

"I move that the test, as outlined by Member Slateri, be given as proposed. If Spar finishes the test as outlined, he will be integrated into the Guild soon after."

The Count seconds the motion.

All members approve, none abstain.

I tele-speak to Mega to come back to the meeting with Spar.

I begin to tell the members about the intelligence we have been receiving on the Horde of Barat.

"TASS believes that we'll have a location soon, so we can bring this threat under control. I intend to use the Elite Warriors in completing this task."

Motion, second, pass. I ask if there are any members who would like to be more involved in the process with this issue. None volunteer.

"Not everyone is a soldier," the Count says, while looking at his feet.

"Are there any other business matters which need to be addressed?"

Even more silence. The Count concludes the meeting. I stand and ask anyone who wants to stay to have dinner with me.

The whole room agrees.

"Well, at least they have a firm grip on politics," I sigh to myself.

While we eat, I inform Mega about witnessing John talking drugs with a guard at the Ranger post. I ask him to send an Elite team to handle this for me. He responds that he'll assign a team and let me know when he finishes it. I didn't bring it up during the meeting because I want it completed. I don't need advice making these decisions.

The guys, Mega, and Jericho follow my lead in the attempt to befriend the High Guild. When the Count comes and sits beside me, not me going to him, I'm pleased. We make small talk before I ask how he's doing. I can't tell if the pain showing on him is from grief or shame. A little of both, maybe. I'm going to keep this man busy, I decide.

"Count de Treon," I start.

"It is Clifton, Your Majesty. If you will call me Clifton."

"If you will, call me Kendra in private then. Will you please work with Spar to make the actions for our business today? Assign who you will—I'll back you up. I also need a personal assistant. Would you be interested in the position? I'll understand if you don't think it's your forte."

"Kendra, I am honored."

"Thank you. I'd like to invite you to lunch with me tomorrow night, if you don't have prior plans."

"I would like that. There is someone I would like you to meet."

"Okay, then I'll see you and your plus one tomorrow. Can you put that on my schedule?" I laugh, and he does, too.

"Of course—it's my job." He grins.

I stay to smooth out several problems that other Ceorfan bring to my attention. Before sunrise, Mica takes me to my room. We talk and laugh, and I kiss him good day before he torps. Then, I lie on my bed and sleep like a baby.

32

SKIRMISH

Kendra

The next night, I have lunch with Clifton. We review things I need, and how I intend to meet the needs of the people. He has the best organization skills I've ever seen. He's going to have me regulated and orderly in no time.

He also introduces me to his mate, Morgan. Morgan is a big impressive gargoyle who looks like a wrestler.

"I would not have imagined it," I laugh to the Count.

"You cannot imagine it. Try being me! I'm a small, truculent gargoyle with little time for love and even less regard for the feelings of others. I, too, wonder, 'how did I land Morgan as a mate'? I will tell you what, I do not know the answer, but it is not because I have big hands or feet, if you catch my meaning."

I laugh hysterically as the two of them banter over the various boorish habits of the Count. I come to the realization that much of the persona of the green goyle is an act to keep others from knowing who he truly is. Yet this big Morgan seems to bring out only the best of Clifton, and maybe everyone he is near.

"Morgan, I've heard you're a chef. Chef Ron is in Scotland, so will you be my new best friend? Girl's gotta eat." I ask.

We let the rest of the meal conversation progress naturally. The Count de Treon is much more affable in this setting and carries the discussions. Although he constantly brings it back to Morgan and their hoped-for family. Thankfully, I do remember to enlighten Clifton on my plans to return to work at the Ranger station. I have him include my upcoming doctor's appointment in my schedule, too.

The rest of the night goes by steadily. I can't wait to see Mica, Spar, and Kino. They've been training to make sure Spar is ready for his test, so I make my way there. How sexy they look worn and sweaty! Seriously, damn hot, that's all I got to say about that! Damn hot.

The Ducere and I are all sitting in the dining room when an unmistakable pulse goes through the air. Its meaning tells me—this is not a drill. The Horde is on the move. We've been waiting for the moment when we could meet Barat and his Horde on the battlefield. We want it before they kill more innocent civilians. Mega wants me to stay behind, worried I haven't mastered my gifts yet.

"I certainly will not stay behind. I'm Dragon Queen of the Ceorfan. I'll not shame my people or myself that way," I hiss.

We've been practicing, so we're already dressed in fighting clothes. Everyone goes to their posts. I call Clifton over and request he get me a line to José Brinker ASAP. In less than a few seconds, he's on the line.

"José, our scouts have the Horde in sight. They are converging on a village in the Ukraine. We are portaling now. I'm sending someone to portal your soldiers now," I report.

"We're ready, Queen Kendra. I will meet you there," he responds and then he drops the connection. Wait, what? I didn't expect him to come. I hope he knows what he's doing.

Kino has a portal open for us, and Jericho opens another portal, so he can assist TASS. We all head to our places. True to our training, we take flight through the portal as soon as we have our weapons and our team is gathered. We organize into three gargoyle teams. This gives us the best protection and the quickest response to get through the entries.

I have a sick feeling as I exit. It's a slaughter field. The Crafted are still here, finishing off the wounded. No live enemy combatants remain, only the Crafted.

I reach out with my feelings. I sense death. I touch the feeling of horror. No people or energy to follow.

Jared must be here; it's starting to sprinkle lightly. I swivel to find him.

The Elite and TASS kill and demolish every Crafted they find on the battlefield in seconds.

Three people are alive, all children. I slice my palm with a claw— Kino has them so sharp I don't even feel pain. A pulse comes from me like a big boom! It covers all in a wave like a tidal wave. I know it says let's save these kids and never forget the slaughter here. I demand justice for these dead on this field!

I pick up the first child. She looks to be a small two-year-old. I drip blood into her wounds, telling her it's going to be just fine. Kino is beside me, taking the baby, handing her to Jared.

Mica hands me another little girl, maybe ten years old. I hold her, dripping blood onto her also. She reaches her hand up and cups my face, a little smile on her lips. She closes her eyes. Kino is singing and takes her from me.

Spar stands next to me and holds me up. The boy he is carrying is older. He might be early teens. Spar doesn't hand me the boy, but presses him up to my side. I wrap my arm around my blue love, so I don't wilt to the ground. My hand is on the boy's gaping chest wound. It looks like the enemy has taken a bite out of him, a big one almost half of his chest is open. He's not awake; Kino has sung him to sleep, so he won't feel the pain of his wounds.

TASS has set up a medical area. We take the children there to continue care. The baby is better now. Crying, but better. When Jared tries to hand her to the medical officer she screams and hangs on to him. He tells them he has her. She lays her head on his shoulder and calms.

Jericho opens a portal to TASS in Scotland. They take all the children, Jared with the little one, to care for there.

He says, "It'll be okay Sis. We will catch them next time."

"Oh, dear God, I hope so."

After speaking to Mega, he reports there is no sign of the enemy. All the Crafted are decommissioned. TASS and the Ceorfan are gathering the dead for identification. He tells my consorts to take me home and clean up. He'll debrief us tomorrow at sundown. I'm disappointed we didn't find the enemy on the field or find a way to discover how they got away so fast.

I turn to leave, stepping through the portal Kino has open. I will not give up until this Horde is put to death. There'll be no incarceration for this enemy. I'll make sure when we catch them that they'll never commit such carnage again.

"My queen," Mega says, asking for my attention again.

I catch a tinge of anger on his face, gone almost before I could notice it.

"My queen," he says again, "All except one of the expelled members of the High Guild escaped while we were gone. They had help from the inside. The guard reported being attacked from behind. When he awoke, he saw one of the ex-members flying away."

"Which one did not escape, Mega?" I asked.

"Your Majesty, it was Traver."

"Well, I'm not sure if that is a good thing or not. Thank you, General. Please ensure the guard is set to prevent any further escape attempts."

"Yes, my queen."

***

. . .

WE'RE all in my room tonight. I can't be without Spar, Mica, or Kino. I undress and take a bath. I don't know how my pool works, but even with all the blood that's on me, my water is clear. All the guys take a bath with me. We're quiet and reflective. It isn't about sex tonight. It's about family taking care of family.

We're all clean and dry in my sitting area. One of the guys brings a bottle of something. I pour us all a drink, tipping it back like a shot.

I say, "Thank you. I love that we work together so well. I thought I would be fighting in a battle, not healing the wounded. I think we did the healing thing very well, guys. We were organized, even though we hadn't even thought to practice a scenario like tonight's. I'm proud of you all. I'm sure the children will live. That's better than the last village. Let's count that part a victory.

"Today when you sleep, dream of me. I'll be dreaming of you. If I even think to dream the horror we just saw, I'm changing it into the most amazing beautiful monsters. The ones who held the children tonight."

Sunrise is here. My men are admiring me with love as they torpify. I'm going to sleep, hoping to have more answers in the morning.

33

TRAITOR

Kendra

I've been staring at my tablet, waiting for José Brinker to message me. It's not easy. I want to end Barat and his Horde now. Right now!

I've had enough of feeling behind the curve. I'm getting impatient. After seeing the carnage of the village, last night, I can't find them and bring them death fast enough. My dragon blood sizzles with rage for the murders. Well, I have a portal stone of my own. Tapping out a note for my consorts on my tablet, I ready myself for a short trip to Scotland.

Stepping into the dining hall, my goal is the kitchen to see Chef Ron first. When I get there, he's at work as usual. He comes over, gives me a big hug, sits me down, and hands me a bowl of what looks like cream of wheat with some fruit or jam or something on top. It's hot and steamy. I eat whatever he cooks. It's always good, and this is yummy.

I just start talking. I don't talk about how the battlefield looked, or any gory details. I do ask if anyone had heard if the children were better. One of the cooks says she'd seen them all this morning. She had cooked their breakfast.

"My lady queen, they're whole and healthy. They're in the hospital wing only because that's where we have room. They're healed, not a scratch on 'em."

I'm relieved. Nonetheless, I don't let go wanting to kill the murdering scum that attacked them, decimating their village and left them young orphans. I failed them. I need to double my efforts to make it up.

José puts a hand on my shoulder. I hug him hello. The kitchen personnel move away, so we can converse without interruption as they complete their tasks around us.

A cup of chai tea in my hands, I lean back in my chair.

"What do we know now?" I ask.

"Not much, the older child is named Pi. He's given us the most information. He said that the soldiers who killed his village came all at once. Just appearing, they started killing without a word. No warnings or talking at all. He said a tall man who looked like a shaman in a black robe was in the middle of a bunch of wooden robots. The Crafted is what he was referring to. It's a good guess the shaman is Barat. He said the shaman had a staff with a crystal on top of it. The crystal had lightning in it, as he describes it. That was all he knew. After that, the Crafted started eating him. The two girls do not speak, at all," José answers.

"Do you have any ideas? What we can possibly do to help?"

"It might take a few days, Kendra. I am sorry. We can only wait. I wish it was different. Waiting for another attack makes me feel terrible. I'm in the same situation as you—very little to go on. We had thought we were getting close to a location of his lair. That was this destroyed village. When we see this process again, we can go in faster. We can't be there before the attack, I'm sorry to say, but that's our best chance for now. We have every available agent assigned to surveillance, gathering information, and infiltration rebel factions"

"I'll check with my people. If they know anything, I'll share it as soon as possible. I have to plan a test for my consort Spar, so the gargoyles will trust him to defend them. Crazy, I know. If it were any other gargoyle and not my consort, I'd change the tradition. As it is, I'll let him finish the testing then I'll change it. He's a good fighter, so I have no doubt he'll pass easily.

I give everyone hugs goodbye. I'm going to portal straight to Jericho. I hope that's okay, and he isn't in the middle of something. I make it to the mage's lab in seconds.

"Jericho, are you here?" I call out.

He pops up from behind a table cluttered with old books and what looks like trash. His room in the caves looks like what I would have thought Merlin's cave would look like, right down to a crystal cave off to the side, small but beautiful, like a geode. There's a smooth, man-sized area in the shiny crystal, I imagine he sleeps there.

"That's beautiful. Do you sleep there?"

"Sometimes, I am drawn to sleep there. It's a chance I take. There have been times I slept for months at a time. When I sleep in the crystal cave, it shows me things that have been and some that can be. Sometimes, it even warns me of things that are happening. Before you ask, I have tried to see if I can find Barat, but not even a second of information will it share. You should try, Kendra. It's open to you at any time. I'll guard over you if you should choose to sleep there, do not fear."

"I'll do that soon. I dream nightmares when I dream," I say.

I change the subject, "I've been to Scotland to check on the children."

That puts a smile on his face.

"I believe, I'll go to Fiatril Hall today to see the children myself. I have some toys and books for them. I need to make sure José knows that I need to help them forget the Ceorfan before they find them homes."

"Good thinking, I'll get better at remembering to protect my people. I should have thought of that first."

"Don't worry, you are doing fine. One person cannot be and do everything, even a queen, dear. You really should try the dream cave."

"Do you mind if I do it later? I'm hungry and want to visit the lunchroom. If you go with me, I'll cook for you. I need to talk to you about the TASS intelligence."

We walk and talk as we go. He has a vague memory about a staff with a crystal similar to the one Pi described. He'll look it up later.

I cook us some pasta with sweet peppers, carrots, jalapenos, and chicken with a little white wine in the sauce. He helps me clean up when we finish. "I need to have the High Guild meet tonight to give them the information José had told me earlier today. Then I'm going to the Halls of History to search for clues."

He agrees. "The more who are working on finding a solution the better."

We go our separate ways, intending to share tonight what we find: me in the Halls and him to his cluttered cave laboratory to research the staff.

As soon as I reach my destination I start reading, searching for a clue.

A shuffling breaks my concentration, and I take my nose out of the etching I'm studying. I relax, seeing Spar, my hottest contestant. Time's gotten away from me. I had no idea it was dark already. It's always the same in the cave, lit rooms without windows. One would think I'd miss seeing the sun, but it isn't that way for me at all.

"Are you finding anything, honey?"

"Yes, just not what I want to find. There's a lot of information I need to absorb for sure. I hope if I keep reading the histories, I'll stumble across the one thing that'll help us discover where Barat is hiding by accident. No real logic to my search at all."

"Well, some crazy hot queen called a meeting in the conference hall while we slept. I'm here to make sure you show up. It's almost time to start."

"Oh, great! Let's go. I need to tell everyone what I learned at Fiatril Hall today."

When we get to the conference room, I greet everyone. Then

start giving them the intelligence on why I called the meeting. I don't want to keep them from their families, but I need to find information about the staff Pi saw at last night's massacre.

I say, "The children we rescued are doing well. Jericho, did you see them and talk to José about removing their memories of gargoyles before they're adopted?"

He tilts his head, "José has agreed. He repeated the same information he gave you—that they would have families soon. He has his people working on it as we speak. He also brought up he hasn't found anything about the staff yet. He will keep looking, though."

Jewel, one of the Members, sketches something on her tablet and shows it to me. It's a staff with a crystal on top like I'd described.

"Tell me more Jewel—everything you know, no matter how small."

"My queen, Traver has a family heirloom, a staff called Caor Thintri. The name means 'ball of lightning.' It is a relic found on the battlefield during the old wars by his family. The stories say that it can transport whole battalions at once."

"Someone get Traver, please—bring him here."

What are the odds?

"Does anyone else know any other facts concerning Traver and this staff?"

Member Slateri, said, "I saw Traver with it not long ago, but remember nothing else. I wonder if magical items are common here."

"Jericho, does this ring any bells for you?"

"That staff was actually a tool Baratium had conjured in his days as a novice. It was used by him in the mage wars. It fell from his hands when he was taken. The Traver family was the one who had captured him. That is why they have the staff. It was a gift from Queen Leta to a loyal brave family."

Mica brings Traver to the conference room in cuffs. I explain what we've discovered and that his family staff is a tool being used once again to aid the enemy.

I ask, "What do you have to say?"

"I say anything I can do to aid the killing and eradication of the human pestilence infesting the world is worth any punishment I might have inflicted upon me." States the betrayer flagrantly.

That's when Spar comes in with Traver's wife and father. They're surprised to see him cuffed and being questioned. Glancing at the criminal to see his reaction to his family makes me sick. Via his body language, he doesn't give a rip. There's not a single concern or worry in his demeanor for his supposed loved ones. He definitely has no shame for his actions. I give them the specifics of what's going on and why we believe Traver's an accomplice to Baratium. They both blanch.

His father is mortified.

He asks him, "Why, would you do this, son?"

Traver says, "Because I want to live normally, in the sun and see all the Ceorfan live normally outside if that's what they want. To be free. Barat promised me we could when they kill all the humans."

I'm not sure when it happened, but this gargoyle has gone off the deep end. His perspective is terribly skewed. He's not only endangered the Guild—he's committed treason and has no remorse. He's gone against the highest law the Ceorfan have: to protect others—all others.

"Jericho, will you spell Traver to tell us all the information he knows about Baratium and the Horde, especially their location?"

Immediately he walks over to the chained gargoyle, who is struggling to get out of Mica's strong grip. It's not possible; it's a valiant try, but useless. My partner's very strong, and he holds him steady for the mage.

The wizard is mumbling under his breath. He touches a stone to Traver's temple. It looks like it sticks there then we all see a holo-like projection of him giving the staff to Barat. Jericho asks where Baratium is located. He tells us exact coordinates of an underground facility.

"Place him in confinement," I say.

I'm not even sure where we incarcerate prisoners. I need to get more acquainted with Navan. Lots of questions here.

"Count de Treon, I need the Chairman of TASS on speaker. Does anyone else have any information on this subject?"

Traver's wife forces her voice out of a dry throat. "I overheard a conversation last night. Another invasion is planned for tomorrow. I didn't understand, but now it makes sense."

She gives us every detail she remembers of the conversation.

Traver's father is another subject; he's crying, completely depressed.

He says, "I did not raise my boy to be that way."

"What do we do with gargoyles who break the law? Is this new, just since I've been queen?" I ask no one in particular, addressing the entire High Guild.

The Members describe they'd had gargoyles who went bad, but it's rare. They state that some of the Ceorfan in the last few years have had similar feelings to Traver's. No one would act on those feelings as he did, though.

I need to think. First, I need some advice from Mega.

I tele-speak to him. "Will you please escort Traver's family to my office? They do not need to be a part of his sentencing."

"Yes, my queen. I am sorry you are put in such a situation. I'll be in your office with them until you tele-speak for me to return.

The wife helps the father, letting him lean on her for support when they leave the room with Mega.

I rub my hands over my face. "Traver, do you have anything to say in your defense?"

He goes on for several minutes about how he's proud of what he's done. The last thing he says is that he'll kill me, too, when he gets the chance.

When he finally shuts up, I ask everyone in the meeting, "Go around the room, what punishment would you give this traitor?"

Clifton repeats the consensus and says, "Death. You can't change what happened, but to let him live after endangering the entire human race and the Ceorfan would be a case of punishing the victims to let him go. It's the law. This is the consensus of the members."

I say, "Thank you all for your honesty. I'm sorry. It grieves me that I'm the queen who must institute the punishment, taking another gargoyle from us. I see no other way. He will be put to death tonight. I'll ask his father and wife if they wanted it in private or public, and if they would like to see him first."

Tele-speaking to Mega again, I say, "Please bring them back in. Traver will be put to death. I need to inform his family."

I advise them of the verdict as gently as I can. They're both crying. They both decide a private death, with a pulse after to the Guild, is best. They want the chance to say goodbye.

"Let's go—I don't want to delay the inevitable. Jericho, please, walk with me. All who are in attendance, come with us."

Mega takes us to a series of cave rooms where they have magic forcefield walls to hold incarcerated.

Traver stands behind one of these walls.

Jericho is mumbling.

Mega turns off the barrier. He tele-speaks, "It is safe. The mage is holding the prisoner still with a spell.

"Jericho also says, to tell you it is not the same as with Eltira. It is all spell."

"Thank you, Mega."

I announce, "Traver, you have been found guilty of treason. Genocide of the human race will not be tolerated, nor will the endangerment of the Ceorfan Guild, our people. You are sentenced to death. Your father and wife would like to tell you goodbye."

We back up to the other side of the room to give them a little privacy.

"Jericho, I'm so sorry. It's not my intention to make you the royal executioner. Please forgive me."

"Pulse of our hearts, I feel your pain. I wish it were not so. Make sure that when you pulse after this deed is complete, tell everything. Including how hard it is to make these decisions, but why they are necessary. You have the authority as queen. Be strong—do not waver in your resolve."

"Okay. Let's get this over with."

I face Traver's father and say, "His name is still etched in the city. He will be remembered. Are you both sure you want to stay, or shall I have someone escort you home?"

"No, we will stay."

Jericho comes forward with another stone. He holds it out. It shines like a flashlight. Everywhere it shines on Traver he dissolves. Shortly, there is only a pile of dust.

His family leaves first, with tears in their eyes. One by one, we leave also.

I reach a hand out to Mica. He gathers me to his chest. I cry my aching grief out in his arms. He stays there for me.

Spar is at my back holding me as I press into him and Mica.

Kino is at our sides with his head leaning on my neck. My head presses on his when I've finally cried enough.

Lifting my head, I dry my eyes with the back of my hand. My goyles are here for me, I can feel their heartbeats. I can also feel they hurt for me. I want to make them feel better.

I ask, "Will you pulse the Ceorfan Guild with me?"

As soon as I say it, I know it's a very good decision. Our people need to see us as unified and strong. They all agree. We stand right where we are, arm in arm. I start the pulse, putting my heart into it— but a strong message also. I sense Kino join in first, then the others. The wave goes through all of Navan, telling the story of today, of our danger and grief.

We go back to the conference room where Clifton has the TASS chairman on the line. I ask him if he has any questions, or if what my assistant has told him is clear.

He says he has enough and will get back with me when they

investigate. He's sending soldiers to the coordinates Traver has given. No delay. We need to know if they're still at the same location, how many are there, what their defenses are. Then we'll have more planning to do later.

I hang up after I say, "I'll be waiting for your call, José."

34

TEST

Kendra

Tonight is the night.

Tonight, Spar will conquer his final test. The moon's full, and the emotions of almost everyone are electric. When he defeats the fifth and final test, Spar will integrate into the Ceorfan as one of the Elite Warriors.

He is testing, and I'll command. I will not put my finger, or claw, on the scale of the test. I will, though, make damn sure no one else does, either! Finally, I will act as regent before the entire Guild. This will be entertaining, inspiring, and it'll most certainly be memorable. Rare as it is for a Carved to be admitted to the Guild, it's rarer still for a Carved becoming an Elite Warrior. This night, I'll help my people live with joy.

Through my assistant and High Guild Member, Count de Treon, I ensure the High Guild convenes. Their job, oversee the test and to integrate Spar into the Elite Warriors after he completes his task. My final act in this upcoming spectacle is to instruct the High Guild to hold the beginning of the test in the arena. I want all the Ceorfan to attend.

The festival-like atmosphere around the arena, has brought out the cosmopolitan gargoyles. The oddball, the kooky, the laborer, the elegant, and the regal all compete for a view of the coming event.

Gargoyle vendors are selling all kinds of food and drink. Some I know, others I'm interested in, and still others, I'd prefer to never see again. Goyles are selling various whimsical trinkets, edgy stickers, and cards—some with Spar's nude picture. Others sold some styluses and tablets with his likeness and name on them. There are still other vendors with many types of imaginative doodads.

The oddest item sold is a framed picture of Spar and me together.

Surprised, I ask, "When did they get those?" to no one in particular.

***

Spar

The Count brings the crowd noise to a halt when he steps into the arena. In his most authoritative voice, he announces the beginning of the test. He calls me forward. This is the worst part, I'll bet.

A member of the High Guild comes forward and faces me. He's a medieval-looking gargoyle, a real demon; his name is Grit. In a serious, 'take-no-shit' voice, he tells me the rules. They are few.

"We have placed this stone—"a hologram of a large green, pillow-cut topaz is blown up for everyone to see "—in the Ranger post building ten. You are to collect this stone and return it to the hands of the Pulse of Our Heart. Then, and only then, will your test be complete.

In this test, you will battle five gargoyles along your journey. You will not know when or where they will show up. They are not friends. They will do their best to stop you. If anyone interferes, they will void your test. You will be given another test at a later date. You must prove you are a master in battle to become integrated with the Elite. If you complete your task, you will be a member of our finest warriors and added to the Ducere. Good luck, young Spar. I bless your going with stone and magic. When the pulse is echoed, you must start."

A big holo in the middle of the arena starts a countdown from ten. The crowd joins in, shouting the counting down numbers. When they say zero, the pulse thumps. It beats 'go' though my body.

I launch myself into the air, dodging around the crowd. Many try to follow me, but I can't let them. I have no problem getting to the cave city's entrance and out into the moonlit sky. I'm going to try my best to finish quick.

Flying toward the Ranger's post I feel a sting on my right wing and hear the sizzle of a laser that's burning me. I can still fly, but wow, that hurts. Not enough to stop me. I never would have thought they would shoot at me from the ground. Especially not with a laser. How are they able to mark me, anyway? I'd have to have a chip or something on me to guide the laser. They could find me with heat-sensing sights, but those wouldn't be accurate at this distance. Unless it's magic. No way would Jericho do that to any of us.

Going over a large hill, I drop. Running back, I find a mage I've never met in a deer stand. He's searching for me in the direction of the hill I dropped under. I need answers, but he's a mage. He'll be able to use magic if I stall, so I can't risk leaving him conscious. I seize him from behind. I grab him in a choke hold, putting extra pressure on his carotid artery. In seconds he's out.

That should hold him a few hours. I hope I'm finished by then. But, just in case, I drag him over to a big boulder. Placing my hands on his I use my gift to press his hands into the rock, then I let his hands go and pull out my own hands. This leaves his encased in the boulder. I tug on his arms to see if his hands stay encased in the boulder, and they do.

Woohoo, that's awesome! I tear off part of his shirt and gag him. I want to be able to come back and release him without him being able to spell me. Where did they find this guy? I didn't know mages worked with us—well, besides Jericho. I better remember this. One down, four more, and I'm safe.

. . .

***

Kendra

I send Mega a tele-message. "Do you have someone following to make sure he's okay?"

He answers, "Already on it Kendra. Already on it."

I'm anxious. My donum is tingling. I'm going to call it my dragon sense. That fits me better. The boys will get a laugh out of that.

Amber's by my side, says, "Spar is a good soldier. He'll do this just fine."

She also brings me a plate full of fruit and some kind of dip for it.

Mica brings me a drink. We sit and eat, talking while we wait for news of Spar's progress.

My consorts and Ducere are sitting with me.

I say, "My dragon sense donum is tingling. I'm going to the cave entrance to see what I sense from there."

I can't see anything wrong, but I've got a bad feeling. I don't want to interfere with the test because I'm worrying over my lover, either. I trust in him. I'll leave it at that. I'm waiting right here. They can't make me leave.

***

Spar

I take off flying again, getting to the post, where building 10 is located, in a few minutes. The top of the building where the stone is waiting is where I perch. After verifying it is clear I sink into the ceiling. I discern the rock and start to grab it, but there's another barrier.

Again, I sink into it, grabbing the gem, then I rise back through the barrier. The second barrier must have been an alarm. Once I tripped it, all four of my remaining combatants converge on me. I put the stone in a pocket of my jeans. The High Guild member telling me they aren't my friends wasn't kidding.

I don't know any of them. In fact, I haven't ever seen any of them before. They're gargoyles. Huge, like Megahir. If the looks on their faces are a sign of their intent, I'm dead meat. Before I can think, they rush me, each one landing hard punches.

I go down. They're brutal, beating me. One keeps shouting that I'll never be part of the Ceorfan. I'm dirt beneath his feet. Die, human scum. They're all over me. All I can do is protect my head. This is a great time to sink into the floor.

I catch my breath laying on the dirt under the structure. Ouch, they must have broken my ribs. I know it's supposed to be hard, but this is worse than I thought. They're trying to kill me.

A ring on the one telling me to die is especially noticeable every time he hit me with it. It's a big ring, with an old-time coat of arms on its face. I need to sneak back, so I start crawling. It's quiet, I keep going. Once I'm on the outside of the building, I stand. Holy fuck, the pain is amazing. Holding my ribs helps. I know I need to fly. Determining I can handly the funcking pain, I take off. As painful as it is, it'd be harder to walk all the way to the cave and my Kendra.

Odd, there's no follow-up attack on my return. Now that I see the entrance to the cave city, my adrenalin takes control. Before I can pulse the coded echo to the sentries, something hits me in the head. I drop to the ground and roll to face my attackers. They're like an angry mob bent on killing me. I take one out, latching onto him and using him as a shield. One of the others hits him in the face and knocks him out. Okay, three to go.

I see Kendra rushing out of the cave with a crowd. "I'm okay, hun —don't help me. I got this."

I attach the one who knocked out his cohort and punch him in the throat. There isn't a second to stop, I spin not forgetting the other two. I kick out as hard as I can. The kick lands hard on the side of a remaining attacker's knee, and he's done.

One more to go. This one is going to use his gift. I can tell because we all get this look of concentration when we use our gifts. The question is, what can he do? I see what looks like a throwing star come out of his hand. I dodge, but it strikes me in my shoulder. There are others hitting me all over as I grab his head and twist. I kill him.

I see Kendra; she's cutting her hand for me. That's nice. I can't stay awake and fade out.

***

Kendra

I'm sitting next to Spar in the medical room. He's going to be fine. I never want to have to see him like this again. The worst thing was when he told us not to help him. For a stupid test! I'm going to give the High Guild hell!

If I hadn't been there, I don't think he would've made it. Dragon blood pulls us out of a jam, once again. Mica and Kino are questioning the assholes who did this to him.

My blue goyle groans and opens his eyes. There's a stupid grin on his face as he reaches into his bloody pants and brings out the topaz. I hold out my hands, and he puts it in them gently.

"Kendra, I think those assholes were trying to kill me. I left a mage in the desert on the way to the Station. We need to send someone to get him. Where is everyone?"

"Can you tell me what he might be close to?"

"Yeah, he is tied up in a deer stand about five miles from the cave entrance, going north."

I take my tablet and call Mica and Kino. I want them to know first that Spar's awake and talking. They say they're finished with what they're doing and will be here soon.

They're here in minutes. I'm giving Spar some water and he's sitting up. His clothes are a bloody mess. I'm glad that when he fights, he wears a vest made of Kevlar. It's a male version of the ones I wear. Lots bigger, it velcros around his waist and neck the same way. Way sexier. It caught some of the sharp little stars the strange gargoyle threw at him. He's going to need new everything anyway.

"Do you want to know the information we collected from the prisoners?"

Kino lets Mica do the talking.

"Yes, here's fine," I answer, not wanting to leave.

"They're nomadic gargoyles hired by the High Guild member Traver and four others. Each of them had been hired by one of the members who left the meeting last week. They all chose to leave Navan instead of loyalty to you. They do have family here who know where they're staying. They're all in Cueva Hallow. We have the Elites collecting them now. They should be in cells before sunrise.

The ones who attacked Spar were paid half last week. They were paid very well—$500,000.00 apiece. The terms of the contract were to deliver Spar tonight. Dead. The attackers believe he is going to destroy the Ceorfan from within. They have a mage working with them. But they think he ran off, because they haven't seen him since before the test."

"How do we know what they told you is true, Mica?" I ask.

"We're sure, because Jericho spelled them to tell the truth. They had no idea Spar was consort to the queen, or that there is a new queen. They believed their prey was an outlaw, a rogue carved gargoyle, and they had been sent to kill, lawfully by the High Guild."

Spar tells them where the mage is located, and Mica calls Mega, so he can tele-speak to one of the Ducere to apprehend him.

"Tell them I stuck his hands in a boulder. They can give him water, and I'll be able to go get him free tomorrow if no one else has a gift to get him out. I don't feel up to it right now," he whispers then drifts off.

I reflect, "The question is, how many Ceorfan believe like Traver and his crew? We need to ask each gargoyle. Fuck, this is a mess! I'm going to need some time to think. When you guys torp today, I want to go talk to José. Mica, given the situation can you get some rest now and stay awake with me?"

"Of course, Princess. Good idea. I'll go rest now. I'll be in my own quarters if you need me, okay?"

I watch as he leaves. "I need some rest, too, guys. As soon as you torp, I'm laying down. This is my new normal. Crazy. I have one thing to do—call Clifton and give him this dratted topaz."

I send a message to José Brinker to let him know I need to speak with him today, so I won't be a total surprise. I don't get into a lot of detail, but do tell him my subject.

Then I message Jared. I'm not surprised when he messages me right back, saying he is not at Fiatril Hall. He's checking out some potential sources of information on the Horde. I caution him to please be careful and call when he can.

35

FIRE

Kendra

I can't sleep, no matter how hard I try. Is Mica still asleep? I reach out to see if I can detect his presence. I can sense he's here. I can't tell if he's awake.

I practice feeling Kino and Spar. Yes, my perception of them is a little stronger because they are right here in my room. I get up and get dressed. I'm in the mood for some fun, so I put a bra on top of Spar's wing. Taking a pair of panties, I put them on Kino's. I've got to do my best to be here when they wake.

I'm going to find Mica, so I can crawl into bed with him. Maybe that'll help me sleep. Reaching for him with my mind, I start off. I haven't been to his room before now. That gives me pause. What if it's his private space? What if he doesn't want anyone in it, including me? Well, I guess I'll find out.

To get there, I must wing my way up. It's off the training room. It looks like there are lots of little cave rooms up here. I go quietly into his room. Yay, he's lying in a bed, not an upright torpefied stone statue. I take off my shoes and pants then, creep over to him, get into bed, and squeeze up close to him. I'm sleepy now. I close my eyes to drift off as he wraps me up in his muscle-bound arms. That makes me feel better about barging in without asking.

I wake to a noise and locate it when I figure out Mica's up, getting dressed. I lift myself onto an elbow to see him better. He's putting on his pants without underwear. Well, commando fits him well, better than boxers or briefs. He notices me watching.

"I had the best present this morning, princess, when I woke up with you in my bed, all warm and sexy," he flirts.

He hops onto the bed, bouncing me up a little, right as my tablet beeps a notification.

I can't ignore any messages when the Horde is still wreaking havoc through the world. It's from José, in answer to my message to him last night. He says he's going to be interviewing couples who want to foster the children today. He's free right now, for about an hour. I message back that I'll see him in fifteen-ish minutes.

"Well, Mica, I guess we're going to talk to José right now instead of me making out with your hotness." I kiss him quickly, so I won't get caught up. I still want more.

"Mica, after we talk to José, let's spend some time together, okay? I don't have any ideas, but if you do, I'll be happy with whatever you want to do." I ask.

"I'd love to spend some time with you. What're we talking to the Chairman about? What happened with Spar last night?"

"Yes, I need to make some decisions. I keep coming back to the idea the structure of the current Ceorfan government isn't working. I want advice before I jump in and change it. That could backfire on me. What do you think, Mica?" I ask, getting dressed.

"Whatever you do, I'm sure you'll do it for the benefit of our people. I'll back you all the way, my fair lady. I trust you. It's possible you'll do everything right, ironing out all the problems. If you do something wrong and make a mistake, I'll still be here for you. I do believe José's a good choice for this kind of advice. I'm a good choice for other stuff. Like fun." He grins, gathering me close to give me an idea of what kind of fun.

"Good thing I'm dressed, or I'd delay talking to my friend the TASS Chairman," I flirt in return.

We meet with José and learn they'll place the children in homes today. "Kendra dear, these children are as healthy as possible. If you had not been there, as fast as you were I do not think they would have survived." He's using his 'Chairman' voice as he speaks. It's clear he wants me to know the actions the Ceorfan took saved these children without question.

"I wish we could catch the sociopathic piece of shit. We have to stop him before he hurts anyone else."

"Ah, thank you. About that—we found the installation from the coordinates you gave me. It's empty. No one there at all. In fact, it doesn't look like anyone's been there in weeks. Your man may have been fooled into thinking their base was there to keep their real location secret. I believe it was used for the one meeting. It is a wonderful place to hide, I'll give you that, but no sign they were using it. Only the front rooms had any sign of use in the past month."

I say, "Shit! I thought we'd be able to end him. Back to the fucking drawing board."

"We are following up on clues. I'll be in touch as soon as I find out anything," he says.

Calming down, we eat breakfast with José, talking all the while. He gives me some great advice. "Take it slow, get to know your people, they will let you know the best way to go. No need to rush. Be patient, little queen—these things usually take care of themselves."

Mica and I leave, but not back to Navan. He portals us straight to Oahu. He says this is big wave season. We can watch the daredevils surf the North Shore. It's not hot, not cold. Chickens are everywhere. The ocean is choppy with huge swells. It takes my breath away to see the surfers surf those big waves. No one is getting hurt. It's astounding to watch.

"Oh Mica, how do they do that?"

"Well, it takes lots of practice. Look, there's a two-hour whale tour. Would you like to go do that?"

"Yes, that'd be so cool. Let's do it."

He gets us tickets, and we're off.

"You know, I'd never been out of New Mexico until Scotland, and now here. This is wonderful," I say and lean back on him. He's steady and strong. Of course, he's getting his share of looks from the ladies.

He laughs when I point that out. If the Rock had a fair, blond twin, he would look a lot like my partner in his glamour. If they could only see his horns. I want to stick a sign on him that says he's mine. It makes me feel good that he only has eyes for me when we are around so many beautiful people.

We can already hear whale song. No matter how nice the movies are, it's much more exciting to hear them in person. When a giant humpback whale jumps, it surprises me, and I jump back into my consort. I hold my breath at the marvelous sight.

He folds his arms around me. Bending close to my ear, he blows his hot breath on me and kisses me. Oh, Mica, too bad we're limited out here.

It's over before I know it. I love every second. Just being alone with my sweetheart is nice. I want to move faster in this relationship, but it's a little scary. Today was wonderful. In summer, we will discover if I can learn to surf or not. He loves it, dare devil that he is, makes a lot of sense. I love the water. Swimming is lovely. These are great plans.

"Let's go to the lunchroom and get something to drink," Mica tells me.

We find a private place to portal back home. We are the only ones in here, so I get us some tea. I like mine with lemon; he likes his with lots and lots of sugar. I decide I'll make us some cookies. I start, and he joins in. We make lots of plans. I can't keep my hands off of him and kiss him as much as possible.

Finishing the cookies, I take them to a table, still hot, when Jericho arrives. Several other gargoyles come in, so we know it's dark already. This day went by fast.

We're talking to the mage, Kino and Spar enter the lunch room. Oh, great! I'm going to die of embarrassment. They still have my underthings stuck on the top of their wings.

"Get over here, you jokers," I order.

I take off my bra and panties from their wings.

They sheepishly say, "How did those get there?"

"I get it, you got me back." I can't help but laugh.

"Come on, guys, let's fly. I have business tonight."

We've been making it a habit to fly first thing after dark. We want to look around the Ranger's Station to ensure everything is up to scratch. That's when we see a fire in the south, close to the tourist caves. We hurry over to see if we can help without being seen. Mica and I take more chances at being seen since we look human. It's dry here, and the fire is spreading fast.

I call the sheriff's department from my tablet. They're sending help. There isn't much we can do except make sure the people and any animals are safe. I knock on several of the cabin doors in the area and tell them to pack; they may need to evacuate. I give them details to start getting medicines and clothes packed.

Mica pulls me to move in another direction. I follow. The fire is spreading farther and faster than before. The winds have whipped up. We warn everyone we can find, "Leave now."

When the fire trucks get near us, we clear out.

The others have rejoined us, and we're flying again. About a mile down the road, there's a car with its top down. Inside are a couple of young people putting their clothes on, fast.

"The car isn't the only thing with its top down," I say.

"I figure they must have been getting busy and didn't notice how bad the fire was." Spar chuckles.

The fire's already surrounded them.

"Mica, we need to get them out of here now," I say.

We both turn to Kino and he sings the two teenagers to sleep. My partner flies in and grabs the boy, while my blueness grabs the girl.

The kids are dead weight, but my goyles lift them like they're babies and soar with them to safety.

The best thing we could think to do was to bring them to the Ranger's Station. I fly ahead in stealth mode. Quiet as I can, I land and change, letting my human blood take over my appearance.

Mica and Spar set them down on the ground. I walk up to them and the guys melt into the forest behind them. I've got to put on the act of my life.

When Kino stops singing, they wake up. "Hi there, my name is Officer Macbard. How do you feel?"

The guy takes his girl's hand and looks at her, his mouth agape. She doesn't hesitate and starts talking. She goes into her story, starting with the devil saving them from the fire. I'm doing everything I can to not roll my eyes as Mica, in glamor, comes up behind them.

He says, "I have been called many things, ma'am. I might have been called the devil a time or two. When I pulled you from your car, you were both knocked out. You probably dreamed the devil part."

"What are your names?" I ask the surprised teenagers.

"Jimmy Danforth and Vanessa Cutter," they tell me. Two of the most prominent family names in Cueva Hallow.

"Well, Jimmy and Vanessa, it isn't safe right now, so we can't call for someone to pick you up. We'll take you home. I just need to call our boss and check out a vehicle."

I call Murphy telling him about the fire. I use the excuse that Mica and I were riding around to see if I could handle working again, so I can tell the doctor I've tried, and it's all good.

He says, "No problem. Take the Ranger SUV you usually drive. I drove it yesterday, and the tank is full. Text me the kid's names, and I'll fill out the report. Oh, also text me the location of the car."

"I'll do that," I do it, right then, so I won't forget.

"Hey, kids, I'll get the SUV and be right back. Stay here with Officer Jacobs."

I can detect , my other consorts in the forest after I round the side of the main building. I take off toward them. They wait for me.

"Are you both okay? No burns or anything?" They both reply they're fine. "You guys can go home. You heard that we need to take those teenagers home. It'll take me about two hours to get back to Navan. Alert Mega and make sure he knows there's a fire."

We take Vanessa home first. Her family lives right on the river—meaning the river is about a football field away from her back door. Ritzy neighborhood. I walk her up to the front door. Using my persuasion, I try to back up Mica's story, so I can reinforce the belief. Making sure she locks the door, I leave. I do the same with Jimmy, only he wants us to leave him at the diner.

After finishing with the kids, we make good time back to the Ranger Station. We head straight into the woods before we change and fly home.

"Mica, do the Elites patrol around here at night? If not, let's set that up. Just to keep people safe."

We head back home at top speed. We clean up in my room again. This is also becoming a habit. I like it. I'll see if Dana will create some closet space for my consorts' clothes. We have a meeting with the High Guild, and we're already late, according to the calendar Clifton made for me. I send him a short message to let him know we are on the way as soon as we shower off the smoke smell.

"Come on, Mica, shower with me."

The look on his face is so serious. "I won't be able to keep my hands to myself, Princess."

"Neither will I, but we need to hurry. I don't want our first time to be a quickie. Is that okay with you?"

"Everything with you is okay with me."

This is going to be a test. I can't help it I start lathering up, and as soon as I touch myself he groans.

Can I come just from the sound? Maybe not, but I'm well on the way. I smash myself up against him. I'm the queen boss here and they'll have to wait a few for me. I'm glad my shower is open like in a locker room. Mica wouldn't fit in a regular-sized shower. Checking out his erection I can't wait to see how that fits. I have never seen junk quite that large in my life. I look in his eyes, asking if I can touch. He says yes. I take him in my lathered hand and pump softly. He steps closer to me kissing my neck, sending tingles to my toes, best feeling ever.

He reaches for my hot, wet pussy, and nope, I was wrong—this is now the best feeling. He holds my hand still and tells me he can't wait, it's been a long time. He's too excited and can't hold back. Okay, me first then. He slams me against the wall. I can balance by putting the sole of my foot on the wall and my knee on his shoulder. He leans in and kisses my clit. I lean into him, putting my hands on his horns. My body takes over with perfect rhythm. I grind into his tongue. In seconds, I orgasm as he holds my ass. It's too much, and I try to back away, but he doesn't let me, and I rapidly come again. Oh, that's good. I reach for his rock-hard penis, sinking to my knees and lick the head while pumping him with my hand. He comes for me quickly.

I stand. My legs are shaky. I'm going to have to start working on them more. We clean each other up. I tell him he's amazing, and I never want to be without him. How can a woman be so lucky anyway?

He tells me I'm the prize, not him. I'll never be without him if he can help it.

36

TERMINUS DEBRIEF

Kendra

When we enter the conference room there're a few grins, as Clifton says, "Your Majesty. Now we can start the meeting."

"Your pardon, my most ardent taskmaster," I reply and grin at him. "You may start."

He starts, "The first order of business concerns the ex-HG members who paid for Spar to be killed."

I interrupt, "Excuse me, what do you mean by 'ex-HG?'"

"My pardon, I mean the High Guild members you removed."

"Thank you, Count," I say.

I like it. I must be rubbing off on him.

His smile was genuine as he continued. "We traced the money, discovering it came from the four ex-HG members' accounts equally. Those funds were dispersed among the five nomads who tried to kill Spar. We also found these ex-members had been spelled into hiring the hitmen by the nomad mage. This was done as soon as Spar was brought into Navan. They were spelled again when you removed them from the High Guild. This time, the spell included disloyalty to you, my queen. Each of them said they were told to hire help to kill

Spar and his girlfriend. They knew you were the rightful queen. The spell convinced them they were doing the right thing anyway."

"Did Traver or his family add any funds to this mutiny?" I asked.

"Your Majesty, we found Traver did not contribute to this fund. We assume he was trying to lay the groundwork for laying the blame on others."

"Thank you, please continue."

"The nomads did not even know there were dragons in the world again. The mage is one of Barat's rejects. He has been trying to get away from Baratium with his life for ages. He spelled the traitorous gargoyles under the impression he was protecting the Ceorfan. According to Traver's account, you are not a real dragon, one who should not be queen. He was told you are a puppet of Jericho's. You and the mage were to have hatched a plan together, so you could procure the dragons' treasure."

Jericho says, "That is preposterous!"

"Wait! What? There's dragon treasure?" That's something I haven't thought about! I almost want to laugh at the mage's outburst, if it weren't such a serious problem.

"Shall we try the same options as before, but with a protection? They can leave, never to return, and have their names etched in the city as traitors. Or stay and pledge fealty with a spell that they can't work harm to anyone, man or beast? We'll do the pledges in the arena for all the Guild to see and take part in. I want to have a short speech concerning our purpose as the Ceorfan Guild. In it, I'll welcome all the nomads to be friends and known to us."

Clifton seconds and the vote carries. "General Mega, you take all actions for the prisoners. I'll plan the pledge party at the arena."

The little green count begins again, "The next order of business concerns John Cooper, your old ranger friend. Evidence was collected by the Ducere team assigned. Pictures, video, telephone calls, receipts proving his location, and witness accounts verifying conduct unbecoming a Federal Officer, dereliction of duty, possession of a controlled substance with intent to distribute in a Federal Park, colluding with a foreign government—the list goes on... you get the picture. This information was mailed in a file to Captain Murphy's home address. The criminal ranger has already been detained and is now awaiting trial. He implicated the others he has been working with. They have also been detained."

"That's wonderful! Brilliant job, too," I comment.

Count de Treon, continues, "I have two dates open for Spar's integration party. Saint Patrick's Day, March 17th, or the 24th. We can also combine it into an integration and naming the royal Consorts as your princes' party. What are your wishes, Majesty?"

"I like Saint Patrick's Day and, yes, let's make it a dual party, if that's all right with Spar?"

"I'm fine with a dual party," says Spar.

Mica seconds.

The motion carries.

Clifton is assigned the task of setting up the party.

"Now, Majesty, do you have news to report?"

"Yes. I want to tell you all the children from the battle are healed and doing well. TASS has found them foster parents, and they should be in their new homes soon.

"Likewise, my Ducere and I have practiced many battle and fighting scenarios. But we missed everything to do with helping the wounded. That's something we'll be working on. It went very well, having my consorts with me. But in a real battle, I'd need someone to help with the wounded and others to protect the medics.

"I would like you, Jericho, to start a medical corps for battles. I'll, of course, need to work with them to plan how we'll handle the flow during battles. Hopefully only one battle. Does anyone want to help Jericho with this task?"

One of the guild members, Amethyst, says she would love to if Jericho is agreed. Seconded and carried.

"I'd like the Elites to set up a patrol of the area around Navan at night. I'd also like to invite more humans into our city. These humans are those who can be trusted to guard during daylight hours. I can ask

TASS if they're able to provide them. That being said, loyalty is an issue. TASS requires that personnel sign a non-disclosure agreement. It acknowledges all property owned by the party would be forfeit. Given that requirement, they have had very few violators."

Mega seconds.

Motion carries.

"I'd also like a daily meeting of this guild. I'd like it to be a breakfast meeting. Thirty minutes after sunset is when I want the meetings. I want them over quickly, lasting only thirty minutes to, at most, one hour. I ask each member here to bring me a topic of interest for the Ceorfan Guild as a whole. We need to meet the Guild's needs, and I can't if I don't know what we need."

Amethyst seconds, motion carried.

Clifton asks if there are any other subjects that need to be taken care of tonight. Finding none, he dismisses us with the closing, "You are dismissed. Have a good night and thank you for serving."

I like that closing. It reminds us why we're here.

"Come on guys, I'm starving. I want pizza. You think they'll deliver?" We all laugh.

A SNEAK PEEK...

Turn the page to read a chapter of the next book in the
Ceorfan Gargoyle Series–

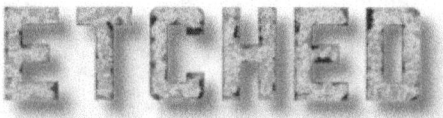

ETCHED, CHAPTER ONE
Work

Kendra

Here I am, sitting in the pristine examination room at Dr. Vargas's office. As he's finishing his exam, I have a good idea he's happy. "Kendra Macbard, I've known you since you were a little girl. If I didn't know how you heal, I wouldn't believe these tests results and would run them again." Doctor Vargas flips through my records. "I think you are more than ready to go back to work at the Ranger's Service. No restrictions. Do you agree, or do you have a problem that we need to discuss?"

"No sir, no problems. I'm more than ready to return to work." But I'm also thinking I'll be able to get inside information much more accessible at work; meaning I can protect and care for my people better. On another note, I can't continue to let them down like I feel I have. Having to have two of our number executed for treason in the short time I've been queen is terrible. I think about that a lot. Well, at least they can't call me Bloody Mary—though I've got to do better. I must find ways to improve their lives.

On my way out of the doctor's office, I overhear two ladies in the waiting room gossiping about the Cutter girl. The one says to the other, "Did you hear? She has gone perfectly insane. Spouting that drivel about the devil saving her and that awful Danforth boy."

Oh no, this is my fault. I sigh. I've got to help Vanessa. Gossip—it only hurts people.

I'd made a date with Chris to meet for lunch. Today is her day off, and I'm in the mood for pizza, so we're going to get some. I'll also take some home to the guys too. Wow. I view Navan as home instead of my dinky little apartment. A dinky little apartment that I need to check on while I'm in town.

I get to Mama's Bistro on Main, and there's the always-dependable Chris, waiting for me. I get a hug before we sit. "Well, chica, I've been given a clean bill of health by the good Dr. Vargas. He says I can go back to work tomorrow. Am I back on the schedule?"

"You better believe I put you on the schedule, Kendra. We're short-handed so it'll be a blessing for you to be there tomorrow. Your new partner was back today. Too bad about him losing family and all, but he's back. Did you hear about John?"

Chris tells me all about John selling drugs then getting caught. I act surprised before I ask a few questions to further cement her belief in my falsehood. I'm learning to better conceal the things I know from those I care for. Chris and I laugh throughout our lunch. She's such an easy person to talk to. I momentarily forget some of the burdens I'm carrying and have a good time. She has a hair appointment, so she needs to go. "Kendra, you look great. Maybe I should get shot, so it'll make me look better." We laugh. I tell her she's a pretty lady, and she knows it.

I order three large, thick, stuffed crust pizzas to go for the guys. On second thought, I better make that six and load them with protein, extra sausage, and pepperoni. I secure them in Jasper's back seat, and head to my apartment. When I get there Brian, the door-man, greets me with his usual smile and expression of how beautiful a day it is as he opens the door for me.

I'm disjointed as I exit the elevator, this place belongs in an old movie, not my life. Unlocking my door, I close and lock it behind me. It's different, not like home anymore... no this isn't home anymore. I'll keep it because we need a place in town for a base, but that's it.

I pack a few of my uniforms for work. Check the fridge to be sure nothing is ruined. No, it's empty and clean. Huh, I'll bet some stone dude is taking care of me. I love them. Wait, yeah, it's true. I'm not denying it. I'm not going to choose between them either. I want to love and be loved. I'm going to do my best and see what happens.

I take my uniforms to Jasper, my truck, load up, and drive away pausing to look back at my life. I'll leave Jasper at one of the Ranger cabins that no one visits. Then I'll stop to pick up Mica from work. He won't mind helping me carry stuff when we fly home.

***

Back in Navan, my room has had a makeover. Yay! Dana has been here and put in some closets made of stone—like my cave walls, but more functional. I see Dana's touch in the kitchen too. He's manipulated the stone; I have several gorgeous rock shelves. We spend a lot of time here. I bet that I can fit in more supplies instead of having to go to the lunchroom for everything. He's put up some of the prettiest red glass lights for me. I set the pizzas on my table. Mica gets some out and starts to eat right away.

"Work is going well. There's a lot to catch up on. I'll show you everything tomorrow," he says between bites.

"Yeah, I suspected we might be behind. Get your shower. I'm changing. The others should be awake by the time you're finished. We can go to the High Guild meeting together. If we get it over fast enough, we can get back here, watch a movie, eat pizza, drink a beer, and then go flying."

"Sounds good to me beautiful," Mica says.

After taking care of showers and food, Mica, Spar, Kino, and I go to the HG meeting—I laugh at the acronym coined by Clifton—he brings the meeting to order.

Jericho interrupts, "This cannot wait, Your Majesty."

"What can't wait, Jericho?" I ask.

"The crystal cave is lit up with lights, all of its own making. Usually, it's a signal to enter and sleep so I can dream. Do you recollect my informing you of the dreams one has while sleeping in the cave? It would not let me enter today, so I desire your presence, or that of one of your brothers, to ascertain whether it will allow one of you to sleep in the cave," he says anxiously. In the past, the dream cave was used by the dragon kings and queens... well at least until I was the only one available to use it.

"I'll go with you when this meeting is over if you don't mind waiting," I plead.

We finish the rest of the guild business in short order after he agrees. Rising to leave, the guys and I follow Jericho to his laboratory.

I step up to the little enclave, and its strobing colored lights. My skin thrills from the display. I feel it's saying it needs me. Taking a deep breath, I sit on the smooth stone seat inside the cave.

I tremble as my body understands more than my brain. "I'm here," I say out loud. My mind is captured by a vision. My body tenses as I lean back into nothingness. Suddenly I'm transferred to another space, another time. I'm gliding like a bird, then abruptly I stop in mid-air. I'm suspended in front of a stunning gargoyle on the side an exquisite palace, surrounded by lofty towers and giant palisades. She—I'm sure it's a she—is speaking to me in my vision. I ask, "What did you say?"

Oddly, I see both her human form and her dragon avatar simultaneously. Her dark face and shoulders show the strength her body held. She stares into me with her crystal blue eyes. Her magnificent orange dragon head avatar seems to radiate energy, strength, and power. Together they turn to face me.

Her voice is a haunting rhythmic whisper as she speaks clearly, "*Kendra, i agapiméni mou kóri, férno tous agapiménous mou gious, ton Jared kai ti Dana, kai érchomai se ména sto Troa.*"

I have never spoken this language before. However, I understand it clearly. As a child intrinsically understanding her mother... the caressing tone, the gentle flute-like fluctuations, the love... "*Kendra, my dearest daughter, bring my well-favored sons, Jared and Dana, and come to me at the Troad.*"

My heart swells with joy. I know with all my being that I have found my grandmother.

My vision continues, "*My daughter, I have waited for you for more than a thousand years. It is difficult to speak to you from atop my monument. The distance... You must come to me. Your memories are not complete. You must be etched. I cannot reach you as my physical tether prevents me from joining you. You must find me before the next full moon, or the Ceorfan will turn from you. Doing so, they will be destroyed by the enemy. Divided, they will be weak. You must unite the gargoyle clans. Bring the surgeon. I will etch you for your reign.*"

My heart is racing. The beating seems to fill my ears and begins to overwhelm the dragon's lilting voice. It fades further replaced by only my breathing and heartbeat as I travel back to my body, back to Jericho's gem-like cave.

I take a few seconds to adjust. "Oh guys, I think we're in trouble." I proceed to explain, repeating every word I heard the dragon queen say in the vision. I'm not sure vision is the right word. It's the closest description I have though. I try to think of a way to explain my emotions to them, the way I felt... feel, and I can't. I have a sinking feeling and a sudden racing of my heart. Fear strikes me, and I break out in cold sweats and heavy breathing.

Jericho, however, is amazed. He's never seen anyone speak to an ancestor that way from the cave. The cave now appears much the way it did the day I was previously here visiting with Jericho. No lights. Again, it's only a beautiful colossal geode, not the harbinger it became.

"Don't worry, beloved we will figure out the puzzle," Kino's calm voice settles me. "Jericho, do you know where a beautiful orange dragon queen's head might be?"

"I am acquainted with exactly where she is located. It is exceedingly difficult to get there. It will not be an easy journey. Turkey is restricted to Americans, and you cannot show up as a dragon in daylight. This will take some planning and quite a lot of luck."

My heart sinks. I must do this. There's no way out of it. Now that I'm out of the vision, the pull of the journey is on me. What am I going to do about work? How am I going to get there? Who the hell is the fucking surgeon?

GLOSSARY

(This short glossary is not a complete character list. More a list of terms we think you might want to remember and a few main characters.)

Amber - Elite Warrior specializes in undercover surveillance. Mate to Mason.

Ceorfan - (Key-or-fan) Carved or born grotesques, gargoyles, and dragons. Anyone different who wants to become family and is accepted by the Guild.

Chiroptera - Hand Wing or Little Wing, usually a hand with four fingers located at the top of many wings.

Crafted - Evil mindless robot created gargoyles made from wood and magic.

Cursed – The Ceorfan who were captured and tortured in the Mage Wars.

Dana Macbard - (Dan-uh) Brother of Kendra and Jared Macbard. Aqua dragon, Duke of Stone.

Donum - A gift, the knowing that the dragon breed has when there is a need between family members or guild. It can show up as a feeling or thoughts similar to ESP.

Ducere - (Doo sah ray) Small specialized team of the Elite Warriors Guard. The Ceorfan Special Forces.

Edling - Noble child, heir.

Ef - An effigy or statue of a gargoyle.

Elite Warrior Guard - The warriors/soldiers of the Ceorfan race.

Findare - Took over as temporary king in the interim between viable queens.

Flint - Elite Warrior undercover agent. Member of the Ducere.

Gortanik - A Mage who had been held prisoner of Barat and infiltrated Navan. His nickname is Kick and he is helping the Ceorfan find Barat.

Grotesques - People of the Ceorfan Race that look like what humans call gargoyles.

Guild - The word is used for the race of the Ceorfan people.

High Guild - The advisors to the Ruler of the Ceorfan.

Jared Macbard - Brother of Kendra and Dana Macbard. Blue dragon, Duke of Storms.

Jericho - Mage. Trusted member of the High Guild.

Kokkino Petra – Kino - (Key-no) Mega's third in command of the Elite Guard. Nephew to Findare. Love of Kendra, Consort of the Queen.

Mage - Human with the ability to perform spells of magic.

Mage Jar - A glass jar of liquid lighting used and powered by the magic, in Navan.

Mason - Elite Warrior specializes as a thief and undercover surveillance. Mate to Amber.

Megahir/Mega - (Mega-here) Commander of the Elite Warrior Guard.

Mica Jacobs - (Mike-ah) Second in command of the Elite Guard. Love of Kendra and her partner as a Federal Park Ranger, Consort of the Queen.

Navan - (Nuh-van) The cave city of the entire guild of Ceorfan people.

Pulse - An echo pulse is a form of communication between the Ceorfan Guild. Similar to the sonar pulses of bats.

Resurgere - 'Restore our family' literally, when a gargoyle has an ingot carved from his body in the seconds prior to hardening into a torpified state to sleep and heal, for the purpose of giving it willingly to another in exchange for a bone of their own body. Each party is implanted with the other's stone or bone.

Spar Megason - Resurgere gave him a new life from David's body he becomes Mega's son. Love of Kendra, Consort of the Queen.

Torpefy/Torp/Torped - Past tense: torpefied. Meaning: make (someone or something) numb, paralyzed, or lifeless. This is an early 19th century word from Latin [torpefacere], 'be numb or sluggish'. It is when gargoyles turn to stone in the daylight.

INTERESTED IN THE CEORFAN HISTORY?

The Myth - The Fairytale - The History
From the Halls of History

The ancient goyles tell a story....

Once long ago on a cold majestic mountain, lived a young woman. She was beautiful with long orange-red locks, skin like velvet, and gentle eyes. Her parents had been beaten by greedy highwaymen. Beaten, abused, and left to die on a cold road where the short ones live. She had tried to help them, but to no avail they were bound for the heavens. Her father's last words to her were, "Run up onto the mountain, find shelter, stay away from the others. I love you, little bird." Then his spirit fled his earthy shell. The tears ran from her eyes unrestrained.

She went to her mother to give her comfort. She hoped she might be able to help her. She could find a shelter for them both to stay in while her mother healed. Her father had taught her the ways of the mountain. She knew she could survive. "Mother, you must get up. I cannot carry you." She lifted her mother into her lap, rocking her. "Oh, Mother, please don't leave me," she cried.

"I have to be with Father, sweet girl. I cannot last. You must remember to always help others. Do not be as the ones who have abused us. Always love first. It costs, but in the end, it comes back to you bigger than your original gift, usually from an unlooked-for source."

She promised her mother she would love first, all the while knowing there would be none for her to love.

"I love you, my beauty. You have always been my greatest happiness." Mother's spirit then fled, flying to the heavens with Father.

She had lived on the mountain for a while when one day, the girl was wandering abroad collecting herbs and bark. There was a cart coming, she hid behind one of the large trees. The short ones dumped a body on the frozen road. She was so close. She held her breath, so they would not chance upon her. Her heart was beating loudly in her head. She held herself still, until she heard them no more. Peeking out from her hiding place, she looked at the still body in the road. She crept up to him. His bruised bleeding body was blue from the cold. They had left him with nothing to cover or protect himself. She hurt for him as she scans his damaged body. Taking off her cloak, she laid it on the ground beside him. Turning him over, she laid him on her cloak. She dragged him up the mountain to the cave, that had become her home. She washed his wounds and put on an ointment made from lavender and animal fat before covering them with broad leaves. She had a blanket, fashioned from scraps found discarded in the forest. Covering him gently, she sang a song over him, asking for the gods to heal his pain-ridden body.

Her guest awoke early. In the days to come, they become fast friends. They did not agree about all things. He thought the short ones were evil. She thought they needed help. As the years went by, they fell into a deep, abiding love for one another. They stayed isolated from the short ones. On occasion, the short ones rid themselves of their kind, calling the outcasts on the mountain 'demon spawn' or 'devils.' The girl and her love took the outcasts in. They cared for them, teaching them the way of the mountain. How to survive.

One day, the short ones dumped a baby, to be rid of it, calling it evil. One of the mountain people took it up to the girl. They wanted to know if she would kill it. It was obviously one of the short ones. Not one of their kind at all.

"Of course, we will add the child to our number. Always walk in love. It is our way," she taught them. "Love even when we are wronged greatly."

As the child grew into a strong man, he learned honor. He learned the way of the mountain people, the ways of the girl and the others who the short ones refused the common decency of living on the Earth.

One day, more short ones were in the forest. It was discovered he was to be a king of the short ones. The old king had tried to have all his brother's family killed, including the baby who, as a man, was the spitting image of the king's brother. Now the king was on his own death bed, with no heirs.

The short ones had found him. They believed he was the next king. They took him home to live in a castle, where food, drink, and warm rooms abounded.

The old king was dead. The baby who had been left to die on the mountain, now a grown man, was made the king. The king invited the orange-red-haired girl, who raised him with such great love, to live in the castle with him. She was the mother of his heart. She brought with her all of the foundlings who had been abused by the short ones. They were now part of a great country. Protected by the king, none of them lacked in any way. They were no longer scorned, but included in all ways. The orange-red haired girl and all her loves lived happily ever after.

ACKNOWLEDGMENTS

Miki

Thank you, our Fans and Readers of Carved and the Ceorfan Gargoyles Series. I appreciate each and every one of you. You are my prize.

My family who is always supportive and helpful. My husband, I love that you are in my corner. Thank you, Mom, for always being here for me. Thank you, Dad, for giving me a great imagination. My son Kit, LaRay, my son Kyle, and daughter-in-law Callie, my step sons John and Jeffery. All my grandchildren, you help me keep being. Our cousins are so wonderful! I hope everyone has people in their lives that are as amazing as you all. We are blessed to have you!

All my friends who are precious to me. Zoe Parker, you are the most giving amazing friend. Thank you for encouraging me to even admit I had a dream. You have helped me beyond measure. Kelly Stephens, you are such a great help and friend. You're always there when I need you. Amy Naylor, you make this world a sunnier place to live, thank you for all your help. I'm better for knowing you ladies.

Craig and Rob, you make everything in this so much more possible. What good dragons! You have always been my best friends.

Garrett, you really are the best co-author ever! I love you all. Thank you for your support! Yours, Miki Ward

Garrett

Thank you, fans, fellow countrymen, and Deadpool . . . hehe. You! Look in the mirror if you are not sure who I mean. I hope we brought some form of happiness to you. Thank you from the bottom of my petrified heart for giving us the opportunity to play around with your feelings for a bit.

I would like to thank my beautiful wife Kathi. Without you I am not a person. Also, thanks to each of my children, David, Christina, and Taelor, for the pure joy, and terror, you continually provide. Because of you, I push myself to a higher standard and sometimes, near the edge of a cliff. . . .

I would also like to thank my sister for having so much unfounded faith in my imagination and author abilities. Writing on your coattails, I fulfilled a long-sought dream. You were my sounding board and problem solver through this whole process. All my other family and friends . . . most of you are wonderful, and I love you. Others are only keeping me informed as I trudge from one mistake to another.

I, like Shrek, am a believer. I believe in the power of any individual to control their own destiny. I believe that if you try hard enough you can accomplish things that no one thought you were capable of. I believe that love has always been the greatest under-used asset in the world. I believe that enthusiasm can make up for shortcomings in knowledge. I believe in you! So, don't be afraid of mistakes. Make as many _responsible_ ones as you can and do them with gusto. – Garrett V. Ward

OTHER BOOKS BY MIKI AND GARRETT WARD

The Ceorfan Gargoyles Series

Carved

Etched

Hewn

The Ceorfan Gargoyles Novellas

My Tormented Mage

Shivers Series

We See You

Double Mirror

Elser Books are stand alone

Flesh and Bold

Stand Alone from Miki Ward

My Phantom Queen

FIND US

Miki & Mine FB Group - https://bit.ly/2CpH3BM Miki's FB
Author page - https://bit.ly/2yMlVSG Garrett's FB Author page -
https://bit.ly/2P3USwv Instagram - https://bit.ly/2Ro5utp
Bookbub - https://bit.ly/2J3FRFh
Follow Miki on Amazon - https://amzn.to/2Ey3qrk Follow Garrett
on Amazo - https://amzn.to/2yNYOr7